DEAD HEAT

A SEPH VERMILLION WESTERN ADVENTURE

DAVID FITZ-GERALD

CONTENTS

1. Chapter 1   1

2. Chapter 2   17

3. Chapter 3   34

4. Chapter 4   48

5. Chapter 5   62

6. Chapter 6   75

7. Chapter 7   87

8. Chapter 8   99

9. Chapter 9   112

10. Chapter 10   124

11. Chapter 11   136

12. Chapter 12   149

13. Chapter 13   161

14. Chapter 14   174

15. Chapter 15   187

16. Chapter 16   201

17. Chapter 17   215

18. Chapter 18   228

19. Chapter 19   242

20. Chapter 20   257

21. Chapter 21   274

22. Chapter 22   288

23. Chapter 23   300

24. Chapter 24   314

25. Chapter 25   329

26. Chapter 26   343

27. Chapter 27   357

FOREWORD

The inspiration for this series came while attending high school baseball games and observing the interactions of the players over the course of a season. Rather than call each other by their names, every player went by a nickname instead, or simply, *kid*, kind of like Billy the Kid.

On television and in movies, cowboys are often played by middle-aged actors, but most or many cattle drives were staffed by much younger men. A notable exception is the 1971 movie, *The Cowboys*, starring John Wayne, which featured children plucked from a one room schoolhouse. In this series, A Seph Vermillion's Western Adventure, the characters are young men who at least claim to be adults.

This story is told without profanity, but utilizes euphemisms. At times, this is a violent story.

Young men riding for the brand in the 1800s inhabited a very different world. Maybe what they want and need hasn't changed as much as we might think. Perhaps there's little difference between team spirit and riding for the brand.

But, when the day was done, there was no escaping the trail without traveling that last mile.

Chapter 1

Late August, 1868

Seph Vermillion sensed something was wrong from a mile away.

As he rode closer, the distant cries of a woman in distress grew more urgent.

Seph urged Win forward, scanning the rolling plains ahead. When the clearing beside the Canadian River came into view, his gut twisted. There were two men and a struggling girl. There was no mistaking what was happening, and no time to think or plan.

He kicked Win into a gallop and drew his Colt from its holster as he closed the distance. The native girl, her wrists tied, stumbled as one of the men yanked her by the arm and ripped her dress.

The other man laughed and spat on the ground.

Seph pulled Win to a stop. "Let her go."

Both men froze, turning to see him with his gun drawn. The taller one, his hand still on the girl, smirked and shook his head. "Ride away, boy. This ain't none of your business."

The other outlaw's hand dropped to his holster, but Seph fired first. The shot hit true, and the shorter man collapsed. Seph dismounted in a flash.

What a shame, Seph thought. Life was precious, but a man who'd do that to a woman shouldn't be mourned. Seph figured he had done what he had to do.

The tall man's grin vanished. He shoved the girl aside and charged at Seph, who was already sliding his pistol back into its holster.

The outlaw barreled into him full force, knocking him off his feet. They hit the ground hard, rolling in the dirt before scrambling back up.

The man's fists flew wildly, but Seph blocked the punches and drove his elbow into the man's ribs. He was strong and eager, but predictable. Maybe he wasn't used to tangling with men who fought back.

From the corner of his eye, Seph saw the girl moving away. He thought her heard her gasp for air.

The outlaw grunted, staggering back. Seph slammed his fist into the man's jaw, just as Dunk had taught him to do. One hit. Then two. The outlaw crumpled and begged for mercy.

Seph breathed hard and rubbed his sore knuckles as he stared down at the stranger. "What kind of man are you?"

The outlaw hadn't put up much of a fight, but that didn't matter. It was the way they had treated the girl that Seph couldn't abide.

"Get out of here," Seph growled.

He scooped up the dead man like a sack of grain and threw the corpse over the back of a horse. "Take him with you and ride out before I change my mind and shoot you too."

The outlaw scrambled to his feet, leapt into the saddle, and rode off without a word. Seph watched him disappear before turning back to the girl.

She stood frozen at the edge of the clearing, wide-eyed, her chest rising and falling with rapid breaths.

For a moment, their eyes met. Dark and deep, her gaze held something more than fear—something that made Seph's heart lurch. He couldn't look away.

"You're safe now," Seph said, his voice soft. He stepped closer, unsure why the moment felt so strange.

The young woman didn't move. She stared at him, her breathing slowing, but there was something in her eyes that he couldn't explain.

He scooped her into his arms. Her trembling body was light, but she didn't resist. Gently, he lifted her onto Win's back. "Which way is home?"

She pointed east along the river. "Thank you, friend. Our village is that way."

The sound of her voice was pleasing. There was no denying she'd been afraid when he rode up—but not now. Her tone was sweet, her words kind, and her English surprisingly good.

When they reached a small village of half a dozen teepees, the girl's parents rushed out to meet them. She slid off the horse and ran into their arms, speaking quickly in a language Seph didn't understand.

Her father nodded at Seph. "Thank you for bringing back our Tala."

Seph dismounted. Standing among teepees, speaking with Indians, was something he had never imagined doing. "Tala," he echoed.

After a pause, he said, "I did what anyone would do."

The man introduced himself. "I am Tsah Kaum. You say Tense Owl." He gestured toward the woman still holding their daughter. "This is Amo Tho."

The girl glanced at Seph from the corner of her eye. Stepping away from her mother's embrace, she said, "Mother's name means Warm Water."

Tsah Kaum nodded. "You sit. Have dinner."

His words were crisp but spoken warmly. Seph knew better than to refuse the invitation. He sat as Tala led Win away, and Tsah Kaum settled cross-legged beside him.

The run-down ranch, west of San Antonio, sprawled before Grim—dusty, worn, but full of potential. He led his five partners up the dirt path toward the small, weathered house.

Each of his men carried a freshly forged branding iron, the metal still black from the heat. Each one bore the Three Bar Box insignia—a mark of their past, present, and future. It was more than a brand; it was their bond.

The brand was simple: a rectangle for the window frame, with three vertical lines inside for the bars. Looking at a branded steer would be like peering into a dark prison cell.

Six men. One brand. In search of a spread.

Zachary Smith and his son, Tobias, stood stiffly by the porch, clearly unprepared to receive visitors—especially men like these.

Grim noticed the nervous way Tobias shuffled his feet and the way the older man leaned in to speak to his boy. He couldn't hear what was said, but he could guess.

Good advice. Not that it would help.

The dry ground cracked beneath Grim's boots as his gang spread out behind him like a dark wave. They drifted toward the barn, the bunkhouse, and the surrounding fields as if they already owned the place.

Zachary introduced himself and his son.

Grim fixed his gaze on the man and gave his legal name—Ward Decker—but didn't offer his hand.

Cautiously, Zachary asked, "What brings you fellas out this way?"

With a sneer, Grim said, "We're looking to make an investment. Looks like you're fixing to sell this place. We was hoping for something in better shape than this dump." He turned his head and looked toward the Medina River. The ranch might not look like much, but he figured the land had potential.

Zachary hesitated, glancing at Tobias before nodding. "We run on hard times. We talked about selling."

Grim grunted. "Good." With a single nod, he added, "Looks like we're the answer to your prayers."

One of Grim's men, Mitch, stepped to Grim's side and spoke to Zachary. "Looks like you've got something like a hundred head, Mister."

Zachary nodded, his voice rough. "Yeah, that's about right."

Mitch twisted the branding iron in his hand. Grim knew he was eager to get started.

Zachary's eyes locked onto the business end of the branding iron as it turned in Mitch's grip.

Grim waited patiently. He could guess what was going through Zachary's mind and didn't want to interrupt. At times like these, a man made calculations.

Zachary was taking stock of his life, measuring his odds. Grim had seen it before. If he played his cards right, a man like Zachary might even beg.

Zachary croaked, "How much are you offerin'?"

Grim tilted his head, letting the silence stretch. He could feel Zachary's discomfort growing, and that suited him fine.

"Seven hundred and fifty dollars," Grim said smoothly. "That's what we've got."

Zachary blinked, clearly caught off guard. "But... that's... that's not nearly what the place is worth. Maybe we could come up with somethin' higher—"

"Higher?" Grim cut in, his faint smile vanishing. "Look at this place."

He turned slightly, gesturing toward his men. They wandered the property—running their hands over fence posts, kicking at barn doors, sizing up the land.

Slowly, Grim drawled, "You ain't kept the place up good."

As if summoned by his gesture, the men made their way toward him.

Zachary swallowed hard. "What about them longhorns. How much more for them?"

Grim didn't answer.

Zachary whined, "Last year was hard. Mother died, my two older boys run off, and my girl married up and moved to town. Me and Tobias figured to fix up the place before selling."

Bert chimed in from where he stood. "Ain't no fixin' this place without money, and you ain't got it. We're your best shot, Smith. Take the deal."

Zachary shifted uneasily, his son looking at him—a silent plea in his eyes—as the six men moved closer, crowding them in.

Tobias was young, but he wasn't naive. He could see the writing on the wall.

Zachary said, "How about a thousand dollars? Lock, stock, and barrel. Critters included."

Grim's voice softened, almost as if he were showing mercy. "I'd love to offer more, Zachary. I really would. But like I said, we ain't flush with cash, and as Bert explained, it's gonna take some money to fix up the place."

He let out a slow breath, his eyes narrowing. "Six hundred sixty-six dollars. For everything. And a job for your boy if he wants it."

Zachary hesitated again.

Grim could tell by the look on his face—he had the man. Beaten. Broken. No two ways about it.

The destitute rancher shook his head, but his words said otherwise. "All right," he muttered, "but my Tobias stays with me."

Grim nodded slightly. "Good man. Six hundred sixty-six dollars, you help us get those beeves branded, then we'll head into Hondo to make it legal."

As Mitch and the others moved toward the longhorns, Grim stood back, watching as they pulled the cattle into a small enclosure. The gang's movements were calm and methodical. They knew their way around a ranch.

As Mitch heated the branding irons in a fire, the conversation shifted.

John Quincy Long spoke first, grinning. "Huntsville was a real good teacher, wasn't it?" He chuckled. "Learned a lot there."

Zachary shifted uncomfortably, glancing at Grim.

The mention of Huntsville Prison was no accident. Grim knew his men enjoyed intimidating folks with words just as much as with their presence—and he allowed it.

Long kept talking, his voice low but pointed. "Learned real quick that if you weren't tough, you didn't last. Ain't that right, Mitch?"

Mitch grunted as he pressed the Three Bar Box brand onto the hide of a longhorn. The stench of burning hair fouled the air. "Sure did," he replied. "Either you make it, or the place makes you."

Bert shook his head. "Most men came out soft. Not us, though. We came out hard. Smarter. And itchin' to find opportunities."

Zachary's shoulder sagged as he watched his cattle—the remnants of his life's work—branded like they were nothing more than renegade mavericks.

"Prison didn't take nothin' from us," John Memphis Short added. "Just gave us more reason to get what we deserve."

As the last of the cattle were branded, Grim walked up to Zachary and clapped him on the shoulder. "Don't worry, Smith. Your cattle are in good hands now. Just look at that spiffy new brand on them hides." It wasn't lost on him that the stark Three Bar Box brand blazed fresh next to the faded Circle Z that memorialized the transaction not yet recorded in town.

Zachary forced a nod, his face tight with barely concealed emotion. "And after we head to Hondo...."

Grim smirked. "We'll come back, and you and Tobias can pack up and ride on outta here. Just like that."

Tobias, who had stayed silent the entire time, finally spoke up. His voice was quiet, almost shaking. "What happens to us after that?"

Grim's smile was cold. "That's your problem, not ours. But I'd suggest headin' far from here."

He mounted his horse and called to Mitch and Bert. "Let's go get them papers signed."

As they rode off toward Hondo, Grim glanced back at the ranch. Behind them, Dick, John Quincy Long, and John Memphis Short stayed behind.

For Grim, this wasn't just a land deal.

It was the beginning of an empire.

Clive Deatherage sat across from his grandmother. His fists clenched in his lap as he watched her carefully fold and unfold a letter.

The air between them felt thick. His back muscles were tight, and sweat gathered beneath his shirt. He had felt this way in her presence ever since he returned from driving cattle from San Antonio to Sedalia.

Now, he worked for wages on the dock, moving other men's fortunes while his own ambitions rotted. Stuck in a rut he couldn't climb out of.

Martha's voice interrupted his thoughts. "Clive, we need to be realistic about this. Buying back your grandfather's business... it's not a smart investment."

Clive stared at her, his jaw tight.

Realistic. That's what she always said. Ever since he was a boy, she'd clipped his wings with that dream-slaying word. "You don't understand. This is our chance to bring it all back—to be something more. Grandfather built that freight line from nothing. We could make it even bigger than it was."

Martha shook her head softly, as if explaining something to a child. "That took your grandfather decades, Clive. He took way too many risks. Times are different now."

Clive's blood boiled. She talked like he didn't know anything, like years of cattle drives with his uncles hadn't taught him anything. He'd worked as hard as any man.

And now, stuck in Springfield with a job that was leading nowhere—all he could see was his future slipping away.

"You don't get it, Grandmother," he spat. "I've been working—heck, I've learned more in the past few years than most men my age. I could run that freight business. I know I could."

Martha looked at him, her eyes soft but annoyingly calm, dissecting him with that cool stare of hers. She always had that way of making him feel small, like he was just a boy—destined to live in his grandfather's shadow instead of rising on his own.

"You're a hard worker, yes. But owning and running a business is risky."

She paused, glancing at the letter still in her hand.

Clive gritted his teeth, forcing himself not to snap. Too risky. She always wanted to play it safe. There was no arguing with Grandmother when her mind was made up.

Martha's fingers tapped lightly on the envelope, and a knot tightened in Clive's gut. She was about to lecture him again.

"Dusty wrote to me," she said quietly, her voice too even. "He thinks there's a place for you at his ranch."

Clive's chest tightened. "I don't need Dusty's charity," he said through clenched teeth.

Martha lifted the letter, her expression neutral. "It's not charity, Clive. When Pierce died, he lost his partner. He's offering you a ten percent ownership stake. That's a chance to be part of something real—something stable."

Clive stared at her, his thoughts running dark. Ten percent. That was it? A pittance.

Grandmother's unwillingness to take risks gnawed at him. She was content sitting here, growing older, living off bank interest. She'd never cared about his ambitions—only her dull, comfortable security.

"He's offering you a place to build," she continued, her tone like nails in his ears. "I think you should consider it."

Clive shot up from his chair, pacing the room. "Why go all that way for ten percent? We could have a hundred percent right here, right now. Why won't you help me?"

Martha stood, her gaze unwavering. "I've invested in safe places, Clive. At my age, I can't afford to gamble. You're young. You have time to take *realistic* chances."

Clive glared at her, the resentment curling tight in his chest. Safe bets. That's what she'd always done—kept everything locked away, out of reach. She hadn't even fought for the business when Hiram died. She let it go.

And now, she was going to let him rot on the docks.

"I'm not asking for the world, Grandmother," he said, his voice low. "Just a chance."

Her face softened, and for a moment, Clive almost thought that she might say something he wanted to hear.

But then she spoke, her tone firm. "Go out there and make your own way, Clive. Take Dusty's offer. Build something real."

His heart pounded. "You think I'm not good enough, don't you?"

"No," she replied softly. "I think you have the potential to be more than your grandfather ever was. But you need to take the right steps. You also have the potential to make bad choices."

The words burned on his tongue, but he bit them back. Turning on his heel, he muttered, "Fine." He grabbed his hat. "I'll figure it out myself."

Clive slammed the door behind him.

As he walked away, the echo of his grandmother's disapproval followed him.

He didn't need her.

He'd find his own way.

Seph rode non-stop for weeks after leaving the Kiowa village.

When he left Abilene alone, he needed time to think. He had been foolish—falling in love with Hazel, a painted lady, after one night alone together. How could he have known she begged every man to take her away?

Yet the days and nights since hadn't changed anything. She was his favorite memory. If he could live one night over and over again, it would be that one.

It took all the fortitude he could muster not to turn around, ride back to Abilene, and beg her to marry him.

But in his gut, he knew the truth.

She had meant everything to him.

But to her, he was just another cowboy.

At the Kiowa village, he thought he'd felt a spark of attraction to the beautiful woman he'd rescued. She had kissed his cheek and sweetly asked him to visit again.

But the moment he rode away, Hazel invaded his thoughts.

Miles of traveling alone hadn't helped him sort himself out at all. He was just as mixed up as before.

Seph rode into Fort Worth and searched for the man he'd met on the way to Abilene. It took a couple of days to find him.

To save money, he slept under the stars rather than taking a room at a boarding house—but he splurged on meals.

At the Prairie Hen, he tasted chicken and dumplings. At the Iron Spur, he savored beef steak and gravy. The Painted Horse Tavern served fried fish with cornmeal, and he couldn't get enough of La Cocina de Estrella's enchiladas.

Each night, Seph walked past the cantinas, saloons, and brothels.

Did he want another beer? He decided he could take or leave the bitter brew.

The calico queens were another matter.

His heart beat faster as he strolled past the establishments. He knew it was a sin, but he had visited Hazel anyway.

The temptation of visiting another brothel only made things worse.

He'd stayed in Cowtown too long.

When Seph finally found Charlie Coppedge, he watched the one-armed man—the man who knew his father—enjoy his favorite hearty stew.

Charlie shared a few stories he hadn't told the first time they met.

Before leaving Cowtown, Seph asked, "Do you have to live here?"

The old man sucked his teeth. Then, with a pop of release, he proclaimed, "Naw. I just sort of landed here. Whatcha thinking?"

Seph hesitated, "I don't know."

Was it crazy to think of having the old codger along on a cattle drive?

He knew better than to suggest something like that without asking the boss. Instead, he said, "How about San Antonio?"

If Charlie were closer to the Deatherage spread, Seph could get away now and then to buy him a meal.

Charlie smacked his lips. "I'll think about it, son."

When Seph rode out of Fort Worth, he already missed the old man.

But he didn't fail to notice the man from the clearing on the Canadian River—just at the edge of his vision.

Some men couldn't let things alone. Instead they felt they had to settle a score.

Seph knew right off—he was being followed.

Did the man plan to ambush him?

CHAPTER 2

A KNIFE FLASHED IN the moonlight.

Seph's eyes snapped open. His heart pounded as the outlaw came down on him. No time to think—only to move.

His hand shot to the pistol beneath his blanket. In one motion, he pointed the barrel and squeezed the trigger.

The bullet tore through fabric and struck the outlaw beneath the chin. The sickening impact sent the knife clattering beside him as the man collapsed in a heap on top of him.

Why feel sorry for the dead man? That outlaw had planned to slit his throat.

The gunshot rang in Seph's ears as he shoved the body aside. No surprise—it was the tall man from outside Fort Worth. The same filthy scoundrel who had tried to assault Tala on the banks of the Canadian River.

Even in death, his face held the same lascivious sneer.

Seph kicked his blankets away, rose to his feet, and stared down at the body.

He didn't need to check for a pulse.

Dang outlaws. They were everywhere?

He began to wonder if Woodsy's Colts were cursed.

The would-be lawman had been brutally slain on the way to Abilene last year. Maybe inheriting Woodsy's twin Colts wasn't a blessing after all.

But if he hadn't fired first, he'd be the one lying dead on the ground. He hadn't wanted to kill another man, yet here he was—staring at the consequences of life on the frontier.

Seph holstered the gun, shaking his head.

"Why'd you have to come for me?" he muttered, kneeling beside the outlaw's body.

He rifled through the man's saddlebags, searching for anything that might tell him more. His fingers brushed against a folded piece of paper.

Even in the dark, he could make out neat but shaky handwriting. He squinted, struggling to read.

It was a love letter.

The envelope was addressed to George Bowman. The woman who wrote it promised to wait for him.

This man had somebody waiting for him. He wasn't just a nameless outlaw. He had been loved.

But how many women like Tala had he forced himself on?

Seph sighed, folding the letter and tucking it back into the saddlebag.

Maybe he'd write the woman a letter—tell her not to wait for George.

He hadn't wanted this, but he'd known the man was following him. What choice did he have?

He glanced up at the stars. He always loved sleeping under them. The vast, twinkling heavens stretched endlessly above, full of unfathomable possibilities.

But life on the frontier was brutal. Danger lurked everywhere.

He had learned the hard way—a man always had to be ready, wary, and armed. Especially when he traveled alone.

Seph crouched beside the body, hands resting on his knees.

Should he bury the man who tried to slit his throat?

The answer came quick enough. If it weren't for that love letter, he'd have let the buzzards have Bowman.

Instead, he picked up a rock and began to dig.

By dawn, a mound of dirt covered George's corpse. Seph wiped the sweat from his brow and stretched his aching back.

"You're one lucky scoundrel, George Bowman," he muttered. "She's the only reason wolves ain't fighting over your bones."

The soft, familiar notes of a harmonica floated through the cool evening air.

Seph nudged Win forward. His chest tightened at the sound. Could a *homecoming* be just over the hill?

Anybody could be camped along the waterway, playing a harmonica.

But how many would play *that* song?

Seph knew he had found his people—his brothers of the trail.

As the Guadalupe River came into view, he spotted the Deatherage outfit, gathered around a campfire. Orange flames danced to the music, illuminating the faces of men he hadn't seen in far too long.

His heart pounded a little faster as he guided Win down the slope and through the brush.

The moment he came into view, Torp leapt to his feet.

"Seph!" Torp hollered, rushing toward him like a kid brother waiting on penny candy. "You made it!"

Seph slid off his horse, grinning as the rest of the men gathered around him.

Chops reached him first, yanking him into a bear hug that nearly crushed his ribs. Even in the dimming light, it was hard not to notice a fresh constellation of pimples scattered across his face.

"About time you made it, Vermillion," Chops laughed, thumping Seph on the back. "Figured you'd fallen in love with some girl and forgot about us."

Seph chuckled, shaking his head as he pried himself free. "You should be so lucky," he shot back, though the memory of leaving Hazel still stung.

Blaze ambled over, grinning. "We were about to send the kid," he jerked his thumb at Torp, "to drag you back."

Seph laughed. "If anybody could find me, I reckon Torp could."

The familiar faces of old friends made Seph feel like Christmas dinner was on the table—but he took note of a couple of new cowpokes too.

When Seph glanced at Stoke, the top hand barreled through the crowd. He grabbed Seph's arm in a handshake so violent it might've dislocated a lesser man's shoulder.

"I was afraid we'd find your bones beside the trail, you knucklehead. Shoulda known you'd make it home to Texas. Don't know how these jaspers got along without you."

Stoke hotfooted it over to the new guys, slinging an arm over each man's shoulder.

"You haven't met the new boys, Seph. This here's Whirlwind."

Seph nodded to a tall, wiry young man with long, dark hair falling into his eyes. Looked like he could run as fast as a horse if he had to.

"From Denton," Stoke added.

Whirlwind nodded, a quick grin flashing across his face. "Heard you make a mean biscuit."

Seph raised an eyebrow.

Before he could reply, Stoke gestured to the second recruit. "And this here's Tumble. He's from Waco."

Tumble, a freckled, red-headed kid, stepped forward with an eager grin.

"If you can cook half as good as you shoot, we'll be just fine."

Seph gave him a nod. "We'll see about that."

Why were these men he never met talking about his cooking?

Before he could ask, Dusty stepped up. His usual serious expression softened—just a touch.

"Glad to have you back, kid," Dusty said, his voice gruff. "Got something important to tell you."

Seph straightened up. Should he be alarmed? He glanced around, but the whole gang was there—and then some.

"What's that?"

Dusty never beat around the bush. "You're the new camp cook."

Seph blinked wildly, as he often did when caught off guard. "Camp cook?"

Dusty didn't smile. "That's right. I need someone I can trust to keep these boys fed, patch up their boo-boos, and shoe the horses. With Dunk run off to Dayton, I can't think of a better man to call *Old Lady* than you."

Seph shook his head slowly in disbelief. "I declare. That's the last thing I expected you to say."

Dusty gave him a hard look, his voice steady. "Do the job no one wants, and you'll find out what you're made of. Do the job no one else can, and you'll be a legend."

Before Seph could process that, Stoke busted in.

"Instead of *Old Lady*, how about *Little Sister*?" He guffawed, slapping his kneecaps. "Anything but *Nanny Joe Jo*—cuz I promised, don't ya know?"

Seph groaned and palmed his forehead, nearly knocking his hat off. He glanced around at the grinning faces in the crowd.

Every single man was shorter than him.

Slowly, he planted his hands backward on his hips—just like Dunk always did when somebody called him *Old Lady*.

"Little Sister? *Me*? Do you know what my specialty is? Corn mush. That and biscuits is about all I can make."

Hork stepped in. "Hope Dunk didn't teach you how to make them nasty beans. I swear, that's all he ever wanted to make. Beans—all the time."

He pretended to vomit, scoring a round of laughter from the crew.

As the chuckles faded, Seph caught the sharp look Hork shot at Trinket. The shorter cowboy sat by the fire, staring into the flames, jaw clenched tight.

Hork muttered under his breath—sounded like, "I ain't talkin' to him. Not after what he pulled."

Seph's eyes flicked to Trinket, but he didn't so much as flinch. His face was set, his silence saying plenty.

Whatever had gone down between them, it wasn't settled.

Lullaby stepped forward, shifting the mood. The black cowboy gripped Seph's shoulders, his deep voice rolled smooth and slow.

"Good to see you again, friend." Then he turned to face the crowd.

"Before we get comfortable, boys, we've got business to tend to."

The group fell quiet as Lullaby led them toward a small, solemn spot near the river.

Slaw's grave.

A simple wooden cross stood as a marker for Seph's fallen childhood friend. They lost him at the start of the drive last year, and Slaw was never far from Seph's thoughts.

Lullaby knelt, his hat in his hands. In his usual low voice, he said, "Lord, please watch over Slaw and keep him close."

The prayer was short, especially for Lullaby, but it hit Seph hard.

As the men drifted back toward camp, Torp lingered. "Why'd you ride off alone, Seph?"

Seph met the kid's eyes. "Didn't Stoke tell you?"

Torp shook his head. "Just said you needed some time to yourself and you'd meet us back at the ranch."

"Oh." Seph hesitated. What could he tell a kid about a man's problems?

The San Antonio River twisted like a thick brown snake through the landscape beneath the blazing Texas sun.

Seph was eager to return to the Deatherage spread, though he generally preferred the trail to the compound.

The ranch was impressive and spacious, but it fit its surroundings. The buildings were new, uniform in style, and built from local materials. Rather than having a dull patina, they shone like a sugar frosted donut.

But something was off—like a teeter with no totter.

Smoke curled lazily from the chimney. Unfamiliar horses stood hitched by the corral.

Dusty slowed his horse. He tipped his head forward, shielding his eyes with his hand. "Someone's been makin' themselves at home."

Seph's stomach knotted as Dusty cursed under his breath. "Danged if they ain't taken over the place."

Seph tightened his grip on the reins, instincts kicking in. The closer he looked, the more certain he was—these weren't just wanderers seeking shelter. They looked like fighters.

Dusty raised a hand, signaling for the group to stop just beyond the trees. "We take it back. Now," he said firmly. "It's ours."

Stoke warned, "They won't leave easy." His warning wasn't disagreement—far from it. "We'll have to be quick, or this could get bloody."

Seph glanced at the men. Chops stood tall, hand on his revolver, a determined glint in his eye. Beside him, Hork looked a shade paler. Lullaby had already dismounted, reciting a prayer, as always.

Seph's gaze swept the buildings. "We've got the advantage. We know this place. They don't."

Dusty nodded, glancing at Stoke. "You take Blaze and Whirlwind around the back. I'll head straight for the ranch house with the rest. We hit them hard, but keep your heads down—I don't want any dead heroes."

They fanned out, moving swiftly but quietly.

Seph followed Dusty's lead, excitement shooting through his gizzard. As they approached the yard, a shout went up from one of the squatters near the barn. "We got company!"

Gunfire erupted.

Seph dove behind a water trough, his heart hammering as the sharp crack of shots echoed across the ranch.

Dusty fired back, his gun thundering in response. He took cover beside the house, grimacing as he crouched, a hand pressed to the small of his back.

Seph peered around the trough just in time to see Stoke charging forward from the opposite side of the complex, rifle raised.

The man never hesitated.

Stoke and Blaze circled the barn, firing on the run. A squatter crumpled, clutching his chest, but the others weren't giving up easily.

One of them—a scarred man with wild eyes—rushed toward Seph, brandishing a rusty shotgun.

Seph's blood surged. He ducked just as the squatter fired, pellets whizzing overhead, some pinging off the water trough.

Without hesitation, Seph drew Woodsy's Colt, popped up like a prairie dog, and fired.

The shot caught the man in the leg. He howled, dropping to the ground, but kept crawling, fumbling to reload.

Seph moved in, booting the gun out of his hand. "Not today," Seph muttered, standing over him.

Another shot rang out—somebody put another bullet in the wounded squatter.

Seph retreated back to the cover of the trough.

From the corner of his eye, he spotted movement at the ranch house window.

A squatter lifted a rifle and fired. The bullet jettisoned toward Hork who had just dived for cover.

"Hork, get down!" Seph shouted—but he was too late. The skinny cowboy was already plastered to the ground.

Hork yelped in pain but scrambled for his gun. Blood soaked his sleeve where the bullet had grazed his arm.

Seph fired again.

The young squatter hadn't been smart enough to back away from the window. Seph's shot hit him, and he fell back, clutching his wound.

Seph didn't have time to watch.

Another squatter burst from the barn, roaring—swinging a piece of timber like a club.

Chops was on him in a flash, fists flying. The two men grappled—the squatter swinging wildly, while Chops moved with precision.

It wasn't long before Chops delivered a brutal punch into the man's gut, knocking the wind out of him.

But just as Chops was about to finish him, a rifle cracked from another window. The bullet grazed Chops' shoulder, then tore into the winded squatter.

"Youch!" Chops howled, stumbling back, clutching his shoulder as blood seeped through his shirt. In a high-pitched squawk, he yelled to Seph, "Did you see that? Serves him right—he killed one of his own!"

The squatters weren't backing down. They fought like they owned the place, and the Deatherage men were taking hits of their own.

Lullaby, his usual calm hardened, took aim. One shot. A squatter dropped. That tipped the balance. "They're retreating!" Lullaby called as two squatters fled toward the trees.

The rest were dead or dying.

Dusty didn't let up. "Drive 'em off! Stoke, cover the left! Seph, you and Whirlwind—take the house!"

Seph and Whirlwind darted across the yard and ducked into the ranch house.

Inside, the air was thick with the smell of sweat and gunpowder. They found two more squatters. One dead, slumped against the wall. The other, wounded. He struggled to crawl toward the back door.

Seph grabbed him by the collar, hauling him upright.

"You picked the wrong place to roost," Seph growled.

The man, bleeding from a wound in his side, spat at Seph's feet. "It was free land," he wheezed.

"Wrong again."

The injured squatter gave one last shudder and went still. Seph let him crash back to the floor.

Outside, Dusty holstered his gun and surveyed the scene, jaw clenched. "This is my home. Our ranch. They should have left it alone."

Seph glanced around. The thrill of danger still juiced his gizzard.

The ranch was theirs again, but it had come at a cost. Hork and Chops nursed their wounds.

Dusty walked up to Seph, his eyes hard.

"We'll bury the bodies. Then we rebuild." He scowled. "Don't bury 'em on Deatherage land. I don't want 'em here."

Most of the cowboys lounged at the tables under the portico in front of the bunkhouse. They hadn't played much faro on the trail, but now that they were home, they returned to their favorite pastime. After a long afternoon dislodging squatters and cleaning up their mess, it felt good to finally relax.

Then Hork let off, fouling the air, disturbing the pace, and griping about beans again.

Trinket had enough. "I am sick of hearing it, Hork. Why you always gotta stink up the place?" He waved a hand in front of his face, grimacing. "I do not know what is worse—the stink or the whining. You gotta do that, go someplace else. Sheesh."

Hork scowled. "I can't help it. Maybe you can handle it, but I can't. Maybe I should just ride outta here and find someplace that serves something else."

Trinket nodded sharply. "Maybe, fine. Good idea. *Adios, amigo!*"

The bickering cowhands fell silent as approaching riders thundered toward the ranch.

Seph squinted, trying to make out the figures. He didn't recognize them. Strangers usually meant trouble. And these riders were coming in fast.

They skidded to an abrupt stop.

Seph stepped aside, hand near his holster. Were they looking for the squatters? Or something else?

One rider sat out front. The other three shadowed slightly behind him.

Dusty stepped out of the ranch house, stepping fast—like he did before his back started bothering him.

"I don't believe it. Clive! I wasn't sure you'd come."

The man smiled but didn't dismount. He sat tall in the saddle, his sharp features shadowed by the fading light. His nose was crooked. Jawline marred by a jagged scar. Cold blue eyes surveyed the ranch like he owned it.

Seph stiffened. *Clive? Who is Clive? And what is he doing here?*

"Boys," Dusty called out, "this here is Clive Deatherage from Springfield, Illinois—my nephew."

The crew exchanged glances.

Dusty pressed on, "He'll be ramrodding our drives and overseeing ranch operations."

Seph's heart sank.

He glanced at Stoke. The man's expression didn't change, but the way his jaw tightened told Seph he wasn't too happy about this.

Clive nodded once. "That's right. And these are *my* men."

Dusty frowned.

Seph caught it—the boss hadn't expected his nephew to bring his own crew.

Clive motioned toward them. "Sparrow. Scorch. Rooster."

Sparrow looked sharp, but friendly. Scorch looked like he was already halfway to losing his temper. Rooster flashed a cocky grin.

Behind Seph, somebody whispered. "Sounds like a bunch of bird brains to me."

He glanced to the side. Torp stood stiff, arms crossed. Conjure looked like he was trying to disappear behind Stoke. Hork scowled. Yodel fidgeted with his harmonica, flipping it over and over in his big hand.

Dusty cleared his throat. There was more. "You should also know—Clive's got a stake in the herd. He'll be gettin' ten percent."

Seph never expected to hear such a thing. It hit hard. What had this man done to deserve ten percent? He glanced at the others. Chops raised an eyebrow. Even Lullaby wore a scowl.

Seph locked eyes with Hork, who grumbled, "There's always a nephew. Or cousin, uncle, brother—some kind of kin to make work miserable."

Seph said nothing. He had a bad feeling. He turned back to Dusty and Clive.

Clive shook his head, smiling brazenly. His voice was smooth. Strong. "Sorry, Uncle. That won't do."

An icy prickle ran down Seph's spine. Nobody talked to the boss like that. Was this good news? Was the man refusing his uncle's offer?

Clive dismounted, swaggering toward Dusty. "Uncle Pierce got half. I want half too."

Seph had seen Dusty angry before. But this—this was different. Seph reckoned the boss wanted to rip his nephew's face off.

Dusty stepped forward, widening his stance. "No, Clive. If ten percent won't do, you'd better head back to Illinois."

Clive tilted his scarred chin toward Dusty. "Then I guess we've got ourself a disagreement."

Dusty didn't flinch. "That we do."

Seph's heart pounded. He blinked rapidly.

No telling what might happen next.

CHAPTER 3

THE LAST SIX MONTHS had been rough as the Dagger D, Angry R rousted three thousand squirrely longhorns from the thorny mesquites and wild hills.

Dusty planned to hit the trail by mid-April. But as the drive got closer, tempers flared.

One second, Stoke and Scorch were trading insults. The next, angry words turned hostile. There was no question what was coming.

Seph watched, unsurprised. *What took them so long?*

Since Clive arrived and decided to stick around, the rivalry between Stoke and Scorch had simmered, waiting to boil over. It reminded Seph of his own fight with Stoke last year. Only this was different. Seph couldn't figure out why or how, but it just wasn't the same.

Scorch barked, "Couldn't they find a real man for your job? You ain't fit to shovel behind my horse. What kind of fool made you top hand round here?"

Stoke shot back, "You ain't nothin' but a snot-nosed brat. Too bad your mama never knew a real man. What a disappointment you musta been."

Scorch growled. "You talk about Ma again, you'll regret it. Least she could tell me who my daddy was. Bet you can't say the same."

Before Stoke could react, Scorch swung. His knuckles cracked against Stoke's jaw.

The blow only fueled Stoke's rage. He fired back, fast and hard—his meaty fist slamming into Scorch's cheek with a sickening thud.

Scorch staggered but didn't go down. The man was even tougher than he looked. He spat blood, grinning as his lip swelled. "My mother punches harder than you."

The rest of the cowboys crowded in, watching. Nobody moved to stop it. This fight had been brewing too long. It had to happen.

Stoke's eyes darkened. He took a step forward, fists raised. "You look like the sort of man that would punch a woman," he said coolly. "But your own mother?"

Scorch's smirk vanished.

The air thickened. Stoke didn't flinch. "I got plenty more," he growled.

Seph knew Stoke had been through worse. Much worse. But Scorch was fast. Faster than most.

They clashed again. Scorch swung first—again. A right hook, straight to Stoke's ribs. The blow landed with a heavy thud.

Seph winced. He could almost feel it himself.

But Stoke didn't flinch. The man was made of stone.

Seph leaned forward, studying the fighters. If he got any closer, he might've gotten clobbered. Still, if there was going to be a fight—he might as well learn something.

Stoke threw a punch, aiming for Scorch's midsection.

Scorch danced back just in time. Then he snapped forward, landing a sharp left jab to Stoke's forehead.

Seph's heart thundered. He'd seen fights before—but this was different. This was what happened when two men hated each other. When they put off a fight too long. When the only way forward involved cracking knuckles.

Stoke grunted and pressed forward, driving a sharp blow into Scorch's ribs.

Scorch stumbled, gasping, but didn't fall. The man had fire in his veins. He wasn't going down easy.

Seph's hands curled into fists. For a moment, he imagined himself in the fight—wondered how he'd fare against Scorch. He saw the mistakes, the openings. If it were him, maybe he'd duck under Stoke's punch, pivot right, catch him with a hook. But Stoke was in the thick of it, and Seph was safe within the crowd.

Scorch swung wild, missing Stoke altogether.

Seph snapped out of it.

Stoke pounced, driving his fist into Scorch's gut. The impact was brutal. Scorch doubled over, gasping.

Stoke grabbed his shirt and yanked him up. One final blow—right to the face.

Scorch crumpled. Blood dripped from his nose, darkening the dust. He twitched and groaned, barely moving.

Stoke stood over him, chest heaving, eyes burning with fury.

Seph's breath caught in his throat. The fight was over. Stoke had won—but not easily. Scorch was tough, mean, and quick. But not quick enough. Stoke's legendary strength carried him through.

From the corner of his eye, Seph spotted Clive. The man stood on the edge of the crowd, arms crossed, frowning hard. He watched like he was taking notes. Making plans.

Seph looked down, uneasy. Was he any different? Hadn't he been studying the fight too? His stomach churned. Clive was trouble. No doubt about it. He hadn't lifted a finger to stop the fight. Hadn't said a word to back his man down. That meant something. Seph couldn't shake the feeling—this was just the beginning.

Stoke spat into the dust and stepped back, wiping blood from his knuckles. He glanced at Seph. "He's dumb, but he's got grit."

Seph nodded, his throat dry.

Scorch lay sprawled on the ground, barely conscious.

Stoke nudged him with a boot. "You done?"

Scorch tried to sit up, but failed. He slumped back, coughing blood. "Yeah," he rasped. "I'm done."

Stoke nodded once. He turned his back like the fight was nothing. But over his shoulder, he made sure Scorch heard him. "Let that be a lesson to you. You'd be smart not to forget it."

Seph's hands curled into fists. His mind replayed the fight. Would he have made it out of a scrap like that? He had speed. Strength. But what about endurance? Could he outlast someone like Scorch?

His gaze drifted back to Clive. Their eyes met for a second. Then Clive looked away—back at Scorch.

Seph's gizzard tumbled like a walnut in a crate. One thing was certain—trouble was coming for the Deatherage outfit.

Grim Decker stood on the porch of what used to be Zachary Smith's ranch house. He scowled. The place was still a mess. Broken fences. A sagging roof on the pole barn. The bunk house looked like a chicken coop. One day, he'd have a real compound. But this? This wasn't it. "Couldn't they have fixed the place up before sellin' it?" he groused.

John Quincy Long chuckled beside him, leaning on the railing. "What do you expect, Grim? You saw how it was. Those folks was barely scraping by."

Grim grunted, watching the men below. Five new recruits mingled with the earlier arrivals and his original crew. The three groups sized each other up, circling like wolves. It reminded him of Huntsville. New arrivals thrown into the yard. Testing boundaries. Searching for weakness.

New or old, every last man had done time.

Mitch stood nearby, cracking his knuckles. His gaze swept over the yard, reading every movement.

John Memphis Short fidgeted with his knife, watching. Listening.

Grim's lips twitched in a sour smile. He'd built this crew from nothing. Hard men. Just like him. Everything to gain.

He gestured toward the herd grazing under the midday sun. "We got a good start," he said. He turned, slightly. "But I tell you what, Mitch. We're gonna double our herd along the way."

"Legally—right boss?" Mitch asked, cracking a grin. He wanted to be sure that they stayed on the free side of the prison walls.

Grim nodded. "You'd better believe it. Long as we get a bill of sale, it's legal." His smirk curled. "I bet there's all kinds of *bargains* we can find along the way."

John Memphis Short snorted. "Like that fella who sold us the ranch. Right, boss?"

Grim's smile widened. "You got it, Mitch. No murders. No hangings." His voice stretched slow, like he was savoring possibilities. "Not if we can help it. But driving beeves is dangerous business. Anything can happen to an outfit on the trail." He tapped a finger against his temple. "Maybe we mess with their gear. Send 'em off in the wrong direction. Spook their beeves. No tellin' what we might come up with." His gaze slid across the men. "You see?"

John Quincy Long laughed. "That's the long and short of it, right there, Boss."

Grim glanced from man to man—Mitch, the two Johns, Dick, Bert. They were his core crew. The men he trusted most. They'd done time together. Rode together before prison. Walked free together. He knew what made them tick—what they were capable of. Now, with a full fifteen-man roster, he was ready. It was time to muscle his way up the trail.

"I like what we got here," Grim bragged.

Mitch nodded, eyes on the herd. "Sure as shootin', Grim. Nobody's gonna get the best of *us* on the way to Abilene."

Grim's eyes narrowed, the fire of ambition burning hot behind them. "Darn right," he said. "That gives me an idea."

He let it simmer, working the angles in his head. It was brilliant. By the time he spoke again, he'd already forgotten Mitch had sparked the thought.

"Yes," he said, stretching out the word. "That's just what we'll do. Wager the herd. Double or nothing. All we gotta do is find some fool dumb enough to take the bet—someone who thinks their herd will get there first."

Grim's gaze settled on Mitch as he thought about the men around them. They were tough—tough enough to pull this off. "And when the chips are down, these men ain't afraid to do what needs doin'."

Grim exhaled slowly, letting the idea settle deep in his bones. Freedom plus power—it was intoxicating.

He thought, *Ain't nothing gonna stand in my way.*

Seph stood at the kitchen counter, plucking the last of the chickens Dusty had brought in. Feathers floated through the air, some clinging to his shirt. He had been at it for hours, his mind elsewhere—on the trail, on the food, on making sure no one went hungry. If he could get dumplings right, maybe he'd earn a few points with the men.

Dusty and Clive were in the next room. Their voices rose, and Seph could hear every word. He had tried to tune them out, focusing on the rhythm of his hands working over the pimply-skinned poultry. But the argument was impossible to ignore.

"You're just like Grandmother!" Clive's voice was sharp. "Always playing it safe. We need to push harder. Bigger herd, bigger payday. Five thousand beeves. Think of it!"

Seph winced. Five thousand longhorns? That was more than last year by a mile. He kept his head down, but his stomach tightened.

Dusty's reply was firm. "We barely made it with three thousand last year, Clive. That's what we're driving again. And I want to leave now. It'd take months to round up another couple thousand mavericks."

There was a heavy thud—probably Clive's fist hitting the table. "You think small, Uncle. So you had some troubles last year, but me and my men weren't there. This year, we are. We could do better than three thousand. Trust me."

Seph wiped his hands on a rag and moved closer to the doorway, just enough to see them.

Dusty stood tall, arms crossed, his face like stone. Clive paced, eyes blazing, jaw clenched tight. Seph couldn't shake the feeling that this argument wasn't just about cattle. "Late herds get lower prices, Clive. I want to leave tomorrow."

Clive shot back. "That's not always true, and you know it."

"You're right," Dusty conceded, "But I'm the trail boss. I own the ranch and ninety percent of the herd. We leave tomorrow with what we've got."

Clive stopped pacing, locking eyes with his uncle. "We can't afford to stick to what's comfortable. Wouldn't you rather have ninety percent of five thousand than ninety percent of three thousand? I'm telling you, *I* want more."

Seph knew Clive still felt cheated—he had expected half the herd. Dusty and Squat were fifty-fifty partners, and Clive figured he deserved the same.

A cold sweat pricked the back of Seph's neck. He'd seen Clive push before, but never like this. Not since that first day he arrived at the ranch.

Dusty's voice dropped even lower, like the calm before a storm. "We do what I say. You don't like it, get on your horse and light out of here."

The room fell quiet.

A knock on the door shattered the silence. Seph snapped his head toward it, relieved for the interruption.

Dusty exhaled hard. "Who is it?"

The door creaked open, and two men stepped inside—Zachary and Tobias Smith. Zachary looked worn from years of ranch work, his hands thick and callused. His son, Tobias was young but looked like he'd been through his fair share of hard times.

"Lookin' for work," Zachary said. "Heard you might have some."

Dusty's face softened for a moment. He looked them over, his gaze lingering on Tobias. "What do you know about longhorns?"

Zachary straightened. "Ran a hundred head before we lost our place. We know cattle."

Dusty nodded, glancing at Clive before making his decision. "We could use the help. I need someone watchin' the ranch, and we're down a few hands."

Clive's eyes narrowed. "I'd like to ask these men a few questions first, Uncle."

Dusty ignored him, focusing on Zachary. "You'll be the caretaker while we're gone. Is the kid old enough to join us on the drive?"

Tobias blurted, "Please, Pa? Please can I go?"

Zachary sighed. "I dreaded this day, but I always knew it would come." He bit his lip and looked at Dusty. "We're much obliged."

Tobias didn't say another word. His eyes squinted at the room around him, sizing it up—like he was already settling into his new life.

When Dusty returned from showing Zachary to his room in the house, he turned back to Clive. "The herd's three thousand. We leave tomorrow. That's final."

Clive's lip curled in anger, but he didn't push it any further. Instead, he muttered, "We don't see things the same, you and me."

Dusty crossed his arms again. "*That* is one thing we agree on."

Seph watched from the kitchen as the argument fizzled out, but Clive wasn't done pushing. Seph could see it in his cold blue eyes.

Zachary and Tobias reemerged from the caretaker's quarters to help Seph prepare the cowboys' last supper. Meanwhile, Seph listened as Dusty went through the roster. Normally, the ramrod would have a word to say about job assignments, but Seph understood why Dusty didn't ask for Clive's opinion.

Dusty declared, "Trinket will be our scout. Stoke and Scorch ride point." Seph frowned. He would never have given that job to Scorch, but Dusty was the boss. "We'll have three pairs riding swing: Tumble and Whirlwind; Yodel and Lullaby; and Rooster and Blaze. Hork and Conjure ride flank. I want Chops to wrangle the remuda again. At drag we have the new man, Tobias, plus Sparrow and Torp. Seph's got the chuckwagon."

Seph chewed the skin at the edge of his thumbnail.

Dusty turned toward the kitchen. "Dinner better be good, son. Our boys need a meal to remember."

Twenty-four days up the trail, Seph gritted his teeth as he hauled buckets of water from the Trinity River back to the big water barrel strapped to the chuckwagon.

He wiped sweat from his forehead, pausing for a quiet moment before setting up camp for the evening.

Hoofbeats sounded behind him. Seph turned, positioning himself for trouble. He'd learned to be wary.

Two riders approached with purpose, dismounting swiftly. These men weren't like the Deatherage cowboys. They were older and looked tougher.

"Howdy," one of them said, his voice edged with steel. "I'm John Quincy Long. This here's my partner, John Memphis Short."

Short nodded, his eyes glinting with mischief as he crossed his arms. "Nice day for fetchin' water, ain't it?" he said with a smirk.

Seph kept his stance ready and his expression neutral. "Good day. Name's Seph." These men looked like trouble. The less he said, the better.

Long tipped his hat. "We're with Grim Decker's crew—Three Bar Box outfit. Maybe you seen our brand?" He chuckled, flashing yellowed teeth. "Means a lot to us. Represents three bars in a window, you see—prison bars. We all done our time, paid our debt to society, and walked away free men. Just so you know—we ain't ever goin' back. No sirree."

Short chuckled darkly. "That's right. We're looking to move forward, not back to Huntsville." His face twisted into a sneering grin, contradicting what he said next. "We're on the straight and narrow path now."

Seph's pulse quickened. These weren't just trail riders—they were ex-convicts, proud of it, and they didn't care who knew.

Long stepped closer, eyeing the chuckwagon and mules. "Looks like you're packin' up the trail yourselves. Headin' to Abilene?"

"Yep," Seph answered, crisply. "With the Deatherage outfit. Dagger D, Angry R."

Short scoffed. "Ooh. Scary," He feigned a shiver. "Death *and* rage. We better watch out in case you fellers start trouble along the way."

Long laughed. "I got a feeling we're gonna see a lot of each other. When you see us coming, you kids better get out of the way and let us go by."

Short added, "That's right. Now that we're law-abiding citizens, we ain't a gonna break no laws—" he smirked, "but we're sure to bend them as much as we can. Long as we're in the states." He didn't have to add that Indian Country might be another matter.

They turned back to their horses, but before riding off, Short grinned over his shoulder. "And that's the Long and Short of it!"

Their laughter trailed behind them as they disappeared down the trail. Seph exhaled slowly. The knot in his stomach tightened. The Three Bar Box outfit was going to be troublesome.

As he finished setting up camp, the feeling only grew stronger. Stoke helped him build the cook fire as Seph told him about the encounter.

"Who were they?" Stoke asked.

"Couple of ex-cons out of Huntsville. Ride with a man named Grim. Every one of 'em did time."

Stoke shook his head. "Great." The top hand was never one to back down from a challenge, but his voice was dry. "It's gonna be a long ride to Abilene."

Chapter 4

Clive tugged his hat low as he stepped into Gert's Griddle House. The smell of frying bacon and fresh biscuits lured him in. The place wasn't fancy, but after weeks on the trail, he relished Cowtown's hot meals and warm beds.

Gert, a sharp-eyed woman with a no-nonsense look, waved him toward a table. "Sit anywhere, cowboy. Coffee?"

He nodded, barely looking at her, and picked a quiet spot in the corner where he could keep an eye on things.

As she poured his coffee, Clive noticed a man a few tables over—broad shoulders, sharp jawline, eyes like he'd seen his share of trouble. The stranger glanced up, tipping his head almost imperceptibly. Something in the way he looked at Clive—like he was sizing him up—set his nerves on edge.

Gert returned with a plate of bacon, eggs, and oversized biscuits. "Anything else, honey?"

Clive shook his head, turning his focus to the food. But as he ate, the stranger shifted in his chair and cleared his throat. "Long ride, huh?"

Clive glanced up, fork halfway to his mouth. "Yeah. Something like that."

The man leaned back, stretching his arms. "Name's Ward Decker. Folks call me Grim."

Clive raised an eyebrow but didn't offer his own name. "You run cattle?"

Grim chuckled. "In a manner of speaking. It ain't for everybody."

Clive studied him, taking in the hard lines of his face, the way his eyes swept the room. This wasn't just another cattleman.

"You look like you've been at it for a while," Grim said casually, nodding toward Clive's dusty clothes. "Ever think of running things yourself?"

Clive shrugged. "Maybe. I'm running day-to-day operations now, so I'm set up pretty good."

Grim's stare bore into him. He leaned forward, lowering his voice just enough to hook him in. "Then you know how it is. Sometimes, a man's gotta do what's best for the herd—even when the boss don't see the big picture."

Clive stilled, fork hovering. The words struck a nerve. Dusty was stuck in the past. He was cautious, unwilling to take risks. Not like Clive.

"I've been thinking the same thing," Clive muttered, taking a swig of coffee. "Some men are too set in their ways. You got a ranch?"

"Bought a place down south," Grim said. "Fixer-upper, but it'll do. Thing is, building a herd is slow work. Unless a man's got the right opportunities."

Clive set his cup down. His curiosity was piqued. "What kind of opportunities?"

Grim smiled faintly, leaning back in his chair. "The kind that could double a herd. Maybe more."

Clive's interest sharpened. "Go on."

Grim toyed with the rim of his coffee cup, his eyes gleaming. "I'm just saying, a man in the right position could... combine forces. Grow the herd, make a real name for himself. But the ones in charge? They gotta be willing to... take chances. Know what I mean?"

Clive chuckled, finally letting his guard down. "Dusty's about as cautious as they come. You want to talk about taking chances, you're looking at the wrong man. He used to be alright, but ever since his back started bothering him, he's become grouchy as a grizzly."

Grim raised an eyebrow. "Dusty?"

Clive nodded. "Yeah. Glenn Deatherage. My uncle. Runs a tight ship, but he's afraid of everything. We could drive double the number of cattle this year, but he wants to stick to last year's numbers."

Grim tilted his head slightly. "And what if you had a say in things?"

Clive exhaled. "I'm only getting ten percent. Ten lousy percent, just because I'm his nephew. He doesn't think I'm worth any more. Pierce, my other uncle, got half, but me? I get crumbs."

Grim studied him, then tilted his head. "You ever think about taking the reins? I mean really taking control?"

A flicker of something dangerous lit in Clive's chest. "Oh, I've thought about it."

"Well, you ain't alone," Grim said with a sly grin. "If you were willing to work with someone like me, I could guarantee you more than ten percent. Heck, I could make it twenty percent of everything we bring in. All you gotta do is... persuade your uncle to take a little gamble."

Clive raised an eyebrow. "A gamble?"

Grim's smile widened. "There's a doctor in town. Deals with folks who have back issues like your uncle's. He's got something that'll loosen 'im up—make him more agreeable to the idea of a little wager. Nothing crazy, just a race to the Smoky Hill River. My herd against his."

Clive hesitated. "A race?"

Grim nodded. "Winner takes all. By the time we reach Abilene, you'll have more cattle than you ever dreamed of. And your uncle won't know what hit him."

Clive's grandmother's voice rattled around in his head. "Be realistic, Clive." The word made his skin itch.

This wasn't reckless. This was strategy. Opportunity.

He leaned in, matching Grim's grin. "What's the name of this doctor?"

Grim chuckled. "Doctor Deal. Got an office right next door. Just tell him what you need and slip him some cash. He don't care."

Clive looked out the window, where the sun was just beginning to rise. "All right, Grim. Let's do it."

Gert appeared at the table with the check. Her sharp eyes flicked between the two men as if she knew what they were up to. But Clive told himself such thoughts were ridiculous.

"Good breakfast?" she asked.

Grim leaned back, flashing a smile. "Best breakfast I've had in a long time. Wouldn't you say so, Clive?"

Seph stepped into Hogan's General Store, his mind split between the long list of supplies they needed and the job offer he planned to make.

Charlie Coppedge trailed just behind him, his one arm tucked inside his vest. The old soldier had seen better days, but Seph figured he had plenty left in him. Charlie wasn't exactly a cowhand, but he'd managed to survive the war and its aftermath. Seph had an idea that the trail might suit him better than scraping by in Cowtown.

A bell jingled as Hork and Rooster followed them inside. The mercantile smelled of pine soap, fresh tobacco, and molasses. Shelves lined the walls, stacked with everything from dry goods to tools, furniture to fabric. It was hard to imagine there was anything Hogan didn't carry.

Behind the counter, a sturdy man with a thick gray mustache and a striped vest eyed them from under the brim of his weathered hat. "Morning, boys. Stockin' up to chase beeves to the rails?"

Seph gave a polite nod. "Got a list as long as my arm, only it's in my head."

Hogan grunted. "Figures."

Rooster plucked a tin of tobacco off the shelf with a grin. "How 'bout this? That on your list?"

Seph smirked but kept moving, tallying costs in his head. He ran his hands over sacks of flour, cornmeal, and beans, gauging what they'd need for the long drive ahead. Every dollar mattered.

"I want to make sure Hork eats somethin' besides beans," Seph muttered, tossing a sack of cornmeal over his shoulder and nodding at a pile of potatoes.

Hork grunted his approval. "Mighty kind of ya."

Charlie Coppedge grinned from ear to ear. "Not many men would think about another fella's belly on a cattle drive. Most cowpokes only care about fillin' their own."

Seph turned, glad for the distraction. "Glad to have you along, Charlie. Dusty said to offer you a job—half pay and all you can eat. Reckon you don't eat much."

Charlie let out a dry chuckle. "Son, I'd take no pay if it meant ridin' free and not beggin' in Cowtown no more. You got yourself one crusty old hand. Half pay sounds right fine to me."

Seph extended his hand. "Done, then."

Charlie shook it, his grip surprisingly firm. "You won't regret it."

Rooster barked a laugh. "Half pay? Don't that beat all. You gonna live on half rations, too?"

Charlie gave him a withering look. "Heck, I'll eat more if the food's good."

Hogan shuffled from behind the counter, adding more beans to the shelves. "You fellas got your sites set on Abilene?"

"That we do," Seph said, still running figures in his head. The tally was just under what Dusty had given him, with a little left over. "We'll take it."

Hogan gave a firm nod. "I'll get it packed. You'd best load up before dark. Some folks 'round here got sticky fingers."

The Green Garter was louder than any place Seph had ever been. Tinny music plinked from between the keys of an upright piano in the corner. Smoke billowed from the ceiling nearly to the floor, thick as river fog, mingling with the sharp bite of whiskey. His boots gummed to the tacky floorboards, like someone had spilled molasses on them. Cowboys, gamblers, and roughnecks crowded around tables, slamming down mugs, shouting bets, and tossing cards with the reckless abandon of men who had nothing to lose.

Rooster spun a round-faced saloon girl across the floor, her skirts flaring high, flashing bright green garters with each lively step. She let out a throaty laugh as he pulled her close again, her curls bouncing to the music.

Seph stuck close to Hork, taking it all in. He had a beer in hand but had barely sipped the foam from the brim. He'd been in a few saloons before—mostly at the end of last year's drive in Abilene—but he still wasn't sure he liked them. The noise, the stink, the feeling that trouble could bust loose any second—it set his teeth on edge. Made him wary.

Hork nudged him. "Look at Dusty, will ya?"

They wove through the crowd, edging closer.

"Never seen him drink like that," Seph fretted. He watched Dusty's reflection in the mirror behind the bar. What he saw troubled him.

Hork shrugged, rolling a chunk of licorice between his teeth. The black stain on his lips and tongue made him look like he'd been gnawing on boot polish—not that he cared. He swore licorice settled his stomach, especially after too many dang beans. A trickle of black juice dribbled from the corner of his mouth as he said, "Dusty's back's been killin' him. Doctor gave him some medicine—maybe that's why he's pourin' whiskey on top of it tonight."

Seph frowned and scanned the room again, like watching over a herd of beeves after midnight.

Closer now, he saw Clive leaning toward Dusty, speaking low. Seph couldn't make out the words, but the posture said it all. Too smooth. Too intent. Clive was up to something. Like a gambler grooming a mark.

At a nearby table, Grim Decker and his men watched Dusty and Clive like hawks. Grim lounged back, his chair tipped on two legs. One boot rested solidly on the table. He looked every bit like a man who ran an outfit of ex-convicts.

One of Grim's men caught Seph's eye. Something about him scratched at a buried memory, like a half-forgotten nightmare. It made Seph's skin crawl.

Grim leaned over and said something to John Quincy Long. Long's lips curled at the corners, just slightly. Was that amusement? Approval? Grim knocked back his drink and bared his teeth like a wolf tasting blood. Whatever burned its way down didn't faze him—he seemed to relish the bite.

Seph studied them. Unlike the other men in the Green Garter, Grim's crew didn't joke, laugh, or let their guard down. Their features were carved in hard lines and sharp angles. They sat still as stone, but their eyes flickered and dashed. Always moving. Always watching, like a mountain lion on a ridge. Seph braced himself, half expecting an explosion of violence.

Rooster leaned against the bar, catching his breath after endlessly spinning saloon girls round the dance floor. He jerked his chin toward Grim's table. "What do you make of them boys?"

Seph peeled his eyes away from the familiar-looking man. "I don't like the look of 'em. Not one bit."

Rooster frowned. "We'd best keep an eye on that lot."

Hork rubbed his chin.

Seph barely noticed them. His attention locked onto Dusty, still deep in conversation with Clive—and a local lawyer named Delmar Deal. The sight of the man sent a fresh jolt of unease through Seph. He edged closer.

The saloon hushed. Even the piano player paused. Curiosity spread through the room like a prairie fire.

Clive's voice slid through the silence, smooth as silk. "What if there was a way to double our herd, Uncle?"

Dusty's reply came too loud. He tipped his chin up like he was talking to the ceiling, arms spread wide. "Why not? Bigger the better, right? Too bad we didn't think of that sooner."

Seph's gizzard caught fire. Dusty didn't talk like that.

Clive played it cool, but Seph saw him work Dusty like a drover hazing a bolting longhorn back into line. "Now you're talkin' Uncle. And what if it weren't too late? What if we could double our herd—without hardly lifting a finger? Easy as buttering a biscuit."

Dusty blinked, swaying slightly. "How?" His voice had the slow drawl of a man wading through thick mud.

"Simple," Clive said, sipping his whiskey. "A bet."

Grim leaned forward, eyes gleaming. His voice boomed over the din of the rowdy saloon. "You boys wanna make a wager? I'm game. Plodding along in the saddle sure drags. Let's liven things up a bit."

Dusty turned, finally noticing Grim. He hiccuped before speaking, but didn't seem to notice. "What're you thinkin'?"

Grim dropped his chair from two legs to four, planting his forearms on the table. His words came sharp as a porcupine quill. "I've got a herd headin' the same way. How about we race for it? First outfit to the Smoky Hill River gets the other's herd."

A drunk shoved his buddy, sending the man crashing into the crowd, sloshing beer onto a card table. Someone hooted, another whistled, and a voice rang out from the back, slurred yet eager, "Heck, I'll put money on that! Who else wants in?" Laughter rollicked through the Green Garter, elbows nudging ribs, men leaning in, eager for a piece of the action.

Seph felt like he'd been kicked in the ribs. No.

Rooster stiffened beside him.

Hork's face turned as green as the saloon girls' garters.

"You can't be serious," Seph gasped, strangling out words like he was choking.

Dusty chuckled, rubbing his back. "Race, huh? And when we win, we get your herd on top of ours?"

Clive stepped in, posing as the voice of reason. "You don't have to do this, Uncle. But I reckon we could take 'em if you wanted to. How tough could it be?"

Dusty considered, swaying slightly. "What're you ridin' with, Decker?"

Grim leaned back, shifting slightly as he planted his palms on his thighs, radiating confidence. "Fifteen men. Seasoned. Hard as nails."

Seph moved closer, fists clenched tight. He couldn't just stand by and let this happen.

Before Seph could speak, Delmar Deal stepped forward, pulling out two half-written contracts. "We'll need to put it in writing."

Seph's breath faltered. This was happening too fast—like a locomotive barreling down the rails.

Seph tried again. "Dusty, you can't—"

Dusty raised a hand, squelching him. "It's alright, kid. We're gonna beat 'em. Ain't nothin' to worry about."

Clive turned his head, the scar on his chin pulsing as he spoke, his lips curing into something too thin to be called a smile. "We tried to talk him out of it, but he won't change his mind."

Seph's eyes darted about, looking for an ally in the crowd. The other cowboys were too stunned to speak. Rooster froze, his shoulders squared at Dusty. Hork's arms hung limp at his sides, useless as a sack of potatoes.

Seph felt like a buffalo was sitting on his chest.

Dusty nodded toward Delmar with a wobbly head. "Let's make it... uh-fish-a-bull."

Mr. Deal gave a curt nod in response and echoed, "Official. Indeed. Yes, sir."

The bartender scribbled down side bets. Patrons crowded closer, shouting wagers.

Seph's head spun. *No. No. No.*

The whole thing gave Seph a cracking headache. Thoughts tumbled in his mind, but the one that stood out was *this can't be happening.*

The lawyer quickly scrawled out the terms of the bet. His pen moved in a blur, the quill scratching the paper's surface. Ink sprawled across the pages. Within minutes, two copies of the contract were laid out on the bar, each one detailing the terms of the race: the first outfit to conquer the Smoky Hill River would take both herds.

Dusty reached for the pen. His hand hovered for a moment. Was he having second thoughts? But then, with a quick, decisive scrawl, he signed his name.

Grim signed next. A satisfying grunt followed his signature.

Seph felt sick. This wasn't the Dusty he knew. This was never supposed to happen.

Dusty called him forward to sign as a witness. Seph tried to back away, but duty compelled him forward.

Grim's witness signed first. Then, Seph inked his name at the bottom. His gaze lingered on the page. There was a reason that man looked familiar, and realization crept across him like a slow chill.

As Dusty and Grim shook hands, sealing the deal, Mitch stepped up beside Seph. "You look like you've seen a ghost, boy."

Seph looked hard at him, then glanced back at the document. He felt as if he had been punched in the gut. "Your name's Vermillion? It can't be."

Mitch grinned. "That's right. It's almost like we're brothers." He slapped Seph on the shoulder. "Well, ain't that something? Looks like we *are* kin, boy. Maybe we oughta be on the same side of this bet."

Seph's mind raced. "From Poesta Creek?"

Mitch nodded. "That was long ago. I ain't been back. Ain't never going back, neither."

Seph could barely breathe. The ex-convict, Mitch Vermillion, was his brother. He struggled to process the thought. *His brother.* It had to be. The man's name was in Ma's Bible.

He spoke before thinking. "Same sides? No, Mitch. I ride for the Dagger D, Angry R. Nothing's gonna change that."

He thought about Hazel, how he almost quit the outfit, and tipped his head forward, shielding his eyes beneath his hat brim. That was different. But this wasn't a time to think of her. He shoved her from his mind, and the thought that remained irked him. *Why didn't his brother want to return home?*

As Dusty and Grim raised their glasses to toast the bet, Seph turned away from the contract on the bar. His stomach twisted.

They were in deep now. And there was no turning back.

CHAPTER 5

THE FIRST HINT OF dawn was still hours away, but Dusty was in a rush to get started. "Up and at 'em, boys! We're burnin' daylight."

Seph rubbed sleep from his eyes and scrambled from his bedroll. He spoke to himself out loud, "It's still dark, how can we be burning daylight?"

Dusty's voice boomed as he clapped his hands together. "Gather 'round the chuckwagon, boys. I got somethin' to say."

Seph stretched and yawned as he made his way to the wagon. Around him, the other cowboys groaned, cursed, and sluggishly complied.

Torp tugged at Seph's elbow, his voice cracking. "What's happening? This can't be good, can it?"

Seph shrugged. "Maybe it's about last night." Dusty looked worn and weary, like an old man at the end of a cattle drive. But this trip to Abilene had just begun. As Seph stirred the fire, he thought, *Dusty is too young to look so old.*

As the men gathered, Seph thought he could see their breath misting in the air. But it was too warm for that.

Hork stumbled, clutching his stomach, while Rooster swaggered over. Even half asleep, the kid moved like a chicken, his head moving forward and back, his chest thrust forward, like he was trying to impress a barnyard full of hens. His nickname suited him.

Dusty cleared his throat and spoke slowly. "Look, boys, I know I got us into a tough spot. By now, you've all heard about that wager with Grim Decker's crew."

Seph watched Clive from the corner of his eye.

Dusty continued, "I wish I could take it back, but I can't. It's done, and we're in deep now. We've got a race ahead of us, and I won't lie—it's gonna be hard. This is gonna be the roughest challenge you've ever faced."

He paused, stopping to drill his gaze into each man's soul, lingering on Seph, Stoke, and even Clive. "But I ain't askin' you to do this for nothin'. Or regular wages. There's a share in it for each of you."

Seph saw Clive's upper lip twitch, and then, as Dusty went on, Clive's face contorted in disgust. His disdain was impossible to miss. Dusty's words stunned Clive.

"That share's forty percent of the profits." Dusty paused, letting the words sink in. "It's all yours, divided fair and square, just like mine and Clive's. But it's only if we win. If we fail, I can't pay you. But if we win, every last one of you walks away with more money than you ever dreamed of making on a cattle drive."

Torp gasped, and Seph turned to look at the kid. His chin hung low, mouth agape.

Stoke whistled. "How about that? I guess that makes us all partners. Real, honest-to-goodness partners." He stood with his legs wide, hands on his hips, shaking his head slowly from side to side. "Dang, I thought I'd heard of everything."

In a weak voice, Conjure said, "Yeah, that's great if we win but I can't see it. Ain't it more likely Grim's men take this? Have you seen them? They ain't gonna make it easy."

Squint burst in breathlessly. "Them's the men that run me and Pops off our place on the Medina River. Took it for their own." He shivered as if he'd just had a run-in with the devil.

Seph's chest tightened at the thought. The reality of their predicament was sinking in fast. He stole a glance at the others. Rooster's eyes gleamed with excitement, while Hork perked up despite his usual complaints. Lullaby's head was tipped back, his lips moving as if in prayer. Seph imagined him asking the Lord for strength. Trinket, half-asleep, nodded along, catching the drift.

Clive leaned against the chuckwagon. His lips were pursed, like he was about to hack a wad of phlegm. Seph was still trying to figure out the boss's nephew. Clive studied his uncle from afar, rarely speaking, but the look on his face betrayed his thoughts. The disapproval faded, replaced by something else. Seph thought he saw the ghost of a smirk. Seph always wanted to trust a man's intentions, but with Clive, he just couldn't.

Dusty barked, "Alright, let's get them beeves movin' before Grim and his gang catch wind of us. We can't afford to waste a minute. Never know when we might need that time later."

Dusty's words spurred the men into action, turning the camp into a fury of movement. Seph hustled to shove out a quick breakfast, glad to have Charlie there to lend a hand. He was thankful he'd tossed wood on the fire before Dusty spoke. Cold biscuits, steaming mush, and strong coffee—it wasn't much, but nobody complained. They grumbled and cursed under their breaths, but they ate.

Clive was the last in line for breakfast and lingered suspiciously. He stood close to Seph, mostly turned away, his shoulder near the camp cook. He turned his head slightly toward Seph. "Hey. Little Sister. Thanks for trying to talk some sense into the boss at the Green Garter."

Seph didn't think much of being called *Little Sister*. Many of the men did it, just as they called last year's cook *Old Lady*. But he couldn't help feeling like the ramrod was trying to butter him up.

Clive rolled his eyes and flashed a quick glance at Seph before looking away. Clive continued, "What was Dusty thinking? He ain't quite right in the head, I'm afraid. We'd better keep an eye on him." He shook his head slowly, frowning, then turned and walked away.

Seph was relieved that he didn't have to say anything to Clive that morning.

Cowboys stumbled over each other to saddle up in the dark. Chops worked quickly, bridling and saddling their mounts, while the boys checked the tack, just to be sure. It was always smart to be certain, especially with the feisty, half-broken cow ponies that liked to test a rider before work even began.

Clive barked orders, telling the cowhands what to do as if he'd been in charge for years.

Seph frowned.

The boss's nephew never passed up a chance to remind the crew that he was ramrodding the drive. It rankled to see the man telling people to do what they were already doing. It made no sense, but Clive did it anyway.

Seph worked to keep up. He had a system for cleaning up after breakfast, loading supplies into the chuckwagon, and hitching the mules quickly enough to ride out near the front of the cow column. Most of the time, the chuckwagon was positioned just ahead of the remuda, due west of the point riders. That meant moving fast to get into position. Sometimes, the plates were washed hastily and needed to be rewashed before being used again. But even with one hand, Charlie was a big help.

The air buzzed all around him. Breaking camp wasn't a quiet activity. The beeves bellowed their complaints, horses stomped their feet in protest, and tired young cowboys groused endlessly about how they never get the chance to sleep in.

Usually, there wasn't much conversation. In the morning, cowboys tended to communicate in grunts. But this wasn't like any other morning.

Things had changed in an instant. It was hard to make sense of what the boss had said. Who ever heard of making common drovers partners in a cattle drive? Or racing longhorns across the prairie?

Hork grumbled under his breath as he lifted his horse's hooves. It was smart to check and make sure they were clean. But Hork was preoccupied. He groused, "Dang fool bet. We'll be lucky if we don't end up in the poorhouse."

Rooster slapped Hork on the back. "We'll be rich if we win, Hork. You can quit cowboying and never eat beans again. How about that? Dusty's put us in the money. He sure has. Don't you get it? We're gonna be rich. Filthy, stinking rich."

Seph poured out the last of the coffee, overhearing Rooster. He liked to believe in the best possible outcomes, but it was hard to ignore the odds. Maybe they were fifty-fifty. More likely, Hork was right. Seph had faith in the Deatherage crew, but Grim's men seemed like the kind who would stop at nothing to win. The challenge gnawed at him. They'd barely made it last year with 3,000 head of cattle at a steady pace. Now, they'd be driving harder, faster, and with every mile, the stakes would rise.

All around him, the camp seemed like a disorganized scramble, but Seph felt his preparations for departure were orderly. Even so, he barely had time to secure the last sacks of flour and beans in the chuckwagon before Stoke nudged Skillet onto the trail, followed closely by a big spotted cow.

Seph climbed into the saddle, bracing himself for Hortense's usual morning fit of bucking. As if protesting the early morning start, she added extra twists to her daily protest. Seph wasn't one to complain, though he'd often griped about that bucking nag. That was last year. It hadn't taken long for him to enjoy the challenge of sticking to the saddle when Hortense tried to unseat him. She'd made him an expert rider, and now he relished helping Chops break the wildest mustangs.

Charlie sat on the wagon bench, driving the mules with a grin stretched wide across his face. He looked like he was having the time of his life. Seph had worried about whether the old-timer would be able to keep the mules moving and handle the chuckwagon, but Charlie proved himself, keeping the rolling pantry perfectly positioned in Skillet's wake. Conjure whined about Charlie, convinced that the *old bag of bones* was a ghost, but Seph didn't care what others thought. He was just glad to have his father's old war buddy along.

The herd was already on the move as the first hint of light streaked the sky. The long line of beeves stretched out in the darkness behind him. The Deatherage outfit drove the cattle north, away from Cowtown, getting a head start before the Three Bar Box crew could catch wind of their early departure. Seph smiled to himself. It might not last long, but for the moment, they were winning the race.

Dusty rode out in front, ahead of the herd. After speaking to the men that morning, he had grown silent. Seph sensed that Dusty was having second thoughts about the wager. Did he regret offering the men shares in the herd? It was hard to know what the boss was thinking. Seph frowned, recalling Clive's insinuation that Dusty was sick in the head.

Usually, Clive avoided Stoke and left the top hand alone. Seph wondered if maybe Clive was afraid of Stoke. When it came to the rest of the men, Clive was quick to give direction. He urged them on like it was the last day of the race instead of the first. Seph frowned as Clive snapped commands at the swing riders and wondered if Clive was harder on Lullaby and Yodel because they were black, or because they had worked for the Deatherage family since they were kids. Seph didn't figure the seasoned cowboys needed any more instruction. If anything, the younger men at the back of the herd might have benefited from a little guidance.

Seph couldn't help but glance over his shoulder, half-expecting Grim's men to ride up fast behind them. They had the trail to themselves, for now, but Seph imagined hordes of barbaric outlaws charging up from behind. He swallowed hard, forcing down the doubts that scraped the pit of his stomach.

There was no time for second-guessing. The race had begun. The only way was forward. They were in the lead but that didn't matter at all. The only thing that mattered was who crossed the finish line first on the last day of the race.

It was a long way from Cowtown to Abilene.

That morning, Dusty's announcement had been met with a mix of surprise and excitement. By supper, the weight of the wager had rooted deep. The cowpunchers had chewed it over all day, ruminating on it like the beeves chewing cud. Now, it was clear—the challenge had gotten under their skins.

Seph stood by the cookfire, watching the men line up with tin plates in hand. They looked tired, but there were hopeful expressions on their stubbled faces. Charlie ladled thick stew onto each plate while Seph passed out biscuits and poured coffee.

Dusty had offered them forty percent of the profits, to be split evenly among the cowboys. Seph had done some figuring. It was hard to imagine cowboys making that much money—just by pushing beeves. But that was only if they reached Abilene first.

They'd have to push the herd hard, faster than any of them were used to. No time for fattening the beeves or long breaks by riverbanks. It would be a relentless march north. Part of Seph still couldn't believe what he'd heard. But he'd seen the deal go down. He'd even signed the contract, officially witnessing the deal.

"Dusty's serious, you know," Stoke said, stepping up beside him looking for a second serving of stew. "Never heard of a trail boss offering shares like that. I'll do 'most anything to make sure we win. But our crew's more boys than men. You and me, we've got our hands full. How we gonna wrangle these sorry tenderfeet all the way to Abilene?"

Seph grimaced. Stoke had put his worries into words. "It sure won't be easy. If we can keep it close, maybe we've got a shot."

Stoke smirked. "I hate to lose. You know that, Seph. Them Three Bar Box men is tough. No telling what they'll do to make sure they win."

Seph handed him an extra biscuit. "That's exactly what worries me."

Stoke moved off, and Rooster took his place, flashing his cocky grin. "Nice to have a night with no beans, Little Sister." He shoved Seph's shoulder roughly, but playfully.

"How about steak and eggs for breakfast?" Seph joked. "Eat up while you got the chance, Rooster. 'Fore long, you'll be lucky to eat twice a day, and it'll be nothing but beans and mush for weeks at a stretch."

Rooster chuckled. "Who cares? I'm gonna be rich." He leaned in close to Seph and asked, "You're good with figures. How's this shake out? How much am I gonna get?"

Seph glanced around. The other cowboys were listening too. He sighed, turning toward the crowd and scratching the back of his head. "Forty percent divided by fifteen men. You're looking at around 2.6 percent each."

Rooster's eyes went wide. "What's a percent? That don't sound like much."

Seph said, "It's your share. A fraction. Let's do the math. Six thousand beeves times 2.6 percent. That comes to 160 head. And 160 times $35 a head. Gosh, Rooster."

Rooster let out a low whistle. "Don't stop now. What's the answer?"

"That's $5,600," Seph said. Some of the men didn't seem to understand. "Each," he added.

"Five thousand, six hundred dollars." Rooster pinched his nose, and Seph recalled him talking about being filthy, stinking rich. The pinched nose made Rooster sound nasal. "I'll never have to work another day in my life."

Seph thought briefly about the cowboy who had ridden in with Clive. Rooster had grown on him, and seemed to fit in, despite his quirks.

"We'll all be rich," Blaze chimed in.

The other cowboys chattered excitedly, nudging each other. Even Hork cracked a smile. For the first time since Dusty announced the wager, the full force of what was at stake walloped them square in the face.

But as the excitement buzzed around the campfire, Clive stepped closer to Seph. His expression was unreadable. He waited until most of the others had moved away before saying, "You're a responsible kid, Seph. More'n most. Having you along, I almost believe we might win this wager."

Seph blinked at the unexpected praise. Maybe Clive was coming around. He should give him a chance, but he couldn't help wondering—what's Clive's angle? But before he could reply, Clive clapped him on the back and moved off to join the others.

Watching him go, a nagging feeling hovered over his shoulders. The old adage about being wary when something sounded too easy rattled in his thoughts and left him with a sense of unease—like he'd missed some important fact or detail.

There was no time to think about it now. Plenty of time to ponder on it later. He glanced over at Charlie, who broke small portions off his biscuit, placed them on his tongue, and mashed them against the roof of his mouth before swallowing.

Seph wiped his hands on a rag and asked, "How you holdin' up, old-timer?"

Charlie tipped his head forward. "Better'n I expected." His eyes misted. "Thanks for asking me to come along. Sure beats beggin' for half dimes on the streets of Cowtown." He looked like he wanted to say more. His jaws flapped, but no words followed.

"Don't mention it," Seph replied. "You're a real help 'round here."

Charlie winked, lifting his tin cup in a mock toast. "Here's to you, Seph. Your Pa'd sure be proud of you."

Seph appreciated Dusty letting him bring the old soldier along. As he finished cleaning up, a howl rang out from the edge of camp. Seph turned sharply, catching sight of Yodel stumbling back, clutching his leg. Seph raced to the chuckwagon and grabbed his small sack of medical gear.

Yodel had tripped over a stray root. His shin was swelling beneath a nasty scrape. He winced as Seph knelt beside him. "That's what I get. Should've watched where I was goin'."

"Sit tight," Seph said, his hands shaking slightly. "I'll fix you up." He worked quickly, cleaning the wound and wrapping it tightly with a strip of cloth.

Yodel grimaced but held still. When Seph finished, he gave a grateful nod. "Thanks, Seph."

Yodel was a man of few words.

Seph nodded acknowledgement, stood up, and wiped the sweat from his brow. Treating patients would take some getting used to.

As the men stretched out on the ground and drifted off to sleep, Seph and Charlie still had work to do. The weight of responsibility pressed on him. The camp cook was always the first up and the last to bed, with no time to rest along the trail. On top of that, he had to handle the doctoring and blacksmithing. But Seph never shied away from a task. No matter how tired he grew, he would rise to the challenge. Still, he missed the simpler days of riding drag, with his childhood friend Slaw on one side and the orphan Torp on the other.

He hated to doubt his fellow men, but he couldn't shake the feeling that they were in over their heads. Way over.

But there was no turning back now.

CHAPTER 6

THE SECOND DAY OUT of Cowtown was grueling. The herd stretched into an endless line and it was hot as an oven. There were no breaks to eat, water the horses, or let the beeves graze. Just a hard push north, with everyone straining to remain ahead of the Three Bar Box outfit.

Seph guided Hortense alongside the herd, balancing canteens across his saddle horn and a burlap sack filled with dried beef and biscuits for the men. He wished he could provide more comfort than dry food and warm water. At least Charlie was handling the chuckwagon and provisions, allowing him to keep the men fed while they worked.

He rode toward the front of the herd, where Stoke and Scorch manned the point position. As he got closer, he noticed that they were out of place. It looked like a confrontation was brewing, and sure enough, they dismounted quickly, shouting at each other.

"You ain't fit to ride point," Stoke snapped, jabbing a finger toward Scorch. "You keep riding like that, you'll get yourself or your partner killed."

Seph reined in Hortense, keeping his distance but remaining close enough to see the veins bulging in Scorch's neck. His face was flushed with anger, and his hands were balled into fists.

Scorch sneered, fury burning in his eyes as he stomped toward Stoke. "You think you're something, don't ya? You've gotten mighty used to everyone doing what you want. But I ain't like that. Quit telling me what to do."

Stoke's face tightened. Seph could tell he was itching for a fight. "I've been riding point longer than you've had fuzzy whiskers on that chin. I tell you what to do because you don't know enough to do this job without being told how."

Scorch's cheeks burned bright red, like he had a sunburn. "You're all talk, Stoke. That's all you ever do. Blah, blah, blah! Always barking orders like you're still in the war. Ain't nobody wanna hear it. Least of all me."

Stoke's eyes flashed, and he took a step closer, his fingers curling into his hands. "I say what I want. You're the one who needs to shut your trap. Keep runnin' that mouth, and I'll shut it for you."

Seph nudged Hortense closer and thought about whether he should intervene. Before he could speak, Scorch lunged.

The hot-tempered cowboy swung a wild fist, aiming for Stoke's jaw. But Stoke moved like a flash, ducking the blow and driving his knuckles into Scorch's gut, landing with a thud.

Scorch doubled over, gasping for air, but he didn't stay down long. He staggered back to his feet, eyes burning with a fiery hatred as he charged again. His shoulder led the way and he tried to knock Stoke off balance. The kid was scrappy, but he lacked control.

Stoke sidestepped, letting Scorch's momentum carry him past. "You got a lot to learn, pup," Stoke growled, grabbing the back of Scorch's shirt and yanking him to his feet.

Seph watched as Stoke wrestled Scorch to the ground, dust swirling up in thick clouds around them.

The commotion caught Dusty's attention. The boss made his way forward and dismounted as Stoke and Scorch scrambled to their feet. Dusty placed a hand on Scorch's shoulder to break up the fight.

Scorch pivoted and slammed a row of knuckles into Dusty's jaw before realizing that he'd just decked the trail boss.

Dusty's voice rang out, sharp and commanding. "That's enough!"

Stoke's fists were still clenched, ready for more.

Scorch's chest heaved with anger, but he barely seemed out of breath.

"What in the blazes is going on here?" Dusty demanded, his gaze burning into Scorch.

Scorch spat into the dust. "Just settlin' things up, boss. That ox aggravated me. That's all."

Dusty's expression darkened as he shook his head. "That aggravating ox is our top hand." He pointed to his cheek. "And this is my face."

"It was an accident, Dusty." Scorch's gaze dropped to his hat, then lifted back to the boss. "I swear, I didn't mean to hit *you*."

Dusty growled, "You ain't got the temperament for this kind of work, Scorch. I can't have a man around that's dumb enough to punch the boss. Pack up your gear and get out of my sight."

Seph blinked in stunned amazement as he watched the exchange. The reality of the firing settled like a stone in his gut. Scorch was a hothead, but Seph hadn't expected Dusty to cut him loose.

Rage twisted Scorch's face. For a moment, Seph thought the red-haired cowpoke might take another swing at Dusty. He could see it in Scorch's eyes—he was considering it. Reason won out in the end, and though he didn't strike, the contempt in his glare deepened and darkened.

"You're makin' a mistake, old man," Scorch hissed. "You think this drive's gonna be easy without me?"

Dusty didn't flinch. "I think you're lucky I'm not takin' that pistol of yours for good measure. Now git. Before I change my mind."

Scorch looked around at Stoke and Seph, then back down the line at the column of cows. His lip curled in disgust. "Yeah, well, we'll see how far you get without me, won't we?"

With that, he stomped back to his horse, yanked the reins, and swung into the saddle. He didn't look back as he spurred his horse hard, galloping away in a fury.

Seph exhaled slowly. His shoulders settled, but a sour taste lingered in his mouth as he watched Scorch ride away. That familiar grinding in his gizzard told him they hadn't seen the last of the red-haired cowpoke.

Dusty turned to Stoke. "Get back to your post. And keep this drive in line. We ain't got time for any more of this."

Stoke nodded, rubbing a hand over his jaw. "Yes, sir." He glanced at Seph, and for a moment, Seph was sure he saw a flicker of amusement in his eyes. The rough and ready top hand had become bearable after Seph saved his life the year before, but now and then, the mean-spirited prankster would re-surface.

Seph turned back toward the chuckwagon. Things had taken a turn for the worse. He watched as Dusty took Scorch's place at point, opposite Stoke.

Seph wiped sweat from his brow as he removed his shirt and tossed it aside. The garment landed in the dust beside the chuckwagon. Heat from the forge radiated against his skin as he crouched to shoe Clive's horse, King, a temperamental gelding. The horse shifted its weight, restless and irritable. Seph couldn't help comparing the horse to his master. King had a habit of pawing at the ground, constantly scuffing his shoes loose. It figured that a man like Clive would fancy a horse like that.

A few paces away, Charlie scooped beans onto tin plates, doling out vittles as fast as his one arm would allow. Seph glanced over to see him offering a potato to Hork, who accepted it with a grateful nod. Charlie beckoned, "Step up, boys, before they get cold."

The cowboys gathered around the chuckwagon. Even in the dark, their exhaustion was evident. They muttered thanks, found a spot to sit, and scraped their plates until every last bean was gone. But Seph focused on his task, working a stubborn shoe into place. It was hard, hot work, but it kept his mind off the miles still ahead—and the wager that weighed heavy on their backs.

He was about to lead the horse back to the picket line when he saw a rider approaching from the south. Straightening his back, Seph set down the hammer and squinted into the darkness. Welcoming strangers into camp after dark was always risky.

The lone rider shouted a friendly greeting as he rode slowly into the ring of firelight. The crew shifted their attention from their meals to the darkness beyond the cookfire. Seph's stomach tightened as he recognized the rider, but it wasn't surprise or fear that cramped his gizzard. It was more a dull sense of foreboding, like a bad wind blowing through the camp.

"Mitch? Mitch Vermillion." It felt strange saying the last name that they shared.

Mitch reined in his horse, sliding easily from the saddle. "Evening, boys," he drawled, nodding at Charlie, who looked up in surprise. Then he turned his attention to Seph. "Good to see you again, little brother."

Seph felt the heat from the forge receding as he stepped farther away from it. What was Mitch doing here?

It had been a shock to learn that the man who witnessed the wager was his long-lost brother. But Mitch's appearance in the Deatherage camp was even more surprising. Seph tried to reconcile the man in front of him with the vague memories of the older brother he hadn't seen in over a decade. Mitch's face was weathered, and his thick beard was unkempt. He looked out of place among the mostly smooth-faced crew of the Dagger D, Angry R. His clothes were worn and stained by years of hard living. And his eyes held a hardness that Seph couldn't relate to.

Finally, Mitch spoke up. "Where's the boss? I'm looking for work."

Seph surprised himself by speaking before anyone else could answer. "You left the Three Bar Box?" He tried to temper his expression and tone, but fiery doubt sparked off his tongue. "Just like that?"

Mitch shrugged as he glanced around the camp, taking in the cowboys who eyed him warily. "That's right. What of it? Grim's a hard man to ride for. But I see you've got yourself a nice operation here. Thought I'd come see if you've got room for one more."

Seph wanted to turn his back to Mitch. It was hard not to be judgmental. A man didn't just up and leave one outfit to join another. "You expect us to believe you just walked away?" Seph asked, crossing his arms. "Who wants to ride with a man who turns his back on his own pals?"

Mitch's expression grew somber. He shook his head, let out a long breath, and said, "You don't know what it's like over there. Grim's got no respect for his men. Treats us like we're still wearing chains. We did our time, Seph. Paid our debts. But he don't let nobody forget where he came from—Huntsville." Bitterness creeped into his tone. "I ain't a slave no more. Figured it was time I made my own way."

Seph studied Mitch's face. There were deep lines carved into his leathery skin. The set of Mitch's jaw hinted at the same stubbornness Seph often saw in himself. Memories from old days crept back. He was surprised to recall the brother who swiped food from his plate, constantly taunted him, and roughhoused as if they were the same age rather than separated by eleven years. Seph remembered feeling small, powerless—trying to swing back at his older brother with a child's rage, only to end up with a black eye or sore ribs.

Mitch stepped closer, his voice softening as he met Seph's gaze. "I ain't looking for trouble, little brother. Just a fresh start."

The other cowboys exchanged glances. Clive pushed forward through the crowd, his face drawn tight. "We ain't looking to take in any drifters, cowboy," he said sharply, crossing his arms over his chest. "Especially not ones who rode with Grim Decker."

Seph wasn't sure, but he thought he caught a conspiratorial wink from Clive as he turned toward Mitch.

Mitch's eyes flickered toward Clive, his smile never wavering. "I ain't looking for a handout, Deatherage. I'll earn my keep. Ain't that right, Seph?" His gaze slid back to Seph. Suddenly his tone turned smooth and buttery. "Remember when Ma used to say I could do anything better 'n you?"

Seph stiffened. He didn't remember any such thing. But he did remember the sharp jab of Mitch's fork into the food on his plate and the way he used to hoard the meaty chunks of stew from the pot. Anger stirred in his chest, but he kept it contained. "You sure about this, Mitch? You left Grim, and now you're just gonna ride with us like nothing happened?"

Mitch's grin faded slightly. "Grim's ways ain't for me no more. Figured I'd try my luck with family instead." He reached out a hand, almost as if offering to shake on it, but Seph didn't move.

Dusty's voice boomed, "You sayin' you want a place on my drive?"

Mitch nodded, his expression casual, but there was a gleam in his eyes that Seph didn't trust. "That's right. I've paid my dues. Now I need a fresh start. Figure you could use another hand."

Dusty's expression hardened. He thought for a moment, sized Mitch up. "We'll see about that." He turned to Seph. "What do you think, Seph?"

Seph hesitated, glancing back at his brother. Memories flashed through his mind until he couldn't make sense of them. He swallowed hard, but his voice was firm. "I figure he's a hard worker and a good hand, Dusty. But I don't trust him."

Mitch's smile returned, but there was a flicker of something darker in his eyes. "That's fair, Seph. Real fair. But I promise you, I ain't looking to cause trouble."

Dusty chewed on the inside of his cheek, then finally nodded. "Alright, then. You want in, you'll ride point with Stoke. But you make one wrong move, and you're out. Understand?"

Mitch nodded solemnly, but Seph couldn't shake the feeling that Dusty just made a terrible mistake. As he watched Mitch settle in, chatting easily with the other men, Seph's unease deepened. What if he was sent to work for Grim by the other side?

When Mitch's eyes lingered on the rifle that Seph had leaned against the chuckwagon—the one named after Uncle Yves—Seph felt a chill creep up his spine.

"Oh, hey," Mitch said casually, gesturing toward the gun. "That's my rifle, ain't it?"

Seph's jaw clenched. "Not anymore."

A foul smile spread across Mitch's face, but it didn't reach his eyes. "We'll see about that, too, little brother. Sure enough. We'll see."

Seph led King back to the picket line. Rain splattered Seph's bare shoulders and ran off the brim of his hat. He glanced to his side and saw Mitch following him. There was a self-assured swagger in his brother's step. The sight twisted Seph's spine. Once they were out of earshot from the others, Seph stopped and turned, fixing Mitch with a hard stare.

"You never came back," Seph growled low. "Ma needed us, and you left me alone. I was just a dumb kid, and I had to take care of everything."

Mitch smirked. The corner of his mouth curled up, but the rain had started to wash some of the smugness off his face. He looked older, more worn, with streaks of gray in his beard. "I ain't proud of how things turned out, little brother. But life's hard. It ain't fair. You should know that by now."

Seph clenched his fists at his sides. His jaw tightened so hard it ached. "Ma said you were off doing great things. All of you. But it ain't true. You're all a bunch of no-accounts. The whole lot of you."

Mitch pitched his head forward. "You know where our brothers and sisters are?"

"No," Seph snapped. "Just Jolie—at a bordello in Abilene. And I hope I never find the rest a y'all."

Mitch took a step closer, getting right in Seph's face, their noses nearly touching. "You think I like hearing that? You think I like hearing my little brother call me a no-account?" He scoffed, and his voice dropped to a rough whisper. "Well, I got news for you, kid. Life ain't nothing but disappointment after disappointment. You're starting to see that now, ain't ya? Boss hired me. You're just gonna have to deal with it."

Seph's hands twitched, and he thought of the rifle. He had left it beside the chuckwagon, and hated the fact that Uncle Yves was beyond reach. It reminded him of all those times outlaws raided their home. Mitch was a convict. Just like those bandits that terrorized him and Ma. Mitch belonged at the Three Bar Box, or in Huntsville, not the Dagger D, Angry R. Seph took a shuddering breath and stepped back, putting a few feet of space between them. "Yeah? Well, forget about me. We will see how long you last here, Mitch."

Mitch raised an eyebrow, the rain now pouring down between them. There was a harsh chill in the air. "Oh, I'll last. You don't need to like it. You just gotta live with it." He tilted his hat against the rain, turning back toward camp without another word.

Seph stood there for a moment, letting the rain soak into his skin. He watched Mitch fade into the shadows. A hollow ache filled Seph's chest. Everything had changed since that magical night with Hazel in Abilene last year. He had intended to take her away—to start a family—but now, here he was, staring down the ghost of a family he wanted to ignore. He tightened his grip on King's lead rope.

The words he'd said to his long-lost brother still burned on his tongue. But he wasn't sorry he'd said them.

Scorch hunched under a scrawny oak. Rain drummed on the leaves overhead and dripped down his back. His teeth chattered as he pulled his soaked coat tighter around him. He glanced back toward the distant flicker of the Deatherage campfire, just barely visible through the sheets of rain. His own fire had long since gone out.

"He can't just throw me out like that." Scorch spat into the mud. "I'll show them!"

The rain soaked into his clothes, plastering his hair to his head, but the fury in his chest burned hotter than a fever. He dug his boot heel into the wet earth. His thoughts turned dark and vengeful. "One hundred and sixty of them critters is mine. I'll be danged if I let them take my beeves."

He turned his back on the Deatherage camp. "This ain't over. It'll never be over. Not till I get what I got coming."

CHAPTER 7

SEPH BOLTED UPRIGHT AT the frantic sound of shouting. It was pitch dark. He scrambled to his feet, yanked his arms through the sleeves of his shirt, and tugged on his boots. Cowboys rushed in every direction, grabbing saddles and lanterns as the shrill neighing of spooked horses made for a rude awakening.

"What in the blazes—?" Seph muttered, rubbing the sleep from his eyes. He barely had time to process what was happening before Dusty's voice thundered in the night.

The trail boss shouted, "The picket line's been cut. Get those horses back before they scatter any further!"

Seph's blood went cold. He sprinted toward the remnants of the picket line, where severed ropes dangled uselessly from the posts. Only a handful of horses remained tied to the lines. The rest of the mustangs had scattered. Seph's mind raced, spinning through one possible explanation after another. Whoever did this knew exactly how to cripple their progress.

Blaze was right beside him, shouting, "Noomoo's gone! If I don't find that horse, I swear—"

Seph grabbed Blaze's arm, steadying him. "We'll find him, Blaze." He scanned the few remaining horses and urged, "Let's ride out and round up what we can."

Blaze nodded. His eyes were wild with worry. Fortunately, a couple of horses were within reach, and they saddled up quickly.

Seph struggled to mount Hortense. She danced to the side every time he tried to put a boot into the stirrup. Then she bucked and reared beneath him, nostrils flaring as usual. She tossed her head, twisted her body, and tried to unseat him. "Settle down, girl," Seph begged through clenched teeth. "I don't know why I always end up on this cantankerous nag," he shouted to Blaze.

Hortense nearly unseated him, but Seph managed to keep his balance. With most of the horses gone, there wasn't much choice. After her morning bucking fit, she settled down.

He spurred her into a gallop, feeling the powerful surge of her muscles beneath him. The cool air whipped against his face as he urged her forward, darting past the other cowboys. Hortense was a fast one.

Dusty's orders rang out behind them, directing the other men in different directions. "Fan out! Don't let 'em get too far! And someone get that chuckwagon ready to roll."

Seph leaned low over Hortense's neck as she flew across the prairie, her hooves kicking up clods of dirt. He spotted Rooster struggling with a pair of skittish mares, their ears pinned back and their eyes wild with fear.

"Need a hand?" Seph called over the wind, barely slowing as he swung his lasso over his head.

"Sure!" Rooster shot back, straining to steady the mares. Seph cast the loop, catching one of the mares around the neck. He hauled back, using his weight to steady the frantic animal as it tried to tear free. Together, he and Rooster turned the horses back toward camp.

As they rode, Seph spotted Blaze farther out, leading Noomoo back with a triumphant grin. But that grin faded when they both saw the sun starting to creep over the horizon. They had hoped to be on the trail by now.

Seph turned Hortense again, pushing her to the north side of camp, where he saw Stoke battling with another runaway. "Get her turned around!" Seph shouted, pulling his lasso free again. He could hear Stoke's labored breaths, his muscles straining against the weight of the wild horse.

Nearby, Chops scrambled to keep track of the few horses that hadn't bolted. Frustration and confusion were written all over his face. His hands fumbled with the lead ropes, and his voice was hoarse from yelling directions. "Come on! Hurry up!" Chops shouted, his eyes darting between the scattered horses and the rising sun.

Dawn had fully broken by the time they managed to drive another group of horses back toward camp. Seph slid from Hortense's back, catching Chops' eye and giving a nod. "Hang in there, Chops," Seph said.

He wiped his sweat-slicked face with a hand, trying to shake off the exhaustion creeping into his muscles as he tried to think of what needed doing next. They had lost hours—hours they couldn't afford to waste. They should've been miles up the trail, not chasing cow ponies across the open prairie.

Seph caught sight of Charlie, doing his best to keep the camp in order while getting breakfast ready. The one-armed man's face was red with effort as he stirred a pot over the fire. He glanced up as Seph rode closer, a knowing smirk on his lips.

"Thought you boys would be back sooner," Charlie quipped. "Good thing I can manage without ya."

Seph glanced toward Dusty, who was still working to round up the last of the strays. His face was set in a grim line as he watched the sun climb higher.

"You alright, Boss?" Seph asked.

Dusty barely looked up. "No, Seph. I ain't alright. We're falling behind already, and I don't like it."

Seph followed Dusty's gaze and felt a rumble in his stomach. In the distance, he saw Grim's outfit snaking its way up the trail ahead of them. He hated to see them pass. A few of Grim's men rode closer, jeering and hollering as they went by.

"Look at them stragglers," one voice called out, followed by a burst of laughter. "Hope you boys ain't planning on winning any races today."

The taunts stung more than they should have. Seph knew the race was far from over, but every minute wasted was a lost opportunity. It was hard to imagine that a race of this length could come down to just a few minutes, but what if it did? Seph was certain that the outcome would be decided by a series of small victories along the way.

Seph's grip tightened on Hortense's reins. He caught Dusty's glance and saw the frustration simmering in his bloodshot eyes. Neither of them had anything to say. The sight of Grim's crew pulling ahead was enough of a blow without needing words to make it worse.

They had no choice but to press on, pushing the beeves northward, with Grim's mocking laughter echoing in their ears.

Scorch leaned back against the rough bark of a blackjack oak. The morning sun filtered through the branches above, shading his face as he sipped coffee. He couldn't see the Deatherage camp from his hiding spot, but he heard the distant shouts of cowboys struggling to round up scattered horses. A slow, satisfied grin spread across his face as he imagined the frustration on Dusty's face.

He set his tin cup down carefully and dropped to his hands and knees, Crawling forward, Scorch inched slowly through the dry grasses, leaves, and twigs. Every few feet, he paused, tilting his head to listen to the Deatherage camp. When he was sure they wouldn't spot him, he hitched closer, his belly brushing the dirt as he slithered through the underbrush.

His palms pressed into the earth as he crawled forward, peering through the gaps in the brush. From his new vantage point, the scene unfolded more clearly—cowboys scrambling after spooked horses, darting through the early morning haze. He could almost taste their frustration.

Dusty's shouts echoed across the prairie, scattering like chaff in the wind.

Scorch took a deep breath, savoring the moment. The sight of the camp in disarray warmed him, the way a double shot of whiskey would. He could feel his heart slow, his pulse steady, as he settled in. It was a thrill to watch them scramble.

"Yeah, that's right," he said out loud. "Run yourselves ragged, boys."

He shifted his weight, careful to stay hidden. He knew they wouldn't spot him. Not while they were all tearing across the prairie like ants whose hill had just been stomped on. The camp remained in turmoil, horses whinnying, cowboys cursing as they fought to regain control.

His mind drifted back to his last conversation with Clive before Dusty canned him. Clive had put a hand on his shoulder, leaned in close, and said, "Don't you worry, Scorch. If it comes to it, I've got your back. Just stick with me, and we'll get what's coming to us."

Scorch snorted. The memory left a sour taste in his mouth. He wasn't so sure about Clive anymore. The man talked big, but Scorch had seen enough to know that folks like Clive and Dusty—they always thought they were better, always assumed they could boss him around. It felt good to put a wrinkle in their plans. Watching them flounder, scrambling to fix the mess he'd caused, gave him a thrill that was better than any reward Clive could promise.

He shifted again. A part of him wondered if Clive suspected he'd been the one to cut the picket line. Clive claimed he was *playing a long game*. But Scorch wasn't so sure anymore.

Most likely, they'd all point to one of Grim's men. Clive liked to think he was the one pulling the strings, but this—this was Scorch's doing. And he wasn't done yet. He wasn't sure what he might do next, but that could wait. He would think of something else later.

The sun climbed higher. Scorch watched as the Deatherage boys finally gathered the last of their stray horses. He would've liked to watch them struggle all day. The thrill began to fade, but as his glee ebbed, he promised himself there would be other mornings like this.

He recalled what Clive had said about helping Grim, but Scorch wasn't concerned with that. What mattered was that Dusty Deatherage would be eating Grim's dust for a while. And that felt good. Dang good.

Scorch slowly rose to his feet, brushing dirt from his hands, stretching, and rolling his shoulders to relax his muscles. He turned his gaze northward. Abilene was still so far away.

There was plenty of time to make Dusty pay for booting him off the drive.

Grim sat erect in the saddle. The scene unfolding ahead delighted him immensely.

The Deatherage camp was in disarray. Grim watched as cowboys frantically scrambled to round up scattered horses. A cold smile crept across his face until his cheeks hurt from grinning so hard. The satisfaction settled deep in his chest like a strong gulp of whiskey.

He nudged his horse, a stocky bay named Thorn, forward a few steps, angling for a better view. Around him, the Three Bar Box crew rode in loose formation. They maintained a steady pace as they drove the herd north. Grim didn't feel the need to rush, especially when the end of the trail was so far away.

Grim's mind drifted to Mitch. He had sent his best man on a mission—to sow discord, exploit weaknesses, and turn Dusty's cautious approach against him. Somehow, Mitch had talked his way in, and it looked like he wasn't wasting time. If the disarray wasn't Mitch's doing, maybe the crew of wet-behind-the-ears cowboys was just careless. Grim was glad he had a mature crew that would never make such foolish mistakes.

He pulled a cigar from his coat pocket and rolled it between his palms before striking a match against his boot. The flame flared briefly and he inhaled the sulfur smell before taking a slow puff. The acrid smoke filled his nostrils, pleasing him all the more as he watched the ruckus unfold.

While Grim lingered, his men pressed on with the herd. A few riders called out to the Deatherage crew, harassing them with taunts and jibes. Grim didn't join in, but the sight and heckling amused him.

He took another puff from his cigar, exhaling a plume of smoke that curled upward into the sky. "Let 'em have their fun," he told himself.

Grim imagined Mitch riding alongside Seph, whispering doubts and sowing discord. Mitch would have Seph questioning Dusty's judgment and Clive's motives. Though Grim had a deal with Clive, he never intended to pay the louse. Grim's grin stretched wider. With the right leverage, even the tightest crew could be ripped apart. The key was finding the cracks—and Grim was skilled at making the most of them.

Grim's smirk faded into a hard line. He flicked the ash from his cigar and watched it drift to the ground. Looking back at the Deatherage outfit, he uttered, "Make 'em suffer, Mitch."

A burn of satisfaction smoldered in the barrel of Grim's chest, like the ember at the tip of a neatly rolled cigar, as he thought about what lay ahead.

With a snap of the reins, Grim urged Thorn forward. He barely spared another glance at the competition. It was better to let them follow close behind, though it was safer to leave them far behind.

His resolve to win by legal means was fading fast. He liked watching men squirm, and following rules made that harder to do. What fun was it to hunt the beast but not see the terror in its eyes? Smell the fear on its breath? Sink teeth into its flesh?

Playing dirty was far more amusing.

Seph stretched his sore muscles as he headed for the edge of camp. It was long past dark, and he had just finished baking a mountain of biscuits and flat bread.

The cowboys were already slumbering.

They'd ridden well past dark, caught up with Grim's gang, and now the crew was wiped out. Most of them collapsed onto their blankets and fell asleep instantly. Seph envied their head start on a good night's sleep, but he chuckled at the odd chorus of snoring cowboys and lowing longhorns.

Despite his exhaustion, Seph longed for a quiet moment to himself. Just five minutes alone, away from the camp. A brief taste of freedom from the weight of his responsibilities.

As he rounded the back of the chuckwagon, Seph heard familiar voices. He hesitated, knowing he should keep moving, but the urgency of an argument made him pause. He stayed in the shadows, just out of sight, and let their words drift to him.

"I'm telling you, Clive, I don't need any more of that stinking medicine," Dusty growled. "I'm fine. Same as always."

Clive didn't back down. "Fine? That's not what it looked like back there, Uncle. You barely kept up today. You think I don't see you reaching for your back every time you move?"

"I can handle it, Clive." Dusty snorted, indignantly. "I've handled it before. No big deal. I'm used to it. You just focus on your job, like I told you."

Clive crossed his arms. "Never mind me. We need to get to Abilene before Grim. Your bum back's gonna make us lose. You know that, right? You're too weak for this."

Dusty's voice dropped lower, rougher. "I'm not weak, Clive. And I'm not about to let you take over. This is my herd. My outfit. Don't you ever forget that."

Seph's grip tightened on his cup, a knot twisting in his gut. He hadn't heard Dusty talk like this before. The weight of that wager must be getting to him.

Clive softened his tone, trying to reason with the boss. "I'm just saying, maybe it's time you think about what's best for the drive. If you don't want to use the medicine, fine. But if you keep pushing yourself, you're going to make things worse—for you and the herd."

Dusty didn't answer right away, and Seph strained to catch the shift in his tone when he finally spoke. "You think you can do this better than me?"

Clive's reply was smooth, too smooth. "I want what's best for all of us. For the Deatherage name. You don't want to admit it, but you're not the same man you used to be, Dusty. Maybe it's time you let someone else shoulder the burden."

Seph's stomach twisted harder. It felt as if a cold pit had opened up beneath his ribs. He glanced back toward the campfire, where the other cowboys slept soundly, oblivious to the power struggle unfolding just beyond their reach. What would happen if Dusty stepped back or returned to the ranch? If Clive took over? The thought sent a chill through him, and he wondered if the others had noticed Dusty's struggle too. It wasn't just Clive. Seph also saw the cracks in the trail boss's iron will.

Dusty laughed. "You don't have what it takes to lead this outfit, Clive. Don't let that ten percent go to your head. If I were to call it quits, there's at least a half a dozen other men I'd put in charge before I looked your way."

A heavy silence stretched between them, thick with the weight of unspoken words. Seph held his breath. Who were these other men? Stoke? Seph couldn't imagine him as trail boss, let alone anyone else in the outfit.

"Humph," Clive griped. "Shows what you know." He grumbled something unintelligible before continuing. "I guess we'll see what happens. Your sore back might just be the least of our problems."

Dusty growled, "I know what I'm doing, Clive." Seph thought he caught a flicker of uncertainty in Dusty's voice, a trembling crack in his usual bluster. It sent a cold shiver through his bloodstream.

"Just take your medicine, Uncle. Is that too much to ask?"

"Fine. I'll take a spoonful. And I don't want to hear another word about it."

Seph took a step back. Questions buzzed in his mind like a swarm of angry bees. What would happen if Dusty couldn't keep up? What if Clive got his way? It was getting harder to see how they could outpace Grim's herd of ex-convicts.

Before hitting the hay, Seph greased the wagon's axles—a task he'd overlooked earlier in the evening.

Chapter 8

It was a rare, cold night, and the air was thick with a creeping fog that swallowed the stars, wrapping the camp in a spectral shroud.

Seph stirred from his bedroll. The faint scent of smoke of last night's campfire lingered in the dampness, suspended within the thickened mist. Dew clung to the prairie grasses, and the chill bit at his skin.

Something was wrong. Seph could feel it in his gizzard.

He reached for his boots, but a distant sound—like the low rumble of thunder—froze him in place. He should have grabbed his shirt and slipped into his boots, but instead he strained his eyes, peering through the mist. Then he heard it again, closer this time.

The unmistakable clatter of hooves rattled through the fog, but the sound was erratic. Was it one horse? Or many? Maybe a longhorn.

Seph lurched to his feet, stumbling out of his blankets, blinking into the darkness as the fog swirled around him. The rumbling grew louder, accompanied by a flickering glow, and a shadow burst from the mist before he could make sense of it—before he could warn the others.

"What in tarnation—?" Seph's words caught in his throat.

A ghost galloped into camp, pale and wild, glowing with an otherworldly light. Seph had never seen a horse like this one. The creature looked like something born of a nightmare, charging in a flaming blur, dragging a bundle of burning branches behind it. Sparks sprayed in its wake, sizzling in the mist.

Seph stumbled backward as the apparition thundered by. The flaming horse careened through camp. Its eyes were like hollow sockets, circled in dark smudges. Its breath steamed like smoke from the underworld. Was it a ghost or a skeleton? Either seemed impossible, but Seph could have sworn he saw dark spaces between its ribs.

Torp shot out of the darkness, grabbing Seph's arm with a tight grip, his fingernails digging into Seph's skin. "Did you see that thing? I think it's the devil. The devil can turn himself into anything."

Seph scoffed, shaking off Torp's hand. "That's nonsense, Torp. Grab a rope. We need to catch it."

Torp's eyes shot back to the flaming apparition, his breath shaky. "Figures you'd say that," he complained before tearing off into the night.

Seph's heart thumped against his ribs. He had to act fast. Sharp stones and prickly thorns jabbed at the soles of his feet, and he cursed himself for not putting on his boots. Sprinting after the ghostly figure, he wondered how anyone could sleep through such a commotion. "Get that horse!" His voice cracked. "Move. Now!"

The spectral figure didn't slow. It barreled through camp, trampling over bedrolls and sending cowboys sprawling.

Conjure's scream made Seph shudder. High-pitched and desperate, it sliced through Seph's ear drums. Conjure scrambled away from his blankets, eyes wide with terror. Frantic, he babbled, "Help. That horse! It's got the devil's eyes. It's come to get us." Tears mingled with snot as he wept like a toddler, looking around in a panic, as if searching for something to hide behind.

The sight of Conjure sent Mitch into a fit of laughter, doubling over, clutching his sides, and howling. When he finally regained his breath, he yelled, "Oh, man, this is priceless! A real ghost story—come to life. You wet yourself, didn't you, Conjure? What a hoot."

Conjure collapsed into a heap, burying his face in his hands, sobbing. Seph barely spared him a glance as he bolted after the horse, but the wild creature veered away, dragging its flames through the mist.

Sparks flew, catching on Trinket's bedroll, and within seconds, the fabric flared up, sending up a sudden burst of flame into the night.

"Trinket, your bedroll!" Seph shouted, wincing as another sharp stone jabbed into his foot. He abandoned the chase for the horse and sprinted toward the spreading fire.

Trinket flailed, his eyes wide with panic as he tried to beat out the flames. "It is everywhere!" His voice cracked as he threw himself onto the burning fabric.

Seph quickly grabbed him and yanked him away. "I'm not letting you set yourself on fire to save a blanket," he growled.

Stoke charged into the fray, shovel in hand. He hurled dirt onto Trinket's bedroll, swiftly smothering the flames.

Trinket's face was slick with sweat and streaked with soot. He opened his mouth to speak, but merely squeaked.

Without a word, Stoke raced off again, shovel raised, searching for another fire to smother.

Rooster and Sparrow, who'd managed to find time to climb into their boots, followed Stoke. They stomped across the prairie, doing their part to keep the fire from spreading.

Seph grunted as he smothered a stray ember making a small orange circle on his pant leg.

Somehow, Chops had managed to sleep through the commotion. Maybe he was overtired from standing first watch.

The horse thundered into camp again. The frantic beast reared up, hooves striking the air before clipping Chops' thigh. As it galloped away, its hind legs knocked into Chops' ribs.

Chops tumbled from his blankets, yelping, clutching his ribs with one hand and his leg with the other. He forced himself to his feet, gritting his teeth and looking dazed.

"Hold still, Chops." Sweat trickled down Seph's face as he examined the wrangler's wounds. The injuries looked painful, but not life-threatening. Gripping Chops' shoulder, Seph said, "Breathe through it. I'll fix you up once we get that horse settled down. You'll be sore, but you'll be fine."

Chops groaned and staggered away. "That nag's got a heck of a kick, don't he?"

Seph looked around to see where the horse had gone. He didn't have time to dwell on it, but it crossed his mind that nobody knew what to do. So, they did nothing. They should do something to help. Anything was better than doing nothing, he figured.

Yodel stumbled up, his shirt singed from flying sparks, clutching his arm where a hot ember had burned through the fabric. "Dang thing spooked me outta my skin," he groused. His lips quivered as he lifted his harmonica to his mouth, blowing a haunting tune. Seph guided him toward the chuckwagon. The melody floated through the fog, sending shivers up Seph's spine.

Yodel kept playing through gritted teeth, but Seph was sure the man was stifling the urge to howl in pain. The eerie tune twisted through the smoke-filled fog. Abruptly, Yodel stopped playing and said, "This place is haunted. We gotta get away from here."

Instead of galloping away, the ghost horse rampaged through camp, bucking and tearing around in circles. It passed through camp again and again, scattering flames in its wake. Its wail—sharp and mournful—mingled with the terrified shouts of half-dressed cowboys trying desperately to capture the suffering beast.

Seph ducked around the chuckwagon, crashing into Blaze.

"It's Win!" Blaze gasped as the ghost horse streaked past.

"Win? It can't be—" Seph bit off his words, his mind reeling.

Charlie, wearing an oversized union suit, hobbled forward with a bucket in hand, barking orders at the cowboys. "Don't just stand around gawkin'! Put out them flames before the whole world goes up in smoke."

Across camp, Lullaby joined the fray, his deep voice rising in prayer as he swung a blanket over a patch of burning grass, smothering the flames beneath the fabric. "Lord, protect us from this devilry," he implored.

Win bolted past them again, the flaming bundle hissing and popping as it whipped through the air.

Seph lunged for Win, trying to throw his long arms around the horse's neck and vault onto its back, but the spooked beast was too frantic. Seph skidded into the dirt, choking and coughing on the thick smoke.

Dusty's commanding voice shot out. "Clive! Don't just stand there with your mouth hanging open. Grab a rope. Get those horses under control! If we lose them, we'll lose the herd."

Clive hesitated, his gaze flicking toward Dusty, but the surprise in his eyes was clear. He was just as caught off guard as the rest of them. But Seph didn't have time to think about Clive. He scrambled back up, his feet bare and stinging, as he raced after the horse.

Blaze had caught up with Win. His hands shook as he grabbed a fistful of mane and swung himself onto the horse's back. Seph was close enough to hear Blaze coaxing, "Come on, Win. Easy, boy. Easy!" Ain't nobody gonna hurt ya, but you gotta stop before you set the whole prairie on fire."

Torp ran up, panting and shouting, "I finally found a rope."

Seph sprinted past him, snatching the lariat as he went. He threw the loop over Win's head but missed.

Win paused just long enough for Mitch to drop an axe blade, severing the rope that dragged the fiery shrubbery. Mitch's laughter had faded, but a smirk still tugged at the corners of his mouth. The drovers gathered around, watching the last flickers of burning branches as they sputtered in the dirt while Stoke whacked the embers into the dust with his shovel.

The next time Seph threw the lasso, he roped Win. The frantic horse calmed almost instantly as Seph whispered soft reassurances.

Blaze slipped from Win's back and doubled over, hands braced on his knees. His breath came in ragged gasps. "I thought we'd lose him for sure. I was sure he would..."

"Yeah, me too," Seph admitted. He glanced toward the east, where the first rays of sunlight streaked across the sky, torching the clouds in brilliant hues.

They had saved the camp from burning, but now what?

They hitched Win to the chuckwagon as Yodel stumbled over. "That horse got a curse on it, I tell ya," he said, shaking his head. "Ain't no good gonna come of this."

Seph stared at Win. His mind churned. Last year, when Slaw was dying after having been dragged by a foot caught in a stirrup, he said he wanted Seph to have his horse. Was Yodel implying that Slaw's spirit had cursed the horse? Why would Slaw haunt Seph or Win? The idea felt absurd, not to mention the ridiculous notion of ghosts being real.

Win was Slaw's horse. That spring, Seph had tried to return him to Slaw's parents, but they'd insisted Win belonged to Seph now. Protecting the horse felt like honoring a friend's last wish, but now, Seph couldn't shake the feeling that he wasn't doing a good job looking out for Slaw's favorite horse.

As Seph looked closer, he saw that charcoal had been rubbed onto Win's hide, between his ribs, turning the white patches into eerie bone-like shapes in the dim light. Someone had put a lot of effort into making Win look like a nightmare.

The crew assigned to night watch trickled into camp.

"What happened?" Whirlwind asked, surveying the damage.

Tumble glanced around at the destruction and said, "I declare."

Squint didn't say a word. He rubbed his eyes, looked again, then shook his head in disbelief.

Torp huddled beside Seph, whispering frantically, "That... that thing looked like it came straight from hell itself, Seph. You think Grim did that?"

Conjure, who had wrapped himself in a half-burned blanket, gasped. "What if it *is* a curse? What if Grim put a hex on us?"

"Shut up!" Torp snapped, his voice wavering. "Win is just a horse, Conjure. That's all. Nothing more. Ain't no such thing as spells. Or ghosts. We been hoodwinked." He paused, then added, "It's sabotage."

Seph placed a hand on Torp's shoulder, trying to reassure him. "You're right, Torp. It's just Win. Man, those Grim boys really got us good."

Torp frowned. "No, Seph. Don't say it's just some kind of prank."

Dusty limped toward them. "Confound it. Grim's got us running in circles, boys. If we don't get moving soon, they'll be halfway to Abilene."

Seph followed Dusty's gaze, seeing the empty space where Grim's camp had been. There was no sign of the other herd. Seph imagined he could hear the faint echo of mocking laughter.

"They were waiting for this," Seph muttered. "They waited until we were distracted and then left us behind." His eyes flicked to the ghost horse.

Win met his gaze, and a chill crawled up Seph's spine.

Seph took a step toward Win, stifling a howl and biting back a curse. His feet felt like they were on fire. He hobbled back to his bedroll, wincing as he rubbed his soles, then grimaced while pulling on his socks and boots.

He glanced around at the other cowboys. Every man was scraped, bruised, or shaken, and there was still a long way to go. A sharp jolt of doubt shot through Seph's gizzard.

How much more could they take?

After hastily packing up the wagon, Seph guided Win toward the creek. The weary horse trudged quietly by his side. Win's once gleaming coat was now streaked with ash, soot, and the remnants of whatever filth Grim's men had smeared on him. Feathers, bramble, and clattering bones were tangled in his mane and tail.

The poor beast's head hung low. Seph could only hope that Win would eventually forget the terrible ordeal he had suffered.

When they reached the creek, Seph loosened his hold on the lead rope, allowing Win to dip his nose into the cool water.

Seph knelt, cupping water in his hands. After splashing his face, he slipped off his boots and socks, rolled up his pant legs, and sank his big feet into the mud. The cool, slippery muck was soothing, but he couldn't afford to dally. Once he rinsed the mud away, the scratches still stung, but he was relieved to have at least washed the grit off his feet.

Seph looked up and blinked, squinting through the rising fog. He could just glimpse a man standing downstream, stark naked, scrubbing something in the water. A second later, he realized it was Conjure—furiously scrubbing his trousers against a rock.

"Conjure?" Seph called, walking closer, keeping a hand on Win's lead. "What in tarnation are you doing?"

Conjure froze. His face flamed bright red as he looked over his shoulder. "Uh—nothing, Seph. Just... doing some wash. That's all."

Seph raised an eyebrow. "At this hour? Buck naked?"

Conjure sighed, his shoulders slumping. "Ain't got no choice. I, uh... well, I soiled 'em. You saw that devil horse tear through camp!" He pointed at Win, just behind Seph. "Scared me half to death."

Maybe someday Conjure would find humor in his predicament, but Seph was sympathetic. "I understand. You mind if I wash Win while you finish up?"

Conjure shook his head, his cheeks still flushed. "Go on. Just... uh, I'd appreciate it if you didn't mention it to the others, Seph. They don't need to know 'bout this."

"You got it," Seph answered. He led Win deeper into the creek, splashing water over him. Seph jumped when Win snorted, seemingly delighted by the cool, soothing water.

Seph paused, giving Conjure a sidelong glance. "How you gonna explain your wet clothes?"

Conjure wrung out his trousers, grumbling under his breath. "I'll just say I slipped and fell in."

Seph chuckled softly, shaking his head. "That might just work."

"It'll have to," Conjure replied. It was a struggle donning sopping wet trousers while standing in the creek. When he finished, he waded toward Seph, glanced at Win, and frowned. "You need a hand with that?"

"Yeah, if you don't mind." Win was covered in smeared charcoal. Seph handed Conjure a rag, watching as he scrubbed Win's withers. They worked in silence for a few minutes, both lost in their own thoughts, until Conjure spoke again.

"I'm scared, Seph," Conjure admitted. "I don't think we're gonna make it. If the convicts don't get us, the spooks will."

Seph paused, unsure how to respond. Part of him wanted to reassure Conjure, to tell him everything would be fine, but the other part—the part that had chased Win through camp—wasn't so sure.

Conjure's voice trembled as he continued, "Why can't we just drive the beeves to market like normal? I don't mind the work, but why's it gotta be so hard? Last year, it was them outlaws. This year, it's this danged race."

Seph sighed, scrubbing at the stubborn charcoal etched between Win's ribs. "Gosh. I don't know, Conjure. Maybe there's no such thing as an easy cattle drive."

Conjure's hands slowed as he stared into the creek. "Remember last year when Dusty said beeves were worth more than cowboys? You don't believe that, do you, Seph?"

Seph hesitated. The memory stung. "No, I don't believe that," he said. "That's just the kind of thing bosses say to make us work harder. I don't think Dusty really believes that."

"You sure?" Conjure glanced up, doubt etched on his face. "I ain't so sure anymore."

Seph scrubbed Win's rump, but the stubborn charcoal smeared instead of washing away. Progress was frustratingly slow. "Dusty's been pushing us hard. But there's a lot on the line, Conjure. I think he knows we're worth more than a herd of cattle. Giving us shares proves it."

Conjure dislodged a clatter of brittle bones from Win's tangled mane. "I just want this to be over, Seph. Ain't no sense in doin' all this if we ain't gonna make it to the end."

Seph glanced toward the horizon. "We'll make it," he said quietly, though he had doubts of his own.

As they worked, Seph noticed movement from the corner of his eye. A man darted from the creek into a nearby swale, disappearing into the divide. Blinking fast, he realized who it was—Scorch.

Seph stiffened, tightening his grip on Win's lead. He glanced at Conjure, who hadn't noticed. "You goin' back to camp soon?" Seph asked, keeping his tone casual.

"Yeah," Conjure answered. "Why?"

"No reason," Seph lied, his mind already racing. He needed to tell Dusty about Scorch, but there was no point in scaring Conjure more than he already was.

Conjure gave a shaky laugh, "I'll just tell 'em I fell in." He stood, toppled into the water, and emerged, laughing. "See, it's the truth. And you witnessed it."

"That I did." Seph grinned, but his amusement faded quickly. Not knowing when they'd have time together again, he added, "Conjure, we're gonna make it. We just gotta have faith and keep pushing."

Conjure nodded, though his eyes were hollow. "I hope so," he said weakly. "But I got a feeling this race ain't meant for the likes of me." He gulped, stifling a sob. "I'm afraid you're gonna have to bury me by a creek like this one. Just like you buried Slaw last year."

CHAPTER 9

A FULL MOON ILLUMINATED the trail, allowing the Deatherage outfit to march the herd hours past dark.

Seph rode between the chuckwagon and the swing position. The evening breeze was refreshing, and despite the wild start to the day, Seph's spirits were high. It was hard to forget the shock of the ghost horse galloping through camp, but Win had settled down once they started moving. They were still in the race, and Seph was proud of his pals for soldiering on.

In the distance, Red River sparkled in the moonlight. The milestone river marked the boundary between Texas and Indian Country. It was an important checkpoint. Seph thought about how far they'd come and recalled how the river had been flooded last year, forcing them to wait five days before crossing.

Seph patted Hortense's neck and promised, "Almost there."

She snorted, as if she understood and was also ready for a break, however brief.

Ahead, Dusty and Clive rode near the front, with Stoke and Mitch at point. Nearby, Charlie drove the chuckwagon. Behind them, the swing riders—Yodel and Lullaby kept the herd in line.

Their arrival was noisy. The herd rushed toward the river, hooves clicking, horns clattering, cattle bellowing, and horses snorting. The mournful sound of Yodel's harmonica rounded out the clamor, heralding their approach.

Suddenly, Yodel's voice trumpeted over the other sounds. "Get lost, buzzards."

Seph reined Hortense in, turning toward Yodel. Two rough-looking men taunted him. "Keep quiet. Can't you see our men are trying to sleep?"

The first man spat at Yodel, insulted his mother, and slandered his race. The second scowled and threatened, "If you stampede our herd, I'll blast you out of that saddle. Y'hear?"

Yodel swung a leg over the neck of his horse, slid to the ground, and started swinging before his feet even touched the ground. Seph blinked in surprise. He had never seen Yodel get into it like that before. The man usually kept to himself, but when riled, Seph could see that Yodel packed a blistering punch.

Grim's man yelped when Yodel's knuckles cracked against his chin.

The second man stepped forward, fists balled tight, and called Yodel's Mama a whore.

Big mistake.

Before Seph could even react, a shove came from behind. The man who shoved him drooled—maybe he always did, whether asleep or on the verge of a fight—but either way, he looked like a mastiff.

Seph didn't waste time. He drove a foot into the man's chest and sent him sprawling.

That was all it took.

The spark ignited, and a full-blown brawl erupted right there on the river-bank, with the Deatherage beeves crowding past them, eager to reach the water.

Stoke had been prepared for a long night, but not a night like this. When that man provoked Yodel, everything went sideways. Stoke, who had been near the front, caught the first punch from the corner of his eye and slid to his feet in a second. He ground-tied his horse, his pulse quickening.

"Alright then," Stoke muttered, cracking his knuckles. He stepped into the fray, fists ready. He had more experience with his knuckles than the rest of the Deatherage outfit combined.

Two of Grim's hardest men charged at him. Their eyes were wild, and their fists were clenched hard, like they'd been waiting for this moment all night. The first blow came fast and wobbled. Stoke ducked it easily, driving a fist into the man's side. He felt the satisfying impact and heard the grunt of pain as the man doubled over.

The second man grabbed Stoke from behind, attempting to wrestle him to the ground. Big mistake. They didn't know they picked the wrong man to tangle with. Stoke had the advantage—strength, speed, and years of brawling. With a quick shove and a fancy spin, he caught the man with a right hook and sent him reeling.

"Two on one?" Stoke smirked, wiping a trickle of blood from his lip. "Why don't you invite another friend over and make this a fair fight?" He glanced back at the first man, who still hadn't straightened up, and said, "That all you got, buckaroo?"

The second man came at him again, but this time Stoke was ready. A sharp elbow to the face sent him sprawling.

The first man tried to capitalize on Stoke's momentary distraction, but Stoke hadn't lost sight of him. He turned just in time to slam him to the ground, then pounced. They rolled in the dirt, fists flying like a blizzard of blows.

Stoke's opponent landed a few solid punches, but Stoke powered through, locking the man's arms and twisting, flipping him onto his back. With a grunt, Stoke ground his knees between the man's shoulder blades, pinning him down. He let up when he thought he heard a crunch—had he broken one of the man's bones?

Stoke stood up, panting, mostly unscathed, with a few bruises to show for his effort. His shoulder ached from a hard hit, and his eye was swelling, but he wasn't done yet. He scanned the brawl around him, looking for his next opponent.

A deep grunt confirmed his satisfaction—and his readiness for more.

Mitch had to play this right. As the fight spread like wildfire, he found himself squaring off against Ted Cross and Marty Price. He had to make the fight look good. And real. That meant being loud, aggressive, and making it believable.

"You boys picked the wrong outfit to tangle with!" Mitch shouted, "These Deatherage boys are tougher than they look." He landed a solid punch to Ted's jaw. The sound cracked through the night, and Ted staggered back, clutching his face.

"I can't believe you just did that." Ted moaned. "I thought we were friends."

Mitch answered, "I got nothing against you. 'Cept my knuckles." He laughed, impressed by his own wit. For a moment, it almost felt natural, like he wasn't just playing a part. It had been too long since he'd had such a fight, and he missed it. So what if he was fighting friends? He threw himself into it, making sure to take a few hits—nothing serious, but enough to sell the performance. To fool the Deatherage children.

When Marty came at him, Mitch winked. He wasn't sure if Marty caught it, but the punches that followed were wild and sloppy. Mitch dodged them easily, but his mind raced. He needed to keep up the act. He couldn't afford to raise any suspicions.

Another punch landed squarely in Mitch's abdomen, and he doubled over, wincing. The pain was real, but it was necessary. He had to admit, it was a good punch. He swung back, sending Marty sprawling with a solid right hook.

Mitch yelled. He made sure that everyone heard him. "Stick with me, boys! We'll show these Grim rats what's what."

Seph ducked as a punch sailed over his head. The sound of the man's fist whizzing past him was almost louder than the grunts and shouts of the fighting men around him. His heart raced, a jolt of energy surging through him as his mind spun with the fury of it all.

Hork was beside him, fending off blows from a rough pair of men who looked like they could be twins. Seph didn't have time to study their faces, but the resemblance was uncanny—stocky, bearded, with wild eyes and bared teeth. Hork looked like he could use some help.

Seph had never been in a fight like this. He ducked, weaved, and swung, his fists connecting with flesh, but a part of him marveled at the confrontation. He was anxious and exhilarated all at once, but one thing was for sure: he wasn't about to back down.

He stole a glance around the battlefield, his tall frame allowing him an almost aerial view. Men were grappling, fists flying, boots kicking up dust in the frenzy. By the chuckwagon, he saw Clive getting backed into a corner. Seph wondered if the boss's nephew would stand his ground or bolt, but he couldn't worry about that now. Not far from Clive, Stoke was in the thick of it, trading heavy blows with a mean-looking cuss. There was no doubt in Seph's mind that Stoke would prevail.

The short, stocky man swung at Seph again, and this time, Seph dodged instead of ducking, driving his fist into the man's ribs. The man let out a snort, stumbling back a step, and Seph felt a rush of triumph. It wasn't a clean hit, but it was enough to knock the man off balance.

Beside him, Hork was locked in a savage struggle with the other man, their bodies rolling in the dirt, thrashing like wild animals. Each of them fought for dominance, grunting and twisting. Seph had worried about Hork. The guttural gasps and the heavy thuds of fists landing on flesh made Seph wince. He thought the ex-convict would've knocked Hork out by now, but the kid was holding his own.

Another punch came flying toward Seph. The twin he had just hit was back. Seph barely had time to raise his arm to block the blow. He swung again, this time aiming higher, and landed an uppercut on the man's jaw. The impact was solid, and the man's head snapped back.

Seph's knuckles burned, his skin scraped raw, but the thrill of victory overpowered the pain. He wasn't just surviving the fight. He was thriving. Last year, Dunk had mentored him well, and Seph was thankful for the time he'd spent training. Though doubt still flickered in the back of his mind, he was starting to believe that the Deatherage outfit would endure this brawl.

Dusty had been in enough scraps to know that fights like this didn't end well for anyone. He'd seen too many good men limping away from battles that solved nothing, leaving behind battered bodies and bruised egos. But tonight, there was no avoiding it. The moment fists started flying, there was no backing down. It was all instinct, muscle memory, and grit.

His back was already protesting. The dull ache that had become his constant companion was worse this year. It had been bad last year, but this year was unbearable. And tonight, every punch he threw seemed to turn that ache into sharp, searing pain. With each swing, his body screamed louder, reminding him again that he wasn't the man he used to be. But Dusty wasn't about to show weakness in front of his men. If they saw him falter, if they saw him flinch, they'd lose faith. So, he squared his shoulders and kept swinging.

His opponent had more scars on his face than Dusty could count. Dusty took note of them in the brief moments between blows. Deep jagged lines crisscrossed the man's face like sunbaked cracks in a withered cactus. This wasn't the kind of man who walked away from a fight. This was the kind of man who thrived on pain, who probably thought of those scars as badges of honor. Not that he'd likely ever seen his reflection in a mirror.

The man came at Dusty with even more force than Dusty expected. Dusty dodged just in time, the other man's fist grazing his jaw. He countered quickly, driving his knuckles into the man's midsection with a solid punch that made him grunt. Dusty knew it was a solid hit. But the jolt of delivering it shot up his own spine. It felt like a hot knife slicing right through him, and for a split second, his vision blurred with the intensity of it. He gritted his teeth, fighting not to show it. The last thing he needed was for Clive to notice him grimacing.

But the truth was, he was barely holding on.

His opponent wasn't finished. The man recovered quickly and charged again. Dusty barely had time to raise his fists up before the man's shoulder slammed into his chest, sending them both crashing to the ground. The impact jarred Dusty's spine even more, and he had to bite back a groan as they rolled in the dirt.

He was pinned for a moment. The man's fist aimed for Dusty's face, but Dusty brought his knee up sharply, catching him in the ribs. The man let out a sharp wheeze, and Dusty seized the chance to shove him off. They both staggered to their feet, panting, covered in dust and sweat.

Dusty landed another solid punch to the man's midsection, zapping him with a spine-shattering jolt. The pain in Dusty's back was unbearable now, but he couldn't stop. Not yet.

He threw another punch, his fist connecting with the man's jaw, and finally, the fight seemed to drain out of his opponent. The scarred man's knees buckled, and he dropped to the ground in a heap, groaning in defeat. Dusty stood over him, chest heaving, but his victory felt hollow. His body was screaming at him to stop, to rest, but there was no time. There never was.

He gritted his teeth, determined to mask his discomfort. He knew the men had noticed, but he couldn't help it.

The worst part was, he knew Clive was watching.

And Mitch, still a mystery to Dusty, had glanced his way once or twice during the brawl.

With that one final hit, Dusty's opponent crumbled, but he knew he'd pay for this fight in the morning. Heck, he'd be paying for it in five minutes if not sooner. His back felt like it had been trampled by a herd of stampeding buffalo, and every breath made his ribs ache. But none of that mattered now.

As the man lay groaning in the dirt, Dusty bent down, gripped him by the shirt and yanked him close. "You stay down, hear me?" he growled. The man gave a weak nod, too winded to argue. Dusty let him drop, turning back toward his crew.

The fight was winding down. Men staggered away from the brawl with swollen knuckles, bloody noses, and bruises that were sure to turn uglier within hours. Dusty straightened up, fighting the urge to rub his aching back. Despite his pain, a sense of pride swelled in his chest. Most of his men had never experienced anything like this before. But they stood their ground, honored the brand, and fought like warriors.

They might be battered, but those boys of his had proven their worth. They might not have the scars of hardened men, but they stood their ground. Dusty couldn't ask for more than that.

With one final glance at the downed man, Dusty called out to the others. "We're movin' out!" he barked, his voice still strong despite the pain. "Let those jailbirds roost. We've got a river to cross."

The brawl was finally winding down. Panting men, bruised and battered, began to stagger back to their herds, but no one was seriously hurt. Dusty, despite his injuries, rallied the Deatherage boys. A few of the younger men were still grumbling, ready to throw more punches, but Dusty shot them a glare that backed them down. He stood tall, his back clearly searing with pain, but determination set in his jaw.

It was a shock to hear the trail boss say that they would cross the river in the dark.

Seph, still catching his breath, hurried to grab supplies from the chuck-wagon. His hands fumbled in the dark as he reached for what he thought was a sack of provisions. His muscles were sore, his knuckles scraped raw from throwing punches earlier, but he wasn't about to let exhaustion slow him down.

His eyes had adjusted to the darkness, and he peered into the back of the wagon. The bag he'd placed on board the night before wasn't exactly where he'd left it, but a bit beyond that point. He reached for the sack and slid it from the wagon. But then he froze.

The bag was moving. He heard a hissing sound.

He released his hold, dropping the sack to the ground, and yanked his hand away as if he'd been bitten. Seph's heart leaped into his throat. The bag twisted and shifted, but remained closed.

From within the bag, he heard the distinctive, unmistakable rattling sound that came with the slithering contents of the burlap bag.

Seph's breath caught, and for a moment, all he could hear was the loud, frantic thumping of his heart. "I wonder how this got here?" he muttered. "Sabotage?" That was the word Torp used. It felt foreign on his lips, but the evidence was right there, writhing on the ground. His mind raced. Who would do this? Grim's men? It had to be one of them.

He backed away slowly, carrying the bag. The faint rattle echoed in his ears, louder than it should have been, as if the danger itself was growing with each step. Poisonous snakes were serious business. They could kill a man. Just one bite, and a man would be a goner. Seph tried to convince himself that such a thing was beneath him. And yet, his fingers gripped the bag tighter.

As he tiptoed toward Grim's camp, carrying the squirming sack by the tied-off neck, he heard Lullaby's voice in his head, saying a prayer and warning about such sins. "Vengeance is the Lord's," the voice reminded him, echoing from the countless nights around the campfire, Lullaby leading them in evening prayers.

But what if the Lord's vengeance took too long?

CHAPTER 10

THE DEATHERAGE OUTFIT FINISHED crossing the Red River hours before dawn. On the north side, Dusty said, "Now we pray for rain."

Most of the men grumbled in agreement. They remembered waiting on the south side of Red River last year until it was safe to cross.

Rather than stop to rest, Dusty pointed north, urging them to keep riding. Dawn was approaching. They would ride all day, and then they could rest. He promised they'd *sleep like babies* that night when they finally made camp.

Seph was glad to keep going. After the excitement of the fight and the late-night river crossing, he couldn't imagine falling asleep anyway. He was weary but in high spirits. Not only had they passed Grim's gang, but they had added miles to their lead.

They were winning.

At dawn, Dusty rode up beside him. Seph nodded and offered a greeting. "Morning, Boss."

Dusty tipped his head forward but didn't say anything. After a quiet couple of minutes, he leaned toward Seph and clapped his shoulder. "Good ride," he said, his voice low but clear.

"Yes, sir." Seph nodded. "Feels like we're pulling ahead."

Dusty rumbled in agreement, the sound coming from deep in his chest. Then he cleared his throat and added, "You did more than just hold your own back there, Seph. You stepped up when we needed it most. You always do. I'm proud to have you with us."

Seph blinked, taken aback by the boss's direct praise. Sure, Dusty had given general encouragement before, but this was personal. Seph could feel pride swell in his chest. Dusty wasn't a man who handed out compliments lightly.

"Gosh. Thanks, Boss," Seph said, his voice quiet but heartfelt. He didn't know what else to say.

Dusty gave a curt nod, then added, "I'd be proud to have a son like you, boy."

At that moment, Seph realized he'd do anything for Dusty. All the man had to do was ask. Better still, Seph thought, if he could anticipate what Dusty might want or need, he'd do that.

He replied, "Any man would be proud to be your son, Dusty."

The boss turned his head, and they locked eyes. Seph thought Dusty looked disoriented. He noticed a flicker of something—regret? Longing? Maybe he was thinking about a woman. Seph found that thinking about the ladies often made him feel lost.

Dusty knocked a knuckle into Seph's shoulder. "Why don't you ride ahead, make some coffee, and juice up them boys as they ride by? It's gonna be a long day."

"Yes sir," Seph chirped as Dusty rode off. He straightened in his saddle, determined not to slouch. Seph was proud to ride for the Dagger D, Angry R.

Scorch crouched in the grass near the top of a hill, a good distance from the herd. His lips curled in a grin so wide it nearly split his face in two.

He watched the Deatherage boys ride further north. The sack of snakes had been swapped. The biscuits filled his gut, made him happy, and he leaned back against a rock, resting his hand on his slightly bulging belly. He gave it a slow, indulgent rub, savoring the fullness. For the first time in days, Scorch felt victorious.

"That'll show 'em," he muttered to himself, licking crumbs from his fingers. The taste of butter and flour lingered on his tongue, and he couldn't remember the last time his stomach had felt so full. With a full belly, he didn't care much about the details. Whether those snakes had been found, bitten someone, or just slithered off—none of that mattered. There was great satisfaction in knowing that he had left a little something for the outfit that wouldn't have him.

He leaned back further, rubbing his belly again. It was almost *too* full. A lazy smile spread across his face. "Biscuits," he muttered with a low chuckle, picking at the crumbs scattered across his chest. "Heck, ain't nothing better 'n that. Only thing I miss about that den of Deatherage wolves is the cooking."

The sack swap had gone off without a hitch. He thought back to the moment he'd snatched the biscuits, the sack of warm bread nestled right where they kept their provisions. He hadn't thought twice—just grabbed it, made the trade, and walked off grinning like a cat who'd caught a mouse.

Scorch shoved another handful of crumbs, plucked from his lap, into his mouth, chewing with exaggerated pleasure. "Bet that sack's crawling right now," he said with a chuckle, spraying a few crumbs as he spoke. "Someone's probably opening it up, thinking they're in for a treat... maybe gettin' a nice surprise when those rattlers uncoil and start hissing and striking."

He wiped his hand on his shirt, leaving a streak of grease and crumbs smeared across his chest. His belly was full, and the biscuits had done more than just take the edge off his hunger. Scorch no longer cared about the stakes of the race, the cattle, or the long drive to Abilene. He'd been pushed aside, overlooked, and left to fend for himself. But now, he was in control, and causing trouble became his purpose in life.

The only thing was, what if the one that made the biscuits got bit? Scorch lifted his hat, scratched his head, and hoped that the cook survived. He thought about the cook's hands—always working, always making food that Scorch had no business eating. He fantasized about all of the meals he might swipe on the way to Abilene.

"Aw, heck," he shrugged. There was more than one way to score a meal, and two herds to raid if it came down to it. He tipped his hat forward, shading his eyes as he watched the herd. "That's how you do it," he muttered, his voice thick with self-satisfaction. "You don't need no big, complicated plan. Just mess things up. Make 'em scramble. That's how to win out here."

He looked down at his shirt again, a crust of biscuit crumbs still clinging to the fabric. He shook like a dog after a swim, wiped crumbs from his face, and watched them fall to the dirt below.

Now it was time for a nap. He tipped his head back, trying to imagine the horror on the faces of the men as the snakes slithered out of the bag.

His last thought before drifting off to sleep was, *They ain't seen nothin' yet. That Dusty Deatherage will pay for cutting me loose.*

Grim stood at the edge of camp, his arms folded across his chest, staring out at the endless plains. The sun was just beginning to rise, but his thoughts were far from the trail. He envisioned a place he had never seen—a land of boundless green pastures, wide rivers, and sprawling estates. Argentina.

In his mind it was as real as the dust beneath his feet. Massive ranches that stretched on for miles. Fat cattle grazing peacefully, tended by gauchos—men who knew how to handle a herd. They would work for him. The thought sent a thrill down his spine. No more struggling. No more marching beeves up a hot, barren trail. No more scraping by. In Argentina, he'd be the king of his own fortune.

One of the men in Huntsville had told him about it. The man had been a cattleman too, before he got caught up in some bad business and ended up behind bars. Grim had listened closely to the man's tales of South America—the vast *estancia*s that stretched as far as the eye could see, the rivers that wound through the countryside like veins of silver, and the wealth that came with owning land down there. "You strike it rich in Argentina," the man had said, "and you could be somebody. A real somebody."

Grim could still hear the man's voice in his head, and he could recall the way his eyes had lit up when he talked about it. "Land's cheap, cattle's plentiful, and the government loves a good rancher." The more Grim thought about it, the more sense it made. There was no future for him here. But down south, in that glorious South American country, he could reinvent himself.

"I'll be King of the Pampas," Grim muttered. The words rolled off his tongue like a prayer. He pictured plumes of gargantuan grasses, as tall as two men, towering over his head, swaying in the breeze. He imagined himself striding across his land, surveying thousands of heads of cattle, his ranch extending farther than he could ride in a day. No one would question his authority.

He'd have a sprawling mansion—bigger than anything he'd seen in Texas or Kansas—grand rooms, chandeliers, plush red carpets, and fine European furniture. The women of Buenos Aires would whisper his name with admiration. Instead of being the kind of man no woman would want, they'd trip over each other to be possessed by him, bearing heirs to his kingdom. The men would tip their heads in respect, and beg for the privilege to crown him. What a spectacular festival his coronation would be.

Grim's eyes flicked over to his men, still asleep in their bedrolls, unaware of the grand vision that was unfolding in his mind. One of them, Ted Cross, had nearly died last night. The sack of snakes from the Deatherage camp had caused a mess in the middle of the night, and Cross had gotten bit. Grim barely gave it a second thought. There would be sacrifices along the way—that was just the cost of doing business.

Cross was still alive, not that Grim cared much about that. He wasn't about to lose sleep over a rattlesnake bitten cowboy. Men came and went. What mattered was to keep moving forward, inching closer to that dream. "There's always another man to take their place," he mumbled. If a few had to fall along the way, so be it.

"Argentina," he whispered. The word tasted sweet and distant, light and airy, like lace curtains behind an open window. "When I get there, I'll have it all." He'd even start learning Spanish. One of his men, Marty Price, had a mother who was Mexican. That fella could teach him. Good thing a snake didn't get Marty.

Grim imagined himself speaking the language fluently, charming high-society folks with his wealth and smooth words. "Señor Grim Decker," he said aloud, trying the name on for size. "*El Rey del Pampas.*"

The more he said it, the more real it felt. The struggles of the cattle drive, the race against the Deatherage outfit, all those years in prison—all of it would be forgotten once he reached that land of opportunity. He'd be a new man, a man of wealth and power. No one would dare question him again.

Grim took a deep breath. Fresh morning air filled his lungs. Soon, he thought. Soon, all of this would be behind him. The endless plains, numbskull cowboys, long cattle drives—it was just a stepping stone to something far greater. He'd leave the scrubby lands of Texas and build an empire in the fertile land of Argentina.

He turned away from the horizon, his chest swelling with ambition, and took a bow.

The Deatherage boys had been through the wringer. Sweat and dust streaked their faces. Their bodies slumped in the saddle. A couple of them had fallen asleep during the day, only to slide from their saddles before experiencing rude awakenings. They had ridden through two long days, a sleepless night, and endured the aches, pains, and bruises from a wild brawl with hard men from the rival herd. But they kept moving.

Seph was feeling it too. His legs were stiff, his shoulders ached, his knuckles were raw, and his eyes felt heavy as lead. Still, he kept his gaze fixed on the horizon, focusing on something—anything—to stay awake. Dusty's praise had lifted his spirits earlier, but that rush was beginning to fade, worn down by the exhaustion settling deep in his bones.

He glanced around at the other men. Yodel hunched forward on his horse, muttering something under his breath, while Lullaby plodded along across the herd from his brother, his head bobbing with the motion of his horse. Most of the men looked like they were sleepwalking, though they were on horseback. Habit drove them forward. They'd gone from being cowboys to zombies in less than a day.

"Could sure use some coffee right about now," Seph muttered to himself. But there was no time for that. Dusty was driving them hard, and Seph understood why. If they slowed down, Grim's men would catch up. That was the last thing they needed.

As the hours dragged on, Seph noticed something that snapped him out of his daze. Ahead of him, Clive and Mitch rode side by side, close enough to whisper into each other's ears. They kept glancing back at the rest of the group, speaking in low voices, their hands cupped beside their mouths to keep the sound from carrying.

Seph's brow furrowed as he watched them. He hadn't thought much about Clive and Mitch before, and would never have imagined them becoming friends. But now something about the way they were acting made his skin prickle. They whispered like conspirators, not like tired men just trying to make it through a long day.

He strained his ears, trying to catch a word or two, but they were too far ahead. The whispers stopped when Clive glanced at Seph. Seph held his gaze, but Clive pretended not to notice. The unease crumbled in Seph's gut like a rock beneath a sledgehammer.

What were they talking about? Seph had no proof, just a growing suspicion that gnawed at him. Dusty trusted Clive—had given him a lot of responsibility and a fraction of his herd—but Seph had a really bad feeling about the boss's nephew. He tried to recall the times he'd seen the two men together lately.

The trail stretched on, and Seph kept an eye on them. They parted and didn't ride together after that, but the feeling of distrust lingered. Seph shifted in the saddle. The hours were wearing on his backside and worry niggled in his head. Maybe it was nothing. Perhaps it was just paranoia. But then again, what if his concern was valid?

He reminded himself that he had learned to trust his gut.

The camp was dead quiet except for a chorus of snores. In particular, old Charlie's hog calling was loud enough to rattle the stars. Clive briefly entertained the idea of putting a bullet in the old coot.

He stepped carefully, weaving his way through the sleeping bodies. A quick glance at Dusty confirmed the man was out cold, a dark lump under a blanket. Same as he'd been every night lately.

Good, Clive thought. It was working.

He slipped past the chuckwagon, keeping his head low, and made his way beyond camp where Mitch was waiting. It was a bright night, but Clive wasn't worried about being seen or heard. Nobody would wake up. Not tonight. He briefly thought of the men he'd assigned to night watch, but his concern for them evaporated quickly.

Mitch leaned against a rock, arms crossed, his eyes flicking up as Clive approached. "Took you long enough."

Clive scowled. "Had to make sure nobody was watching." He crouched down beside Mitch, keeping his voice low. "It's getting easier. Dusty don't notice a thing. I've been upping his dose a little every day. But he ain't seen nothing yet."

Mitch nodded, but there was no satisfaction on his face, just cold calculation. "How much longer you think it'll take?"

Clive scratched his brow. "Hard to say. Bound to kick in eventually. Before we leave Indian country, he won't know what's real. Then we can control him. Make all the decisions."

Mitch raised an eyebrow. "You got enough of that tonic?"

Clive's face tightened. He didn't like being challenged, but was glad he had thought to buy out the doctor's entire supply. He couldn't help sounding defensive. "You'd better believe it." Clive almost said Mitch's name after that, but he never liked saying other people's names if he could avoid it.

Mitch's eyes closed halfway. "And then what? You step in? Take over the outfit?"

Clive's expression grew more intense. "Ain't nobody left to stop me. Not the top hand, the camp cook, nor the Bible-thumping, singing cowboy. Nah, they're all a pack of idiots. Dusty's losing his edge. I make sure of that every morning and evening, and by the time we hit Abilene, this herd will be mine. I'll be running the show, and Dusty won't know what hit him."

Mitch shook his head. He lowered his voice. "You're playing a dangerous game, Clive. And Dusty—he's your flesh and blood."

Clive leaned in, grinning. "Dangerous? Maybe. But you want something, you gotta take it. You don't wait for someone to serve it up to you." He paused, glancing back toward the camp where Dusty's steady breathing was barely discernible. "He ain't got a clue. He's never gonna see it coming."

Mitch shook his head. "You should see the way your teeth gleam in the moonlight. Makes you look like an evil genius."

Nobody had ever said anything like that to Clive before. He tilted his head forward, smiling wider. He was on the verge of something big. His plan was working, and the more he increased the dosage, the closer he came to taking everything. Soon, it would all be his. He gave Mitch a final nod. "We keep this up, Dusty'll be good as gone."

Mitch's voice dropped, laced with caution. "Sure, but what about Grim? Have you forgotten you only get a fraction?"

CHAPTER 11

THE SUN WAS BARELY up, but the Deatherage outfit had already been on the move for hours.

A couple of days had passed since the moonlight march, and Seph felt the grind of relentlessly pushing the herd north. Whenever the others took short breaks, Seph was ready with water, food, and coffee—always coffee. The men expected it.

The camp cook was always the first up, and the last one to crawl under a blanket at night. Charlie said he didn't care. Old men barely slept more than a couple of hours anyway. Seph figured, if Charlie didn't complain, why should he? Complaining wasn't something Seph cottoned to anyhow.

Ever since they passed the Three Bar Box outfit at Red River, the Deatherage boys had managed to stay ahead of Grim's gang. Being ahead was good, but that drive was taking a toll on the horses, beeves, and men. Seph wouldn't have admitted it, but he was way beyond weary.

Everybody was tuckered out. Some of them whined and complained, but Seph thought the worst-off man was the trail boss. Dusty had always been sharp in the mornings, giving orders with a clear head and making quick judgments. But today? He just waved his hand to the north and grumbled. Seph hated seeing the boss slumped in the saddle, staring off into the distance.

Seph rode up beside Dusty, glancing over to find his eyes glazed, his jaw slack.

"Morning, Boss," Seph offered cautiously.

Dusty grunted, not even bothering to look at him. "Yeah. Morning."

Seph's brow furrowed.

The herd plodded on. Seph glanced back over his shoulder, taking in the spread of men and critters along the line. Everyone was tired, sure, but they still did their jobs.

Dusty's stocky frame had always made him look strong and immovable, but now his robust musculature seemed to weigh him down. Seph noticed the wince every time Dusty shifted in the saddle, the way his hand kept circling his lower back. It had been bad before, but now, Dusty looked like he was fighting to make it—mile after endless mile.

"Doing alright, Dusty?" Seph asked.

Dusty turned his head just enough to glance at him. There was no mistaking the glassy look in his eyes and the wobble in his voice. "Fine. Just... fine." He blinked hard, as if trying to shake off a fog. "But I feel like I hit the sauce too hard last night."

A tumble of thoughts churned in Seph's mind. Was the boss getting pickled every night? He knew some men did, but drinking wasn't allowed on a cattle drive, except when they reached the end of the trail.

Before Seph could ask another question, Dusty snapped the reins, urging his horse forward a few paces. He turned his head toward Seph, his face twisting in irritation. "You gonna sit there starin' at me all day, or you gonna get to work?"

Seph blinked, taken aback. "Hitting the sauce too hard, Boss? Is that what you said?"

"No, I ain't been drinking. Feels like I got a case of whiskey fever, son. But I guess that's what it's like, getting old."

Dusty wasn't old, Seph thought. The man was just shy of forty. Charlie was old, but not Dusty.

The trail boss added, "Some days are better than others. Enjoy them young bones while you can, ya hear?" He spurred his horse and rode off ahead of the herd.

Most mornings, Grim liked to move the herd at dawn. But today, they got a slow start.

He watched with amusement as his men had fun at the expense of a man named Gene Stone. Grim didn't know the man well. He wasn't one of his core six. Mostly, Grim left the other members of his gang to John Quincy Long, John Memphis Short, Dick, Bert, and Mitch to contend with.

Poor Gene sat rigidly on a stump, fidgeting as Lewis Kelly brought a razor to his jaw.

Lewis grinned as he scraped the blade over Gene's rough stubble. "There, Gene. You'll be pretty as a picture in no time. Maybe find yourself a nice lady when we hit Abilene."

The others snickered, and Gene shifted uneasily. "Quit your yammering," Gene muttered, trying to hold still as Lewis tilted his head to the side. "This ain't about no lady."

Henry Payne, leaning against a nearby tree, grinned wickedly. "Sure it ain't. Why else would you let us gussy you up like this? You look like you're off to get hitched."

Another round of laughter erupted from the group, but Gene kept his eyes locked on the ground, his jaw tight. He claimed he didn't care much for the attention, but Grim had insisted on the shave. And the haircut. And the stiff new clothes. Gene hadn't been given much of a choice, but the reason for it hung heavy in the air. Gene wasn't asking questions.

Jim McDonald stepped forward, shaking his head with mock disappointment. "If you're goin' after a lady, Gene, you're doin' it all wrong. Ain't no woman gonna want a man who smells like old horse blankets." He leaned in and sniffed, wrinkling his nose for effect. "Might want to think about having you a bath."

Gene rolled his eyes, but he didn't have much of a retort. Instead, he sat still while Lewis finished with the razor, then started in on his hair. Lewis made quick work of it, shearing off the uneven tufts. Then Lewis stepped back and said, "Take him away, fellas." He handed Jim a bar of soap. "Pitch him in the creek and make sure he scrubs himself good. Make sure he's *presentable*."

Grim laughed as the gang lifted poor Gene from the stump and carted him off for his bath. Lewis hollered at them, "Don't let him back into them dirty duds. I'll fetch him something fresh."

When Gene's bath was done, he walked back to the stump on his own and sat down. He looked clean, but miserable.

Lewis asked, "You always scowl like that, or is it just when you ain't got no whiskers?"

Gene moped. "Aw, cut it out." His hair was normally an unruly mop, but Lewis whipped out a comb, parted Gene's hair roughly down the middle.

"Ouch," Gene complained as Lewis patted something minty smelling onto his hair, holding it stiffly in place. "Didja have to slice my head with that thing? Sheesh."

"Well, ain't you handsome," Lewis teased, stepping back to admire his handiwork. "You could pass for a gentleman now, Gene."

Gene scowled, but the camp was filled with grins. Even Fred Hayes, who had been busy oiling his saddle, chimed in. "Hope you got yourself some manners to go with that haircut. Might need 'em if you're going off a courtin'."

"Shut up," Gene growled, though his voice lacked real heat. He glanced around at the smirking faces, then looked down at the new clothes they'd handed him earlier. A clean shirt, dark trousers, boots polished enough to reflect the sunlight. Even before prison, he never dressed like that.

"Don't forget *this*," Thomas Morrison called, tossing a black hat Gene's way. "Can't show up without a proper lid."

Gene caught the hat and stared at the wide brim for a moment before placing it on his head. It felt strange, but he tugged it down over his eyes and stood up.

Payne crossed his arms as a crooked grin spread across his face. "What next? You gonna buy a ring? Or maybe get yourself a bouquet?"

Gene opened his mouth to voice a retort, but his attention was drawn to the side, where Grim had been sitting quietly. Grim wasn't laughing. He wasn't joking. Instead, he reached into a saddlebag and pulled out a small, tarnished object.

The men fell silent as Grim began to polish it with slow, methodical strokes. The silver gleamed in the sunlight as the dirt and grime were rubbed away, revealing a star-shaped badge. He didn't say a word, but his eyes flicked up to Gene, and a knowing look passed between them.

Grim stood and pinned the tin star on Gene Stone, then gave the man a quick pat on the chest.

The Deatherage outfit moved at a fast clip all morning. Instead of giving them a break, Dusty told the boys to slow the pace.

Seph wiped his brow with the back of his hand. His muscles ached from tending to the chuckwagon, and helping prod the herd faster than they liked to move.

"My biscuits disappear as fast as I can make 'em," he muttered, glancing at the empty skillet hanging on the chuckwagon. It had been a grueling day already, and it wasn't nearly half over.

He sighed and looked closely at the wheel of the chuckwagon while it turned. Several of the spokes had cracked. Seph had painted them to prevent them from drying out, becoming brittle, and snapping. But the hot sun and fast miles had taken a toll. Before they went much farther, Seph would have to fix and paint the spokes again.

Seph was surprised to hear somebody shouting. It was hard to remember the last time they had a midday break.

He turned and saw a stranger riding up the line as the herd bunched together and began to graze. The man didn't look like anyone he'd ever seen before.

A clean-shaven man sat tall on his horse, and when he lifted his hat he revealed neatly combed and parted hair beneath it. He looked out of place, too polished for the dust and grit of a cattle trail. His clothes were dark and crisp, and pinned to his chest was a star that gleamed in the sunlight.

"What's going on now?" Seph muttered to himself, leaving the wagon to Charlie as he rode toward the disturbance. Most of the gang had gathered around the stranger, who was glaring with arms crossed, a frown creasing his brow.

"I'm a U.S. Marshal," the man said, his voice loud and authoritative. He pointed at Conjure and said, "What's your name, son?"

Conjure shook as he answered, figuring the marshal wanted to know his given name. "Shelbin Lander, sir."

The marshal grunted, pointing at Hork, and said. "What about you?"

Hork's lips trembled as he said his name. "Ezekiel Salsbury, Marshal."

Shaking his head, he nodded toward Chops. "You, with the pimples and fuzzy cheeks, who are you?"

Chops hated when people mentioned his complexion. With a frown, he answered, "I'm Henry. Henry Shinkle."

"That's my man," the marshal said. "I've got a warrant for the arrest of Mr. Henry Shinkle." He looked at Dusty and said, "Henry's wanted for theft and desertion out of Dallas."

Chops snorted. "Theft and desertion? Heck, I ain't never even been to Dallas." He looked the man up and down. "And who are you supposed to be?"

"I told you. I'm a U.S. Marshal." He puffed out his chest. "Marshal Radcliffe Kingsnake," he announced.

Mitch, standing off to the side, snickered loudly, his shoulders shaking. Seph shot him a look. Why was Mitch laughing at the law?

Chops raised an eyebrow. "Kingsnake, huh? Well, I ain't no snake, and you sure ain't takin' me nowhere."

Marshal Kingsnake's face flushed. He looked uncomfortable in his crisp new clothes, but stood his ground. "You'll come peacefully, or we'll do this the hard way."

The camp grew silent, all eyes on the exchange. Seph's gut twisted. The man might have a badge, but something seemed out of place. Seph didn't have any experience with lawmen, but this marshal looked too clean and sounded like he had memorized everything he was saying.

Dusty stepped forward, his brows knitted together in concern. "Did I hear you right? You expect us to just hand over one of our own and watch you ride off with him?"

Marshal Kingsnake glared at Dusty, his grip tightening on the chains he had just whipped from his saddlebags. "That's exactly what I expect, unless you plan to join us? Who are you?"

Dusty answered and gave his name.

"So, would you like to ride with us to Dallas, then, Mr. Deatherage?"

Dusty sighed and rubbed his chin. "Well, before you haul him off, maybe we oughta have a big meal, huh? Chops here's had a long ride, and so have we. How about some stew, coffee, and biscuits before you take him?"

Seph's jaw dropped. A big meal? They were supposed to be moving north, not sitting around having a feast. How was he supposed to produce a stew? There wasn't time to butcher a longhorn. They couldn't just toss jerked meat in hot water and call it a stew, could they?

The marshal hesitated, his stomach growling. "Fine," he muttered, "but make it quick. I don't have all day."

Seph blinked as Marshal Kingsnake locked thick cuffs on Chops' wrists and ankles.

How could this be happening?

A couple of hours passed by as the Deatherage men gathered for the biggest meal they'd had in days. Stew bubbled over the fire, and biscuits slid from the Dutch oven as fast as Seph could manage.

Chops, still in chains, sat grumbling to himself. But that didn't diminish his appetite.

Marshal Kingsnake, for all his earlier bluster, wolfed down food like a man with no manners.

Dusty leaned back, watching the scene with a hint of unease. Seph caught him rubbing his neck and rotating his head, a faint grimace crossing his face.

Just as the last of the biscuits disappeared, a chorus of laughter echoed from just beyond the camp. Seph's heart sank as Grim's gang rode up, their horses kicking a fresh cloud of dust into camp.

Dick Fowler was the first to holler.

"Well, look at that!" he called, pointing at the Marshal. "I do declare. If it ain't Marshal Kingsnake. He always gets his man. Arrest them all! They ain't nothing but a bunch of common criminals, I'm sure."

More laughter followed.

John Memphis Short shouted. "Marshal Kingsnake, my ear. That there's Gene Stone. Thought you'd joined a circus, not the law."

The rest of the Grim gang joined in, jeering at the so-called marshal, calling him by his real name. It was quickly clear to everyone in the Deatherage camp that it was all a setup.

Seph's stomach dropped. The arrest was a distraction, a ruse to waste their time. Chops stood there, his mouth hanging open in disbelief as the truth dawned on him. "So I ain't gotta go to Dallas? Or prison?"

Gene Stone handed Seph a key and waited for the chains. Red-faced and humiliated, Gene shot a glare toward his fellow drovers, but what could he do? He looked like he expected the Deatherage boys to pile on and give him a good pounding. The jig was up.

As the Grim gang sped away, the laughter spread to the Deatherage outfit. Soon, even Chops was shaking his head and laughing so hard, he had to clutch his stomach to keep his meal down. "Well, heck. If them boys wanted to slow us down, there were easier ways to do it than this."

Seph couldn't see what everybody found so funny. His eyes stayed on Mitch, who was still grinning from ear to ear, thoroughly enjoying the spectacle. Mitch must have known that Marshal Kingsnake was really Gene Stone. Why didn't he say anything?

Mitch was playing both sides. Or he was a traitor.

The Deatherage crew didn't catch up with the Grim gang that night.

Dusty knew the finish line was a long way off, but the boys' morale was better when they were ahead rather than behind. But all that really mattered in a race was who crossed the finish line first. Whoever was ahead on any given day wasn't important.

He sat on his blankets and looked forward to lying down. If only the ground weren't so stiff. And, if only saddles came with stiff backs, like dining room chairs in a restaurant. His mind was foggy, but something about the fake arrest irritated him. They'd lost precious time, and Dusty didn't like being played for a fool.

Mitch wandered over. Hours later, he was still smirking. It was as if the man couldn't help himself. Dusty looked up at him. "Why didn't you say something, Mitch? You knew it was a setup."

Mitch shrugged and crossed his arms. "I was enjoying the show too much to stop it, Boss. Besides, that Gene Stone is the last man I'd ever expect to see wearing a badge. If you only knew half the things he's done...."

Dusty grunted and stretched his neck. "We've lost time, Mitch. Grim's gang passed us."

Mitch's grin widened. "Maybe. But we've got a few tricks up our sleeves too, don't we, Boss?"

Dusty stared at the man. What was he talking about? His gut churned. Something about that cocky grin annoyed him. It was hard to believe that this man, Mitch, was Seph's brother. The Vermillion brothers were nothing alike. His mind drifted back to the pain in his back, and to how strange he'd been feeling lately.

As Mitch walked away, Dusty couldn't remember if he'd answered the man's question—or what that question had even been. The horizon seemed to sway like a restless prairie wind, his vision rippling with each unsteady step. His legs barely held him upright, and a strange lightness in his head threatened to topple him. Slowly, he bent his knees, lowered himself to the ground, and braced his palms against the dirt. He rolled over, and when he was flat on his back, he stared at the sky and wondered, *Is this the end?*

He rubbed his temples. Tomorrow would be another long day. He just hoped that he could keep it together.

CHAPTER 12

THE DEATHERAGE OUTFIT STIRRED at first light.

Yesterday's arrival at the milestone Washita River was celebrated with a long swim and a much-needed opportunity to bathe. The refreshed crew slept soundly and woke at dawn, ready for another long day on the trail.

Seph and Charlie rushed to make a big pot of corn mush and beans for those who preferred it, as well as coffee. As Charlie prepared to serve breakfast, Seph fetched the mules from the picket line. He rushed them back to the wagon, lined them up, and hurried to get the rigging.

It was a shock to see the jumbled mess of straps. He took them from the wagon and stared. Somebody had sliced the straps clean through. In several places. Not just the lines, but the back strap, quarter strap, and girth as well.

He dumped the leather on the ground, kneeled beside the tangled heap, and wanted to scream. It wasn't like him to do such a thing, but that's exactly what he wanted to do.

"Stoke," Seph shouted, his voice loud and urgent. "Get over here."

Stoke had been rolling up his blankets. When he looked up and saw Seph kneeling beside the wagon, he muttered something under his breath. The bedding unrolled as he stood and strode over to see what Seph was shouting about.

Seph pointed at the tack. "See this?" he asked, his finger tracing the clean cut through the leather. "This is no accident. It ain't wear and tear. Somebody's up to no good. Again."

Stoke knelt down beside him, running his fingers over the surface of a severed strap. "That's a clean knife slice, alright," he muttered, his eyes narrowing. "It wasn't done in a hurry, either."

Seph stood and glanced around camp. Most of the crew was awake now, climbing from their bedrolls. Together, they made their way around camp. It wasn't just the chuckwagon's rigging. Half the guys had severed cinch straps on their saddles, and many had sliced up bridles as well.

"Whoever did this was quiet as a mouse," Stoke said, shaking his head. "Ain't nobody heard a thing last night."

Seph clenched his fists. "I'd like to get my hands on the man who done this." They'd been pushing hard to catch up, and now this. He turned to the chuckwagon. One of the spokes that had worried him was now broken. "It's like everything's fallin' apart all at once."

Stoke straightened, looking at the sliced tack with a grimace. "It's gonna take me a while to fix this. I can do it, but we'll lose half the day, if not more."

Seph nodded, frustration bubbling in his chest. "I'll start working on the wagon spokes. We can't afford to lose all this time, but as long as we're stopped, we might as well get some work done."

As he bent down to inspect the cracked spokes, he spotted Torp walking toward him, rubbing his jaw. Instead, Seph stood and waited. Last year they had been inseparable, riding drag together. This year, they worked at opposite ends of the drive. He had taken the young orphan under his wing, looked out for him, and helped him get through a tough year. The kid was still scrawny but taller, and Seph hadn't realized just how much Torp had grown. It was possible that the youngest member of the Deatherage outfit was no longer the shortest.

Torp had taken a hard hit during the fistfight, and the black eye he sported was fading slowly. He'd had a tough time getting his molars to meet when he chewed, but Seph couldn't recall Torp complaining.

"How's that eye?" Seph asked, smirking slightly.

Torp gave a wry grin, touching his bruised cheek. "Still hurts, but I'll live. Jaw's worse than the eye." He noticed the broken spoke and said, "Looks like you got your work cut out for you today."

Seph chuckled softly. "Yeah, and then some. Ain't it funny how things always go wrong around here?"

Torp nodded, tipping back on his heels. "Funny? Nah. Just seems like bad luck has taken a keen interest in us lately."

Seph sighed, running his hands over the wheel's spokes. "It's more than just bad luck, though. The spokes are wear and tear, but the tack, the saddles, the rigging... somebody's doin' this on purpose. I just can't figure out who."

Torp's brow furrowed. "You think it's Grim's gang?"

Seph nodded his head. "Must be." The truth was, Seph could think of several possibilities, but didn't feel like saying names out loud.

The two friends stood in silence for a moment, watching the camp come alive and listening to the early morning sounds. Seph stood up and wiped his hands on his pants. As Torp wandered away, Seph glanced at Stoke, who had already begun working on the tack.

Seph's stomach churned. Time was slipping through their fingers, and with every delay, the gap between them and Grim's gang grew wider. Whoever was sabotaging them had timed it perfectly, leaving the outfit stuck once again.

As he whittled a dowel to fit the rim of the wagon wheel, his stomach growled again. It wasn't just the worry, setting off his gizzard. He'd forgotten to eat, as he often did. But hunger didn't bother him. Long ago, he'd learned how to overlook that.

He knew that the operation was everyone's responsibility. But sometimes, Seph felt like he was in the middle of everything, like a frayed rope pulling a bucket from a well. Only, someone kept slicing that darn rope.

Tears threatened. He was too old for such nonsense, but the frustration was unbearable—always struggling to get ahead, only to fall further behind. He clenched his jaw, determination hardening his stance and steadying his hands. He swallowed hard and stifled the angry tears.

Seph knelt by the fire, poking at the coals while Charlie started ladling mush into tin cups. It was the same every morning—rush to get the food ready, serve up the beans and mush, then wait for the grumbling to commence. But today, the usual clatter of camp chores was interrupted by a different sound.

Slap!

Laughter erupted from across camp, and Seph looked up to see Whirlwind and Tumble, the recruits hired at the end of last year's drive standing face to face, grinning like a pair of idiots.

Slap!

Tumble took the hit and stumbled back a step, but to his credit, he didn't flinch. "That all you got?" he sneered, wiping the corner of his mouth with the back of his hand.

"I ain't even warmed up yet," Whirlwind shot back, rubbing his own cheek from the last slap. The two stood at arm's length, winding up like they were about to slug each other, but instead, it was an open palm to the cheek.

Seph rolled his eyes and got back to his work, but the spectacle had already drawn a crowd. Most of the crew stood around the boys, grinning and placing bets.

Chops held the bets, shouting, "Who wants to bet on the man from Denton? It's either that or the feller from Waco?"

"I got five says Whirlwind drops him!" Hork called out, jingling coins in his hand.

Blaze shook his head. "No way. Tumble's got a chin on him. I'll take that bet."

Slap!

The men cheered as Tumble swung again, this time with more force. Whirlwind's face turned red, but he refused to step back. Seph couldn't help but chuckle under his breath. The whole scene was ridiculous, but it did provide a momentary distraction from the morning's problems.

Just as Seph was about to turn away, Trinket appeared beside him. He tugged at Seph's sleeve, his expression grim. "I need a word with the boss," he muttered under his breath, glancing off into the distance.

Seph stood and nodded. "Alright, let's go." On the way, Seph wondered why the scout fetched him before seeing the boss.

The two men wove their way through the growing crowd, dodging another round of slaps as they went.

"Come on, Whirlwind! Put him on his rear!" Yodel shouted, laughing so hard, he nearly doubled over.

Slap!

The cheer went up as Whirlwind delivered a stinging blow. Tumble's head snapped to the side, but he stayed on his feet, gritting his teeth. "Don't know why I ever partnered up with you anyway!"

Seph shook his head and followed Trinket toward the other end of camp. Dusty was sitting on a stump near the chuckwagon, rubbing his temples as if the weight of the trail was pressing down on him. His eyes were bleary, and Seph couldn't help but notice the sluggish way he moved—like he was still half-asleep.

Just before they reached Dusty, Trinket leaned in close to Seph. "I found him," he whispered.

Seph's brows furrowed. Sometimes, Trinket's accent took a moment for him to comprehend. He heard Trinket say *heem*, but realized he meant *him*. Quick as he could, he blurted, "Who?"

"Scorch. He is camped about a mile south of here. Been stealing our food. That is where all your missing biscuits are going."

Seph felt a knot tighten in his stomach. So it was Scorch. He'd suspected Grim's gang, but hearing it was one of their own left a sour taste in his mouth. He had been banished, but at least he wasn't with Grim.

They reached Dusty, who glanced up at them with half-lidded eyes. He didn't speak, just grunted as Seph knelt down beside him.

"Dusty," Seph said gently. "Trinket's got some news."

Trinket shifted nervously before speaking. "Boss, I spotted Scorch. He is camped nearby, living off the supplies he has been taking from us."

Dusty's head jerked up and for a moment, his eyes cleared. "Scorch?" His voice was gravelly, but there was a hint of his former sharpness.

"Sí," Trinket confirmed. "Saw him with my own eyes. He has been eating like a king off what he has stolen from us. If he keeps this up, his *caballo* is gonna refuse to carry him."

Dusty's hands rubbed his lower back, and Seph noticed the tremor in his fingers. "Son of a...." Dusty grumbled, but his words slurred toward the end after he cussed. He wiped his mouth and tried again, but his frustration showed. "We will deal with him."

From across camp, another *slap* echoed, followed by more laughter.

Dusty looked over toward the spectacle, his brow raised. "What in the blazes is goin' on over there? I can't see a thing with all them guys in the way."

Seph couldn't help but laugh. "The boys are havin' themselves a face-slapping contest."

Dusty shook his head slowly, his face twisting in a half smile. "Never heard of such nonsense. Well, at least they're awake."

Seph turned his attention back to Trinket. "What now? You think Scorch'll come back tonight?"

Trinket nodded. "I expect so. He has been sneaking around at night, raiding the chuckwagon when we are all bedded down."

Seph stood, his mind turning the problem over. "Then we'll be ready for him. Let him slither on in like the snake he is. We'll catch him red-handed."

Dusty blinked hard, rubbing his forehead. "Make sure... make sure he don't get away." His voice wavered again.

Slap!

Dusty's eyes opened fast. "Maybe that's what I need. When them boys get finished, bring 'em over here and have 'em slap some sense into me."

Seph leaned forward and whispered his concern. "You gonna be okay, Boss?"

The man said, "Gotta be. I think I'm gonna have to quit that blasted medicine."

Trinket replied, "That is a good idea. I think it is making you worse, not better."

"Amen, son." Dusty said.

As Trinket and Seph turned to leave, another *slap* echoed through camp, followed by a roar of laughter.

"Somebody must tell those boys they will need their jaws if we run into trouble," Trinket muttered, shaking his head.

Seph smiled. "Let 'em have their fun. Lord knows we could sure use some."

The final slap of the contest cracked loudly. A cheer went up as Whirl-wind's hand connected with Tumble's cheek, sending the younger man stumbling backward, his arms flailing for balance.

Tumble caught himself. He swayed on his feet for a moment before raising a hand in surrender. "I give!" he yelled, his face red and swollen from the barrage of slaps.

Laughter rippled through the crowd as Whirlwind raised his arms in victory.

"I knew he'd win," Blaze hollered, clapping Hork on the back. "You owe me five!"

Hork scowled, tossing a handful of coins into Blaze's outstretched palm. "Tumble nearly had him," he muttered, but there was no real bitterness in his voice. The whole camp had enjoyed the diversion. As far as anyone could tell, the contest had done more for their spirits than any meal Seph or Charlie had ever cooked.

Chops, still holding the betting pot, grinned as he doled out the winnings. "Y'all oughta make this a regular thing," he said, counting out the coins. "Turn it into a tournament!"

Whirlwind, wiping the sweat from his brow, shot Tumble a look. "You game for another round later?"

Tumble, still rubbing his sore cheek, grinned back. "Give me a day or two to heal up, and I'll give as good as I get!"

The crowd laughed, and Seph, who had been watching from the edge, couldn't help but shake his head. He admired the energy, though part of him wondered how they'd fare if they had to put that same strength into fighting Grim's gang again. *It just might improve their fighting skills,* he thought.

As the men dispersed, Seph's attention shifted to more pressing matters. The trap for Scorch was on everyone's mind now. They had agreed to lay out the bait that night—that meant cooking up a mess of food that smelled good a mile away—and leave the chuckwagon's provisions a little deeper in the wagon so that they could catch the rat in their trap.

"We'll set up watch over yonder," Blaze suggested, pointing to a patch of brush near the chuckwagon. "He'll think the coast is clear, and when he gets in close, we'll grab him."

Hork nodded, his eyes gleaming with anticipation. "And when we catch him, what then? March him straight to Dusty?"

Stoke, who had been quiet throughout the planning, finally spoke up. "We ain't gonna hurt him. He's gonna answer for what he's done. Stealin' from your own crew ain't somethin' we can let slide."

Seph nodded, keeping his hands busy as he packed up the last of the cooking gear. He didn't like the thought of confronting Scorch. Even if he'd gone rogue, he was part of the Deatherage outfit. Seph wasn't one for violence that could be avoided, but there was no denying that the other men meant business.

As the group finished setting the trap, Seph's eyes drifted to Clive and Mitch, standing a little way off, talking in hushed voices. They weren't exactly hiding, but there was something about the way they were leaning in close, that made Seph's skin crawl. It reminded him of when he witnessed them whispering secretively after dark several days earlier, when nobody was looking. He couldn't hear what they were saying, but the way Clive glanced toward Dusty's bedroll, made Seph uneasy.

Dusty, still looking worse for wear, had just risen from where he'd been sitting, stretching his back with a wince. His face was pale, his movements sluggish, and he looked like he didn't know where he was going. But then, Dusty turned toward the group, his jaw set, and in that familiar gravelly voice, he made an announcement that caught everyone's attention.

"I'm quitting that dang back medicine," Dusty growled. "I don't care if my back hurts like the dickens, I'll deal with that. What I can't take anymore is feeling like a bowl of boiled mush."

Seph's heart skipped a beat. Dusty was a tough man, no question, but Seph had seen how bad his back had gotten. The idea of him quitting the only relief he'd known sent a wave of concern through him.

From the corner of his eye, Seph caught Clive's reaction. The man's face twitched—just for a moment—but it was enough for Seph to see. Mitch, standing beside him, had a similar look on his face. The meaning wasn't clear, but Seph could tell they didn't like this development.

Dusty's declaration hung in the air like a challenge. Clive's jaw clenched, and Mitch crossed his arms over his chest. Neither man said a word.

Seph's gut twisted. He wasn't sure what was going on between Clive and Mitch, but he didn't like it. And the fact that Dusty was quitting the medicine made him wonder what would happen next. Clive had been giving Dusty that tonic for weeks now. If Dusty was done with it, Seph suspected Clive would have to come up with a new plan—and soon.

As the men started to break up for the night, whispers of the face-slapping tournament still on their lips, Seph kept his eyes on Clive and Mitch. Something was brewing.

CHAPTER 13

THE CAMP WAS QUIET. It was late at night, almost morning, and the stars were fading.

Seph and Blaze hunkered in the blind and watched the chuckwagon. The trap had been set and was baited with the hungry outcast's favorite provisions. Now all they had to do was wait for dawn to catch the thief red-handed.

They took turns sleeping. Seph was tired, but his nerves kept him alert. He scanned the camp and listened carefully for any sound that seemed out of place. But as the sun rose, a growing sense of gloom descended on his shoulders. They hadn't heard a sound from the chuckwagon all night.

Blaze stretched his back and yawned. "You think we missed him?" he asked, rubbing his eyes.

Seph frowned. "Let's go check."

They approached the wagon cautiously. Seph was ready with Woodsy's Colts, just in case.

When they reached the chuckwagon, all they found was disappointment. The provisions were untouched. Not a can, crate, or sack had been disturbed.

"Dang," Seph muttered, his eyes scanning the tree line beyond the camp. "He didn't come."

Blaze kicked at a patch of dirt, his frustration evident. "That slippery snake. He probably caught wind of what we were up to. We'll never catch him if he lays low like this."

Seph nodded, but his mind was already racing ahead. The banished cowboy was unpredictable and it was unsettling knowing that Scorch shadowed them along the trail. What else might that scoundrel try to get away with?

Dusty groaned and slowly sat up. Seph noticed the pale sheen on his skin and the violent tremble of his hands as he reached for his canteen. Day one of quitting that awful tonic was hitting him hard, and they had a long ride ahead. It was a pity they couldn't take a couple of days off. They'd all be better off. But there was work to do.

Blaze shook his head as he surveyed the empty trap. "We'd better pack up. It's a long march to the Canadian River."

Seph clenched his fists. The trap had failed, but at least there was food for the men.

Dusty rode beside Seph. He didn't try to do more than sit straight in the saddle, endure the hours, and survive the miles. His face was slick with sweat. His eyes were glassy and his hands gripped the saddle horn as if he feared he might fall from his horse. Holding the horn also helped steady himself against the tremors that shook through his body.

Seph imagined feeling Dusty's pain himself. He knew nothing about how a man could become so stuck on medicine that it nearly killed him when he stopped taking it, but he was learning fast.

The silence between them didn't bother Seph. He was well accustomed to going a long time without speaking. If it weren't for the boss's condition, Seph might have been unnerved by the silence. But knowing that the man needed him nearby made him comfortable riding quietly at his side.

After a long, quiet hour, Dusty spoke in a low, strained voice. "Seph... I need you to promise me something."

Seph turned his head. "Anything, Boss."

Dusty shifted in the saddle, wincing as another tremor racked his body. "I don't know who else I can turn to or trust." He paused as if speaking was a strain and the words came hard. "But no matter what I say or do... no matter how much I beg, don't let me take any more of that dreadful medicine." He took a deep breath, coughed, and sputtered, "Promise me, Seph."

Seph's stomach tightened. The request hit him like a punch to the gut. He could see how much Dusty was suffering. This was no small favor. It might even be life or death. It felt like a suffocating responsibility. He hesitated, and his voice quavered before he said, "I promise."

Dusty gave a slight nod, but there was no relief on his face. "And no matter what Clive, or anybody else says... Promise me."

"I swear, Dusty. No matter what. I won't let you take it."

"That stupid medicine was Clive's idea. Keep him away from me until I'm myself again, okay Seph?"

"You got it, Boss."

Dusty's brow tightened and he blinked slowly, as though trying to focus on the path ahead. Seph could see the fear beneath the pain. It was hard to believe that someone who had survived the war and braved countless trails could deteriorate so quickly.

As they continued to ride through the morning, Seph kept one eye on the horizon and the other on Dusty. The boss slumped in his saddle more with each mile and his breaths became increasingly labored. The crew, riding just ahead, didn't seem to notice the full extent of Dusty's condition.

By mid-morning, the sun blazed high, and its heat bore down on them. Dusty's condition worsened. He wiped the sweat from his brow, but his hand shook uncontrollably. Seph couldn't imagine what that felt like.

Suddenly, Dusty spoke again. His voice was weak but urgent. "Seph... you sure you can handle this?"

Seph didn't hesitate. "Yes, Dusty. No matter what."

Dusty gave a small, tired smile. "Good man."

The sun reached its zenith by midafternoon. The cattle plodded along, too tired to protest the never-ending march.

Seph's legs and backside ached from hours in the saddle. It was his job to protect Dusty, but he needed to shake a leg, wet his whistle, and answer nature's call before he could carry on.

"Seph!" a voice rang out from behind him. He turned in his saddle, instinctively gripping the reins tighter, his eyes scanning the trail for the source of the call. He hadn't realized that he and Dusty were so far ahead of the lead bull.

Stoke trotted up alongside him, his hat tipped low to shade his eyes. "You look like you could use a break. I'll take over with Dusty for a while."

Seph looked at the boss and considered what to say to Stoke in front of the man. He looked intensely into Stoke's eyes and said, "You gotta stay close. Close enough to grab him if he falls. And if anybody else comes near, chase them away."

"Okay, alright already. Sheesh. You sound like a prison guard. Not that I would know what a prison guard sounds like." He chuckled, but moved his horse closer to Dusty's. "Don't worry, Seph."

Seph nodded, gratefully. "Thanks, Stoke. I don't need long, but I'll fill the canteens, take care of some personal business, and be right back."

Stoke gave him a nod and gestured toward the front of the herd. Skillet had wandered a little too far ahead, but had stopped. "Skillet's gettin' restless," Stoke observed.

Seph glanced at the bull. He was indeed farther than usual, standing still, waiting for the herd to catch up. The massive bull's head hung low. His big shiny eyes reflected the sunlight. It seemed as if the animal was watching the entire herd, waiting to guide them forward again.

Seph nudged Hortense into a trot. "Back in a spell," he added over his shoulder as he made his way toward Skillet.

Seph recalled the day he brought that bull in, and thought about the long scar that its horn had gouged into his leg, mid-thigh to mid-shin. But it wasn't the bull's fault. A wild, cornered beast must protect itself, and Skillet had felt cornered. The bull was hardly docile, but after last year's drive, Seph believed the bull had been tamed.

Skillet stood still, as if he were enjoying a break. His thick neck flexed as he lazily chewed on dry grass. Seph dismounted a few yards away, letting his legs stretch as he approached the big beast without letting go of Hortense's reins. He'd learned the hard way never to trust that mustang.

"Hey, Skillet," Seph murmured, his voice soft and calming. "You waiting on the rest of the gang?"

The bull lifted its head slightly, turning those deep, dark eyes toward Seph. The animal's gaze was calm, yet there was something in it that felt almost... knowing. Seph had always been in awe of Skillet: the way the bull led the herd, never wavering, always steady, like he enjoyed being out in front—as if it were his purpose to be followed. In a way, Skillet reminded him of

Dusty, a powerful leader who'd been through battles and challenges, yet soldiered onward.

Seph stepped closer, feeling a strange connection as he looked into the animal's eyes. The bull's reflection was like a mirror, the shiny orb staring back at him, revealing his weary, dust-covered face. It was a rare moment of stillness. A moment for Seph to see himself clearly. The curvature of the bull's eye distorted the shape of his body, but Seph never felt more at home with himself. That moment crystallized both who he was and who he was becoming.

He reached out and gently touched the bull's neck, feeling the heat of the animal's massive body beneath his fingertips. "I know you're tired too, big guy," Seph whispered. "You, me, and the boss—we're all the same."

Skillet snorted softly, shifting his weight as if in acknowledgment. Seph smiled faintly. He admired Skillet's strength, resilience, and perseverance. The entire outfit depended on him, though they often overlooked his contribution to their success. Seph took a deep breath. Calmness washed over him as he realized something.

He wasn't just following orders anymore. And he wasn't just another cowboy. He had stepped up, made promises, and taken on responsibilities. He felt like more than a cook, more than a rider. Dusty depended on him. The entire outfit looked his way when things got rough. He wasn't the boy he'd been when he joined the outfit last April for half pay. He was the sort of man who could carry the weight of the drive on his shoulders without hesitation.

Seph stood there, his hand still on Skillet's neck. The bull's calm presence grounded him. He felt his own strength return. His resolve had hardened. He knew he was ready for whatever came next.

Just as he prepared to mount Hortense, he realized that he had forgotten to relieve himself. It could be hours before he got another break. "Dang," he muttered under his breath, glancing toward the advancing herd. Skillet shifted his weight beside him, snorting softly.

Seph patted the bull one last time before stepping away. He put Hortense's reins between his teeth, and made quick work of the task at hand. The sound of cattle lowing grew closer, reminding him that time was running short. He glanced over his shoulder. The front line of the herd was closing the gap.

As he finished up, Stoke appeared on horseback, grinning as he rode up. "What's takin' you so long?" he called out, his voice carrying over the noise of the cattle. "Herd's catching up fast. You're gonna get yourself trampled. What a way to go, huh?"

Seph laughed, shaking his head. Removing Hortense's reins from between his teeth, he said, "Yeah, that's the last thing I need—getting flattened by a bunch of beeves."

Stoke chuckled, pointing his thumb back toward the line of cattle. "Better move it then. Skillet might forgive you, but them steers sure won't."

Seph vaulted onto his horse quickly, glancing back at the critters closing in. "I'm comin'," he muttered. He spurred his horse forward and caught up to Stoke with ease.

"Glad you made it out in one piece," Stoke teased, as Seph fell in alongside him. "Now, let's get back to work."

"Thanks Stoke," Seph said. He wanted to ask if the boss was alright, but he could see the man upright in his saddle a short distance ahead.

Seph smiled, no longer feeling weary, though he hadn't yet visited the water barrel.

That moment with Skillet lingered in his mind. He glanced back at the bull, plodding ahead, steady as ever.

"One day," Seph muttered, "I'll be top hand, riding point. Here's hopin' you'll still be workin' the trail, old boy. We'll be pards."

The Deatherage boys reached the Canadian River well after dark, finally catching up with Grim's gang. They unpacked the chuckwagon, quietly but efficiently, and set up camp. The murmurs of tired men floated in the air as Seph, Stoke, and Charlie built a makeshift place for Dusty in the back of the wagon, offloading supplies and lining the wagon bed with blankets.

Chuckwagons weren't made to carry passengers, but they tunneled out enough room for the boss to rest. It wasn't spacious. There was just a small space near his feet, but he had more room for his chest, shoulders, and hips so that he could turn from his back to his side when he wanted to.

Seph was tired, but he kept moving. There was plenty of work to do before he could stop.

Stoke clapped Seph on the back. "Take a break," Stoke said. "I know how you like to gaze up at them stars out there. We'll put the boss to bed. Step away for a bit. Then you can sit up all night if you want." He laughed like he didn't care, but Seph knew better.

Seph nodded, grateful for even a couple of minutes alone. He stepped beyond the flickering light of the campfire, letting the quiet of the night wash over him. The stars were out in full force, scattered brilliantly across the sky. He stood still, just enjoying the view. The cooler air brushed against his face. He recalled seeing himself in the bull's eye and wondered how the cosmos would look reflected there.

As he began to lose himself in the calm, a familiar voice interrupted the silence.

"Star-gazing, huh?"

Seph stiffened, then glanced sideways.

Mitch stepped into the shadows and stood beside him. Seph hadn't heard him approach, and the sudden appearance sent a ripple of unease through him.

"What are you doing out here?" Seph asked, forcing an even tone.

Mitch shrugged, a crooked grin on his face. "Same as you. Enjoying a little peace."

Seph didn't reply. Instead, he turned his gaze back to the stars. He wasn't in the mood to talk to Mitch, but something told him Mitch had more to say.

"You ever think about what comes after all this?" Mitch asked after a long pause. "The drive... the wager... everything. You got a plan?"

Seph shrugged. "Back to the ranch and another drive next year. Someday, I'll make top hand. What else does a man need but to find a place where he belongs—then make the most of it?"

Mitch hacked up a wad of phlegm. "I reckon wherever a man is, that's where he belongs. You can work for any outfit. As for me, I came to say my goodbyes. Gonna rejoin Grim's gang. They've got the winning hand. Figure you'll wanna come with me."

Seph's stomach knotted, and he avoided Mitch's gaze. "No thanks. I got me a place here."

"C'mon Seph," Mitch pressed. "We could make something of ourselves together. You don't owe these boys nothin."

Seph's gaze dropped from the stars to the ground. He thought, *I don't owe you nothin'.* He felt a burden lift from his shoulders and a weight drop from his chest. There was no decision to make. He shook his head and sighed.

"You'll never understand, Mitch. This brand means more to me than you'll ever know. You made your choice. And I've made mine."

Mitch's grin faded a bit. "I just figured we should stick together, brother. Blood runs deeper than the punch of a branding iron."

Seph turned, locking eyes with Mitch. It took all the composure he could muster to speak his thoughts evenly. "My brothers and sisters walked away from our family and never came back. Ma was dying. I had to take care of everything. I was just a kid. That was ages ago. Now, my blood is my own. I ride with my brothers of the trail—brothers by choice, bound by duty, hard work, and loyalty. We don't come and go with the shifting of the wind."

He took a step away from Mitch, turning his back on his brother "I don't give a dang about our bloodline," Seph added coldly. In his mind, he thought, *Hang my siblings.*

Dusty tossed and turned in the back of the chuckwagon. His clothes were soaked in sweat. It was well past midnight, and the trail boss had survived his first day without the tonic. His body trembled in fits, his teeth clenched against the pain that seemed to chew at his innards.

Seph stayed awake in case Dusty needed anything. And to stand guard. His head snapped up as he heard the soft crunch of footsteps approaching.

Clive emerged from the shadows, carrying a small bottle. The dim light from the campfire flickered across his face, but Seph caught the glint in Clive's eyes.

"Ain't lookin' too good, is he?" Clive stepped closer. He held up the bottle, giving it a light shake. "This might just get him through the night. No sense lettin' him suffer."

Seph planted his boots firmly in the dirt, his weight balanced evenly as if ready to hold his ground against a charging bull. He straightened his back, broadened his frame, and fixed Clive with an unwavering stare. "Dusty said he's done with that stuff."

Clive sneered. "Men say things when they're hurtin'. He'll thank me in the morning."

"He don't want it, Clive." Seph's hands hovered near his hips, brushing the grips of Woodsy's Colts.

Clive stepped closer, his eyes cold and hard. "Dusty needs this. You gonna let him die, Seph? We need him strong. Doctor's orders."

Seph set his jaw. "Dusty told me to keep him off that tonic, no matter what. I gave my word."

Clive's face twisted with hatred. "Dusty is my kin. That makes him my problem, not yours. You ain't got no right interfering. Step aside." Clive moved around Seph, bottle in hand.

Seph's eyes flashed, his voice cold. "You come one step closer, and I'll blow a hole through you, big as Texas. And just so you know, Clive—I wear my Colts to bed."

Clive froze, his eyes darting to Seph's steady hands and unyielding stance. Slowly, he lowered the bottle.

"We ain't done," Clive growled before turning on his heel and vanishing into the darkness.

CHAPTER 14

JUST BEFORE DAWN, SEPH rose from his spot in the blind they'd built to keep watch over the trap near the wagon.

A few feet away, Dusty thrashed in his sleep, his sweat-soaked clothes clinging to him after another feverish night. Seph hadn't had much rest, but that was nothing new. Between working with Charlie to keep the men fed, tracking down a thief, and watching over Dusty, there wasn't much time for sleep.

Charlie had the coffee boiling. "Breakfast is almost ready," Charlie said while stirring a pot of mush. "Our boys're bound to be hungry. Been a rough stretch lately."

Seph nodded and crouched by the fire. After checking the beans and making sure the biscuits were coming along, he turned to look at Charlie. "Looks like our trap didn't work," Seph grumbled, glancing toward the wagon where they'd set the bait the night before.

Charlie shrugged, wiping his flour-dusted hand on his apron. "That Scorch is slippery as an eel, that's for sure."

Seph scowled. "I should've known he wouldn't come. Not with Dusty flopping around in the wagon boot."

Charlie sucked his gums, made a popping sound with his mouth, and said, "Betcha Scorch'll strike when you stop standing watch."

Seph stood and looked at the groggy cowboys beginning to stir. Clive wasn't among them. It was uncommon for the boss's nephew to wake up before Seph. Where had Clive gone? What was he up to? The questions buzzed in Seph's mind like a fly.

As if on cue, Clive came into view, riding back into camp on King. He dismounted and headed straight toward the men, barking out orders to men who didn't need to be told what to do.

"Chops, get those horses saddled," Clive ordered. "Make sure the remuda's ready to move. We've got a lot of ground to cover today, boys."

Seph watched Clive, but he didn't say a word.

When Clive finally caught sight of Seph, he barked, "Fetch my breakfast, kid."

Seph complied, delivering a steaming plate of mush with a firm "Yes, sir."

"Coffee. Where's my coffee? I shouldn't have to tell you everything."

Seph brought the ramrod a tin cup full of strong coffee and a weak "Yes, sir." Clive was making a show of his position. Seph didn't question that Clive was in charge, but the way he seemed to need to make a show of it rankled. That's not the way Dusty acted.

Clive griped. "Bad enough I have to get up before dawn to check the herd and see what the Three Bar Box gang is up to. I shouldn't have to beg for my breakfast, should I?"

"No sir." Seph kept his expression neutral, but inside, he didn't believe a word of what Clive said.

As Clive strode off giving orders, Seph muttered under his breath, "Where did he go? Where has he been? What is he up to?"

Charlie glanced over, raising an eyebrow. "You thinkin' what I'm thinkin'?"

Seph didn't answer. Instead, he motioned to Trinket, who had been lounging by the fire. "Trinket," he said quietly, "what if you followed Clive's tracks. Do you suppose you could find out where he went?"

Trinket tipped his sombrero. "*Sí*," he said. "This would be good to know. I will see what I can find out." He slipped off toward the horses.

A few minutes later, Clive returned, his chin jutting forward as he pointed toward Dusty. "I'm gonna need you to step back from him. We can't have him taking up all of your time. I need you to ride with Stoke today."

Seph stood his ground. He did not raise or lower his voice, but said his piece crisp and firm. "No can do, sir. I made a promise to Dusty, and I intend to keep it."

Clive's lips twisted into a sneer, but Seph held his gaze. "We'll see about that," Clive growled before stalking away.

Seph watched him go, then turned back to Dusty, who looked worse than Seph had ever seen.

Trinket crouched low to the ground, studying tracks in the soft dirt. The distinct shape of hoof prints led away from where Clive had dismounted. The boss's nephew had clearly been in a hurry, and didn't cover his tracks. Maybe he hadn't thought about it.

The scout squinted at the tracks and shook his head. Clive hadn't just ridden to this spot—he had led another horse here. Trinket noticed an unusual line across a stretch of wet, dewy grass and surmised that the second horse had been tethered here.

"*¿Qué demonios?*" he muttered under his breath in Spanish. "Why would Clive ride out with two *caballos* and return with just one?" His hand brushed over an irresistible shiny pebble. He slipped it into his pocket, which bulged with the weight of his collected treasures. He indulged his childhood habit before quickly returning to his chief task.

Trinket stepped closer and moved silently through the brush. Up ahead, in a small clearing, he found the remains of a campfire. The ashes were still warm to the touch. When he pressed his hand against the earth, he could feel the residual heat. "*Anoche*," he mused to himself. "Somebody was here last night."

He surveyed the area for more clues. A bedroll had been here, hastily rolled up and thrown over a saddle, judging by the indentations. *This is the camp of Scorch*, he thought. But now Scorch was gone and his trail led east.

As Trinket stood and followed the tracks from the clearing, his father's words came to him. The hard-working blacksmith from Presidio often said, *"Cada pista cuenta una historia."* Every track tells a story. The hoof prints were deep and widely spaced, indicating that Scorch had taken off at a gallop. But why?

He followed the trail for half a mile. The farther east he went, the more the landscape stretched out before him. There was little out there but the open plain and sky. Trinket knew little about what lay to the east.

"¿Qué hay al este?" Trinket muttered, dismounting and squatting down once more to examine the tracks. *Why go east?*

The marks were clear as day. After following closely for so long, now Scorch was putting distance between himself and the Deatherage camp too fast. Too fast for a simple errand. Too fast for a man who had decided to give up and follow a different path.

Trinket scratched his ribs. He loved everything about the bright blue shirt he'd picked out in Abilene last year—the soft fabric, the vibrant color, and the fact that it was not borrowed. He'd never had a brand-new, store-bought shirt before. They'd always been homemade and passed down from his older brothers. He paused to admire it for a long moment before returning to ponder the mystery of Scorch's disappearance.

What could be so important out there? Where was Scorch going in such a hurry?

Trinket stood and cast one last glance to the east, his thoughts galloping away. Sometimes, the more a man knew, the more questions he had. With his thoughts churning, he turned back toward the herd. His job was to scout ahead of the herd, not follow Scorch. He would have to wait to tell Seph what he'd found. There wasn't much to go on, but he had discovered that Clive met with Scorch and gave him a horse.

The unease in his chest only deepened. Curiosity tugged him east, but duty compelled him to ride north.

Grim and Mitch rode into a clearing.

Tense Owl stood, waiting, standing beside his men with his arms crossed. Grim couldn't help but notice how calm the Indian looked.

The Three Bar Box boss pulled his horse to a stop and dismounted, taking off his hat with a respectful nod. He introduced himself simply and added, "We come in peace."

Tense Owl remained silent, his dark eyes watching Grim. The years had worn lines into the Kiowa man's face, but Grim saw that there was plenty of fire in his eyes. Behind him, a few of his warriors stood by, eyeing Grim and Mitch.

Finally, the Indian spoke. "I am Tsah Kaum. You say, Tense Owl."

"Tense Owl," Grim began. He softened his voice and spoke slowly, not knowing how good the Indian's English might be. "There are men over yonder, driving a herd of longhorns toward Abilene. Young men. Strong, but wild. They're not just herders. They're escaped convicts. Broke out of prison months ago. They stole every critter in their herd." Grim's voice was steady and his words were spoken like he believed his own lies. "They're killers. Thieves. Dangerous men who do terrible things. Don't let their looks fool you."

Tense Owl's gaze flicked to Mitch for a second, then back to Grim. Grim knew that the man was judging them. Every second mattered now.

"We know your people have suffered," Grim continued, trying to sound even more earnest. "We ain't askin' you to fight for us, but... those men deserve justice. You help us stampede their herd, and you can keep any cattle that are left behind. Fresh meat for your families."

There was a thick pause. Grim had expected that the Indian wouldn't accept their initial offer.

Mitch stepped forward, holding a rope. Grim thought this would sweeten the deal. Mitch turned the horse, showing the Indian what the horse looked like from different angles like a kid at the county fair. This horse was sleek, black, strong, and fit for a chief.

"Your horse," Mitch said. "A gift. For your leadership."

It was a fine horse, and Grim could tell that the Kiowa leader was impressed.

Finally, Tense Owl spoke. Each word was carefully chosen. "The men you speak of, where are they?"

Grim took a step closer, pointing south and lowering his voice. "These men... they don't belong on this land. They are not like us. They've taken what is not theirs and they plan to take more. If they're allowed to keep driving that herd, who knows what they'll do next? It wouldn't surprise me if they started raiding villages, like yours, along the way. They think that nobody can stop them, but they are wrong. You must show them."

Tense Owl's lips tightened. Maybe Grim had struck a nerve, but he knew he must be careful. It was a delicate moment. The Kiowa man was a proud, respected, leader of his people, not some pawn to be moved around. But that was Grim's objective.

Tense Owl's brow twitched and Grim knew he had his attention.

"You help us," Grim said, his voice taking on a more persuasive tone. "Stampede their herd at noon tomorrow. What they leave behind, it's yours."

Mitch reached toward Tense Owl, inviting the Indian to take the black horse's lead rope.

Tense Owl looked at the horse, tall and proud. Grim was sure the Indian understood what accepting this gift meant. There was a flicker of surprise on the man's face when Mitch took Tense Owl's hand, placed the rope in it, and closed his fingers around it before letting go.

The Kiowa leader held the rope, but he had not yet given his word. As he looked away from the steed, he said, "The men you speak of, what have they done to my people?"

"They're thieves, my friend. Like the men who took your lands. Men like that should never get away with such crimes."

Tense Owl frowned, his face betraying a flicker of bitterness. He looked at Grim for a long moment, then at Mitch. Finally he looked back at the sleek horse.

At last, Tense Owl nodded once. "We will do as you say. We will ride tomorrow when the sun is high in the sky." He looked Grim in the eyes. "We will help you."

Grim nodded. He felt like grinning, but held his emotions in check. "That's all we ask. Stampede the herd and take what's left. You deserve it."

As Grim and Mitch rode away, Mitch let out a low chuckle. "You sure got a way with words, Grim."

Grim nodded. "That wasn't easy, but Tense Owl is a man of his word. Good thing he's a bad judge of character." Hearty laughter felt like a just reward, and now that the Indians were gone, he could let it out.

Mitch grinned. "Them boys are gonna spend days chasing scattered beeves."

Dusty lay curled on his side in the back of the chuckwagon, trembling so violently that the whole wagon seemed to shake. His eyes were glazed and unfocused. Breathing was hard, and came in shallow, ragged gasps. The boss's body spasmed with tremors that showed no sign of letting up. Seph knelt beside him, wiping his brow with a damp cloth, helplessly, as his boss and friend suffered through his worst moments yet.

Dusty groaned, rolled onto his back, and gripped his stomach. Without warning, he lurched upward, his body wracked by another wave of nausea.

Seph barely had time to grab a bucket before Dusty vomited. The harsh, guttural retching sound rose above the clatter of the crowded camp.

The herd had been forced to stop early, hours before nightfall, because Dusty couldn't stay in the saddle. The Deatherage men milled around, grumbling. They were hungry, tired, and unsettled. Supper was late and Seph hadn't started on it. He couldn't. All his attention was on Dusty. They'd have to wait for Charlie to finish cooking for them.

Seph glanced at the sky, which had darkened into hues of gold and orange, but the beauty was lost on him. His mind thundered. Could they still win the race? Could they deliver the herd on time with Dusty in this state? Seph was growing more doubtful.

But what did it matter, he thought bitterly. Dusty's health was more important than any wager, or a herd of beeves.

Seph remembered Dusty's words from last year—that beeves were worth more than cowboys. At the time, it felt like the truth. The cold reality of the trail. But now, seeing Dusty like this, Seph knew it had been nothing but bluster. Dusty never believed that, not really. He'd never choose cattle over his crew, over his boys.

A sharp laugh broke through Seph's thoughts. Clive.

"Dinner's late," Clive sneered, leaning against the wagon. His eyes glinted with malice, his arms crossed over his chest. "You boys think Seph's gonna stop babying the boss long enough to feed us?"

Seph shot Clive a look that could have stopped a stampede.

Clive shouted, "We're falling behind. Give Dusty his medicine so we can have our supper and catch up with the Three Bar Box gang." Clive smirked, his lips curling. His beady eyes looked like those of a rattlesnake—ready to strike. Or a weasel, Seph thought. The way the man slinked around camp, issuing orders made Seph want to vomit.

Seph's temper flared, but he bit down on it hard. Clive wanted a reaction. He wanted to push Seph over the edge, make him lash out. But Seph wouldn't give him the satisfaction.

"Dusty's more important right now," Seph said, his voice tight, keeping his gaze on Dusty's shivering shoulders. "Supper will be ready when it's ready."

Clive's grin faded, replaced by a cold glint in his eyes. "We'll see how long that attitude of yours lasts."

Seph's jaw clenched as Clive sauntered away. He half expected the man to come at him, swinging his fists. But, Seph realized, that wasn't Clive's way.

Despite knowing he was right, it was hard for Seph to blot out the doubt that lingered. He had promised Dusty he'd protect him, keep him off that tonic, but with every tremor, every ragged breath, Seph wondered... How much longer could Dusty survive without it? Clive claimed that the medicine was ordered by a doctor. Could Seph keep his promise? What if not having the medicine killed Dusty?

The thought gnawed at him as Dusty moaned softly beside him. And yet, deep in his gut, Seph knew he would not back down. Not for Clive. Not for anyone.

As Dusty moaned softly beside him, Seph's resolve hardened. He would see this through, no matter what. He would not back down from his promise to Dusty. Not for Clive. Not for anyone.

The campfire had burned down to embers. Supper had come late, and most of the men had already retired to their bedrolls, exhausted from the long day.

Seph sat near the wagon, his eyes half-lidded, but his thoughts tumbled. Dusty was resting, though his body still trembled beneath the blanket Seph had tucked around him. A sudden rustle of hooves brought Seph to his feet.

Trinket rode into camp, his sombrero pulled low. He was barely visible in the dim light. Seph had set aside a plate for him, and without a word, he handed it to the scout as he swung down from his horse.

"Gracias, amigo," Trinket muttered between bites.

Seph waited until Trinket had eaten most of his meal before leaning in close. "What did you find out there?"

Trinket glanced around the camp, making sure no one was close enough to hear. He wiped his mouth with the back of his hand and spoke in a whisper. "Grim's herd is to the north. It will take some work to catch dem." He paused, his eyes narrowing. "But guess what I found this morning."

Seph's brow furrowed. "What?"

"I followed Clive's tracks, just as you said," Trinket continued. "They led me straight to Scorch's camp."

Seph's jaw tightened.

"And that is not all," Trinket added. "Clive... he brought Scorch a horse. A fresh one. Scorch took it and galloped away. East."

Seph's mind raced. *East?* That made no sense. "Why east?"

"I do not know, Little Sister," Trinket admitted, a shadow crossing his face. "But Clive knew exactly where Scorch was. They are up to something and it is bad."

Seph covered his face with his hand. "Betrayal. That Clive!"

The two of them sat in silence for a moment. They couldn't confront Clive without proof. And yet, letting him continue unchecked was also dangerous.

"What do we do?" Trinket asked.

"I don't know, Trinket. We need to come up with a plan. Don't worry. We'll figure something out. Get some rest."

Seph stepped into the darkness beyond camp, scratching his forehead. He spoke as if Trinket was still there, listening. "Where can he be? This can't be the last we've seen of Scorch. What is he up to?"

CHAPTER 15

SEPH KNELT BESIDE THE fire, stirring a pot of beans that Charlie had set to cooking. But keeping busy couldn't shake his uneasy feeling.

Dusty was still resting, recovering from another feverish night of shaking. Though Seph was sure the worst had passed, the boss's body remained weak and unsteady.

Normally a robust and imposing figure, Dusty now looked gaunt, his pale face drained of its usual vigor. Even the whiskers of his beard couldn't conceal the sickly pallor beneath.

"How's he doin'?" Charlie asked quietly.

"Better," Seph said, gazing off into the distance. "He still ain't right, though." It was hard to look Charlie in the eyes for fear of betraying his concern. He had seen men worn down from illness before, but Dusty's state worried him in a different way. The whole outfit rested on Dusty's shoulders and without him, the Deatherage enterprise was at risk.

Charlie grunted, handing Seph a tin cup of coffee. "You keep watching over him, and he'll pull through. You always been the stubborn type."

Seph smirked, accepting the coffee. "Ain't that the truth."

Just then, movement at the edge of camp caught his attention. Clive appeared, trotting in from the east. King was lathered in sweat and Clive's expression was guarded. Seph stood, his attention fixed on the ramrod's approach.

"Where have you been?" Seph growled under his breath. It made him suspicious when Clive rode out before dawn.

Clive dismounted and brushed the dust from his hat as he approached Seph and Charlie. "Thought I'd take a look at the trails ahead," Clive said. "Didn't find much worth mentioning."

Seph wasn't buying it. Clive had gone scouting alone, without saying a word. He exchanged a glance with Charlie who raised an eyebrow but kept silent. And if he saw nothing, why was his horse so sweaty?

"Oh," Seph said slowly, his distrust all but confirmed. "What did you see?"

Clive shrugged again, his eyes shifting slightly. "Like I said, not much. Certainly nothing for a camp cook to concern himself with."

Seph bit his tongue, but he had many questions. Before he could press further, Clive strode past him, issuing orders to the men. "Let's get the herd moving. We're losing daylight."

A deep sense of doubt settled over Seph as he watched Clive go. The man had disappeared before dawn, and now he was back with a weak story and a sweaty horse. They had a scout—Trinket—and Clive had not been known to scout the trails before.

Charlie leaned in closer. "You gonna let that slide?"

Seph shook his head. "No. But I ain't making a scene. Not yet. Not until I have proof of something."

As Clive barked orders to the cowboys, Seph made a quiet decision. "Trinket!" Seph called, waving the young scout over.

Trinket jogged over. "What is it, Seph?" Curiosity sparkled in his eyes.

"Clive's been out early again this morning." Seph glanced over his shoulder to make sure Clive wasn't listening. "See where he went."

Trinket's expression turned serious. "What do you reckon he is up to?"

"I don't know," Seph said, his gaze fixed on Clive as the ramrod supervised the men. "But I wanna find out."

Trinket nodded and slipped away without a sound. As he rode off to trace Clive's path, Seph stayed behind, tending to Dusty.

It wasn't just a matter of keeping the herd together anymore. Seph had an awful feeling that something dreadful was coming their way.

The Deatherage herd trudged through the relentless heat as they moved across the open plains. Sweat ran down Seph's neck as he rode Win, giving Hortense a well-earned day off. The air was dry and stifling. It was the kind of heat that seared a man's skin and cooked his shoulders through his shirt. Seph longed for the cool breeze of night or the refreshing touch of a stream.

Dusty was still recovering, riding in the boot of the chuckwagon. Seph had taken up more responsibility than ever, keeping a close eye on both the men, the beeves, the boss, and the rolling pantry.

Seph missed the easier days of the drive, when there was time for lively chatter among the men. Now, the boys grumbled constantly. Exhaustion had taken its toll, crushing the spirits of the once jovial crew.

He glanced over at Charlie, driving the chuckwagon with a Colt nestled at his side. The old-timer's one good hand was steady as a snake's strike, and Seph trusted him to keep watch.

Something pricked at the back of Seph's mind. That uneasy feeling had been building since Clive's return earlier that morning. It was as if he could smell danger brewing in the still air.

Then it happened.

Out of nowhere, war cries pierced the stillness of the prairie. The shrill, unmistakable whoop of mounted warriors slammed into Seph's eardrums. His heart lurched as his eyes snapped to the horizon, where a group of riders appeared from behind the rolling hills. There were a dozen and a half Indians, charging hard at the herd.

"We're under attack!" Seph shouted. The cry echoed up and down the line of cowboys as the Deatherage crew scrambled to react.

Horns and hooves churned up the earth. The herd broke loose in every direction, but Seph noticed that the warriors weren't hurling arrows at them. They seemed intent on driving the longhorns wild and scattering the herd.

Seph's mind raced. He spun in the saddle, glancing back at the chuckwagon where Dusty lay. "Charlie! Watch Dusty!" he yelled over the din. He couldn't afford to leave Dusty unguarded, but he had to act fast.

Charlie grabbed the Colt from the bench beside him and gave a sharp nod. His eyes gleamed with determination as he parked the chuckwagon and positioned himself to protect Dusty at all costs.

Stoke had never seen anything like it. One moment, the herd was moving steadily under the midday sun, and the next, everything exploded into mayhem. Hooves thundered, dust filled the air, and the ground trembled beneath him. The cowboy who thought of himself as invincible couldn't help recalling the moment last year when he was almost killed during a stampede.

"Confound it!" Stoke cursed as he wheeled his horse around, eyes wide as the longhorns bolted in every direction. Forcing thoughts of last year from his mind, he kicked his horse into a gallop and raced alongside the frenzied herd. Skillet whizzed past him in a blur. "Get those beeves under control!" he shouted to the nearest cowboys, his voice straining to rise above the noise.

But it was no use. Arrows whizzed overhead and the beeves ran wild. Stoke knew better than to chase them down one by one. His focus had to be on stopping the mass of bodies before they lost too many doggies.

Ahead of him, a steer broke free from the pack, its horns slashing through the air as it barreled toward Torp. Torp froze in place.

Stoke's stomach dropped. "Torp! Move!" he bellowed, but there was no time to wait for a reaction.

Digging his spurs into his horse's flanks, Stoke surged forward, his hand reaching out to whack Torp's horse on the rump just as the steer charged through where the young cowboy's horse had been standing.

Stoke heard Torp shout, "Thanks!"

"Don't thank me yet," Stoke muttered, glancing back at the stampede. The herd was still moving fast. Too fast. He had to do something.

Stoke urged his horse forward again, looking for Skillet. If they could steer him in the right direction, the rest of the herd should follow. His eyes locked onto the bull's massive frame, its powerful muscles straining as it thundered ahead of the herd.

"Come on, big guy," Stoke muttered under his breath. "Help me out here."

He spurred his horse toward Skillet, trying to get beside the beast. Sweat dripped from his forehead as he closed the distance. It was dangerous and exciting. He was always happiest when his heart thundered in his chest, but it was his job to get the herd under control.

An arrow whooshed past his head. Stoke swore under his breath but kept pushing forward.

If they lost too many critters now, they might never catch up with Grim's gang.

Blaze tightened his grip on the reins, his heart drumming in rhythm with the thunder of hooves. The blood of his Lipan Apache ancestors coursed through his veins and instinct guided him through the melee. While others scrambled to control their mounts, Noomoo wove through the herd with effortless grace, carrying Blaze unscathed through the fray.

A sharp whistle escaped his lips, and Noomoo shifted beneath him, cutting left just as a steer barreled toward them. Blaze leaned low, balancing himself before lifting slightly off the saddle, one hand gripping the horn, the other guiding Noomoo as though they were one being.

Dust clouds swirled, choking the air as the herd spiraled into a frenzy. Blaze spotted a steer breaking from the line and urged Noomoo forward, weaving between panicked beeves. He glimpsed Hork and Sparrow struggling to control their horses, their shouts drowned out by the deafening roar of hooves.

Blaze spurred Noomoo toward them. In an expert maneuver, Blaze swung from the saddle, clung to Noomoo's side, balancing parallel to the ground. Shifting his body weight forced his horse to veer sharply away from a wild-eyed longhorn, and protected Blaze from its slicing horns.

Returning to the saddle, Blaze locked eyes with Hork, who looked like he'd seen a ghost. "Don't just sit there!" Blaze yelled. "Grab them reins and pull tight before we get trampled!"

Without waiting for a response, he spun Noomoo back toward the twist-ing herd. Dust filled his lungs, and his muscles burned, but Blaze knew he couldn't falter.

This wasn't his first stampede. Riding through danger ran deep in his blood.

If Trinket hadn't dallied, he'd have missed the stampede.

He trusted his instincts, but it was nearly impossible to stand still when men, horses, and longhorns were panicking all around him. The thunder of hooves rattled through the ground and up into his bones. He gripped the reins tighter, guiding his horse to the outskirts of the stampede. Dust swirled in the air, rising like storm clouds, and he tugged his sombrero lower to shield his eyes.

He scanned the herd, looking for patterns. There—some of the cattle were moving in a tight cluster, funneled toward a specific direction. Trinket frowned. Why were they moving like that?

A flash of movement caught his eye. Beyond the herd, hidden in the brush, was a man where no man ought to be. Trinket gasped. "What the... Hey!" He dug his heels into his horse, edging closer for a better look.

The man moved deliberately, staying just beyond the churn of the stam-pede. Trinket squinted, his heart skipping as recognition hit him. It was

Clive. The man wasn't panicked. He was watching. It was as if he were studying the herd.

Trinket tasted the burn of bile in the back of his throat.

He couldn't get closer—wild cattle tore through the space between them—but he had seen enough.

Trinket spun his horse and galloped away. The urge to flee overpowered him. Things were worse than they seemed, and they'd already seemed bad enough.

Seph was in the thick of it now, his heart hammering against his ribs. The stampede roared like a river of dust and thundering hooves. Longhorns bolted in every direction, their massive horns cutting through the prairie grass like thousands of scythes. Win danced beneath him, agile but straining to keep his footing among the surging bovine waves. Seph pulled hard on the reins, sand in his mouth and dread gripping his shoulders.

"Steady, boy," he muttered, trying to clear his mind. Through the haze of charging beeves, something caught his eye—no, someone—riding toward him from the far side of the melee.

His stomach sank.

There, mounted on a sturdy paint horse, was Tense Owl. He could never forget the man whose daughter he had rescued. But now, the Kiowa chief was leading riders straight into the herd. Not at the cowboys—at the herd itself, scattering the longhorns.

Seph spurred Win, weaving through the stampede as fast as he dared, steering clear of the lethal horns. His chest tightened as he drew closer to the chief. Tense Owl, calm and steady atop his horse, locked eyes with Seph as their mounts approached.

"Tsah Kaum!" Seph shouted, lifting his voice above the dying roar of hooves. "It's me. Seph!"

The chief's eyes flashed with recognition. His stern expression softened. Raising a hand, Tense Owl signaled his riders, who immediately slowed and pulled their mounts away from the herd.

Seph urged Win closer.

"You use my Kiowa name," Tense Owl said, his voice deep and composed. "Why do you ride here?"

Seph placed a hand over his heart. "I ride with this herd, Tsah Kaum. We're in a race to market. A gang of ex-convicts drives the other herd."

The chief leaned forward, his expression unreadable. "They said you were thieves and killers."

Seph shook his head firmly. "No, sir. You know me. You know my heart. If they told you that, then they lied to you."

Tense Owl studied him, tightening his grip on the reins. The chief's silence felt like an eternity, but Seph met his gaze without wavering.

Finally, Tense Owl's tone softened. "Grim spoke of men who escaped their chains. But you—you are not those men."

"No, sir," Seph said earnestly. "We're just honest, hard working cowboys trying to finish this drive."

The chief glanced over his shoulder at his riders. Turning back, he spoke quietly. "My daughter... Tala. She is safe, because of you. I remember."

Seph's throat tightened. He hadn't seen Tala since that day. He had been drawn to the woman. For a moment, he wondered if she was the woman for him. But after he rode away, all he could think of was Hazel in Abilene. Nevertheless, he still felt a protective whenever he thought of Tala. "I'm glad she's safe, Chief."

Tense Owl nodded slowly, his hand rising again. "You saved her. Today, we help you."

He gave the signal, and his riders began retreating, their horses pulling back from the scattered herd. The thunder of hooves began to fade, leaving the cowboys to gather the wayward beeves.

Seph exhaled deeply and his shoulders relaxed. Glancing over the scene, his gaze locked onto Clive watching from a distance, scowling. The man's face twisted with anger, and Seph knew that Clive resented not being the one to resolve the conflict.

But there wasn't time to dwell on Clive's bitterness. They had critters to round up. Seph had averted one disaster, but he knew the trail ahead would bring more.

It took most of the afternoon to round up the herd and point north again. The Kiowa riders, alongside the Deatherage crew, worked in tandem. The beeves had scattered for miles. It felt strange to work with the same men who had led an attack only hours earlier. Yet, an unspoken understanding bound them to the task.

When the last of the longhorns was brought in, Tense Owl rode up beside Seph. Their eyes met, and a nod of mutual respect passed between them.

"You fight well, young man," Tense Owl said, his voice heavy with authority. "And you speak true. Those men who lied about you, they will face the consequences."

Seph dipped his head in gratitude. "I owe you, Tsah Kaum. Thank you for your help. Take these fifteen beeves as a token of our thanks—for your people."

Tense Owl raised an eyebrow but nodded. "Your gift is generous. It is good that we meet again."

Seph hesitated before asking, "How is your family?"

Tense Owl's expression softened. "My wife and daughter are well. They often ask about the cowboy who saved Tala's life." A rare smile flickered on his lips. "You have friends among the Kiowa."

Seph felt a mix of pride and humility but had no time to respond.

"Seph!" Clive's voice rang out sharply, interrupting them.

The Kiowa riders turned their horses and began to ride away as Seph turned in his saddle to face Clive.

Clive approached, irritation written across his face. His eyes burned with accusation. "Why didn't you wait? You had no right to speak for this outfit." Clive's tone was sharp and his eyes were hard.

Seph tightened his grip on the reins, meeting Clive's hard stare. "I know Tense Owl. Giving him those beeves was the right call."

Clive's jaw twitched, his lip curling in frustration. "That's not your place. You should've let me handle it."

Seph's frown deepened. "Where were you anyway?"

Clive bristled. "Never mind where I was. Just watch yourself, Vermillion. One more stunt like that, and I'm booting you out of this outfit."

Scorch barreled eastward, one horse beneath him and another trailed behind—ready to be swapped when the one beneath grew weary. Each mile carried him farther from the Deatherage outfit.

Why am I doing this? he wondered, squinting into the night. *Fellas get fired all the time. Ain't no shame in it. I should just keep ridin'. And keep goin' till I'm gone.*

Clive had promised he'd make it worth his while. Scorch had spent too much time on the trail not to get paid for his troubles. But he wasn't sure about Clive's plan. The odds of success didn't trouble him. It was the way Clive seemed willing to cross any line that Scorch wasn't sure about.

Yet he rode like his horse's tail was on fire. To make it to Fort Smith and back in time, he would need to cover fifty miles a day, swapping horses as often as he could and trade them for fresh horses whenever possible.

Once he reached Fort Smith and completed his business, he'd have to decide whether to keep his promise to Clive or ride away with nothing.

CHAPTER 16

GRIM SAT BENEATH A cottonwood tree. With a clenched jaw, he ran his thumb over the silver concho on his belt. His eyes were fixed on the horizon as he waited.

Clive rode up, dismounted, and stepped toward Grim, looking over his shoulder. He wanted to make sure nobody saw him.

Grim grunted and gave Clive a curt nod. "We still got a deal?"

With a shrug, Clive answered, "Why wouldn't we?"

The older man tilted his head and directed a probing gaze at the younger. "Maybe your uncle gave you half the herd instead of ten percent. Maybe you took the whole herd. Who knows what could have happened?"

Chuckling, Clive shook his head. "No such luck."

Grim tipped his head forward. "You're a smart young man. Full of ambition. If you thought you could make more with the Deatherage outfit, you'd forget all about our bargain. Wouldn't you?"

As he said the words, "Never occurred to me," Clive lifted his upper lip and scratched his chin. The lie spilled from his lips like it was the truth.

Grim said, "Here's the thing. You make a deal with me, you had better plan on keeping it. No matter what. Because if you double-cross me, you're a goner. That isn't a promise that can be broken but a threat. And not an idle threat at that."

Clive gulped hard.

"And another thing. I don't think you're working hard enough. Y'all boys should be falling way behind by now."

With a couple of nods, Clive agreed. "I have had my hands full with a couple of Dusty's men. They buck me every chance they get. But I got plans for dealing with them."

Grim said, "Well, see that you do." He tucked an arm behind his back and began pacing, before speaking again. "Because I like you, Clive. Because we see things the same, I've decided to offer you a better deal. But you gotta move faster. So, instead of twenty percent of the combined herd, I'll give you twenty-five percent of my herd and fifty percent of Dusty's."

Clive crossed his arms and he whistled.

Grim took a deliberate step closer. "We'll be rich. Both of us. More than rich. All you gotta do is make sure Dusty's herd loses the race. Do you think you can do that?" He paused just long enough for Clive to answer. "Well?"

Clive's giddy expression betrayed his greed. He knew the stakes. It truly was an offer he could not refuse. "You get seventy-five percent of your herd and fifty percent of the Deatherage herd? Is that right?"

Grim's grin widened. "That's another way of putting it. Imagine it: next year you could run an outfit bigger than Dusty Deatherage ever dreamed of."

Clive wondered if Grim knew about Dusty's plan to split forty percent of the herd with his men. Mitch must have told him. Grim's plan would cut Dusty's men out of the deal.

It was risky, but he was already living on the edge. Taking chances thrilled him. With the kind of money Grim was talking about, he'd have enough to bankroll his dream of buying back his grandfather's freight company. It wasn't right that strangers owned it now.

"What's the catch?" Clive asked, shifting uneasily.

Grim leaned in, his face hardening. "No catch. Dusty loses, you win. Dusty wins, I slit your throat. So I suggest you do whatever it takes."

As Clive mounted his horse and turned back toward the Deatherage herd, his thoughts whirled. He *had* just made a deal with the devil, and there was no turning back.

At supper, Seph watched Dusty standing beside the chuckwagon, talking to the crew as they passed by. His color had returned, and there was a spark in his eyes that had been missing for weeks.

Seph felt relieved, but couldn't stop thinking about the Kiowa attack.

Clive stood on the outskirts of the firelight.

Seph took a deep breath and approached him, clearing his throat as he neared the man. "Clive," Seph began. "Got a minute?"

Clive turned slowly, his eyes unreadable beneath the brim of his hat. "What do you need, Seph?"

Seph glanced around to ensure they were out of earshot. "I wanted to talk about the Indian attack. Trinket mentioned he saw something. Said you were missing when things got heated."

Clive's jaw tightened. "Is that so? What exactly did Trinket think he saw?"

"He didn't think it. He saw it," Seph said crisply. "You weren't where you were supposed to be. Instead, you were hiding behind a bush. Why?"

Clive took a step closer, lowering his voice to a frosty whisper. "You're treading on thin ice, Little Sister. Exactly what are you accusing me of?"

"I ain't accusing you of anything—yet," Seph said, his tone firm. "But I think you're up to something. I aim to find out what it is."

Clive scoffed. A humorless smile twisted his lips. "You need to remember your place. My family owns this outfit. I'm the ramrod here. And you are the camp cook." Clive spit on Seph's boot. "Or have you forgotten how a cattle drive works? I give the orders and you follow them."

Seph's eyes flashed with irritation. "I haven't forgotten a thing. But I won't stand by while someone is putting the herd and our crew at risk. Not even you."

"Careful, boy," Clive warned, his gaze hardening. "I'm warning you. You're overstepping your bounds. Dusty might have let you play nursemaid while he was laid up, but he's back now. It's time for you to step back and let me run things."

Seph felt a muscle twitch in his jaw. "Dusty's on the mend, but he's not at full strength yet. Look Clive, we need to win this race. We gotta pull together to get it done. We need to be honest with each other around here."

Clive leaned in, his breath cold and dripping with disdain. "Honest? You wanna talk about honesty? Maybe you should look in the mirror. You knew them Indians, didn't you? I'll bet you put them up to stampeding the herd. What were they gonna give you in return?"

Seph briefly explained how he had saved Tala and met Tense Owl, but Clive was impatient. The boss's nephew stomped his feet, rolled his eyes, and flopped his hand around, signaling his impatience.

When Seph finished, Clive said, "Likely story. Sounds like make-believe to me. And what about giving away beeves? Without so much as a word to me or Dusty. Like you're in charge. Like you own the outfit."

"I did what needed to be done to save the herd," Seph shot back. "And I'd do it again."

"That's your problem," Clive snapped. "You think you're smarter than everyone else. But you're just a cook who got a taste of the big time while Dusty was down. It's time for you to get back to the chuckwagon where you belong and remember your place."

Seph took a slow breath, reining in his temper. "Maybe so. But I'll be watching, Clive. If I find out you're hiding something—"

"You'll what?" Clive interrupted, a sneer creeping into his expression. "You don't have the authority to do a blasted thing."

Before Seph could respond, Dusty's voice called out from near the fire, sounding concerned. "Everything all right over there?"

Seph had barely slept. His mind churned after his confrontation with Clive the night before. He stood by the chuckwagon, helping Charlie get the coffee started when Clive strode over like nothing happened.

"Morning," Clive said. He gave a brief nod to Dusty, who was sitting nearby, sipping from the edge of his tin cup. "Got a long day ahead, so let's get things moving. Seph, we'll be heading out soon. Make sure the chuckwagon travels on the east side of the herd today."

Seph raised an eyebrow. "East side? We always keep it on the west side, closer to the wind, to keep the dust out of the food."

Clive shrugged. "A little dust won't hurt a man. Besides, the creek runs on the east side, so you'll be able to reach the water. I'll have Trinket scout a good spot to fill the barrel."

Clive didn't linger. He continued giving orders to the other cowboys, making sure everyone was ready to move out.

As Clive mounted his horse and rode away, Seph couldn't shake that uneasy sensation that had become a constant companion lately. He had watched Clive amble through camp, barking orders, and thinking about it made him shake his head in disgust.

The men packed up quickly, eager to get moving. Dusty, though still weak, was improving. He mounted his horse slowly, wincing with each movement, but determined. "Let's get this show on the road," he rumbled.

Trinket crouched in the tall grass near Uncle Johns Creek. His fingers twitched as they brushed the dirt by his feet, tracing the tracks of a rider who'd come in from the opposite direction.

But it wasn't the tracks themselves that had him on edge. It was the voices coming from just beyond the creek bed.

Trinket had delivered Clive's orders to fill the water barrel. Seph had driven the wagon near the river, but instead of riding back to camp, Trinket scampered along the creek.

He hadn't expected anything out of the ordinary, but when Mitch Vermillion appeared on the far side of the creek, a lump rose in his throat. Mitch wasn't supposed to be here. And neither Seph nor Mitch had noticed him nearby.

Trinket crept closer, his sharp eyes focused on the two men. Seph's stance was tense as Mitch dismounted and approached him. Though their exchange wasn't loud, Trinket overheard every word.

Mitch's tone was insistent. "Come on, Seph. Let's go. Grim's got a plan. We could be on the winning side together."

Seph shook his head and spoke firmly. "I told you already. I ride with the Deatherage boys. That's all there is to say."

Trinket frowned. Seph had always been loyal, but Mitch was pushing hard.

Mitch stepped closer, but Seph didn't flinch. "This could be your last chance, little brother. You're making a big mistake. Grim's gonna win this race. You're just wastin' your time here."

Seph's jaw clenched and he stepped back, away from Mitch. "Maybe, but at least I'll be able to look my friends in the eye at the end of it. I ain't running off just 'cause things got hard."

Trinket felt his stomach tighten. They didn't act like brothers should.

Finally, Mitch sighed and his shoulders slumped. "Suit yourself," he grumbled. As Mitch turned to leave, Trinket ducked lower, his heart pounding. He was afraid that he would be seen.

Trinket's fingers curled around a small rock near his foot. He weighed it in his hand, feeling the coolness of the stone as his mind chugged. Seph was being set up.

He remained still, waiting until Mitch mounted his horse and rode off in the opposite direction. Seph stood alone by the creek for a moment, staring after his brother.

As Seph finally turned away, he went back to filling the water barrel with a big pail. Trinket straightened, his heart heavy. "Oh Seph," he called out. "What happened?"

Seph blurted, "Mitch keeps trying to get me to join Grim's gang. That will never happen. How many times do I have to tell him? Why won't he leave me alone?"

Clive watched the column of men and cattle moving steadily toward Uncle Johns Creek as the midday sun beat down. Sweat glistened on his brow, but he paid no mind to the heat. He was focused. Everything was falling into place.

He rode slightly ahead of the herd, keeping his eyes on the chuckwagon and maintaining a clear view of Seph by the creek.

As the herd stopped for a break, Clive slowed his horse and turned to Dusty who was riding near Stoke. Dusty was tired but alert. Most of the cowboys were scattered around taking advantage of the brief respite.

Clive hadn't felt this good in weeks. Not long ago, he'd sent Trinket to have Seph fill the water barrel. He knew that Mitch would be there. And he made sure he, his uncle, and a couple of the other men had a good view.

"Dusty," he called out, loud enough for the riders at point and swing to hear. "You might want to take a look at something."

Dusty frowned but reined his horse to a stop. "What is it?"

Clive pointed toward the creek. "Take a look over there, down by Uncle Johns. Looks like Seph is meetin' up with some stranger he didn't tell us about."

Dusty squinted, following Clive's gesture. Sure enough, there was Seph, standing by the water.

"Who is that?" Dusty asked.

Clive shrugged. He tried to sound casual and suspicious at the same time. "Don't know. That kid's got too many secrets if you ask me."

The surrounding cowboys eyed Seph and the stranger. Clive hoped seeds of doubt were already taking root in their minds. He had to press his advantage now, while the moment was hot.

"Don't look like a stranger to me. Ain't that Mitch," Clive said, feigning surprise. "Why is Seph parleying with him?"

Dusty stiffened and pulled his chin toward his chest.

Clive gave an exaggerated shrug, raising his voice just enough for more of the cowboys to hear. "Could be nothing. But it is hard for brothers to be on opposite sides. It's tough to separate kin, wouldn't you say?"

Dusty's face darkened. Clive could see that his uncle was considering what he had said. Dusty and Squat had served on opposite sides during the war.

"I'll talk to him," Dusty said after a moment, his voice gravelly.

Clive kept his expression neutral, though a satisfied grin threatened to break through. The setup was perfect. Let Dusty think Seph was plotting behind his back. It didn't matter that Seph was likely just as blindsided by Mitch's appearance as anyone. What mattered was planting doubt in everyone's minds.

Finally, everything was going exactly as he had planned.

Seph drove the chuckwagon back from the river. He couldn't stop grumbling to himself, frustrated by his brother's latest attempt to get him to leave the Deatherage drive for the Grim gang.

He noticed the expressions on the men in camp right away. Those he called partners, brothers, and friends eyed him with suspicion.

Clive stood by his horse, arms folded, watching as Seph climbed down from the chuckwagon bench. There was a sharpness in his gaze, and Seph thought he saw a gleam in Clive's eye.

Then it hit him. Clive had set a trap. The men had seen him with Mitch.

Dusty stepped forward. "What was that about?" His voice was gruff.

Seph looked Dusty in the eye. In a level tone, he said, "Mitch found me at the creek. Said he wanted to talk."

Clive snorted. "Talk, huh? Ha!"

Seph looked at Clive, but before he could respond, Clive pushed away from his horse and walked closer. "A man like Mitch ain't lookin' to catch up for old times' sake, right? Grim sent him. Didn't he?"

Dusty's eyes flicked between the two men. "Is that true? Did Grim send him?"

Seph nodded. "I don't know why Mitch keeps insisting I join up with Grim. I keep telling him to leave me alone."

Clive's voice dripped with condescension. "Well, it sure looked like a cozy, family chat to me."

A few murmurs of agreement rippled through the crowd. Seph felt a surge of anger rise in his chest. "I don't care what it looked like, Clive. I ain't conspiring with Mitch, Grim, or anybody else. You know I'm loyal to this outfit."

Clive shook his head. "Loyal? Ha! Like when you gave our beeves to the Indians? That Tense Owl fella, he knew you. Your brother rides with Grim. We'd be fools not to question your loyalty."

Dusty raised a hand. "Enough, Clive." He turned to Seph, his gaze searching. "I know you've been lookin' out for me, but this don't look good. Clive's got a point. You gave away our beeves without asking me. And now you're meeting with Mitch behind our backs."

Seph's heart sank. He had expected Clive's pushback, but Dusty's hesitation stung. "Dusty, I swear to you, I didn't plan that meeting. And I didn't mean to go behind your back with the beeves. It happened so fast, I didn't have time to think."

Dusty rubbed his temples, his weariness showing. "I don't know, Seph. Maybe it's best if you step back for a bit. Give me some time to think."

Seph's stomach twisted. "Step back? What do you mean, step back?"

Dusty nodded, avoiding his gaze. "Just do your job. I'll decide what to do next. Later."

The streets of Fort Smith were ghostly quiet. Only the occasional flicker of light penetrated the shadows along the wooden sidewalks.

Scorch moved swiftly through the alleys, keeping his head down. He'd ridden hard to get here, swapping horses whenever he could to cover more ground. Now, with both horses traded for fresh mounts and hitched to a rail a block away, he crept toward his target—a plain warehouse at the edge of town.

Clive's instructions had been clear: get in, grab the goods, and get out. Scorch reached the side door, just as Clive had described and, with one quick motion, he pried it open. The warehouse was cold, dark, and smelled of dust and rot. The faint glow from an oil lamp on the wall barely illuminated the rows of crates stacked high along the walls.

Scorch made his way through the shadows, eyes peeled for the mark Clive had described. And there it was. A crate marked with a faded red "X."

He approached cautiously, working quickly to pry the lid loose. Inside, he found exactly what he had been sent for. He reached in and carefully removed the contents, his hands steady but his mind buzzing. He wasn't sure about this job, but Clive had promised it would be worth his while.

Scorch wrapped the items in cloth, stowing them carefully in his saddlebags, which he had carried over his shoulder. There was no time to think about it. He got what he came for.

As he tiptoed from the warehouse, ready to leave, doubt troubled his mind. *Why am I doing this? I could just keep riding. Disappear for good.* But the promise of what lay ahead—whatever Clive had in mind—kept him moving.

Mounting his nearest horse, Scorch gave one last look toward the dark streets of Fort Smith before quietly walking his horse out of town. As soon as he was a safe distance away, he spurred the horse into a gallop, heading westward into the night. He rode fast, the wind whipping against his face.

It was an exhilarating feeling, sneaking into town and completing his mission.

CHAPTER 17

"WHO THE HECK TIED my horse's legs together?" Hork howled. Half-awake cowboys shot up from their bedrolls. Getting up before dawn was bad enough without being jolted awake in a needless panic. Hork had sparked their ire.

Seph stepped away from the cookfire and headed toward the picket line. It wasn't just Hork's horse. Several of the horses were hobbled, but not in the usual way. The hobbles featured intricate knots, layered one over another, each pulled tight.

Groggy cowboys gathered around. Agitated grumbles ricocheted through the crowd as they squatted or kneeled. Some tried to untie the knots, while others sliced ropes from their horses' legs. But everyone was annoyed.

Chops threw his hat to the ground in frustration. "Who was supposed to be on watch?"

"I was," Blaze snapped, standing up and wiping his brow. "I didn't hear or see a thing all night."

"Me too," Squint echoed. "And me neither," he added.

Seph crouched beside one of the horses, his nimble fingers deftly working through the knots. Whoever had done this had real skill. "Quiet as a ghost," Seph said to himself. The knots were too intricate to be a prank. This was another act of sabotage.

Hork spat on the ground and stomped his foot. "I bet it's Scorch. Slipping in here, messing with us, trying to get back at Dusty for canning him. That's just how he is."

Seph frowned. Scorch hadn't been seen in days. Was it possible? Or had someone else picked up where he left off, stirring up trouble?

The crew slowly worked through the tangled ropes, freeing horse after horse.

Seph stood, brushing the dirt from his hands, and glanced over at the chuckwagon. Dusty hadn't stirred yet, but since his recovery, Dusty was often one of the last to emerge from beneath his blankets. Clive, however, stood near the chuckwagon, arms crossed, watching with an air of casual indifference.

"What's your take on this, Clive?" Seph called out. His challenge shot through the air, and his tone carried the unspoken question: *Was this your doing?*

Clive shrugged. The corner of his mouth twitched. "Looks like somebody wants to make sure we don't get ahead. Probably Grim's boys. You know how low they'll stoop."

Seph didn't respond. Clive was too calm, too smug. But without any proof, Seph couldn't do anything but seethe.

By the time the horses were freed, valuable time had been lost. Again. The men snapped at each other like coyotes fighting over a buffalo bone. It was frustrating, being delayed over and over again. It wasn't much fun to start the day swearing at each other.

Seph's mind niggled at the problem. If it wasn't Scorch, and it wasn't Grim's gang, then who was behind this? Clive wouldn't risk getting caught doing such a thing. Maybe it wasn't just Clive they needed to worry about.

Was there another traitor among them?

The Deatherage crew reached the Cimarron River just as the sun began to set. The day's ride had drained them, and Seph knew everyone was weary. They were beginning to unpack and set up camp—when trouble struck.

Stoke had wandered off, scouting for a good place to lay his bedroll near the riverbank. Meanwhile, the rest of the crew busied themselves with chores—unsaddling horses, gathering firewood, and setting up the chuck-wagon.

Suddenly, a sharp snap rang out.

It was followed by a pained grunt and a shout: "Blast it!"

Seph sprang to his feet. Stoke clutched his leg. His face twisted in pain, his foot was caught in a rusted bear trap, and jagged metal teeth bit deep into his boot. The trap had been hidden in the tall grass near the riverbank, just waiting for an unlucky step.

Rushing to his side, Seph ordered, "Hold still!" He dropped to a knee and pried at the trap with his hands, but it wouldn't budge.

Stoke gritted his teeth, his face pale. "Get this durn snapping turtle off my stinking foot!"

The others quickly gathered around as Seph wrestled with the trap. The metal was old and rusty, but strong enough to make freeing Stoke's foot a struggle. With a final grunt of effort, Seph wrenched it open just enough for Stoke to yank his foot free.

Stoke winced as he inspected the damage. His boot was torn and blood stained the leather. The wound was ugly, but not deep. "Stinking trap," he grumbled, gingerly testing his weight on the injured foot.

Hork stood nearby, scowling at the rusted metal.

Trappers set traps—that was common enough. But placing one where cattlemen crossed the river? That was something else.

Hork grunted. "Who the heck would put that thing there?"

"Could be Grim's men," Blaze suggested, glancing at the surrounding brush. "Maybe just for us. Or maybe somebody else wants us out of here."

Dusty strode over and inspected the bear trap. "Let's not jump to conclusions," he said. "We've got to clear the area. Make sure there aren't more of these bear traps waiting for us."

Seph nodded. The light was fading fast, and they couldn't afford to let another man's foot get clawed. As the crew spread out to check the area, his thoughts drifted back over the day's events. There was no other explanation that made sense. It had to be another sabotage.

"We're losing time," he warned, watching the men search. "Too much time."

Across the camp, Clive met his gaze. That same look. The one Seph had seen at the start of the day.

Seph clenched his fists. One thing after another kept slowing them down, knocking them off course. It had to stop.

At this rate, it'd take a miracle to win the race.

Tempers frayed as the men scoured the terrain for more traps. By the time they disarmed the last rusted device, the sun had slipped over the horizon. The Cimarron River loomed before them. The dark waters reflected the dim light of an array of stars. The current was sluggish, but there was no mistaking the strength of the current beneath the surface.

The herd clustered near the water, restless and lowing. Seph wiped sweat from his brow. His eyes darted across the camp as the men began to settle in. The earlier discovery of the traps had shaken everyone, and even the toughest cowboys griped under their breath, casting wary glances at one another.

"It's Grim," Hork spat, fists clenched. "He's trying to slow us down."

Seph nodded, though his mind was elsewhere. The bear traps were one thing, but it was Clive's reaction that stuck in his mind. He had no proof, so he tucked the moment away with all the others that lived in his memory.

The men gathered around the campfire, nursing their frustrations. Hork and Blaze argued about how they should handle the situation, and soon, the bickering spread. One by one, complaints surfaced. Frustrations multiplied. The forty percent stake they had riding on this drive ratcheted up their fury over endless delays.

Near the fire, Stoke sat with his bandaged foot propped up. He growled, "We're getting nowhere fast. If we don't push harder, Grim's gonna win, and we'll be left with nothin' but dust. No high times for us in Abilene this summer."

Clive, who had been pacing near the chuckwagon, stopped short. Folding his arms, he fixed his gaze on Seph. "That's right," he said coolly. "We are falling behind, and we can't afford any more distractions. Maybe it's time we got our priorities straight."

The conversation stilled. Slowly, the men turned toward Seph.

Seph straightened, sensing the shift. "What're you gettin' at, Clive?" His tone was neutral, but his eyes were sharp.

Clive took a step closer to the firelight, arms still crossed, a smirk tugging at his lips. "I'm sayin' maybe those hobbled horses last night weren't the result of Grim's gang after all."

Seph's eyes narrowed, but he said nothing, waiting for Clive to lay it out.

Clive's voice turned sly. "Seems to me it could've been someone a little closer to camp. Someone who's been actin' real suspicious lately. Like maybe... you."

A ripple of murmurs passed through the men. Seph's pulse kicked up, but his face remained unreadable.

"You're outta line, Clive," Seph said, low and firm. "I've done everything I could to keep this outfit together, and you know it."

Clive chuckled and shook his head. "Do I? All I know is, we woke up to horses that couldn't run and traps that only a man on the inside would know how to avoid." His gaze hardened. "And we know you met up with Mitch, out there by Uncle Johns Creek."

Seph's head pushed forward. He insisted, "I didn't know Mitch would be there."

"Yeah, yeah, we've heard all about that," Clive sneered. "You meet with a known convict—your own brother, no less—and next thing we know, traps are snapping at our feet like alligators by the river. Sounds like somebody's tryin' to sabotage this drive from the inside."

The men around the fire exchanged uneasy glances.

Clive added. "And I think that somebody is you."

Seph's face burned hot. "You really think I'd sabotage the herd I've busted my back to bring in?" Seph's voice rose in anger. "That's insane."

Clive stepped in closer, dropping his voice so only Seph and a few nearby could hear. "Or maybe you've been makin' deals of your own. Maybe Mitch set those traps, and you put him up to it—so you can take down Dusty's herd." He stepped back and made a dramatic face, like the thought had just occurred to him, and surprised him.

The words hung in the air like a noose swinging in the breeze.

Seph felt his fists tighten at his sides. He looked at the crew, and saw doubt in more eyes than he liked.

Clive's poison was spreading.

Morning found the Deatherage crew preparing to cross the Cimarron River. The camp was quieter than usual. Yesterday's arguments still hung thick in the atmosphere, souring the mood like curdled milk.

By the chuckwagon, Seph adjusted the straps securing the last of the supplies, his hands busy but his mind elsewhere. Clive's accusations from the night before still rang in his ears. Worse than the words had been the looks—doubt settling in the eyes of men he'd ridden alongside for hundreds of miles. Even Dusty, though clearer of mind, hadn't spoken up in his defense.

"Think they'll believe you today?" The voice came low, laced with challenge. Seph didn't need to turn to know it was Clive.

"I don't care what you think, Clive," Seph replied, not pausing his work. "I know where my loyalties lie."

Clive chuckled, stepping closer. "I think your meeting with Mitch proves otherwise."

Seph spun to face him, his fingernails digging into the palms of his hands. "I didn't know he'd be there. I keep telling you that. And I ain't answering to you."

Clive didn't waver. "Maybe not today. But Dusty ain't been himself. He's still not thinkin' straight. When the time comes, you really think the boys will follow you?"

Seph exhaled slowly, forcing himself to look away. The herd was gathering near the river, restless and shifting. "You think I'm gonna let you ruin this outfit?" He shook his head and spat. "You think I'm gonna let you lead them down the same path you're walking? You're the one in Grim's pocket, Clive. Not me."

Clive raised an eyebrow, feigning surprise. He was getting good at that. "Got any proof of that, cowboy?"

Seph's chin jutted forward. "Not yet. But I will. And when I do, you'll be the one answering to Dusty."

Clive smirked, brushing off the threat. "You think you're so smart. But are you smart enough to prove it?"

Before Seph could answer, a shout came from across the camp.

"Chuckwagon's ready to move!" It was Hork, giving the signal for the morning's departure.

Seph shot Clive one last glare, then turned on his heel and swung into the saddle.

The river crossing lay ahead.

So did a reckoning.

The Cimarron River stretched wide before the Deatherage outfit, its waters murky and swollen from recent rains. Seph sat on the bench of the chuckwagon, his grip firm on the reins.

Charlie stood beside the wagon, arms loose at his sides as he watched the river warily. "You sure you wanna be the one to drive this across, Seph?"

Seph nodded, watching the current. "Someone has to, and you can't steer with one hand if things go sideways."

Charlie stepped back, giving a slight nod of respect. "Be careful. This river don't look like it wants to play nice."

The mules stirred restlessly as Seph urged them forward. The wagon groaned under the weight of its load, wheels sinking into the muddy bank before they hit the water. As they stepped in deeper, the river surged against the wagon sides, rising higher as the current pushed against the mule's legs.

"Easy now," Seph pleaded, keeping a steady hand. Stoke rode up alongside him, watching closely. "You reckon the wagon will make it?"

"Don't know," Seph said, squinting ahead. "But we don't have a choice. We've gotta get across."

The mules strained, hooves slipping on the slick riverbed. Then—a sudden drop. The rear wheel plunged into a hidden dip, and the wagon lurched violently to one side.

"Dang it!" Stoke yelled as the supplies shifted dangerously.

Seph gritted his teeth, yanking the reins, but the weight was pulling the wagon deeper. "Everyone, get over here!" he bellowed. "We're losing it!"

The crew splashed into the river, grabbing ropes and pulling with everything they had. Charlie shouted orders from the bank, trying to direct the frantic effort.

Bit by bit, they fought the current. The wagon groaned as it slowly righted itself. A few sacks of provisions were lost to the rushing water, but the rest held fast.

Seph didn't look back—he kept his focus, urging the mules forward. Finally, after what felt like hours, the chuckwagon rolled onto the far bank, soaked but intact.

A ragged cheer went up as the last wheel cleared the water.

"We did it!" Blaze whooped, pumping a victorious fist.

But the celebration was short-lived.

Clive stormed toward them, his face a mask of fury. "What in the blazes were you thinking, Seph?" he spat. "We lost precious supplies because of your recklessness!"

Seph wiped a splatter of mud from his chin. He said nothing, but glanced at the river, where their provisions floated out of sight.

The cheers faded into uneasy whispers. The men stood by, soaked and spent, their exhaustion turning to unease as Clive stomped about. He lit into Seph. "Do you have any idea what you've done?"

Seph kept his temper in check. "We got the wagon across, Clive. Could've lost more if we hadn't pushed hard."

Clive's hand curled into a fist, but he didn't swing. Instead, his voice hissed, coiled with venom. "We lost valuable supplies. Enough to set us back. And you—you wanna act like you saved the day?"

The men exchanged nervous glances. Some lowered their heads, avoiding the fight. But Blaze and Torp stood firm beside Seph.

"You'd rather we lost the whole wagon?" Seph shot back.

"I'd rather you start listening to orders and keep your nose out of business that don't concern you!" Clive snapped. "But instead, here you are, playing the hero."

A rumble rippled through the group.

Seph squared his shoulders. "I ain't trying to be no hero, Clive. I'm just doing my job. I'm the cook. This is the chuckwagon."

Clive's eyes narrowed. He stepped in close. "I know exactly what you're up to, Vermillion. You've been cozying up to Dusty for months. You think you can replace me, don't you?"

Seph blinked, caught off guard. "What are you talking about?"

"Don't play dumb," Clive sneered. "Everyone sees it. You're aiming for my spot, but it ain't yours to take. You're just a cook who thinks he's more'n he is."

Before Seph could answer, Blaze stepped forward. "He's been keeping this herd together, Clive. Ain't nobody replacing you, but someone's gotta make sure we finish this drive."

Just as Blaze finished, Torp angrily blurted, "Seph's the reason we're still movin'. He's doing right by Dusty."

Clive's face darkened, his gaze sweeping the crew, assessing their loyalties. "You all see what's happening here, don't you? He's getting too big for his britches."

Dusty stood back, watching the argument unfold. His expression was unreadable, but his silence carried weight.

Seph met Clive's glare head-on. "I'm not interested in your job, Clive. But if you think I'm gonna stand by while you make a mess of things, you're dead wrong."

The Deatherage outfit had survived the Cimarron River. But a deeper battle was brewing—one that could tear them apart from the inside.

Clive's lips curled into a bitter frown. "Fine, Vermillion. Maybe Dusty will tolerate you making threats. But mark my words. Someday I'll be trail boss, and you'll regret ever crossing me."

CHAPTER 18

THE SUN HAD BARELY risen. The cowboys stirred sluggishly, weighed down by exhaustion. Seph felt it too, deep in his bones. But he forced himself upright, sparked a fire, and stepped toward the water barrel strapped to the chuckwagon.

Except—it wasn't there.

He blinked rapidly. Scrubbed a hand over his face. But his shock and disbelief remained. He scratched his backside and stared at the empty ledge where the dip drum should be. Finally, he turned away and looked around, but didn't see the barrel.

They were all looking forward to reaching the Salt Fork of the Arkansas River, but it felt like weeks, not days since they'd left the Cimarron. They had made a dry camp last night and needed that water. It was dangerous to be without it on the open prairie, especially in the heat of summer.

Seph searched for the missing barrel. Could it have fallen off yesterday? That had never happened before. But he knew for sure it had been there last night—he'd lifted the lid himself. After nearly a half an hour of searching, he found it. The barrel lay on its side about fifty feet away, half-hidden behind a thick clump of grass.

The good news was that the barrel wasn't broken.

The bad news—it was bone dry.

But the worst part was Clive appeared just as Seph found it. Chops and Torp had followed Clive, who spread his arms wide and shouted, "What have you done now?"

Seph turned to face him. "I went to make coffee, but the water barrel was gone. Found it here."

Clive rolled his eyes, shook his head, and threw up a fist. "You expect us to believe that? I swear, you'll stop at nothing to help your brother and them jailbirds win this race."

Seph exhaled sharply, his patience frayed. "So let me get this straight. Now you think I dumped the water, rolled the barrel all the way out here, and hid it just so I could *find it* again."

Clive lifted his lip, exposing his front teeth in a hideous sneer. "That's right. You're always looking for ways to make yourself seem like the hero when you're really a traitor. I've got you figured out now, Little Sister. Looks like I'm just two seconds too late to catch you red-handed."

Seph turned his back on Clive. "Chops, help me carry this."

Chops didn't hesitate. He grabbed one end while Seph hoisted the other. Walking backward toward the wagon, Seph let Torp call out trip hazards along the way.

By the time they reached camp, Clive had already spread the word. "No water, no coffee. Just another act of sabotage. Seph *claims* he didn't do it." The way he said claims made it clear he intended to cast doubt.

Dusty stepped up as Seph and Chops lifted the barrel onto its wooden ledge and secured it to the wagon. "At least it ain't smashed," Dusty said. "Better make the water in your canteens last, fellas. It's gonna be a long, hot day."

From the saddle, Clive's voice grated. "Morning's wasting. If there ain't no breakfast, there's no reason to dally."

Seph had learned to hate the sound of Clive's voice.

"Hurry up, men. Let's move," the man added needlessly.

A few cowboys cursed under their breaths, but no one challenged him. Clive had grown more domineering by the day, throwing his weight around, always reminding them he was in charge.

Seph glanced at Dusty. He wasn't trembling anymore, and his color had come back, but he still moved like a man far older than his years.

Dusty was watching Clive. His eyes sharp. His patience thin.

Dusty set his plate down and stood, favoring his back as he marched toward Clive. "They don't need you riding over 'em like that, Clive," he said. "We've picked up ground. These men are working harder than ever."

Clive turned, his expression darkening. "Working hard is one thing. Keeping them sharp's another. We ain't ahead of Grim yet."

"Let 'em breathe," Dusty growled. "We've been riding herd on these boys, non-stop."

Clive's eyes flicked to Seph, then back to Dusty. "You sure that's all we need to worry about, Uncle? Pushing the boys too hard? Or maybe we oughta be more concerned about where some of these fellas' loyalties lie."

The camp went still.

Seph felt every eye shift toward him. He wouldn't take the bait.

Dusty snapped, "What are you getting at now, Clive?"

Clive's smile was thin. "Just saying we need to keep our eyes open. Lotta funny things happen on the trail. Men switching sides. Dealing with the enemy. Slashed leather, knots in the rope, empty water barrels—seems like there's all kinda ways to sabotage a drive." He tipped his head toward Seph, and made a face. He let his expression make accusations without having to say the words.

Dusty's face darkened. "I told you before, Clive. This outfit is solid. If there's a problem, I'll deal with it. But you keep stirring things up, and you'll be the problem."

Silence. Heavy as a yoke.

Seph saw it now—the anger simmering beneath Dusty's expression. This wasn't the man who had started this drive back at the Deatherage compound—strong, sharp, in control. Dusty was stretched thin. Like a rope about to snap. And Seph was sure that Clive knew it too.

Dusty glanced at Seph, his voice quieter but still firm. "Keep your wits about you. I don't want to see any more foolery like this." He gestured toward the empty barrel.

Seph gave a short nod.

Clive turned and rode off, barking more orders.

Dusty moved slowly toward his horse, where Chops had it waiting.

The boys set out with nothing but two-day-old biscuits for breakfast. And nothing to wash them down with.

Seph couldn't shake the feeling that the worst was yet to come.

Scorch's horses stumbled across the Salt Fork of the Arkansas River, hooves splashing in the sluggish current. He sagged in the saddle, his shirt plastered to his back, grime streaking his face.

One hand clung to the reins as he wiped sweat from his brow with the other, squinting at the sky. Heavy clouds gathered to the west, smudging the horizon with bruised streaks of gray. A storm was building.

He spotted a pale rock by the riverbank that looked to be just the right size, and in the right spot to be seen by northbound herds. Sliding from the saddle, his legs nearly buckled beneath him. He dug into his saddlebag, fingers closing around the chunk of coal he'd carried from his last campfire.

Kneeling, he scratched a large X onto the stone, dragging each stroke deep until the black mark stood bold and unmistakable.

"That'll do." He tossed the coal aside.

Straightening, he looked to the saddlebags strapped tight to his horse. The precious cargo inside was the reason for his hard ride to Fort Smith. His job was simple—deliver it, no questions asked.

Scorch tugged the reins, leading the animals up the bank and westward.

A mile from the crossing, he found a shallow swale and dismounted. The horses stood like worn-out ghosts, their heads drooping, legs trembling on the edge of collapse. Scorch barely noticed. His mind was elsewhere as he loosened the cinch, eased off the saddle, and picketed the nags.

Under a modest cottonwood, he knelt beside his saddlebags, unfastened the straps, and removed the treasure. His eyes were wide with wonder. "Treasure!" He mouthed the word as he gazed at it.

He told himself he was just checking the cargo, making sure it was still in good condition. But he knew the truth.

He just couldn't stop looking at it.

The contents were intact, dry, and looked exactly as they had the day he stole them from that warehouse in Fort Smith. Carefully, he repackaged the bundles, tucking the oilcloth snugly around them. When he finished, he gave the saddlebags a gentle pat, like a man settling a restless child.

He didn't have to guess what Clive planned to do with this so-called treasure. "Ain't my problem," Scorch said under his breath.

The first fat drops spattered the dry earth as he leaned back, tipping his head toward the sky. Why hadn't he built a fire when he had the chance?

The clouds churned, thick and swollen. It smelled of wet dust and coming fury. A storm was brewing. Thunder rumbled, low and rolling. Moments later, the sky split open, unleashing a soaking downpour.

Scorch huddled under his slicker, cursing himself for not starting a fire, for not having dry clothes, for not carrying a thick blanket beneath his rain gear.

"Clive owes me for this," he groused. "He'd better pay me good."

Late in the afternoon, the sky shifted without warning.

A gust of wind howled across the plains, picking up speed with every passing second. Dust and sand whipped into the air, swirling into thick, choking clouds. Within minutes, the entire landscape vanished, consumed by a blinding storm. The wind shrieked. Its force was so powerful, it felt like it might shred everything in its path.

Seph yanked his bandana over his face, squinting against the sting of flying grit. Beneath him, Hortense danced nervously, nostrils flaring as the storm lashed across her flanks.

The longhorns he'd been pushing north were now all but invisible through the thick curtain of dust.

"Steady, gal." He forced the calm into his voice. His grip tightened on the reins as Hortense pranced sideways, spooked by the storm. "C'mon! Steady now."

The wind howled across the prairie. Horses whinnied in terror. There was a constant clatter of hooves and horns. The panicked herd made all sorts of frightening sounds: bellowing, bawling, snorting, and even screeching. It took a lot to make trail-worn cattle screech like that. Most cowboys never heard such a sound. It was enough to rattle the bones. He strained to hear anything over the storm—a voice, a signal, anything. He had to find the others. Had to help settle the herd.

Was the chuckwagon holding? He shivered at the thought that it could be destroyed. And Charlie was out there. Helpless and alone. But there was no finding him now.

The storm had swallowed the outfit whole, scattering men and beasts like leaves in a gale.

Through the madness, he thought he saw Blaze—just a blur, gone in an instant. Later, he caught a glimpse of Hork. At one point, he was almost sure he heard Clive's sharp voice barking useless orders, commands no one would hear over the roar.

Mostly, though, it was just him and Hortense. Alone in the storm.

The herd was falling apart. They'd lose days' worth of progress in minutes if the storm wasn't done with them soon.

Seph dug his heels into Hortense's sides, urging her forward. The wind lashed at them, but he pressed on, guiding her blindly through the swirling dust. He had to stop the herd from scattering.

And then—a shadow.

A rider emerged in the storm. Just for a heartbeat, a rider on horseback appeared like a ghost in the swirling gloom. It looked like there might be another rider behind him, then the apparition appeared to vanish.

Seph saw it so fast, he wasn't sure if it was real. His heart kicked against his ribs. Cold dread flushed across his skin.

That stranger didn't belong there. Who was that? What were they doing out there in the storm? Or—was his mind playing tricks on him?

He shook his head, trying to focus, but the image burned into his mind.

The wind howled louder. Then—the sky split open.

And the rain poured down.

The wind finally died down. Then the work of bringing the herd back together and bedding them down for the night began. The crew had recovered most of the beeves when Seph rode in alone. He hated to admit it, but he had been lost. At least he'd made it back in time to help set up camp.

Dust still hung in the air, clinging to everything. The cowboys coughed and spat, rubbing dry, bloodshot eyes. Grime coated every inch of skin, making the youngest cowboys look like old-timers.

Everyone was bone-tired. And thirsty.

Nobody had more than a few precious drops of water left in their canteens. Seph craved the feeling of cool, clear water sliding down his throat, but there wasn't even enough to make coffee.

Charlie swore, scowling at the layer of sticky dirt that clung to his pots and pans. "I cain't even wash 'em."

There was no hope of a hot meal. Instead, they picked through scraps of dried jerky and crumbled biscuits at the bottom of a burlap bag. Somehow, the dust had invaded its way into everything, including the vittles. There was no choice but to eat it as it was. Complaining wouldn't change a darn thing.

Seph had just settled down to rest when Clive stomped up. "What happened to you?" he barked.

Seph's shoulders stiffened. He fought to keep his temper in check. "You say something, Clive?"

Clive puffed his chest, scowling. "Dang sure did. While everyone else was wrestling the herd, where were you?"

Seph turned to face him. "I got carried away with the herd. Couldn't see a thing. I ain't proud to say I got lost."

With a huff, Clive rasped, "Why didn't you stay with the chuckwagon, Little Sister? Ain't that your responsibility? But no, you're always making that old man do all your work."

Charlie snorted. "Don't worry yourself none. Me and them mules did right fine."

Seph dusted off his trousers. "I was trying to help with the herd."

Clive bared his teeth. "Maybe you should mind your business and stay with the wagon."

Seph tried to bite his tongue but failed. "I don't recall asking for your opinion on how I do my job, Clive."

Clive leaned forward and shouted, inches from Seph's face. "Leave the herd to the real cowboys, and from now on, don't do nothing without asking me first."

Before Seph could respond, a familiar voice interrupted.

"That's enough." Dusty looked stronger than he had in weeks. His hands were steady and his eyes were sharp.

"Seph's doing just fine," Dusty said. "I asked you not to ride herd on these men, Clive. Mind your place and do as I ask."

Clive scowled, stepping back, his hands twitching at his sides. The men exchanged glances, but none spoke.

Seph exhaled slowly, giving Dusty a nod of thanks, but anger boiled his blood.

The fire crackled softly in the center of camp. Most of the men had settled in for the night, more than half of them already snoring away the day's exhaustion.

After greasing the chuckwagon axles, Seph stepped through camp, counting bedrolls, and making sure that everyone was accounted for.

His gut tightened.

Someone was missing.

"Torp ain't here," Seph stammered.

Despite camping in a different place every night, most cowboys bedded down in nearly the same spots—creatures of habit, just like the horses and beeves. Maybe Torp had decided to unroll his blankets somewhere different tonight.

But that wasn't likely.

Seph widened his search, stepping beyond the dark edges of camp.

Torp was nowhere to be found.

Seph's pulse quickened. He turned and scrambled over to Dusty, who sat by the fire, rubbing the small of his back and yawning. "Dusty, have you seen Torp?"

Dusty looked up, concern in his eyes. "Torp?" He paused, frowning. "Ain't seen him since this morning. He ain't bedded down?"

Seph shook his head, trying to squelch a rising sense of dread. "No. He's gone."

Dusty pushed himself upright, scanning the camp.

Clive sauntered over, wiping his hands on his untucked shirt tail. "What's all this fuss about?"

"Torp's missing," Seph said sharply. "Ain't nobody seen him since I don't know when."

Clive shrugged dismissively. "Probably off watering the weeds. Maybe he strayed." He rolled his eyes and added, "Addle-brained cowpoke's likely gawking at the stars instead of getting some shut-eye. I wouldn't fret over it. Dang fool'll turn up sooner or later."

Seph's intuition told him otherwise.

Charlie ambled up and chimed in. "I ain't seen him since before the storm hit."

Seph turned. "Who's on night watch?"

Charlie frowned. "Whirlwind and Tumble. Not Torp."

A fresh wave of unease crawled up Seph's spine. He strode toward the slumbering cowboys who rode drag and shook Sparrow and Squint violently. "Torp! Where's Torp? When did you last see him?"

Sparrow and Squint exchanged a look, both waiting for the other to speak first. By now, Seph had woken up everyone. Squint groaned. "Aw, Seph. We thought he was with you. Half the time, he's always trying to ditch us to go chasing off after you."

Seph dropped his head for a second. "Dang it, Torp." Then he straightened. "We can't just sit here. We have to find him."

Clive scowled. "We ain't got time for search parties, not with the pace we gotta keep. We can't spend half the night looking for one man. He don't do much anyway."

The other cowboys shifted uneasily.

Seph's frustration boiled over. "We can't leave Torp out there."

"You don't even know if he's in trouble," Clive shot back. "For all we know, he's just shaking hands with the devil, if you know what I mean. Ain't no use in us getting all worked up for nothing."

Dusty stepped forward. His voice was firm. "We can't lose a man."

Nobody said anything. There was only silence.

Then, "We'll send a couple to search. The rest stay in camp."

Clive let out a sharp exhale but didn't push further.

As the men prepared to search, Seph waited at the edge of camp, staring out into the dark, endless expanse beyond the firelight.

His mind raced with questions.

Had Grim and his gang started picking off cowboys, one by one—like the outlaws that hunted them last year?

Seph clenched his fists, a bitter hopelessness creeping in. How could he save Torp when he had no idea where he was —or what had happened to him?

And then—the memory crashed into him. That apparition in the storm. At the time he'd convinced himself that it wasn't real.

But now, it seemed all too real.

CHAPTER 19

THE PALE SLIVER OF a moon was shrouded behind drifting clouds. Seph guided Hortense carefully across the prairie, though the sure-footed mustang could see better in the darkness than he could.

Trinket took the lead. His sharp eyes swept the terrain while Chops trailed behind. Lullaby rode beside Seph.

They searched every shallow swale, every dip in the land—scanning for any sign of Torp. A crumpled form. A piece of clothing caught on a shrub. A spot of blood. Anything.

Occasionally, they dismounted to peer behind clusters of sagebrush or beneath the gnarled, thorny limbs of a mesquite tree. The stillness of the night was unnerving, broken only by the soft rustle of grass and the occasional creak of saddle leather.

"Where could he be?" Seph muttered. He gazed into a shadowy dip that seemed to stretch forever.

Chops grunted, his voice rough but tinged with worry. "That undersized orphan's really grown on me. Be a dang shame if something happened to him, just when he's turning into a passable cowboy."

Seph glanced back, his throat tightening. There was an affection in the wrangler's voice he hadn't expected, and it only deepened the ache in Seph's chest.

Lullaby shifted in his saddle. "We'll find him, brother. Don't let the dark play tricks on you, Seph. The devil hides doubts in dark places. Keep the faith, Seph."

"We need more'n faith about now," Seph replied.

Lullaby chuckled softly. "The good Lord's got His eyes on us, even when we can't see our way through the darkness. Trust in that, and in the work you're doing. Ain't the Lord more likely to hear the prayers of hard-working men who stick to the task?"

Seph hesitated, chewing on the thought. "I don't know. Is He?"

"I like to think so." Lullaby's warm soothing voice compelled confidence.

The group pressed on, scouring every shadowed crevice and hollow.

After two hours, Trinket reined his horse to a stop. "That is enough," he said wearily. "No sense in breaking ourselves out here. The trail is more likely to share her secrets in the daylight."

Frustration burned in Seph's gizzard. But Trinket was right. Reluctantly, he nodded and they turned back toward camp.

He hated returning without Torp.

As they rode, Lullaby's voice intruded on Seph's dark thoughts. "One bad thing after another—that's the trail. But you've got what it takes to handle it. The Lord don't give us more than we can carry, brother."

Seph didn't answer right away.

Lullaby always had a way of lifting his spirits. But it was hard to feel hopeful when the trail seemed determined to chew them up and spit them out.

Still, as they neared camp and the faint glow of the chuckwagon fire came into view, Seph felt a flicker of something.

Maybe faith. Maybe stubbornness.

Whatever it was, he held onto it as tightly as the reins in his hands.

It had been a long night. And yet, morning came all too soon.

Seph rubbed his gritty eyes as the sun peeked over the horizon. The men gathered around Charlie's fire, heads low and shoulders slumped.

Torp was still missing.

News of the failed rescue spread through camp. A dark mood hovered over the outfit. To make matters worse, the water barrel was still empty and there wasn't a drop left in anybody's canteen.

Seph glanced at Dusty, who sat beside the fire, face drawn but alert. His back was clearly giving him grief, but he wasn't letting it show as much anymore. That was a relief. Dusty was still sore and stiff, but his mind was sharp again. His voice was steady as he directed the men to prepare for the day ahead.

At the edge of camp, Clive spat into the dirt. "Can't figure why we've lost sleep over a man that don't do much anyway."

Seph's fist clenched instinctively. But he forced himself to stay quiet.

Clive was baiting him. Trying to rile him up in front of the men. Seph wasn't going to give him the satisfaction.

But the truth was, he had never wanted to bash out the man's teeth more than he did right now.

Dusty stood slowly, wincing as he stretched his back. "Trinket's gonna keep looking," he said. "The rest of us must press on. We've come this far, and we ain't about to quit now. We're closer than we've been in ages to catching Grim."

Seph glanced at Chops. His arms hung low and dark circles bagged under his eyes.

Lullaby tipped his head back, whispering to the heavens, no doubt imposing on the Lord once again.

Sparrow and Squint dragged their feet as they made their way forward, and Seph wondered if they had lost as much sleep as the men who searched the darkness half the night looking for their partner.

The men nodded.

It was hard to accept that they had to move forward while one of their own was missing. It showed in their posture, in their eyes—they were exhausted. It seemed as if every cowboy suffered from *slouched-posture plague* and *tired-eye malady*.

Stoke tried to lift their spirits. "If he's out there, Trinket will find him."

Clive turned his back, palming his forehead, and bellyached about stupid cowboys.

Lullaby's gaze turned to Seph before dropping to the ground.

Chops twisted a bridle in his hands, like he was wringing out water from a wet shirt. He shook his head. "That boy. I sure hope we find him. Things ain't gonna be the same 'round here without him." He met Seph's gaze briefly before heading off to prepare the mounts for another grueling day.

Stoke poked a hole through a hunk of leather with an awl. If he wasn't pacing, his hands always needed to be busy, and working with leather fit the bill.

Trinket studied Seph, and it made Seph nervous. Trinket's expression was unreadable. Was he worried that he'd never find a trace of Torp?

Dusty stepped forward. "We ain't giving up on Torp, but we gotta move forward. We got a race to win, and we gotta find water. We ain't got no choice in the matter."

Stoke tossed the scrap of leather into the fire. Brashly, he winked at Dusty. "We ain't got a chance, but let's win this anyway." He rotated his shoulders and cracked his knuckles. "That forty percent is shouting my name."

Lullaby knelt beside the fire and started his morning prayer. The men bowed their heads out of habit, even if their thoughts were elsewhere.

Seph closed his eyes. He prayed for Torp.

As the prayer ended, Dusty gave Seph a firm nod. "Let's keep it together, boys. We've lost sleep, not time. We still got a chance."

The herd plodded forward, their pace sluggish and uneven.

Seph rode alongside Dusty, feeling grit coat his tongue and the corners of his mouth. His throat burned with a thirst that no amount of swallowing could ease.

The canteen slung across his saddle was bone dry. Its presence was a cruel reminder of how long it had been since his last drink.

Dusty shifted in his saddle, resting a hand lightly on the horn. His posture was tense. Alert.

Seph followed his gaze, squinting against the shimmering haze of heat. Then he saw it—movement.

Faint. Distant. A line of cattle and riders blurred by dust. His stomach knotted tight.

Grim's herd.

The sight was like a spark to dry tinder. Seph's cracked lips pressed together and he leaned forward.

Water.

It wasn't just a race anymore. It was a matter of survival. The men, the cattle, the horses—they needed it desperately.

He glanced back at the others.

Blaze's hat brim drooped low, his face gaunt, lips chapped.

Lullaby pulled his bandana tighter across his mouth, his shoulders hunched as though even the weight of the air pressed on him.

Behind them, the herd stumbled forward, tongues lolling. The dry clatter of hooves against the parched earth echoed in Seph's ears.

"There they are," Dusty croaked.

Seph nodded. His throat was too dry for him to form words.

Grim's herd wasn't just ahead—it was moving toward water. That was the real prize now. Not just the lead. If they didn't reach it soon, the animals wouldn't last.

Clive rode up, his face pinched and sour. "Maybe we wouldn't be so thirsty if we hadn't wasted half the night looking for a man who's probably halfway to Texas by now." His voice was scratchy and bitter.

Seph mashed his teeth. His knuckles whitened on the reins, but he kept his gaze forward.

Dusty turned in his saddle, his face hard. Brow furrowed. Jaw tight. His eyes sharp with authority. "You think losing sleep over Torp is what put us behind?" His voice croaked, but his words shot at Clive like a swift arrow. "We're right on Grim's tail, Clive."

Clive's lips twisted into a sneer. But he didn't respond.

Dusty sat straighter. Shifted his shoulders. Seph caught the flicker of pain crossing Dusty's face before he yanked his hat lower and squared his jaw. "We've been through worse, and we ain't quitters."

Seph swallowed against the dryness in his throat. "Amen." The word rasped like gravel but tasted good on his tongue.

Clive muttered something under his breath and rode off, kicking his horse harder than necessary.

Seph glanced at Dusty. "That back still bothering you?"

Dusty took a deep breath. "My cross to bear, son. But don't you worry yourself none. I'll carry it."

The Deatherage outfit reached the banks of the Salt Fork early in the evening. The river shimmered in the slanted light, and for the first time in days, there was a spring in the cowboys' steps.

Horses snorted and tugged at their reins as the men unbridled them, letting the animals wander to the water's edge.

The herd surged forward, hooves splattering mud as they jostled for space to drink.

Cowboys waded into the shallows, cupping water in their hands, gulping it down. After days of choking on dust, it was impossible to fully slake his thirst.

Seph knelt by the riverbank, letting the cool water run over his arms and splash onto his face. It eased the worst of the heat, but his throat still burned. He envied the cattle their noisy gulps.

Once the herd was watered and began to settle along the riverbank, the men turned to chores.

Lullaby and Yodel, buckets in hand, called for help filling the battered water barrel. "C'mon, boys, let's make it quick!" Lullaby hollered. A bucket brigade formed, sloshing water as they worked.

By the chuckwagon, Sparrow and Squint scrubbed pots and pans. Charlie had bribed them with seconds if they helped out. Sparrow flicked a handful of water at Squint, who retaliated with a sharp spray from the pot he was scrubbing. Charlie barked a laugh, and Seph caught himself smiling at the tomfoolery.

Yodel waded into the river, tossed his hat onto the bank, and dove under water. Whirlwind let out a whoop, stepped out of his boots, stripped to his drawers, and plunged into the water. Tumble followed, cannonballing into the deepest part.

Within minutes, the river was full of rowdy, laughing cowboys.

Stoke, grinning ear to ear, called out, "Who's next for a mud bath?" He flung a glob of wet dirt at Whirlwind.

Blaze, shaking his head but unable to resist, rolled up his sleeves and tackled Stoke into the water.

Seph didn't realize he was laughing until Blaze grabbed him by the arm. "You're too clean, Seph!"

Stoke grabbed Seph's other arm. He might have been able to stand his ground against Blaze, but not against both. They hurled him forward and let go. Seph landed on his backside in a deep bog of mud. The thick gunk oozed between his fingers and squelched under his toes.

The antics escalated as Stoke and Whirlwind locking hands, launching Tumble high into the air. He hit the water with a resounding splash, coming up sputtering but laughing.

Mud flew in every direction.

Blaze let out a sharp whistle, holding up a harmless water snake. "Who wants a new scarf?" he called, sending the snake wriggling through the air.

Whirlwind dodged with a yell.

Near the chuckwagon, Dusty smiled.

Charlie stood beside him, shaking his head. "A bunch of toddlers. The whole dang lot a ya!"

Charlie clapped a hand on Dusty's shoulder and shoved him toward the river. "You need this as much as they do, Boss. Go on!"

Dusty stumbled forward. He turned back, eyebrows raised. "You'd better hope I don't pull you in with me, Charlie."

Charlie chuckled, leaning back against the wagon, smacking his lips. "Don't make promises you can't keep."

For a moment, Seph thought Dusty might actually jump in. But the trail boss shook his head. "Let 'em have their fun." His voice was lighter than Seph had heard it in days.

Charlie, grinning like a fox, had already shed his outer clothes. His union suit was threadbare, sagging at the knees and elbows. The threadbare relic looked like it was riddled with bullet holes. Before anyone could warn Dusty, Charlie let out a war cry, launched his rickety body forward, and crashed into Dusty with all the grace of a falling tree. They tumbled into the river with a tremendous splash.

The crew roared with laughter. Dusty surfaced, sputtering. Charlie floated lazily on his back. "Told ya you needed a bath, boss!" Charlie cackled.

Dusty wiped water from his face. "You're lucky I don't drown you, old timer."

Charlie grinned. "Lucky? I'm the luckiest son of a gun on this whole drive! This is tons more fun than begging for change for a living."

Meanwhile, Stoke piled globs of thick mud on his head and crowned himself Mud King of the Salt Fork. He dared the others to follow suit, and everybody did. Everybody but Clive, who stood at the river's edge, scowling.

Seph laughed as clammy globs dripped from his hair. It felt like they had a day off, though it was just a couple of hours.

After dark, the men dragged themselves onto the bank, dripping and grinning like boys let loose from chores. Seph wrung water from his hair and tugged on a clean shirt. The carefree clamor restored his spirits. But as he looked toward the horizon, his thoughts shifted. Trinket and Torp were still out there. They would have enjoyed larking about in the river.

Seph spotted Sparrow and Squint seated near the water, bare feet skimming the surface. He joined them, lowering himself to the ground with a soft grunt. "How're you boys holding up?"

Sparrow shrugged. "Doin' alright. Just feels wrong, ya know?"

Squint rubbed the back of his neck. "Torp's tough, though. That kid don't have any quit in him."

Seph nodded. "You're right. And Trinket? He knows how to handle himself."

Sparrow let out a humorless chuckle. "Be a dang shame if we lost Torp now. We're just gettin' him broke in."

Seph smiled faintly. "We'll find him. We sure enough will."

As Seph rose, Clive swaggered forward. He exaggerated a stumble, slamming his shoulder into Seph. "Why'd you go and trip me, kid?" His voice dripped with mockery. "You trying to get fired?"

Seph stiffened. "Didn't trip you, Clive, and you know it."

Clive smirked. "Sure you didn't. I swear, you're always up to something." He stepped closer. "If it ain't one thing, it's another. Herd's dragging, boss is limping, and you've got one trick after another up your sleeve." His tone turned sly. "Tell me, kid, what's the plan when it all falls apart?"

Before Seph could answer, Dusty's voice interrupted them. "Clive, you got something worth saying, or just flapping your gums again?"

Clive's expression hardened. "Just trying to keep things on track, boss."

Dusty grunted. "Good. Then keep your head down and mind your business."

Clive glared but nodded sharply before turning and stomping off toward the remuda.

Dusty exhaled, shifting his weight carefully. "Don't let Clive get to you, son. He's been a thorn in my side since the day he could ride. I should have known better than to give him a chance."

Seph nodded.

Dusty stepped closer. He confided, "When this drive's over, I'm sending him back to Illinois with his cut. I don't care if he is kin—he's worse than a bad back."

Seph blinked, in surprise and relief. "You're serious?"

"Dead serious," Dusty's tone left no room for doubt. "Don't go spreading it around, though. Let's keep it between us."

Seph grinned. The thought of seeing Clive ride away for good, never to bother the crew again, was almost too good to be true.

Dusty added, "But first, we finish this race and get paid. *Then* we send Clive back to his grandmother where he belongs. And that'll be the end of it."

Seph felt a flicker of hope reignite.

Dusty wasn't ready to quit. And neither was he.

Most of the crew had fallen asleep. As Seph worked on finishing the day's chores, the triumphant mood from the riverside frolic faded and was replaced with a bad feeling. It clung to him. It was like something terrible was coming. And they were doomed. He should hit the blankets, get what rest he could. But it was hard to sleep with a head full of tragic possibilities.

Seph had just stretched out when he heard hoofbeats. Trinket returned from his scouting trip. Seph sat up and then stood.

The scout's expression was grim. "I searched all over," he whispered. "I cannot find any sign of Torp. It is like he vanished."

Seph's heart sank, but he forced himself to stay calm. "We'll find him," he said, though the words felt hollow in his mouth. "I don't know how, but we will."

He clapped Trinket's shoulder and told him to get some rest. Then returned to his bedroll. But sleep didn't come. His thoughts pitched from one worry to the next. Torp was missing. Grim's herd was still ahead. And Clive—Clive was up to something. Seph was sure of it. But what?

A shiver ran through him. His thoughts drifted back to Torp. The kid was out there somewhere, maybe suffering, and Seph felt guilty. Torp needed him.

But what could he do?

CHAPTER 20

SCORCH HUDDLED CLOSE TO a small campfire, staring into the glowing embers. His heart pounded like the hooves of the horses that had carried him so far, so fast.

Across from him, just beyond the firelight, Clive paced like a caged animal. Between them, the saddlebags bulged ominously.

Dynamite.

Scorch's throat felt tight. "Look, I did what you asked," he whispered, his eyes darting between Clive and the saddlebags. "But I don't wanna kill nobody. I thought we was just gonna scare 'em. Scatter the herd."

Clive's lips curled into a sneer.

Even in the dim light, Scorch could see the fury in his clenched jaw, and the wild gleam in his eyes. He wasn't sure, but for a second, it looked like that jagged scar on Clive's jawline glowed in the dark. A man who could make his scar glow? That was someone to watch out for. Scorch considered himself brave. But everybody had their limits.

Clive's voice was threatening. "You're not backing out now, are you?" He tilted his head, making his crooked nose look even more bent. Scorch always thought Clive was scary enough in the daytime. But in the dark? He looked even more dangerous.

Clive stepped closer, blocking out the firelight. "The plan hasn't changed." His posture was rigid. Coiled. He looked like he might spring from his feet. "We take out the remuda. No horses, no drive. We get what we came for. As for Dusty...." He let the words hang.

It was too dark for Scorch to see his face, but he could easily picture Clive's lips curling. He jumped when Clive spoke again. "He should have given me my fair share when he had the chance. The world's better off without him."

Scorch's stomach heaved.

He glanced at the horses, then back at Clive. He didn't need to see the man's face to read his expression, and there was no mistaking his posture. Legs planted wide. Shoulders squared. Arms bent slightly, ready. Like he was about to pounce.

A log popped in the fire. A quick burst of light illuminated Clive's face. Then it went dark again.

Scorch's breath hitched. He'd never seen that look before. Clive wasn't just angry. He was unhinged. There would be no talking him out of anything.

Scorch swallowed hard. "You always hated him." The words slipped out before he could stop them.

It was a bitter truth that Clive didn't bother denying.

Scorch could kick himself for missing the opportunity to keep riding east instead of stealing that dynamite. Fort Smith could have been his stepping stone to something else. *Dang, I missed my chance.*

Clive crouched beside the saddlebags, his fingers grazing the dynamite like they were relics of untold power.

Scorch's hands trembled no matter how hard he tried to still them. His own fingers had touched that dynamite. Even then, he'd known it wasn't right. Now, he saw just how wrong it was to do Clive's bidding. He'd longed to see what would happen when the fuse was lit. He hated Dusty too. But not enough to kill him.

He'd wanted to watch things explode. The idea was thrilling. Titillating. But this? This was madness. He didn't want people to die.

He'd come too far to turn back now. Or had he? He never figured on being a murderer.

Scorch's breath came in ragged bursts. "Look," he stammered, "I brought what you wanted, but I ain't gonna set them things off. I... I just can't."

Clive didn't even look up. "You don't have to. Just keep watch. I'll handle the rest."

Scorch's gaze snapped back to the horses. A thought hit him like a gunshot. *Run!*

If he got on a horse now, he could just ride off into the night.

But where would that leave him?

He knew Clive had a plan for what came next. It involved heading straight to Grim's camp. Scorch wasn't sure if he was a part of that plan. Clive had promised to take care of him. But he'd never been specific. A terrible thought struck Scorch. He gasped at the notion. What if Clive *took care* of him like he planned to take care of Dusty?

What if he did run? Then he would be safe. If only he could escape. Scorch frowned. If he ran, that would leave him with nothing.

This was bad.

Clive stood, lifting a stick of dynamite from the bag, rolling it slowly between his fingers. His eyes met Scorch's. For a second—Scorch swore he saw doubt flicker in them. Maybe it was the pause rather than the look in his eye. But then, just as fast, it was gone. Replaced by steely determination. Cold. Sharp. Unshakeable.

Clive's grip tightened around the dynamite. "Stay sharp," he commanded. "Our time has come."

Scorch nodded. But then he realized that Clive wasn't talking to him. He was talking to himself. Scorch's mouth felt as dry as desert sand.

As Clive turned away, Scorch's gaze stayed locked on the dynamite in his hand. Its potential unraveled in Scorch's mind like a slow-burning fuse. The consequences of what was about to happen loomed like a mountain. A towering, jagged peak, ready to break loose. And Scorch wasn't sure if anyone would survive the violent avalanche.

Clive was the kind of man who always got what he wanted. Scorch tried to convince himself that meant that everything would work out.

But he didn't believe it.

Not anymore.

Clive crept through the dark, the stick of dynamite cold and solid in his grip.

Every step closer to the Deatherage remuda sent a thrill racing through him—the kind of reckless exhilaration that made his palms sweat and his mouth go dry.

This was it.

Dusty's outfit was as good as finished without the remuda. No horses meant no drive. And no drive meant no payday. That's what he'd told Scorch, and he'd meant every word. But it wasn't just the herd that spurred him forward.

It never had been.

Clive's lips curled into a smile. He imagined Dusty's downfall. His uncle, the almighty trail boss, toppled by his own kin. He could practically hear Grim's boys cheering as they welcomed him into their fold.

His empty pockets already felt heavier, just thinking about how rich he was about to be.

Clive had always known he was destined for more. For something bigger. Grandmother was wrong. And Dusty had underestimated him. Now, Dusty would pay for it.

Everything hinged on this moment.

Clive crouched behind a pile of brush, studying the camp in the dim moonlight. The Deatherage boys were all tucked in—oblivious to the danger in their midst. The campfire's last flickers barely reached the edges of the sleeping herd.

Everything was going according to plan.

Except for Scorch. Clive's teeth clenched. The man had gone soft. Whining about not wanting to kill anybody. Clive had seen it—the uncertainty in Scorch's eyes. The way his fingers trembled when they touched the saddlebags. It made Clive nervous. More nervous than he liked to admit. But he couldn't afford to let doubt creep in. Not now.

He was in control. Finally. And he wasn't about to let anyone or anything stop him. Soon, he would be rich. And powerful.

Clive crept closer to the remuda, slipping a hand into his coat pocket. His fingers brushed over the box of matches.

Just a few more steps.

The horses nickered softly, swishing their tails. One snorted, sensing something unseen.

He bent low, planting the first stick of dynamite near the edge of the herd, pressing it carefully into the dirt.

Then—

He froze.

From the corner of his eye, something moved at the edge of camp. His gaze snapped toward it. His heart thudded against his ribs. It was Win, the dapple gray ghost horse.

Clive gulped air. It was just a horse.

Win stood still, watching him. His eyes were dark and unblinking. Like he knew exactly what Clive was planning.

The dynamite suddenly felt heavier in Clive's hand—like an anvil. For the briefest moment, Clive's confidence wavered. A chill crawled up his spine.

It's just a horse, he reminded himself. An old nag with a spooky coat. Nothing more.

But the horse didn't move. Didn't so much as twitch. It was an eerie sight. But ghosts weren't real. And ghost horses definitely weren't real.

Its presence unnerved him.

Clive crouched, shoving another stick of dynamite into the dirt, just a few feet from Win. Clive muttered under his breath, "Let's see how ghostly you feel after this."

The horse didn't flinch.

Clive counted the number of sticks he'd placed. Calculated how many more he needed. Plotted his escape. Gallop away after lighting the last wick.

Speed would be everything. His escape had to be perfect. He flexed his fingers around the matches.

There was no turning back now.

Blaze had night watch. He sat atop his horse, his hat tilted low, watching over the bedded-down beeves.

He hadn't expected anything to happen. Not tonight. The past few days had been hard enough. He'd rather be asleep, but instead, he was stuck nighthawking with Sparrow and Squint.

Then it hit.

The ground shook beneath him. A deafening boom ripped through the night.

Noomoo reared in terror. Blaze snatched for the reins, barely holding on. He was an expert rider, but it was hard to stay in the saddle as the panicked horse bucked beneath him.

Then—

Another explosion. A blast of fire and light tore through the darkness. For a moment, it lit up the sky, turning night into a blazing, flickering dawn.

Blaze's heart slammed against his ribs.

What in the devil was that? Before he could gather his thoughts, the remuda lost its mind. Horses snorted, screamed, and bolted. Wild hooves pounded the earth. They scattered in every direction, Their eyes flashed white in the moonlight.

He had to act fast. Blaze spurred Noomoo hard. They lunged forward, tearing across camp. He barely heard himself shouting over the madness. "The horses. We're losing them!"

Seph had been dozing by the fire, his head resting on his saddle after baking extra provisions for the hard days ahead. He wasn't sure if he'd even been asleep.

Then—

The first explosion hit. Seph jerked upright, his heart hammering, instinctively reaching for Woodsy's Colts.

A second blast followed. Closer this time.

The ground trembled. Chunks of earth rained down. A solid thud cracked against his skull, knocking him off his feet.

His ears rang. His vision blurred. For a moment, he didn't know which way was up.

Through the swirling dust and smoke, Seph spotted the remuda in the distance. Horses were scattering in every direction. Blaze was there—charging after them.

But then—

A third explosion ripped through the night. Seph saw Blaze thrown. One moment, he was on horseback. The next, he was gone—vanished into the haze.

Seph's gaze darted sideways. Beyond the fray, he saw it—

A shadow moving. Tiptoeing through the darkness.

Clive.

Seph's stomach flipped. He wanted to vomit.

This wasn't an accident. This was sabotage. And Clive was behind it. The realization hit like a boot to the ribs. He'd known Clive was up to no good. But it had never dawned on him just how far the man would go.

Clive wasn't just an opportunist. He was ruthless. Didn't care that his own uncle lay asleep. Trusting. Unaware. Just yards away.

And still—Clive had lit the fuse.

Seph's blood ran cold.

This was war.

Stoke hobbled around the outskirts of the camp, trying to work out the stiffness in his leg. The bear trap injury from days before hadn't healed right. Now, every step sent a hot blade of pain shooting up through his hip. He gritted his teeth, refusing to let it slow him down.

Then—

The world erupted.

The first blast knocked him flat on his back.

The ground bucked, the shockwave rattled his ribs and rumbling deep in bones.

A second explosion followed. Dirt and debris rained down, stinging his face, clogging his throat with smoke and dust.

Stoke groaned, rolling onto his side as the pain in his leg surged to a white-hot peak. His fingers clutched his thigh, his breath coming in ragged gasps. The blinding throb blurred his vision.

But there wasn't time to wallow.

Stoke forced himself to his feet, staggering against the force of his own injury. Through the haze, he barely made out the shapes of horses tearing through the smoke.

Then he heard it—

Blaze. Shouting. The pounding of hooves as the remuda bolted into the night.

Stoke gritted his teeth. His leg screamed in protest. Every step was a battle. But his mind locked onto one goal. Reaching Seph and the others.

Another explosion shattered the air. For a moment, he felt completely alone. Separated from the rest of the world by sound, smoke, and peril. Like he was living in a nightmare.

He shouted. His voice was raw and defiant. Even he didn't know what words came out.

His leg throbbed. Each step sent new waves of agony through him. He was determined not to pass out—forcing himself forward. Through the smoke. Through the fire. No fear.

He wouldn't let the night swallow them all.

Not without a fight.

Clive crouched low. Just beyond the mayhem. His heart pounded.

He tried to count the explosions. Had they all gone off?

The blasts felt endless. Echoes rolling through the night like thunder. Each more frantic than the last. It was spectacular. More than he hoped. More than he imagined. But it wasn't enough.

Sweat dripped into his eyes as he fumbled with the last stick of dynamite. His fingers were slick. Unsteady. The plan was slipping.

Horses thundered through the haze. Men shouted in the distance. The ground beneath him trembled.

He struck a match. The small flame flickered, barely clinging to life in the smoky air. His hand shook as he brought it closer to the fuse.

Just one more. Finish it.

Then—

Something moved. Like a specter.

Clive turned, and a lump blocked his throat.

It stood at the edge of the firelight. That horse. The once proud dapple gray, was now nightmarish. Its mane hung in jagged, singed patches, still smoldering in places. What remained of its tail was a charred stump. Shreds of hide were peeling away, exposing glistening muscle.

It stared at Clive through the smoke.

It's eyes. Milky. Hollow. Reflecting the orange glow of the flames.

It stared through him. An unholy, knowing glare.

He hated that horse.

Clive's hand trembled. The match flickered as he stared at the beast.

How was it still alive?

His mind screamed, but his body refused to move. The dynamite in his palm felt impossibly heavy. Like a lead weight.

The batch burned low, singeing his thumb and forefinger. He helped, jerking his hand away.

The horse snorted.

The sound sent a shiver down Clive's spine. And he swore he could feel the splatter from the horse's muzzle. It pawed at the ground, scattering ash and dirt. For a brief moment, Clive believed that the zombie ghost horse was glaring.

That it knew. That it was judging him.

Clive blinked as the creature took a step forward. He stumbled backward, the dynamite slipping slightly in his sweaty grip. His breath came in shallow gasps. *It's just a horse. Just a danged horse.*

But the horse kept coming. Its battered body floated forward.

The cold grip of fear closed around him. He felt utterly powerless.

He fumbled for another match. His hands shook so badly, he nearly dropped it. His eyes darted between the dynamite and the fast-approaching specter. The match caught. A weak flicker of flame.

Then—

A shout. Somebody called his name.

Through the haze, Seph emerged. Charging toward him. Like a hunter closing in on prey. Eyes locked. Sharp. Focused. A Colt in each hand.

Clive felt as if he had swallowed his own tongue. The match fell from his fingers.

The dynamite remained in his grip. Clive snatched another match, struck it hard, and touched the flame to the wick. The fuse sputtered to life, hissing in the dark.

A wild grin split Clive's face.

Seph stepped fast through the smoke and debris.

The explosions had rocked the camp. His ears still rang, muffling the distant clatter of destruction.

Through the haze, he saw Win. Slaw's ghost of a horse, gliding like a phantom across the prairie. The sight of the scorched, battered animal sent a chill through him.

But Seph locked his gaze onto Clive.

Seph snapped Woodsy's Colts from their holsters. The familiar weight steadied him as he leveled both barrels.

"Freeze," Seph barked.

Clive's head jerked up. Panic flashing across his face. He crouched low, gripping a cylinder with a long wick. Like a candle. And it was lit.

Seph's eyes darted. He had never heard of dynamite. But instinct screamed—put it out.

The flame flickered.

It sputtered.

Then—it faltered. And died.

A slow breath rushed from Seph's chest.

For a second, Seph thought Clive might try something. But he froze. His fingers tightened around the dynamite like it was his savior. But the man's candle had gone out.

Beyond Clive, Seph caught movement. Scorch! He scurried into the night. Seph watched briefly. He'd deal with Scorch later. Right now, Clive was the problem in front of him.

Clive lowered the dynamite slowly as Hork hustled to Seph's side. The kid was panting. Pale. His words hit like bullets. "It's bad, Seph. Chops... he's gone."

Seph's stomach lurched.

"Didn't stand a chance."

Seph gasped for breath. His wind stuck behind the lump in his throat. "Chops? Gone?"

His hands clenched the grips of Woodsy's Colts. For a second, he thought he'd empty his stomach right there. He wanted to choke the life out of Clive.

But Hork wasn't finished. "Blaze got hit in the leg. He's bleeding bad, but we patched him up the best we could. Yodel's ribs are cracked, and Rooster's arm... well, it don't look good."

Seph's eyes darted to the camp. Bedrolls. Supplies. Scattered gear. Charred and smoldering. The injuries, the shouting, the destruction—it all churned in his head.

Hork's voice pulled him back. "Dusty's alive, but we can't wake him. It's like he's in a deep sleep."

Then—Stoke hobbled up. He dragged his injured leg. His face was grim. His gaze locked on Clive. Like he'd crawl through fire to get him if he had to.

Seph glared down at Clive. Standing there. With nothing left but his dead man's candle. "Start talking."

Before Clive could speak, a voice piped up from behind. Sparrow. "What now, Seph? What should we do now?" The question lingered.

Seph looked at the battered men surrounding him. The wounded. The exhausted. The angry. They all turned to him.

Seph didn't lower his guns.

His mind whirled. One thing was immediately clear. He had decisions to make. And that impossible question... it needed a fast answer.

What now?

CHAPTER 21

THE CAMP WAS STILL.

Seph frowned at the lingering smells of scorched earth and gunpowder. It was sure to be another hot day on the trail, but Seph shivered as he stepped cautiously through the wreckage. It was hard to look at the aftermath of the explosions. But he forced himself to take it in—every shattered piece. He needed to remember.

On his way to spend a few minutes beside Chops' grave, Seph witnessed the full carnage of the night before. The jagged craters where Clive had detonated the dynamite. Debris littering the prairie. The dead bodies of horses at the edge of camp. Seph couldn't wait to leave this wretched place.

But first—Chops.

Seph knelt beside the freshly dug grave, placing his hands on the mound of dirt. He closed his eyes and thought back to the first time he met Chops. It was hard to imagine the Dagger D, Angry R without him. He fought back tears. "We'll never forget you, buddy. May you find peace at God's side." He stretched his arms wide, eyes lifting toward the sky.

Then he stood. And walked back to camp. Their mission had not changed. The Deatherage Longhorn Cattle Ranch had a race to finish. A wager to win. And a herd to deliver.

But first—they had to deal with Clive.

The traitor sat with his hands and feet tied, watching the camp come alive. His eyes were sunken, and Seph hoped that he'd spent a sleepless night, haunted by guilt.

Nobody moved. Nobody acted. It was as if they were waiting for someone to take charge.

Then it hit Seph. They were waiting for him.

Seph didn't hesitate.

To Rooster and Hork, he said, "Let's get him in there." He jerked a thumb toward the chuckwagon. The same spot where Dusty had convalesced, sweating out the tonic. "We ain't taking any more chances with him. Not after what he done to Chops."

Clive didn't fight. Didn't struggle. But he didn't cooperate either. Rooster and Hork dragged him to the wagon and shoved him inside.

Seph turned to Whirlwind and Tumble. "There's nails in the chuck box. Let's board him in."

Tumble frowned. "Don't we need a door?"

"There ain't time for that this morning," Seph said. "We'll worry about that tonight."

It was hard to watch them hammer the boards into place. Harder still to see the chuckwagon—a proud fixture of their camp—turn into a rolling prison.

Seph's mind drifted. He recalled pulling boards off an outhouse to make Ma's coffin. That seemed like ages ago, but it was just last year.

An outhouse shouldn't be a coffin.

A chuckwagon shouldn't be a jail.

Seph reminded himself that it was his job to feed the men. The chuckwagon was his headquarters. But as the miles rolled by, it had become Charlie's place.

Seph glanced at the one-armed man he had befriended in Cowtown. The old-timer stood stiffly, his hand covering his mouth. His eyes looked wide as saucers.

Charlie's expression froze in Seph's mind. He would never forget it. Charlie turned and griped, "I never figured on being a prison warden."

Seph sighed, extending an arm across the old man's shoulders. "Sorry, friend. I wish we didn't have to do it."

Charlie grumbled. "It's just a wagon." Tears welled in his eyes. His voice cracked. "I don't know why you're getting all mushy-faced about it." He stepped away, shaking his head, mumbling, "Kids these days."

Seph cracked a smile. He wasn't the one getting mushy-faced, as Charlie put it. But that was the moment he realized something. He loved that cantankerous old coot.

Seph inspected Whirlwind and Tumble's handiwork. Then he forced himself to look through a small gap between the boards. He could just see Clive's face. Blank. Lips pressed into a thin, pale line. His once commanding presence—gone. Clive didn't move. Didn't speak. Didn't beg for mercy or offer a word of regret. Instead, he went mute.

Seph turned away. Blaze limped toward him, favoring his leg, guided by Rooster. Charlie followed, badgering him about shrapnel wounds. "I lost an arm over a piece of metal just like that!" he fussed.

Yodel trudged behind them, breathing shallow. Every step pained his cracked ribs.

Seph let out a breath. "Looks like I got some doctoring to do."

Charlie threw his arm up. "What are you waiting for? We should've done it last night."

They eased Blaze down beside the fire, propping up his leg. Blood seeped through a hastily wrapped bandage. Blaze's face was pale and drawn.

Seph knelt beside him, peeling back the cloth. A deep gash stared back at him.

Blaze winced as Seph examined the wound. "I'm fine," Blaze muttered, jaw clenched.

Seph huffed a soft chuckle. "Yeah, right. Hold still, Blaze. This is gonna hurt."

With steady hands, Seph worked. He carefully pulled out the jagged bit of shrapnel lodged in Blaze's muscle, making sure not to tear anything worse.

Blaze sucked in a sharp breath.

"Almost got it," Seph reassured.

Finally, the metal came free. He cleaned the wound as best he could, wrapped it tight. "Keep pressure on it if you can. That'll help stop the bleeding."

Blaze's face was tight with pain, but he nodded. "Oh, I can stand it. I can endure a lot, Seph. You should know that by now."

Seph smirked. "You know it, Blaze." Moving on, Seph checked Yodel's ribs—scraped, nothing more. Likewise, Rooster's arm looked better than expected. Merely a scratch.

Lullaby stepped forward. His deep voice trembled as he began to pray. "May the Lord give us the courage to pick up the pieces and go on." His eyes filled with tears.

He prayed for Clive. Then for the wounded. And finally, he delivered a long eulogy for Chops.

Instead of listening, Seph's mind wandered. He had to remind himself that Chops' real name was Henry Shinkle. When Lullaby finished, the men shared stories about their fallen friend. A twenty-year-old kid with a rough complexion and wild sideburns. Loved to deal faro. Suffered from cracking headaches. Had a wry grin and an uncanny way with horses.

Blaze shifted, wincing. "Poor kid. Didn't deserve to go like this."

Rooster rubbed a hand down his face. "He sure was good with a deck of cards."

Seph turned his attention toward the remuda. What would they do without a wrangler?

The explosions had been meant for the horses. Several lay dead, their bodies strewn across the prairie like fallen sentinels. But most of the survivors weren't injured.

Except for Win.

Slaw's old dapple gray stood at the edge of camp. His mane was singed. His tail was burned. His eyes wide, wild—like he'd seen the devil.

Seph approached slowly, extending a calm hand. "You're alright, boy. What a survivor you are! My tough boy."

The creature shivered under Seph's touch. He looked frightful. Would he heal? Physically, maybe. But mentally? Seph wasn't sure.

His thoughts drifted to Sheriff, the claybank dun with the orange mane. He'd grown fond of Hortense. And Win reminded him of his promise to Slaw. But he'd never love a horse the way he loved Sheriff. Seph sighed. It was a pity that the outlaw, Swoop, stole him during his getaway last year. He still held out hope—slim as it was—that he'd see him again. But now wasn't the time for old losses.

Seph turned back to the crew. Their weary faces. Dark bags under their eyes. Sleepless nights, close calls. And Dusty... Dusty still hadn't woken up.

Seph crouched beside him, his heart heavy. He pressed a hand to Dusty's cheek. Softly, he whispered, "We need you, Boss. Gosh, we need you awful bad."

Dusty's eyelids fluttered. A soft groan escaped his lips.

Seph leaned closer, pulse hammering. Dusty's eyes finally opened. But he looked disoriented. Unfocused.

It was hard not to be excited. "Hey, you're alright." He gripped Dusty's shoulders. "You're back with us, Boss."

Dusty blinked, his gaze shifting between Seph's face and the camp. "Where... where am I?" His voice was hoarse. Strained. Like it hadn't been used in days.

"You're here, with us," Seph assured him. "At Salt Fork. We had a bad night. You been out for a while. Do you remember anything?"

Dusty's brow creased. His sluggish mind searched for memories. "I... I remember an explosion. I tried to get up, but then... everything went dark."

Seph nodded, his hand still resting on Dusty's shoulders. "There was—well, I guess it's called dynamite. Have you ever heard of that? It blows stuff up. Clive—" He hesitated. How much should he unload at once? Then, he said it. "Clive tried to blow us all up."

Dusty's face darkened. "Clive?" His lips pressed into a thin line. "Dynamite!" After a long silence, Dusty lamented, "I always knew he was trouble. I thought I could turn him around."

Seph sighed, pulling back. "You ain't the only one who thought that. He fooled a lot of us."

Dusty closed his eyes again. "How bad is it, Seph?"

Seph took a steadying breath. "We lost Chops." He paused, and added, "A couple of horses, too. Some injuries, but we're tough. They'll pull through." He didn't want to mention Clive again, but Dusty needed to know. Seph blurted, "Clive's nailed in the back of the chuckwagon. He ain't going nowhere."

Dusty nodded weakly. "Good... good. Just... just make sure we get to Abilene."

Seph squeezed his shoulder. "We will, Boss. You just rest."

Seph rose to his feet and turned back to the crew. "I promised Dusty we'd make it to Abilene."

Hork frowned. "How in the world are we gonna manage that?"

Seph locked eyes with him. Then, he looked to the others. "The same as we always do." His voice strengthened. "We keep moving." Then, turning to Stoke, he added, "Let's hit the trail and make sure we win. And when we reach Abilene, we celebrate."

Stoke let out a rowdy whoop. The others cheered.

It was one thing to rally. Another to get the job done.

The Deatherage outfit was back on the trail by midday, pushing hard. They had lost time. Too much time.

Charlie drove the rolling pantry that now doubled as a prison wagon, bellyaching about his new job—prison warden.

Seph rode beside Dusty. He remembered sitting beside the boss before, as he fought off the tonic. Now, he had the same dazed look. The same jumbled words.

Stoke claimed Dusty had *brain shock*, which happened when a man took a bad knock to the head. But at least Dusty was upright, in the saddle. That had to be enough.

They had to narrow the gap between them and Grim's gang. They had to move.

A shrill war cry split the sky. Seph snapped upright. He heard a sound he'd learned to fear. The drumming of hooves.

Not again, Seph thought. His mind flashed back to another attack. Had Grim bribed another Indian village to attack them?

Before he could see them, the sky was filled with streaks of fire. Flaming arrows. They rained down like shooting stars, and Seph's gizzard dropped. The chuckwagon was the target.

Charlie yanked the reins, mules braying, rearing in panic. Protesting. But they couldn't run.

The old mule driver slashed the free. One-handed.

The wagon bucked. The flames caught. The raiders were already retreating by the time Seph reached the blaze. He saw them now—Grim's men. Mitch was among them. They used arrows but it wouldn't be possible to claim it was an Indian attack.

"Hurry!" Seph shouted. "Get water! Put it out."

Flames lapped hungrily at the wagon.

Seph reached through the fire, yanking the chuck box cupboards open, heaving supplies to safety. Not much made it. The brittle boards burned fast.

Men scrambled, shoveling dirt onto the flames, but it was useless. The fire spread. It sizzled through the wagon bonnet. It snaked between the boards. It licked the undercarriage. The wind fed it. And then—the whole wagon was ablaze.

Flames roared higher. Thick black smoke spiraled into the sky. Seph's gut knotted. His chuckwagon was ruined. Destroyed. Their supplies were gone.

And Clive.

"Clive's still in there!"

The realization hit all at once.

And then—Clive screamed. A horrible, soul-ripping sound. The crew froze. The water barrel was strapped to the wagon. There was no way to reach the water barrel. They weren't anywhere near a river. There was nothing they could do to save the wagon or the man inside.

The flames crackled fiercely, torching into the sky.

Clive's screams weakened.

Seph gritted his teeth. He tried to think of a way to save him. But it was too late. The wagon was an inferno. No man could get close without burning himself.

He stumbled back, arms raised to shield his face from the heat.

Clive's screams stopped, and Seph knew he had perished.

The fire died out almost as fast as it had started. Smoke rose from the wreckage. The wagon was gone, and so was Dusty's nephew.

It all happened so fast. He had never wanted it to end this way. If he had known that this was going to happen, he would have found another way to confine the man. No man deserved such a fate. Not even Clive.

A hand touched his shoulder. Seph turned to Hork. The kid's face was pale with shock. "You... you saved the coffee." The words came fast, breathless. "But that's all we got left."

Seph's gaze shifted back to the smoldering wreck. His voice shook. "That ain't true." He swallowed hard and spoke. "That ain't true at all." His voice rose. He practically shouted. "We still got our horses. We still got the herd. And more than anything, we got each other. That, and we got a job that needs doing. A trail that needs riding. A bet that needs winning. After all we've endured—we just gotta win. Now more than ever."

Hork gasped. "But Seph, we ain't got no food. We'll never make it."

Seph grinned. "Well, Hork. Listen to you, making such a fuss over dang beans. But let me tell you what... from now on, we eat beef. By the time we reach Abilene, you're gonna be so sick of beef, you'll be begging for a plate of beans."

Hork threw his head back, laughing. "Ha! That'll be the day. Let's get back to the herd, boys."

The crew rallied.

As the last of the cowboys returned to their positions, Seph turned.

Dusty had arrived on the scene.

Seph clasped a big hand on the boss's shoulder. His voice was gruff, but he didn't mince words as he gave him the gruesome news. "I'm mighty sorry, Dusty."

The boss's chest deflated. His head hung low.

The Deatherage herd pressed on beneath a sky heavy with clouds. The betrayal, the explosions, the fire—all of it trailed behind them like ghosts.

Seph rode near Dusty, but his thoughts scattered. They wouldn't settle.

Up ahead, a single ray of sunlight pierced the cloud cover, spearing through the gloom. It landed squarely on Skillet. The massive bull strode forward, his muscles rippling, his horns catching the light, gleaming like polished ivory. And he stood still before continuing forward.

Blaze galloped up beside Seph, eyes wide. "It's an omen," he said. "A blessing from the Great Spirit."

Seph wasn't sure about that. But he couldn't deny that the sight was striking. Maybe it was a sign. And Lord knew, they needed one.

Dusty, still groggy from the explosions, rode in silence beside Seph. He didn't notice the beam of light trailing Skillet for several minutes, nor did he react when Blaze galloped forward. His back looked worse with every mile.

Seph hesitated. Then, softly, he suggested, "Maybe we should stop for the night."

Dusty shook his head without looking at Seph. "Don't ya dare," he grumbled. "Keep moving," he said firmly, waving Seph off.

A rider approached.

Seph shifted in the saddle to get a better look. It was Trinket. Seph was relieved to see the scout, but the emotion was short-lived. He had hoped and prayed that when he saw Trinket again, Torp would be riding beside him.

But Torp wasn't there.

He didn't want to ask. But he had to. He shouted, "Did you find him?"

Trinket shook his head slowly. His expression was hard to read, but there was no hope in his eyes. With a heavy sigh, he said, "I rode miles up and down the trail. But there is no sign of him. I been everywhere. It is like he vanished without a trace."

Dusty rubbed his eyes and let out a weary grunt. "That little boy's tougher than old boots. But this don't look good. It's been too long."

Seph's jaw clenched. He fought down a surge of frustration. Days had passed since they'd last seen Torp. And with every hour that passed, the likelihood of finding Torp alive faded. Like sand through his fingers. They could no longer afford to have Trinket searching for something that wasn't there. Could they?

Seph stared off to the north. His mind turned over the question. Where was Torp? The orphan wouldn't up and quit or ride away for somewhere else. He had no place else to go.

And yet—he was gone.

CHAPTER 22

THE DROVERS HAD PUSHED hard all day. By sunset, they made camp along Bluff Creek.

They crossed the estuary and shouted joyfully about leaving Indian Country behind. To celebrate their arrival, the men had planned a feast. But their mood soured fast.

Dusty condemned a gaunt longhorn. "Ain't nobody gonna pay for this sorry critter in Abilene."

The steer bucked weakly against the rope as Seph tightened the halter and led it to slaughter. Its labored breaths fogged the air in the fading sunlight. Bony ribs jutted through its hide like the posts from a sagging fence. The tortured critter had been driven beyond its endurance.

Seph ran his hand along the beast's neck, muttering a soft apology and telling the animal he hated to have to turn him into dinner as he gripped his knife and positioned it against the thick, pulsing vein beneath the animal's throat.

With one swift motion, it was done. Warm blood gushed onto the dry Kansas soil, pooling darkly as the longhorn collapsed. Seph stepped back, his stomach growling loud enough to feel the vibration in his chest. The men behind him were quiet, their eyes fixed on the lifeless animal.

"You sure picked a sorry lookin' steer," Stoke complained, breaking the silence. He leaned on his shovel. "There ain't enough meat on that thing to feed a magpie."

"It'll feed us," Seph countered. He crouched down and sliced through the tough hide. His hands moved quickly. He hadn't much experience butchering cattle, but growing up, he'd butchered plenty of chickens and hogs.

As the last rays of sunlight faded, the cowboys scattered around camp, tending to chores with the urgency of men racing darkness.

Hork muttered curses under his breath as he hammered picket pins into the hard-packed soil. "Ground's packed solid like a brick," he growled, tossing a glare toward Sparrow, who was struggling to untangle a rope. "Coulda picked a softer spot."

"Coulda picked a better crew," Sparrow shot back, the rope slipping from his fingers again. "Why you always gotta whine about stuff? Shoot, I got my own complaints. Here's one. It's you. You're slower than molasses in January."

Hork snapped. "Shut your mouth before I shut it for you."

"Both of you, knock it off!" Stoke barked, stomping over. His limp was less noticeable, but the anger in his step was enough to make both men turn back to their work without further complaint. Normally, the top hand might enjoy the amusement of a dust up. But not now.

Seph glanced up from the carcass, shaking his head. He couldn't blame the men. With the chuckwagon gone, they couldn't even count on proper meals. On top of that, Torp was still missing. They hadn't had the chance to properly mourn the loss of Chops. Seph wondered how much longer they could keep going before somebody snapped for real.

Squint stood by the fire, his arms crossed tightly over his chest. "I'm telling you, Torp didn't just get lost," he said, his voice strained. "How does a man just disappear?"

Sparrow sighed, rolling his shoulders as he secured the last picket pin. "I don't know, Squint. Maybe he fell behind. Maybe he wandered off to take a dump. We don't know nothin'."

"That's the problem," Squint muttered. "Ain't nothin' we can do about it, neither."

Sparrow said, "Hey, is that coffee ready?"

Squint piled on. "I want some too."

Seph answered, "Probably. Go ahead."

After they filled their cups, Squint said, "Where's the sugar?"

Seph frowned. "I'm sorry, men. We lost the sugar in the wagon fire."

Squint protested. "But you saved the coffee."

Seph nodded. "Yes, I managed to save the coffee."

Squint couldn't understand. "Why would you save the coffee but not the sugar? It don't make no sense. Wasn't they in the same place?"

"No. Sorry, Squint," Seph answered. "I wish there was time to save more than just the coffee. But that fire burned too darned fast."

Squint turned his head and looked at Seph from the corner of his eyes and whispered, "You sure there ain't just a little squirreled away somewheres around here?"

Seph understood how the kid felt. He had a hard time acquiring a taste for black coffee himself, just last year. The trio that rode drag didn't mind going without meals, but doing without sugar was another matter. Seph advised them to do their best to choke down black coffee for the next couple of days. "You'll find it ain't so bad once you get used to it."

Sparrow refused. "Nope. No way. I ain't gonna touch this stuff if there ain't no sugar. There'd better be sugar and there'd better be a chuckwagon next year or I ain't signing on again."

Squint said, "You could always bring your own sugar."

Petulantly, Sparrow stomped his foot. "A man shouldn't have to carry his own sugar. That's the cook's job."

Seph agreed. "You're right, and I'm mighty sorry."

He turned his focus back to the longhorn, ignoring the pang of guilt that twisted in his gut. Torp's absence pained him, but fretting over it wouldn't bring the kid back. The best he could do was to keep moving and make sure the men got fed.

By the time the meat was roasting over the fire, the sky had turned a deep indigo, the stars beginning to scatter across it. The smell of charred beef filled the air, but it did little to lift their moods.

Lullaby stood by the fire, his broad shoulders hunched and his hat pulled low. He stared at the meat, his lips pressed into a narrow line. "I don't feel like praying today," he said finally, his voice barely above a whisper. "Somebody else can do it."

The men exchanged glances until Yodel stepped forward, removing his hat. He bowed his head. In a low and solemn voice, he prayed, "Lord, please bless this forsaken cow and the stringy, gristly scraps of meat that cling to its bones. Amen."

A few chuckles rippled through the group, but the mood remained somber. The cowboys took their portions in silence, chewing mechanically. Stoke spat a piece onto the ground, his face twisted in disgust. "This is the worst beef I ever ate," he grumbled, tossing his tin plate into the dirt.

Seph sat by the fire, the last to eat, his plate resting on his knees. He stabbed at the meat, his stomach twisting with hunger, but the first bite was tough as leather and just as flavorless.

As the men chewed in silence, Blaze leaned closer to Seph. "You reckon Scorch ran off to join Grim's gang? Or is he just out there running wild?"

Seph titled his head and frowned, stabbing his meat with a little more force than necessary. "Don't know. But I doubt we've heard the last of him."

Blaze nodded, looking off into the darkness. "Feels like there's trouble coming."

Seph didn't answer. He chewed until his jaw ached and spat the indigestible hunk of gristle into the fire. The night felt heavier than usual. Somewhere out there, Scorch was running wild, Torp was missing, and keeping up with Grim's gang felt impossible. For now, all they could do was gnaw on chewy scraps of beef and keep marching forward.

"We got meat," Seph muttered to himself, his voice low and bitter. "We got coffee. That'll have to do."

The horse's flanks foamed with sweat, her sides heaving as Scorch leaned low, driving her forward with sharp kicks. The reins burned his raw palms, and grit stung his sun-cracked lips. Behind him, a dusty trail stretched like a scar across the prairie.

"Git along, nag." His voice rasped against the dry wind. "A little farther. Just a little more."

The mare snorted, her ears flicking back, but she kept running. Scorch wiped his sleeve across his face, smearing dirt over his sunburnt skin. His stomach gnawed at itself, but it wasn't just hunger that churned in his gut.

Dang that Clive.

The name clawed at the back of his mind. Scorch thought back to the promises Clive had made. Smooth as snake oil. He cursed himself for being so gullible.

He spat into the dust. "Hang you, Clive. If there's justice in this world, it'll catch you first. Hang you for getting me into this mess."

The mare stumbled and Scorch eased the reins, letting her catch her footing. He slowed her to a walk and groaned, "Don't die on me yet, you ol' nag. We're almost there."

But the truth bit harder than the wind. He didn't know what he'd find in Abilene. A warm meal? A place to sleep? Or just more trouble? The Deatherage outfit was far behind, and Clive's promises were ashes in his mouth.

Scorch shifted in the saddle, the pistol on his hip jabbing into his ribs. He fished into his vest and pulled out three silver dollars, the last of his money. They gleamed faintly in the evening light.

"One for food," he muttered, flipping coins in the air. "One for whiskey." He caught the second coin. "And one for...." he hesitated, staring at the third coin. A lascivious smile curled his lips. "We'll see what that buys me."

Scorch saw what could only be buildings. The first shapes of Abilene wavered in the distance. He sat straighter, pulling his hat lower against the setting sun. The town looked small but busy.

The mare staggered as they reached the edge of town. Scorch dismounted, his knees buckling as his boots hit the ground. He tied the reins loosely to a hitching post. The mare's sides heaved and Scorch fought the urge to kick her.

He straightened, squaring his shoulders as he stepped onto the bustling main street. His eyes darted to the saloon, the general store, the bordello.

Each provided a temptation, like greedy fingers tugging at his pocket, competing for his meager funds.

"Somebody's gotta pay me," he griped bitterly. "Somebody's just gotta."

He paced the length of the street and his gaze bounced from one storefront to the next. The saloon's batwing doors swung open, spilling laughter, sour smoke, and lively piano music onto the street. His stomach tumbled at the smell of roasted meat.

"Food first," he declared. "Then whiskey. Then...."

His thoughts trailed off as his gaze lingered on the bordello's bright lanterns. The knot in his stomach tightened, and his hands fisted at his sides.

But first, he needed a plan. Something to get him out of this mess. To get him back on his feet. He rubbed his jaw, pacing faster now, his boots scuffing against the wooden planks of the boardwalk.

He stopped in front of the saloon, tilting his head back to look at the peeling paint on the sign above. A plan was forming, half-baked and desperate, but it was something. And for Scorch, something was better than nothing.

He thought about Grim's gang. When they came riding into town, he'd tell them about what he did to help them beat the Deatherage outfit. They'd pay him. He was sure of it.

He just had to wait.

With a sharp breath, Scorch shoved through the saloon doors and into the smoke and noise, clutching his last three dollars like a gambler fixing to place his final bet.

The camp was quiet now. The restless stirring of the herd and the soft snoring of exhausted cowboys filled Seph's ear.

The fire had burned low. Seph added fuel to the fire and turned his back to it. He crossed his arms and gazed at the stars.

Dusty stepped up beside him. "Mind if I join you?" he asked.

Seph glanced over and nodded. "Of course not."

Dusty rubbed his back as he stood, then bent his elbows and rubbed the back of his neck. For a moment, neither man spoke. The silence hung between them like a fragile thread. Then Dusty tipped his hat back, revealing a face lined with weariness but tempered by quiet resolve.

"Hard day," Dusty said, breaking the silence. "Hard trail, too."

Seph gave a faint nod. "It sure ain't getting any easier."

"Nope." Dusty leaned forward, then back. He spoke softly as if hoping to avoid disturbing the sleeping lumps of cowboys scattered around the camp. "But we ain't finished yet. That's something, ain't it?"

Seph rocked his head slowly back and forth. "I suppose. But the fellas are worried about the dangers ahead. What do you say to guys at times like these? They're not wrong and we can't lie to them."

Dusty tittered and replied. "Tell 'em what you know. Tell 'em what you can. And tell 'em the truth. But don't take away the hope they need to see them through.

Seph didn't immediately reply. He mulled over Dusty's words. It sounded like the boss wanted him to be cheerful, but he didn't have it in him. "Feels like we're one step away from losing everything, Boss. I don't know how much more these guys can take."

Dusty grumbled agreement.

Seph added, "Ain't we been through enough already?"

Dusty chuckled lightly, though the sound held no humor. "That's the trail, son. It'll strip you bare, make you doubt yourself, force you to wonder if you've got anything left to give. But you keep putting one boot in front of the other. You keep riding. That's the only way to make it to the end."

Seph glanced at him. There was a strange expression on Dusty's face.

"I've come to depend on you something fierce, Seph," Dusty continued. "You've held this outfit together when everything else was falling apart. You've done things I wouldn't have dared ask of you. And you've done 'em without being told."

Seph shifted uncomfortably, his throat tightening at the unexpected praise. "I just did what needed doing."

Dusty smiled faintly. "And that's what makes you different. Anybody can do what they're told. But you see what's gotta be done, and you do it. That's rare, son. Dang rare."

Seph looked down, scuffing the dirt with the toe of his boot. He wasn't sure what to say, so he said nothing.

Dusty leaned back, his gaze sweeping the quiet camp. "Look at 'em, Seph." He gestured toward the sleeping men. "Every one of these boys has given more than they had to give. I'm proud of every last one of 'em."

Seph whispered, "Me too."

Dusty paused, his eyes lingering on the darkened shapes of the cowboys scattered around the camp. "But you... You've got something special, Seph. You've got a head on your shoulders and a heart in your chest. You've got grit, but more than that, you've got the kind of loyalty that makes a man want to follow you."

Seph swallowed hard. "Follow me? I don't know if I'm ready to be followed, Dusty."

Dusty reached out, gripping Seph's shoulder firmly. "Ready or not, you're doing it. You've already done it. This ain't over yet, son, but the finish line ain't far off now. I reckon we've got one last punch in us, and I know you'll see this through."

Seph understood that Dusty was depending on him, had faith in him, and it didn't feel like a burden. It would be challenging. Their purpose was clear.

Dusty sighed deeply, his hand dropping away as he leaned back again. His voice softened, almost inaudible over the crackling fire. "There's one thing we gotta talk about, though."

Seph turned to him. The boss's words sounded serious.

Dusty's gaze dropped to the ground between them. "We gotta face facts, Seph. Torp's gone. I hate to say it, but the kid ain't coming back. It hurts like the dickens, but we've done all we can."

The words hit Seph like a punch in the face, and for a moment, he couldn't speak. He looked away, turning his face toward the dark prairie. He wanted to argue, deny it, but deep down he had to admit that Dusty was right.

Dusty's hand returned to Seph's shoulder. "Get some rest, son. Tomorrow's another day, and we've got a long way to go."

As Dusty walked away, Dusty's words sunk into his soul. He squared his shoulders, letting the fire warm his backside.

He refused to believe that Torp was dead. Let Dusty give up on the kid. Seph would hold out hope as long as there was a chance of finding him alive.

Chapter 23

It could have been just another night after a day on the trail.

The Deatherage camp lay quiet. A pot of coffee bubbled near the embers. Seph sat cross-legged, sharpening his knife, passing the blade across stone with slow, deliberate strokes. He angled it just right. Firelight danced on the steel, flashing with each pass. Around him, the men finished their chores before settling in for the night.

Dusty leaned back against his saddle, his hat tipped low over his face.

Yodel blew a slow, mournful tune from his harmonica. Each note wallowed in sorrow. Seph wondered if the sound mirrored their present hardships or echoed sadness from Yodel's distant past.

It had been a long, grueling day, but tomorrow they'd reach the Arkansas River—a milestone they desperately needed to reignite their spirits.

Seph eyed the coffee pot. The promise of a hot cup tugged at his thoughts. He was ready to wash away the day's grit. He hadn't eaten yet, but hunger had taken a back seat to exhaustion. His thoughts drifted to Torp, missing for so long that keeping the faith, clinging to hope, felt like folly. He still refused to accept the worst. But it was getting harder to believe that they would find him.

Yodel's song didn't help.

Out of the darkness, the sound of pounding hooves shattered the calm.

Heads shot up. Hands instinctively reached for guns.

"Who's that?" Dusty growled, rising stiffly to his feet.

It didn't take long to find out. That rider was coming in hot.

Seph's pulse quickened. What was he thinking? That's a good way for a stranger to get shot.

"Trinket!" Stoke shouted.

Dusty pushed his hat back. "What the—" His voice stalled. "Something's wrong. He don't never ride in like that."

Trinket yanked the reins, but his horse didn't stop in time. The horse's back hooves skidded, responding to the rider's command. The animal plunged through the firelight and skidded into the campfire. Embers scattered. The cauldron of stew toppled into the fire with a hiss and a splash. The coffee pot crashed, spilling its contents into the ashes.

"Dang it, Trinket! What's gotten into you?" Stoke roared, leaping back to avoid the spill.

Trinket's lathered horse sidestepped, nostrils flaring, eyes rolling white. Steam coiled from its neck and flanks. It had been ridden hard.

The scout barely held his seat. His face was streaked with dirt and his eyes were open wide. He slid from the saddle, staggered forward, and waved an arm. "*¡Sacre Dios!* I found him. I found Torp!"

The camp erupted.

Seph surged to his feet, his knife still clutched in his hand.

Dusty shoved past him, barking, "What are you talking about? Where is he?"

Trinket stumbled, his legs trembling. He had ridden long and hard and it left him unsteady. How many hours had he been in the saddle, pushing to get here?

"He is alive," Trinket gasped, his breath ragged. His shoulders sagged, like his body hadn't caught up with the relief of his own words. Stoke offered a steadying arm, and Trinket gripped it tight.

"He is alive," Trinket repeated. Then, his voice dropped. "But he is at Grim's camp."

A stunned silence fell over them.

Seph's grip tightened on the knife. "With Grim? What do you mean?"

Trinket nodded, still catching his breath. "I tracked Grim's gang. Spied on them. Their chuckwagon... they have got Torp tied to the back of it. Like a trussed-up calf on branding day."

Yodel's harmonica hit the ground. The cowboy shot to his feet.

Dusty's jaw clenched. "How far ahead are they?"

"Half a day. Maybe less. They are not too far ahead," Trinket replied.

Stoke spat into the dirt. "That skunk. What's he planning, dragging a kid around like that?"

Seph sheathed his knife and stepped forward. "Is he hurt? I swear, if they've done anything to him—"

Trinket's face darkened. "I did not get close enough to see much," he admitted. "But he is alive. That is all I can say."

Dusty paced away, then turned back. "This changes things." His voice rose. "We catch up to Grim tomorrow. No more delays. We push hard, even if it means marching through the night."

"Tomorrow we're gonna cross the river," Yodel said. "Crossing won't be easy. Grim will know it. He's gonna be ready."

"We'll be ready, too," Seph said, his tone like steel, and sharp as a knife. "We ain't leaving Torp behind."

The men exchanged glances, but nobody said anything more. They didn't need to.

Dusty clapped Trinket on the shoulder. "You did good, boy. Get some rest. Tomorrow's gonna be miserable."

The camp began to settle. But Seph lingered by the fire, facing north and looking off into the darkness. The thought of Torp, bound and helpless, spun in his mind. Had they kept him tied up all this time?

His gizzard pulsed, like fire in his belly.

Seph whispered up to the stars, "Hold on, kid. We're coming."

The Arkansas River glistened in the late afternoon sun. Its wide expanse snaked across the prairie like a vein of molten silver. Whitecaps churned across its surface, stirred by a strong wind and the relentless pull of the current.

A shot of excitement pulsed within Seph as he realized that they had caught up to Grim's herd. The Three Bar Box was crossing the mighty river. They had been behind for too long and it seemed like ages since they had seen or caught up to their rivals. Too long since they'd been this close.

The Deatherage boys had pushed hard all day. Now, they didn't need to prod the herd to keep them moving. The beeves bellowed greedily as they caught the scent of fresh water. Seph thought that the way they moaned made it seem like they hadn't had a drop of water since leaving Texas. The longhorns didn't care that another herd occupied the crossing. They wouldn't stop and politely await their turn.

Had Stoke and Dusty seen Grim's gang ahead? They must have. But to be certain, Seph left his usual spot near the chuckwagon and rode over to talk to them.

"They're crossing now," Dusty growled. "I say we catch up to 'em in the water. What do you say?"

Stoke nodded sharply and twisted in his saddle, yelling to the men. "Drive 'em forward! Let's pass Grim."

The cowboys hollered and spurred their mounts as the herd surged toward the river. The gap between the two outfits disappeared quickly. The front of the Deatherage herd splashed into the water as the last of Grim's beeves stepped in.

The river was wider than it seemed. The current was fast and strong. Longhorns splashed and staggered as the current tugged at their legs.

Seph gritted his teeth, urging Hortense into the water. She was a good swimmer, but even she struggled against the pull.

Then Seph saw it.

Near the back of Grim's herd, the Three Bar Box chuckwagon struggled upriver. Grim rode beside it.

Seph leaned forward in his saddle. Was Grim looking back at him? On Hortense, he figured he could reach them quickly.

Seph's heart clenched as he spotted Torp, slumped and bound to the back of the wagon. His head drooped and Seph worried. Was Torp dead or alive?

"There's Torp!" Seph shouted, pointing toward the wagon. He didn't stop to make a plan or wait for others. He spurred Hortense hard and broke away from the Deatherage herd, plunging deeper into the river. The current was strong. Water surged against them, but they aimed for the wagon.

Behind him, a whoop split the air. Rooster—screeching like a banshee and shouting. "I got your back, Seph."

Seph didn't figure on help. But he couldn't worry about the impetuous young cowboy behind him.

Grim turned, spotted them, and let out a sharp whistle, signaling his men.

Seph had barely reached the midpoint of the river when Mitch and another rider charged toward him. Their horses kicked up plumes of spray as they rushed straight for Seph.

"You don't learn, do you, kid?" Mitch jeered, raising his rifle.

Seph veered sharply. A bullet whizzed past his shoulder.

Mitch's companion swung a club.

Seph ducked low, just in time.

A startled steer lunged between them, crashing into Mitch's horse, forcing Mitch to pull back. He yanked the reins hard, cursing.

It was just enough.

Seph pushed forward, closing in on the wagon. Grim wheeled his horse around, eyes blazing. "Get back, Vermillion."

Seph didn't stop. He grabbed the rope tied to Hortense's saddle and leapt from the horse onto the wagon. His boots slipped on the wet wood, but he steadied himself, lunging to rescue the captive.

"Torp!" Seph shouted, gripping his friend's shoulder. The younger cowboy stirred, his eyelids fluttering weakly. "I'm getting you outta here."

Grim growled and lunged from his saddle, yanking Seph back by the collar. They tumbled into the wagon bed, collapsing the wagon bonnet, snapping the bows that held the bonnet aloft. The slick surface made moving a struggle, and the clutter at their feet tripped them up.

Seph swung first, landing a punch on Grim's jaw.

Grim grunted, retaliating with a brutal elbow to Seph's ribs.

"You're in over your head, boy!" Grim snarled, shoving him against the wagon's edge.

The river surged violently. The wagon tilted.

Seph's grip faltered, and Grim took advantage, wrapping an arm around his neck and dragging him into the water. They plunged into the river. The roar of the current was deafening. As he fought to the surface, Grim's weight pinned him down.

Seph thrashed, his lungs burning. His hand found a submerged piece of wood—likely debris from a wagon—and he swung it blindly. The blow connected with Grim's shoulder, loosening his grip just enough for Seph to break free, gasping for air.

Coughing and sputtering, Seph clawed his way to a nearby sandbar. Grim followed, his face ablaze with fury. "You don't quit, do you?" Grim growled, advancing.

Seph planted his feet, steadying himself, but sinking into the wet sand. "Not when one of our men is on your wagon," he shot back, his voice raw.

Before Grim could respond, Dusty's voice bellowed from the river. "Get him, Seph. Don't let him win!"

The two clashed again, their fists meeting flesh with bone-jarring force. Seph ducked a swing and retaliated with a hard jab to Grim's gut, forcing the older man to stagger back.

But Mitch and another rider joined the fray, cutting Seph off from the wagon. Mitch leveled his rifle at Seph, a smirk spreading across his face. "Looks like your luck's run out."

A whistle split the air. Grim raised a hand, signaling Mitch to hold fire. "Not yet," Grim said, panting. He grabbed Seph by the shirt and yanked him close. "You want the kid?"

Seph didn't answer. The question didn't deserve a reply. He wanted to knee Grim's gut.

"Trade me the herd." Grim breathed hard, bloodshot eyes blazed red.

Seph froze, his chest heaving. The sounds of the river and the distant shouts of the Deatherage outfit faded to a dull roar. Grim's ultimatum echoed in his ears.

"The child's life for the beeves," Grim sneered. "Think it over, boy. But don't take too long.

Seph glared at him, his fists clenching. "This ain't over."

Grim chuckled darkly, shoving Seph away. "It is if you make the wrong choice. You don't want a dead kid on your conscience, do you?"

Seph stumbled back into the water.

The hardened felon lifted his pistol. "Let's start with that one."

Grim fired a shot. Blasted Rooster from his saddle.

Seph was shocked. His stomach dropped. He didn't hesitate long before launching himself into the river to grab Rooster before he sank. He had to see what he could do for the young cowboy. Saving Torp would have to wait.

This wasn't just a race anymore.

It shouldn't have surprised anyone that a gang of ex-convicts would start killing their rivals to win a race. A good-sized herd was worth a fortune. Men would do anything to become rich for thirty five dollars a head.

Yet the Deatherage boys were stunned.

First they lost Chops. Now, Rooster was dead. Not to mention Clive. How many cowboys would they have to bury before they reached Abilene?

Above them, the overcast sky hid the stars. A damp chill hung in the air. The soft murmur of bedded-down cattle was accompanied by the occasional cough of a nighthawk. Both outfits had doubled their night guards. Two herds rarely bedded down this close to one another. Both crews were armed. Both were on edge.

Seph lay on his bedroll, fretting.

Torp's gaunt face haunted him. It was hard to think of his friend as a prisoner, tied to Grim's wagon. It was unbearable to think of what might happen next. What was worse, he had told Torp that he would save him, but that rescue had failed.

The more Seph thought about Torp's captors, the more furious he became.

It was bad enough to kidnap the kid. They weren't even feeding him. Torp wasn't that big to begin with, and he didn't eat that much, so as bad off as he was, they must have been giving him next to nothing. And he was filthy. If he never got the chance to wash up, maybe he didn't get enough to drink either. Seph didn't get a very close look at him, but it was plain to see that Torp was in bad shape.

There was no way Seph could abide waiting until morning. He should talk to Dusty and ask for permission, but what if Dusty said no? No. He had to act now.

Carefully, he slipped from his blankets. The gravel beneath his boots crunched softly as he rose, and he froze, holding his breath.

Nearby, Lullaby stirred beneath his blankets, but did not wake. Seph's chest constricted. If anyone saw him—if anyone stopped him—Torp might never get free. There was no telling what Grim and his gang might do next.

Seph grabbed his knife from its sheath. It was comforting to hold the familiar handle in his palm. It felt like it belonged there. He wrapped his fingers tight around it as he crept toward the edge of camp.

Hortense stood at the picket line. Her ears twitched as Seph slipped past. He stopped just long enough to stroke her neck. "Not tonight, gal," he whispered. "I gotta do this on foot."

The darkness swallowed him as he slipped from the Deatherage camp and tiptoed toward Grim's encampment. His cautious ears amplified every sound—the rustles of dry grass underfoot, the creak of leather as he adjusted his belt, the dry cough of another man in the distance. Perhaps some of the worrisome sounds were magnified within the stillness. Maybe others were merely imagined.

Seph ducked low and stuck to the shadows. His heart pounded so loudly, he was sure it would give him away, but he scurried along anyhow.

The river gurgled and whooshed nearby. Seph thought it might drown out the sound of his footsteps as he approached the edge of Grim's camp. The chuckwagon loomed ahead.

Torp was tied to the rear axle. His body slumped and he didn't move.

Seph crouched, scanning the camp.

A lone guard patrolled the perimeter, pausing occasionally to peer into the night.

Seph waited, his breaths shallow, timing his movements with the guard's pace.

When the man turned his back, Seph darted forward as quietly as he could.

The chuckwagon was closer now. Its wooden frame creaked with a shift in the wind. Seph pressed himself against the side, his pulse racing.

He could hear Torp's labored breathing, faint but steady. He peered around the edge of the wagon and saw his friend's face, pale and gaunt in the dim light. If he didn't know better, he would have thought he was looking at an old-timer rather than a teenage drover.

Seph touched his shoulder.

Torp stirred, his eyes fluttering open. "Seph?" he croaked, his voice hoarse and weak.

"Shh," Seph hissed. "I'm getting you outta here."

He slid his knife into the rope binding Torp's hands, sawing carefully.

The fibers resisted, but the blade was sharp, and he worked quickly. His ears strained for any sound of approaching danger.

His nerves were on fire. Every creak of the wagon or snort of a distant horse made it worse.

Then, the rope snapped. Torp's hands fell free.

Seph caught him as he slumped forward, his body limp with exhaustion. "C'mon, buddy," Seph urged, slinging one of Torp's arms over his shoulder. "Let's git."

He thought of sheathing the knife, but instead he put it in his mouth and clamped his teeth on the blade. The dull edge was sharp enough to cut into the corners of his mouth, but his hands were free. He gathered Torp in his arms and stepped away from the wagon.

They were steps away from escaping.

A commanding voice stopped him in his tracks.

"Hey. You there."

Seph froze. His blood ran cold. The voice came from behind him, close enough to send a shiver down his spine.

Grim's man said, "Put that down."

Seph lowered Torp and turned slowly.

Another voice called out, growling, "Step back."

A second man called out. The guard looked away. For half a second.

Seph's feet moved before his brain. He had to get away fast. While he could. He might not get another chance.

He vanished into the darkness. It killed him to leave Torp behind.

Again.

CHAPTER 24

GRIM'S GANG PULLED OUT hours before dawn. The final leg of the race was underway. The Smoky Hill River—the finish line—lay 93 miles to the north. Normally, they'd plan on eight days to make it from the Arkansas River to the Smoky Hill River. It was hard to guess how much faster they'd need to travel to win this race.

The sun was minutes away from peeking over the eastern horizon when the Deatherage outfit surged forward. Urgency burned in their veins.

Seph rode near point with Dusty, his eyes locked on the trail. He hadn't told anybody about his failed attempt to rescue Torp, but he couldn't shake the image of his friend. Bound to Grim's wagon. Slumped and gaunt.

He racked his brain for a new plan.

Then, as they rounded a curve in the trail, Seph saw what looked like a body. It was slumped against a scraggly bush, half-hidden in the tall grass.

Seph jerked Hortense to a stop. "Whoa!" he shouted, pointing urgently.

Dusty was right behind him. "Who is that?"

Seph didn't answer. He was already running. "It's him, Dusty! It's Torp."

Stoke and the swing riders, Lullaby and Yodel, dismounted fast and crowded in behind Seph and Dusty.

Torp lay motionless. His shirt was torn, and he looked like a corpse.

But he was alive.

"Torp!" Seph called, kneeling beside him. He placed a hand on Torp's shoulder and gave him a gentle shake. "It's me."

The boy stirred. His eyes shot open.

At first he looked relieved. Then he snapped, "Took you long enough." His voice was raw and raspy.

Seph grinned despite himself. "Good to see you too."

Lullaby passed a canteen forward. Dusty crouched down, tilting it to Torp's cracked lips.

He gulped greedily.

Seph checked him over for injuries.

Dusty grunted. "He's lucky. This could've been worse."

Seph thought of Rooster and frowned. An understatement. They could have easily killed Torp too.

Torp groaned as they helped him sit up. When they lifted him to his feet, his legs wobbled. Bad off as he was, it was his feelings that hurt the most. "They just... left me," he said. His voice was tinged with disbelief. "All that time-tied to the chuckwagon like an old barrel. Then, when they pulled out in the morning, they forgot me."

Seph and Dusty exchanged a glance.

Grim's gang wasn't just ruthless. They were sloppy. Their hasty departure gave them a little head start that morning, but it also gave the Deatherage gang a victory. Even a little win was just what Dusty's boys needed.

Torp's gaze hardened. His cheeks turned red, and he spoke with a fury. "Them convicts laughed at me. Called me a *damsel in distress*. Then they left me behind like a broken old crate."

"Forget about them," Seph said, steadying Torp as they led him to his favorite horse. "You're back where you belong."

From down the line, Sparrow and Squint trotted forward. News spread fast.

Sparrow grinned ear to ear. "About time, kid!" He clapped Torp on the back. "Good to have you back."

Squint nodded. "Thought we'd never see your ugly mug again."

Torp's lips twitched. "Don't get all mushy on me," he warned. But it looked as if his anger had subsided.

Seph chuckled. The crazy kid was mad about being abandoned by his captors.

The mood was buoyed by Torp's return, but Dusty's voice cracked like a whip. "Back to your places! We got a herd to move."

The men scrambled into their saddles. Torp fell in alongside Sparrow and Squint, reclaiming his spot at drag like he'd never been gone.

As they rode out, Seph felt a surge of pride in his fellow drovers. They'd recovered one of their own, but there was no time to rest. If anything, Torp's return sharpened their resolve.

From the front of the column, Dusty bellowed. "No more delays, boys. Let's ride like our lives depend on it."

Seph glanced back.

Torp rode steady. His eyes burned with a renewed fire. Grim had used Torp to slow them down. Then—they forgot him.

The Three Bar Box might overlook an orphan, but the Deatherage never would.

The finish line lay ahead. And they were riding hard for it.

The sun was a merciless, blazing orb that seemed to press down on the plains, baking the earth and every creature on it. The air shimmered with heat waves, making the horizon ripple like water. The longhorns trudged forward, their tongues lolling and sides heaving. But they couldn't slow down or take a day off, just because it was hot.

Seph wiped the sweat from his brow, but his sleeve was already soaked through. His shirt clung to his back, stiff with salt, and Hortense's coat gleamed with frothy perspiration. Her ears twitched in irritation, nostrils flaring with each breath.

Dusty's raw voice cracked through the haze. "Move 'em along, boys!"

Seph dug his heels into Hortense's flanks, guiding a stray back into the herd. A dust devil spun up near the end of the line, swirling grit into the already blistering air.

Behind him, a hoarse grumble rose from the drag position. "Why we gotta drive 'em so hard?" Sparrow's voice rasped like a frayed rope about to snap. "It ain't right. Poor doggies."

Squint spat into the dust. "Because we ain't losing to that snake, Grim. That's why."

The words were sharp, but the sentiment rang true. Every man on the Deatherage crew knew what was at stake. Winning was more than just a wager. It was everything. Their share of forty percent made them partners with the trail boss. They were more than common cowpokes. Grim wasn't just a rival. He was a thief, a cheat, a man willing to kill for the same dream they were chasing.

Seph glanced back at Torp. The kid rode stead, shoulders squared, but Seph could tell he was exhausted. Grim's cruelty had left its mark—but that kid would never quit.

"Keep 'em moving, Torp!" Seph called. "Don't let 'em string out too much!"

Torp gave an earnest nod. "I'm on it!"

Grim

Grim squinted against the harsh glare of the sun, his shirt unbuttoned to the chest, exposing a V of sun-reddened skin. The heat pressed down like a branding iron, relentless and unyielding.

He rode at the head of the herd, his men strung out behind him in a loose, weary line.

Thorn's ears flicked back and forth, swatting at the endless buzz of flies.

"Pick it up!" Grim snarled.

Mitch rode beside him, his usual grin replaced by a scowl.

"They're gaining on us," Mitch grumbled. "They ain't nothing but a bunch of snot-nosed schoolboys!"

Grim spat to the side, his lips dry and cracked. "Let 'em come. They won't hold the pace. Not in this heat."

But even Grim couldn't ignore the strain. His men were quieter than usual. The frequent ribbing and cackling had faded—replaced by muttered curses and sharp, frayed tempers.

Behind him, one of his riders snapped. "Get off my dang heels, Gene!"

"How about you move your slow carcass faster, Jim?" Gene shot back.

Grim reined in hard, twisting in the saddle. "Both of you shut your traps and ride!"

The men glared at each other, but the silence that followed was thick and uneasy.

Grim turned back to the front. He was in a foul mood. He hated how the heat worked on a man's nerves, turning even his most seasoned riders into bickering fools.

He clenched his jaw, grinding his molars.

This was no way to live.

Day three of the relentless push found the Deatherage outfit flagging but unbroken.

The heat wave refused to break. Seph felt like he was cooking alive in his boots, but he pressed forward, riding swing to keep the herd tight.

"Hey, Seph!" Stoke called from point. "Don't it feel like we're plowing through the devil's back yard?"

Seph managed a grin, though his sunburned lips cracked from the effort. "Gosh, it ain't that bad, Stoke."

Stoke shook his head, scowling. "You're too danged optimistic, Vermillion. Don't you know a fella's gotta gripe now and then? Somebody ought to slap that sunny disposition from your mangy carcass. It's not becoming."

Seph chuckled, but the moment didn't last.

Behind them, Blaze snapped at Hork, who was struggling to keep a steer from straying too far.

"Get it together, Hork!" Blaze barked. "We ain't got time for this!"

"How 'bout you get down here and do it yourself?" Hork shot back.

Seph rode between them, raising a firm hand. "Enough! Both of you. We're all fried out here, but we gotta keep our heads. Got it?"

Conjure lamented, "I'd trade you all to the devil for a basket full of fried chicken and a jug of icy lemonade."

Blaze muttered something under his breath but nodded, while Hork threw a curt, sarcastic salute. When Blaze turned his back, Hork added an obscene gesture.

Seph didn't have time to dwell on their moods. Ahead, Dusty lifted an arm, signaling.

Keep 'em moving.

The heat in Abilene was as suffocating as the heat on the trail. It wrapped around Scorch like a burly buffalo blanket. Sweat soaked his clothes, same as everyone else in town. He yanked his hat low, shielding his eyes from the merciless sun as he trudged down the main street. Dust clung to the grime on his boots. His stomach growled, loud enough that he glanced around, embarrassed. But nobody ever looked at him.

"Dang town," Scorch complained, kicking at a loose rock. "Kansas is worse than Texas. Dang trail. Somebody's gotta pay me."

He flipped his last silver dollar in his pocket. The pitiful coin was all that he had left. Enough for one good meal. Or a couple of drinks. Or one visit to The Fancy Frolic. His lips pressed into a thin line as he weighed his options.

When he passed the saloon, the scent of roast chicken and fresh bread wafted out, taunting him. His mouth watered and his stomach clenched. He stopped, one boot poised on the wooden steps leading inside.

But just beyond the saloon, the Fancy Frolic's painted sign caught his eye. The curling script promised pleasures that he hadn't known since long before leaving San Antonio.

With a resigned sigh, Scorch turned toward the brothel. "To heck with food," he said under his breath. "Might as well have one good memory before I starve to death."

He pushed his chest through the doors.

The shaded interior of The Fancy Frolic provided a welcome reprieve from the blazing sun. Scorch's eyes adjusted slowly to the dim light. He scowled at the smell of perfume which failed to mask the smells of stale whisky, tobacco, and sweat. He figured it smelled better than a cattle drive, and made his way to the back room.

He looked over the girls and chose a beauty. The madam introduced him to Hazel. Her green dress was dazzling, and her demure smile was beguiling. It was enough to make him forget, if only for a moment, the gnawing hunger in his gut. And the wretched pickle he found himself in.

Their time together was brief. It was over in a flash. Ten minutes blasted by fast. When it was over, Scorch sat on the edge of the bed, staring at the floorboards. His satisfaction curdled into self-loathing.

Hazel slipped back into her dress.

"Thanks, Hazel," he mumbled.

She gave him a sympathetic smile. The kind that stung worse than indifference. "Take care of yourself, cowboy."

Back outside, the heat hit him like a blacksmith's bellows. He tugged at his shirt collar, but there was no escaping the heat. Was there? It occurred to him he could find relief in the river.

His stomach growled again, reminding him of his empty pockets. He should have spent his money more wisely. Where did he leave his dang horse?

When he finally found the hitching post where he had abandoned the mare, he set out for the edge of town. Mud Creek offered a murky respite. Scorch stripped off his shirt and boots and waded into the tepid water. It wasn't cool. Not really. But it was wet, and that would have to do. He dunked his head, letting the water slide over his scalp and face, washing away the worst of the trail dust.

Emerging from the creek, he shook himself like a dog and sat on the bank. The relief was short-lived. Hunger clawed at him again, and he cursed under his breath.

"Stupid," he carped, jamming his boots back on. "I should've had me a meal." A man could live without a whore but he couldn't live without food.

What could he do? He pondered on his situation and there wasn't any choice but to wait until dark. And scrounge.

The alley behind the Alamo Saloon was a haven for stray dogs and desperate men.

Scorch dug through the refuse. His nose wrinkled at the sour stench of discarded food and spilled beer. He found a half-eaten loaf of bread, with edges hard as rock, and a chunk of cheese riddled with mold. He had to fight a fat, squeaky rat for the vittles.

"Better than nothin'," he said grimly, biting into the bread and chewing slowly. It scratched his throat and made him thirsty, but he forced it down. The bitter taste of failure was more foul than the dry crust.

Leaning against the alley wall, Scorch stared out at the dusty street. He thought about the trail, about Clive, and about the sorry end to his misadventure. Anger bubbled up again, hot and rancid.

"Somebody's gotta pay me," he growled, his voice low but venomous. His gaze drifted toward the cattle pens in the distance, where Grim's outfit would eventually show up. His fists clenched at his sides.

"I'll get what's owed to me," he whined. "One way or another."

Scorch retrieved his horse and rode out onto the prairie where a man could sleep without paying for the comfort of a bed in an overpriced hotel or rooming house.

Dark storm clouds loomed on the horizon, and he couldn't shake the worry of being caught in a thunder gust. He told himself it was just heat lightning flickering in the distance, the kind that fizzled out by nightfall. Still, with his luck, he was sure he'd have to suffer through a night of misery.

Then, the storm hit.

On the fifth day after leaving the Arkansas River, Grim could almost taste the water ahead.

Thorn snorted beneath him, sensing it too. But his men? They were beginning to crack.

The night before, Fred Hayes had nearly come to blows with Ted Cross. Lewis Kelly tore off his hat, threw it to the ground, and stomped on it.

Grim rode up alongside Mitch, eyeing the horizon. "We're close." Ahead of them, nothing moved. Not a rider, bird, or even the wind. "They'll push hard, but we're gonna cross first."

Mitch nodded, but cautioned. "Don't count on it. We're out of food. And the men are half-dead."

Grim smirked. It wasn't like they were still in prison. They wanted freedom. Well, freedom didn't come with supper. He huffed, "Ain't my fault if they can't hack it."

The herd slowed as they crested a knoll. The Smoky Hill River came into view. It was broad and glinting in the afternoon light. The sight was almost blinding.

Grim turned to his men and barked orders. "Pick up the pace. Move, you flea-bitten dogs."

He closed his eyes and imagined lounging beneath the shade of pampas grass in his massive *estancia*. A grand estate.

Stoke's voice boomed. "River ahead!"

Seph's pulse pounded. "Push 'em!" he shouted, riding hard beside Stoke as the two drove the longhorns faster. Dusty's voice echoed behind them, urging the crew forward.

Skillet surged ahead. His massive hooves churned up dirt, his horns sliced through the wind. Seph flanked him on one side, Stoke on the other, both cowboys whooping, whistling, and hollering to keep the herd charging forward.

The river loomed large now, its shimmering surface rippling in the wind. Seph gritted his teeth. Grim's herd was ahead, already pressing toward the water. They had the lead. They had the advantage.

But they didn't have Skillet.

Stoke let out his trademark yell. That raw, piercing sound could raise the dead. It always made the hair on the back of Seph's neck stand up straight like the quills of a porcupine. More importantly, it made Skillet run like the devil was on his tail.

Seph had never seen a longhorn run faster than that brindled bull.

Grim's point riders hollered and cursed, rushing to drive their cattle into the water first. They thought they had it. Thought they could hold their lead.

They thought wrong.

The powerful bull raged across the prairie like a tornado, chased by a loud pair of cowboys. Seph felt like he had lassoed a comet.

Skillet hit the water first. His massive chest crashed into the current, water splashing in his wake, drenching the drovers who followed him into the Smoky Hill River.

Seph and Stoke plunged into the water, howling gleefully. It reminded Seph of galloping into Abilene last year, guns blazing, celebrating the end of the trail.

Grim's herd bunched in, churning the river into a violent, thrashing mess of muscles, hooves, and horns. The river boiled with shouting men and bellowing critters. But Seph and Stoke didn't let up. Skillet snorted angrily as he swam for the other side of the river. That bull always had to be first.

Seph barely heard the shouts behind him. His vision tunneled toward the far bank.

They were almost there. Then—Skillet's hooves struck solid ground.

The moment they hit the bank, a tidal wave of water gushed off his broad back. He snorted, satisfied with himself, and grunted as he heaved his bulk from the river.

Seph let out a hoarse whoop, but his throat was too dry. He sounded more like a frog than a cowboy.

Behind them, Grim's lead riders were still a hundred feet away.

Every man in both outfits screamed themselves hoarse. But it was too late.

Skillet had won the crossing. He had reached the far bank before Grim's lead steer.

That was it. The race was over. They had crossed the finish line.

But Grim's men celebrated like they had won the wager.

Why?

CHAPTER 25

THE TWO HERDS STOOD side by side on the north bank of the river, dripping wet.

The beeves were restless after the hard race, though they didn't care about wagers. But the cowboys did.

It was sweltering hot. Sweat mixed with river water. Everyone was soaked in sweat, wet to the chests from the wild river crossing.

Both outfits gathered between the herds. The men were prepared for anything. It looked like a brawl was brewing. Or maybe there would be a gunfight. Seph sat atop Hortense, watching their rivals. Grim's crew acted like they thought they had won.

Dusty shifted uncomfortably in his saddle beside Seph, his back stiff from the long trail. "Well," Dusty rasped, "What next?" He coughed into his hand.

Seph shrugged. It was hard to figure. "Anything can happen now."

Grim emerged from his group, his stride unhurried, but predatory. He looked like a wolf closing in on wounded prey. His scarred face twisted into a grin that never reached his cold, calculating eyes. Mitch swaggered behind him, thumbs tucked into his belt.

"You think you've won?" Grim barked. "Ha!"

Seph dismounted. If Grim was going to challenge them, he wasn't going to do it from the saddle. They met halfway.

"We reached the river first," Seph said evenly. "And our lead bull crossed first."

He was taller than Grim, but that didn't make him feel bigger. He felt like he was standing across from a coiled snake that was about to strike.

Grim chuckled darkly. "Reaching the river ain't winning, boy. What matters is who crossed it first. That's us. You know it. I know it. So does everyone here." He gestured broadly. His men jeered in agreement.

Seph squared his shoulders. "That wasn't the deal. First *to* the river wins."

Grim tilted his head, feigning amusement. "Did you memorize the document? What did it say *exactly*? Even when it's writ down, it ain't always black and white. You think you won. We think we won. So... what now?"

Dusty interjected. "Let's just let each man keep his own herd and forget about the wager."

Mitch scoffed. "It ain't a victory unless the vanquished admits defeat."

Grim stomped forward. "No. That ain't the deal. The wager is winner take all. So, I'll offer you two choices. Outfit versus outfit, or man versus man."

The camp fell silent.

Dusty swallowed hard. "Man versus man?"

Grim grinned. "So be it. I will choose the man on your side."

Seph's heart pounded as Grim pointed straight at him.

This wasn't just a fight. This was a fight for everything. And it was up to him.

Grim's next words made his blood run cold. "You choose your opponent." Grim turned and looked at Mitch, beside him. "Perhaps it would be fitting if your fight to the death is with your own brother." Grim tipped his head back and laughed.

He heard Grim say that it was a fight to the death but he had to repeat it in his head to make it stick. And he had to pick who he would battle. Recalling that moment when Grim shot Rooster, and watching the young cowboy blown from the saddle, he knew at once what he had to do.

Seph stepped forward. He had chosen. "No, Grim." Fire burned in his chest. "You ain't gonna weasel your way out of this one." He glared at the man. "You and me. We'll settle this."

Dusty twisted in his saddle to look down at Seph. He looked horrified. "Seph, no—"

"You heard him," Seph interrupted. "This is my fight, Dusty. I will finish this."

Grim shrugged, dismissing Dusty. "Sorry, old man." Then, to Mitch, he said, "Would it be alright with you if I slay your baby brother? He don't seem to want nothing to do with you anyway."

Mitch rolled his eyes and tipped his head back. "I tried to save him. He wouldn't have none of it. What more can I do?"

Grim laughed. "Some people is stubborn."

He pointed to his chuckwagon. "Right there. We'll fight tied to my wagon. Can't think of a better place to clobber a camp cook than the crumb box." The irony delighted him. "Winner take all. Lock, stock, and barrel."

Dusty dismounted, grabbing Seph's arm. "Listen, kid. You don't owe that man nothing. Don't let Grim sucker you in."

Seph jerked his arm free. His jaw set hard. "I'm not doing it for him. And I'm not a kid."

Grim whistled sharply. "Testy, young 'un."

His men began to prepare the wagon, clearing space and tying ropes to the front axles, just inside the wagon wheels.

Seph felt the eyes of the Deatherage crew on him. He saw doubt on some, wonder on others, and grim resolve on the faces of the rest. Lullaby's lips moved in silent prayer. In Seph's mind, the words rang clear. "May God have mercy on their souls."

As he stepped toward the wagon, Stoke appeared beside him. His limp was barely noticeable. His voice was quiet, but firm. "You sure about this, Seph?"

"No," Seph exhaled sharply. "But it must be done."

Stoke nodded, clapping him on the shoulder. "Pound him into the ground." Then, his voice darkened. "But listen, this fight is different." His hand tightened on Seph's shoulder. "You must kill him. Don't go soft. You might want to spare him. But I'm warning you, that ain't how this sort of thing goes. He will not spare you. We don't wanna bury you. Got it?"

Seph bit his lip and nodded. Things were happening so fast.

The ropes tightened around his wrists. The crowd formed a tense semicircle. The lines between friend and foe blurred in anticipation of violence.

Seph's hands clenched into fists. His breathing was slow. Deliberate.

Grim looked like a predator who already tasted blood. "Let's see what you're made of, Vermillion," he sneered.

Seph whispered under his breath, "Yeah. Let's see."

When those ropes came off their wrists, one of them would be dead.

Only one man would walk away from this fight.

The ropes were taut. Coarse fibers bit into Seph's wrists as he tested their tension and weight. He stood opposite Grim, tied to the other end of the chuckwagon.

The space between them was charged with a current, like the air during a thunderstorm. The makeshift battlefield had gone eerily quiet. Cowboys from both outfits stood in hushed anticipation. Even the cattle had gone still.

A horse nickered loudly. Seph looked over at Win. His last thought before the fight began was of his childhood friend, Slaw. His neighbor who wanted nothing more than to be a cowboy.

With a frown, Seph looked back at Grim.

Both fighters had stripped to the waist. The contrast between them was stark. Grim was stocky and solid, built like an ox. Seph had hoped for flab, but no. The older man's arms were thick with muscle, his chest dense, and his shoulders powerful. Seph, in contrast, was lean and long-limbed, but farm work had made him strong. His loose shirt hid it well, but he knew his own strength. Pushing a plow and fighting with a stubborn mule had made him strong. Cowboying made him stronger. His chest was cut squarely, his arms were thick as fence posts, and he wasn't soft.

But Grim was solid, like a bull. He rolled his shoulders and taunted, "You ready, boy? Or do you want your mama?"

Seph didn't answer, but Ma's final words of advice swept through his head. "Don't be timid. Be tenacious." Clearly, this was one of those moments that required tenacity.

He clamped his jaw firmly. He didn't like the feeling of having his wrist tied, or the limitations of fighting in the shadow of the convicts' wagon. It felt like a trap, like a noose, but he forced himself to concentrate. It was frightening, but he would not worry or hesitate.

Excitement shot from his gizzard, that pulsing beacon of determination that powered him during dangerous moments. It was time to finish what Grim had started. It was time to end the idiotic wager that began in Cowtown, and all that came with it.

Mitch stepped back into the crowd, chanting, "Fight!"

Torp yelled, "Knock his block off, Seph."

"Clobber 'im," Stoke hollered.

Grim moved first. He propelled his bulk toward Seph with surprising speed and agility.

Seph sidestepped, narrowly avoiding a blow aimed at his gut. The thick rope around his wrist pulled taut as it anchored him to the wagon.

He countered with a jab, catching Grim in the shoulder, but the older man barely flinched.

"You fight like my baby sister," Grim teased.

Seph tried to dance backward, but Grim was relentless. He swung again, this time landing a fist squarely on Seph's ribs. Pain lanced through his side, and he stumbled into the wagon, steadying himself quickly.

"That all you got?" Grim laughed. "Can I kill you now?"

Seph told himself this would be a long battle. He must pace himself and let the older man tire himself out. *Don't let that man goad me*, he thought. *Keep quiet.*

The crowd was a blur in Seph's peripheral vision, but he could hear them. Dusty's gruff voice barked orders for the Deatherage men to hold their positions. Mitch jeered with every punch Grim landed. *Some brother he turned out to be.* Stoke shouted for Seph to keep moving.

Seph surged forward, using the slack in the rope and his longer limbs to his advantage. His fist connected with Grim's jaw, snapping the thick-necked man's head back.

A cheer rose from the Deatherage crew. Seph pummeled Grim relentlessly.

There was a tingly sensation at the back of Seph's head, just behind his ears, and something came over him like it did sometimes when he was digging graves or chopping wood. It was an almost supernatural burst of energy. Boom. Boom. Boom. His fists pounded into Grim so fast that spectators could barely see between the punches. His arms thrust, jab after jab into his foe.

Grim backed away and shook like a wet dog. He spit blood onto the dirt and grinned like a man who thrived on pain. "That was impressive, kid, but you'll have to do better than that," Grim snarled, yanking the rope hard. Seph stumbled toward him, lost his balance, and Grim seized the opportunity, driving his knee into Seph's stomach.

Seph doubled over. The wind was knocked out of him.

Dusty's voice boomed. "Stay on your feet, Seph. Don't let him pin you down!"

Seph staggered but straightened. His vision blurred.

He feinted left, then drove his fist into Grim's sternum. The impact was solid, and Grim grunted. Had he found a weak spot? Seph pressed his advantage, landing another punch, this time to Grim's temple, spinning his head.

The crowd surged forward, voices blending together like the dust at Seph's feet. Dusty's voice reached him again. Maybe he imagined hearing the words, "Come on, kid. We're depending on you."

It was hard to know what was real.

Grim was far from finished. With a roar, he threw his full weight forward, slamming Seph's back against the wagon. The impact rattled the wooden frame. The boards it was made of creaked ominously. Seph gasped, but he kept his arms up, blocking Grim's fists as they rained down on him.

Through the haze of pain, Seph heard a sound that sent a chill down his spine. A horse screamed, sharp and haunting. It was followed by a menacing snort. The crowd stilled, and for a moment, even Grim hesitated. His fist stalled, mid-swing.

It was Win. The ghost horse stood at the edge of the battleground, his dapple-gray coat marred with burn scars. His mane and tail singed to uneven tufts. His eyes gleamed eerily. He pawed the ground and snorted again before tossing his head, rearing up, and galloping away.

Seph's heart surged with renewed determination. The moment passed in a heartbeat as Grim shook off his unease and grabbed Seph by his belt, yanking him forward. But the distraction had restored Seph. Twisting free, he slammed his elbow into Grim's cheek and made space between them.

The battle raged on. The wagon groaned under the weight of the combatants, its boards creaking and cracking with every shift and blow. Thick, stifling air made each breath harder to draw than the last. Every strike landed with a sickening thud that reverberated through his body, shaking his resolve but not his determination. Each hit echoed in the crowd's winces and gasps.

Seph locked eyes with Grim again. He saw the faintest flicker of doubt in the older man's gaze. It gave him hope that he might win. And he clung to it.

There was a chance he might win.

Dusty held his breath as Seph and Grim circled the wagon, their bodies battered and streaked with blood. Seph moved quickly, his long reach keeping Grim at a distance, but it was clear the older man's brute strength was wearing him down. Each feint and blow edged Seph closer to his limit.

It should be me, Dusty thought. Maybe if I'd fought harder, insisted on another way, this wouldn't be happening. If only I hadn't gotten hooked on that blasted tonic. Dang regrets. Maybe Seph had a chance. Dusty knew that if it had been up to him, the fight would already be over. He should have done it anyway. Dusty clenched his jaw. It was hard to admit, even if just to himself.

Seph was exhausted. His movements had slowed, his punches had lost some of their snap, and his dodges were noticeably sluggish. "Keep moving, man," Dusty shouted, reminding himself not to call the strong young man a kid anymore.

Grim was relentless, driving Seph back toward the wagon's edge with a series of heavy blows. Each punch landed with a sickening, bone crunching crack that made Dusty wince. The chuckwagon groaned under the strain as Seph slammed against its side, and Grim capitalized, gripping Seph by the throat and pinning him.

"Get out of there!" Dusty barked. He turned to Stoke, who was watching with equal intensity. "What's he thinking? He's gotta break free!"

Stoke didn't respond, his eyes were glued to the fight, but a muscle in his jaw ticked. Around them, the Deatherage cowboys murmured anxiously. Dusty thought their glances conveyed distress. The men were worried.

Dusty's gaze shifted to the opposing side, where Grim's men jeered and laughed. Their confidence swelled with every passing second. Mitch crossed his arms, smirking triumphantly. Dusty felt his stomach churn. How could a man cheer for the death of his own brother?

"Come on, Seph," Dusty growled. "You can't let him beat you."

Grim shifted his grip, wrapping the rope around his forearm for leverage as he dragged Seph toward the wagon wheel. With his free hand, Grim reached down and grabbed an iron poker from the wagon. It wasn't against the rules, for there were no rules. Dusty's breath caught as Grim shoved the poker lengthwise under Seph's chin, forcing the younger man's head back.

The crowd gasped as Seph struggled, his boots digging into the ground for purchase.

Grim's men roared their approval.

Dusty felt a hand on his arm and turned to see Lullaby, his expression grim. "We could sure use a miracle about now, Boss," Lullaby fretted. It was almost like a prayer.

Dusty's eyes flicked back to the fight, where Seph's face was clenched in pain, his hands gripping Grim's arm as he fought to push him away. Dusty swallowed hard. "That's for sure," he said. "That's just what we need."

The crowd surged forward slightly as Seph bucked against Grim's grip, twisting away just enough to escape the poker's push against his windpipe. He brought his knee up sharply, catching Grim in the stomach. The older man grunted but didn't let go, his determination as unyielding as the iron in his hand.

Dusty's heart pounded as he watched Seph's strength waver. He knew that Seph had grit, but Grim was tough—relentless and brutal. "Seph," Dusty muttered, his voice barely audible now. "You've gotta find a way."

Dusty's stomach churned as he realized the tide of the fight had shifted. Grim was in control now, and it didn't look like Seph had much left in him.

In the periphery of Dusty's vision, Win appeared again, pacing along the edge of the battlefield. The horse's presence seemed to cast a spell over the crowd, silencing even the most boisterous jeers. Dusty's breath hitched as the animal's eyes appeared to lock onto the fight.

As quickly as Win had come, he was gone, galloping off into the distance, leaving a stunned silence in his wake.

The momentary distraction gave Seph a chance to slip free of Grim's grasp, but it was clear he was running on fumes. Seph scrambled to the top of the chuck box at the back of the wagon.

Grim didn't give him a chance to recover. He lunged forward, grabbed Seph's ankle, and hauled himself to the top of the wagon. With a forceful yank, Grim toppled Seph and dug his knees into Seph's gut. The poker was still in his other hand. Seph squirmed to escape as Grim twisted the poker back into place, just beneath Seph's chin. This time, Grim would choke him for sure.

Dusty's knuckles whitened. "Don't give up now, man," he whispered, though his voice was thick with doubt. Dusty felt the bitter taste of despair creeping in.

Seph's eyes bulged as he tried to keep a trickle of air flowing into his lungs. His arms and legs hung over the edge of the chuck box, and with a little bit of movement, he was able to get his head over the edge as well, but he couldn't escape the iron bar throttling his neck. It was about to shatter his windpipe.

Grim's breath came ragged, his sweat-streaked face twisted with effort, but his grip never wavered. He licked his lips, as if tasting victory. But he looked tired.

Dusty felt helpless, knowing the next move could end it all.

The crowd seemed to hold its breath, waiting for the moment when Grim would crush the life from the young cowboy's body.

Dusty tipped his head forward. What a valiant effort. He had tried to stop it, but he should have been more insistent.

If he lived to be a hundred years old he would never forgive himself for letting Seph fight Grim.

CHAPTER 26

SEPH'S VISION BLURRED AT the edges, darkening with every second that Grim pressed the iron bar beneath his chin. The cold metal bit into his skin. It was hard to breathe and he panicked. It felt as if the world around him was falling away. Flailing desperately, he tried to grab hold of something, but his strength was waning.

The crowd's gasps and whispers blurred into a steady hum, drowned out by the pounding of Seph's heart. This was it. He could feel it coming. His defeat was inevitable.

His limbs twitched, uselessly. Stars popped behind his eyes. His lungs screamed. Darkness crept into his soul. The world shrank to the press of iron against his throat. There was no way out. He tried to reconcile himself to dying. Slipping away. Letting go.

But then, from deep inside, something stirred. A spark detonated. The faint memory of his mother's voice. The way she whispered to him: *Never give up.* The vision of Slaw, running a dirty hand through the tangled shreds of his hair. The strength of Win, standing proud and defiant in the aftermath of dynamite explosions and dragging flaming bushes from his tail. Those sparks surged through him like a prairie fire, carrying the promise of everything he fought for: the herd, the men, and the life he wanted to build.

Seph's body stiffened as a final jolt of power ignited his muscles. With a violent twist and heave, and using the power and leverage in his long legs, Seph throttled his knees upward and pitched Grim over his head. The hulking convict sailed over the edge of the chuck box.

The crowd screamed.

Seph felt the wagon rock beneath him as the man's weight pulled hard against the rope binding them. For a moment, it seemed like the force would crash the whole rig onto its side.

Grim dangled off the edge, his weight dragging Seph closer to the precipice. The younger man braced his heels, and squatted to keep from toppling over the edge himself. The rope cut into Seph's wrist, but he held tight, veins bulging in his arms as he hauled Grim back up, inch by agonizing inch.

Grim's head appeared over the edge. There was fury and disbelief on his face. He snarled, "You... you ain't strong enough, boy."

With one final heave, Seph dragged Grim onto the perch, his chest heaving as he stood over his opponent. The iron poker lay nearby. What kept the object from rolling over the edge?

The jagged point caught Seph's eye. Stoke's warning replayed in his head. He knew what he must do.

There was no hesitation in him as he grabbed the poker. The weight of the staff felt familiar in his hand, like the grip on his knife. His throat tightened and it almost felt as if the iron bar was still pressing beneath his chin. That poker almost killed him.

He planted his boot on Grim's chest to hold him down. "This is for the men you've destroyed. For the lives you've taken. The things you've stolen. The people whose lives you've ruined." Seph shook with rage as he heard himself say those words. It felt surreal, like somebody else was saying them. He moved the sharp end of the poker toward Grim's chest and shouted. "This is for Rooster. For Torp. And the Dagger D, Angry R brand."

Grim's eyes widened, darting wildly between defiance and terror. Searching for escape. His breath came in choked gasps, his body twisting, fighting the inevitable. For the first time, he looked afraid—truly afraid. A look of terror flashed across his face. His lips parted. He mouthed the word—Please. Grim squirmed. But he was unable to escape.

Grim's fear was plain now. Seph could see it in his eyes. But Seph felt no sympathy. No mercy. Stoke had warned him about that. They knew the stakes going in—only one man would survive this battle. Seph raised the poker high and drove it down with a primal scream. But no amount of justice could bring back his friends. Chops. Rooster. The ones Grim had stolen. He drove the sharp tip deeper, through the flesh, through bone. The poker plunged through Grim's chest and pierced his heart with a sickening crunch.

Seph exhaled. He felt dizzy. The world swayed around him. He had done what he had to do. So be it.

The air stilled and the crowd froze in shock. Grim's lips trembled as his final breaths came in shallow gasps. Blood burbled at the corner of his mouth, and his once-fearsome eyes dulled.

"I was supposed to be king," Grim rasped. *"El Rey del Pampas...."*

His head lolled to the side, his body slackening beneath Seph's foot. His fingers clawed weakly at Seph's boot, then stilled. The terrible reign of Ward "Grim" Decker, King of Huntsville Prison, and would-be King of the Pampas, had ended.

Seph stood over the fallen man, the iron poker still in his hands. Blood dripped from the jagged point, dripping on the top of the chuck box. His sweaty chest heaved. Every muscle screamed with exhaustion. But he stood upright, the embodiment of triumph and vengeance, and the pride of the Deatherage Longhorn Cattle Ranch. The setting sun bathed his glistening form in a fiery glow, making him look like a hero in a painting.

For a moment, no one moved. No one spoke. Then, Seph heard Torp's voice. "I declare."

That was followed by Stoke's ear piercing yell. It sounded like it could curdle milk and raise the dead at the same time. A chorus of cheers erupted from the Deatherage side, swelling into a thunderous roar of victory.

Seph looked down at Grim's lifeless body one last time. He exhaled, his ribs aching. "It's over," he whispered, more to himself than anyone else. He uncurled his fingers. The poker tumbled from his grip.

The clang of the falling weapon echoed. Like the chime of a church bell.

Most of Grim's men disappeared into the shadows.

Five remained, clustered near the chuckwagon: Mitch Vermillion, John Quincy Long, John Memphis Short, Dick Fowler, and Bert Knight. Their hands hovered near their holsters. It must have been hard for them to accept the death of their leader.

They intently watched the Deatherage cowboys, who were celebrating Seph's unexpected victory. The contest was over. The battle to settle the wager was finished. The Three Bar Box beeves now belonged to Dusty Deatherage. But Grim's most loyal men wanted to fight on.

Except for Mitch.

He stepped forward and raised his hands, palms out, in a gesture of command. "That's enough," he said.

John Memphis Short stepped toward Mitch, his hand resting on the butt of his revolver. "You expect us to just walk away?" he growled. "We can't let them take what's ours. We owe it to Grim."

Mitch's expression didn't waver. His eyes were hard, unflinching. "Look around. Grim is dead. The herd is lost. Our crew has turned tail and gone. It's time to face the facts. It's a bust for the Three Bar Box brand. Besides, loyalty is for suckers. You can only count on yourself."

They looked at each other in disbelief. John Quincy Long said, "But they're just a bunch of kids."

Firmly, Mitch said, "No. They're not. Don't be fooled. They don't look like much, but together they're unstoppable."

The Dagger D, Angry R boys gathered around, arms crossed over their chests, ready to take on the last of their foes if it came to another fight.

Mitch stretched his arms wide, like they were fence rails, corralling his partners. "We've been together a long time. Too long. It's time to go our separate ways."

Dick Fowler spat. "I never liked you to begin with, Mitch."

Bert Knight sneered. "Me neither."

"Why should I care?" Mitch said. "My family don't like me neither. Why don't you all just ride out, find some corner of this country where nobody knows your name, and start fresh. That's what I aim to do."

Bert said, "I'm going north. To Chicago, maybe."

Dick figured to go east.

John Quincy Long and John Memphis Short mounted up and headed south, back to Texas. John Quincy said, "We was born there."

John Memphis Short added, "And that's where we'll die."

When they were gone, Mitch said to Seph, "Help me bury him. Would you?" He dragged Grim's body from the top of the crumb box. And hopped back as Grim's corpse landed on the dirt beside the wagon, with a thud. Mitch knelt beside his fallen partner and tipped his head forward. "You don't owe him, Seph, and you don't owe me, but I'd sure appreciate it." Mitch turned away from Grim and looked at his brother.

With a frown, after a brief hesitation, Seph nodded. Together, they dug a modest grave at the edge of the camp. When the hole was deep enough, they lowered Grim's body into the earth, covering him with the same soil he had spent his life trying to conquer.

As Seph packed the dirt with the flat back of his shovel, Mitch stood at the grave's edge, his hat pressed to his chest. "He was rotten to the core," Mitch said. "But he was my partner. I guess that counts for something."

Seph didn't respond immediately. He straightened, resting his hands on the shovel's handle, and looked down at the grave. "He wanted to be a king," Seph said softly. "But he never knew what it meant to take care of people."

Mitch nodded, a faint, bitter smile playing at his lips.

Without another word, Mitch rode off.

Seph watched as his long-lost brother disappeared into the western horizon. A memory from the year before crossed his mind. The outlaw, Swoop also rode west. Again, he thought of his favorite horse and yearned to be reunited with that claybank dun. He would not miss Mitch. And he hoped he'd never see Swoop again. But he yearned to get his horse back.

Seph turned back toward the camp and ran into Charlie. The old-timer sucked his cheeks, smacked his gums, and said, "It's time to feed them boys again."

After racing all the way to the Smoky Hill River, it was hard to remain in one place.

Dusty kept them from town for six weeks, moving them west along the river to let the herd graze and bulk up before driving the critters to market. He forbade the men from going to town, and set the example himself by sending a homesteader to buy their provisions, making it well worth the man's trouble.

They had twice the number of beeves, but they were down three men. But watching grazing cattle was easier than driving a herd. After a month and a half of doing nothing but daydreaming about whooping it up in town, the boys were more than ready to deliver the herd to market.

Dusty finally gave the word on the 4th of August, a Wednesday.

The combined herd, just shy of six thousand beefy longhorns clattered toward Abilene. The Deatherage drovers rode with heads held high.

Dusty rode at the front of the column. He commanded the travel-wise cowboys who didn't require his instruction, but were nevertheless glad to hear his strong voice. His back was still stiff, his movements wooden, but he looked years younger than he had along the trail.

"Keep the swing riders tight!" Dusty hollered. "Yodel, Lullaby, flank those stragglers. Don't let up now, Stoke. We're almost there. Bring 'em on home, Skillet!"

The cowboys obeyed without hesitation. Despite the constant bellyaching, six weeks of lollygagging restored the men as much as the herd.

Seph rode opposite Stoke, leaving Grim's rickety chuckwagon in Charlie's care at the Smoky Hill River crossing. It was an easy mile and a half ride, but the familiar sight of Abilene quickened his pulse.

As the stockyards came into view, Seph's chest swelled. It was a triumph. The dusty town stretched out before them. Empty pens and chutes were about to be filled to capacity.

Seph noticed a cowboy sitting nonchalantly on the fence near the stockyard entrance. It could have been any old drover, but it wasn't.

Stoke howled, squinting ahead. "Is that—"

"It can't be." Seph shook his head, but it was. "Scorch!" He'd almost forgotten about Scorch.

The wiry young man looked equally stunned as he straightened up. His face twisted in disbelief as he took in the sight of the victorious Deatherage outfit, his hand lingering near his boot.

"Where's Grim?" Scorch called, his voice cracking. He jumped from the fence and approached cautiously, as if fearing they might shoot him.

Dusty dismounted, his brow furrowed. "You'll have to ask the Devil about Grim. What are *you* doing here, Scorch?"

"I came to get paid," Scorch snapped, his confidence returning with a sharp edge. "Figured Grim's boys'd be the ones rollin' in, not you. Guess that means you've got all the money. What the heck took you so long?"

"We don't owe you nothing," Dusty said flatly. His tone left no room for argument.

Scorch's face darkened. "Clive promised to pay me."

Dusty said, "You'll have to ask the Devil about Clive's promises too, Scorch."

In a swift motion that looked so smooth it must have been practiced, Scorch pulled a stick of dynamite from his boot and a match appeared between his thumb and forefinger. The cowboys froze.

"You better rethink that, Boss," Scorch snarled, holding the dynamite aloft. "I've had about enough of getting hoodwinked. Somebody's gotta pay me, or I'll blow myself up."

"Easy now," Seph said, stepping forward and raising his hands. "You don't want to do this, Scorch. Think about what that'll get you."

"It'll get me the respect I deserve!" Scorch shot back, his grip tightening on the explosive cylinder.

"Respect?" Seph frowned. "Or pity? Look, maybe we lend you a few bucks and you can have your old job back. You've got skills, Scorch, but this ain't the way to prove nothing."

Scorch hesitated. Seph couldn't tell if he was defiant or desperate. He was clearly hungry. Maybe starving. He'd missed far too many meals. His grip on the dynamite wavered.

Just then, a loud voice interrupted them. "No need for that."

The sheriff, accompanied by Hork, who had tipped him off, stepped into view. The lawman kept his hand near his holstered revolver and his gaze locked on Scorch.

Scorch's eyes darted from the sheriff and the dynamite in his hand. "I—I just want what's mine!" he stammered, his bravado crumbling.

The sheriff took a step closer. "You want what's yours? Then let's settle this the right way. Put that down, son."

Scorch's shoulders slumped as he lowered the dynamite. Two deputies closed in, cuffing his wrists before he could protest further. He looked back at Seph with sad eyes. "I told you—I just want to get paid."

Seph met his gaze. "I know, Scorch. But you've got to earn it the right way."

As the lawmen disappeared into the town, with Scorch in tow, Dusty turned to his crew. "Alright, boys," Dusty said. "Speaking of getting paid... let's go get paid!"

The cowboys let out a raucous cheer.

The streets of Abilene pulsed with the sound of cowboys whooping it up. Their hooting and hollering carried over the clatter of boots and the wails of fiddles. Seph walked slowly down the wooden walkway, his hands tucked into the pockets of his new trousers. His fresh haircut and shave made him look sharp, and his new boots creaked with every step. But none of it made him feel at ease.

His fellow cowboys were scattered across the town, spilling out of saloons, shouting at the stars, and raising their glasses in celebration. Dusty sat on a rocking chair outside the general store, just as he did last year. He remained nearby in case somebody found trouble they couldn't handle. Otherwise, he believed in letting the boys be boys. And, he also believed as Stoke did, that riding the trail from San Antonio to Abilene earned a man the right to howl and run hog wild as Stoke liked to put it. For those who felt otherwise, Dusty invited them to remain in camp on the Smoky Hill River.

Most of the men were ready to celebrate. But Seph wasn't in the mood.

He stopped outside a saloon. The windows glowed with lamplight and the sounds of music and laughter spilled over the batwing doors. He tipped his hat back and considered going in, but the thought of whiskey burning his gullet turned his stomach sour. He didn't want whiskey.

His feet carried him down the street toward The Fancy Frolic, and his heart thudded harder with each step. The painted sign above the door gleamed in bold letters. Seph stopped in front of the building and stared at it, his brow furrowed.

The memories of last year haunted him. Hazel. Her warm smile, her soft laugh, the way she had made him feel like he was the only man in the world. He had spent the entire year convincing himself that he wasn't the kind of man who visited places like this. And yet, here he was again.

Seph frowned, pulled his hat low over his brow, and stepped inside.

The interior of the Frolic was gaudy and bustling. The smell of perfume powdered the air. The main room bustled with laughter, music, and clinking glasses, but Seph's eyes went immediately to the sign at the back that read *Jolie's Girls*. His steps felt heavy as he made his way forward.

Jolie, the madam, intercepted him before he reached the doorway. Her arms were crossed, and her expression was stern. "Aw, Seph," she said, shaking her head. "I told you not to come back here."

Seph pulled off his hat and clutched it in both hands, his eyes downcast. "I... I can't help myself, Jolie. Is Hazel here?"

Jolie sighed, her hard demeanor softening just a little. "I'm sorry, Seph. She ain't."

The words hit Seph like a punch to the chest. His shoulders sagged. He wanted to ask for more information about the young woman, but didn't. "Oh," he said quietly. "I see."

Jolie placed a hand on his arm. "Remember what I told you, honey? This ain't the place where a man comes to fall in love. That's not what we do here. Pick somebody else, Seph. That's what you need. How about Ellen?" She indicated a pretty young woman standing by the wall, waiting for a customer. "She's sweet. And nice. She'll make you happy."

Seph shook his head, his voice firm but pained. "No. No thank you, Jolie. I'll just go then."

He turned to leave but hesitated at the doorway, his hand on the frame. "Before I go," he said, "I wanted to tell you about Mitch. I met him... our brother... on the trail." Last year, he had found his long lost sister, Jolie, working in the Abilene brothel. Now he'd also found Mitch.

Jolie's face froze, her eyes narrowing. "Mitch?"

"Yeah," Seph said, still not meeting her gaze. "He's just out of Huntsville. I guess he done a mess of time there. Just thought you should know."

Jolie's lips tightened, her expression unreadable. "Okay, you told me. Alright then."

With that, Seph stepped back out onto the street, the door swinging closed behind him. He dropped his hat back onto his head and tipped it low, shading his eyes as if hoping to hide his disappointment. The night was cool, but it did nothing to soothe the ache that had settled deep in his heart. He had hoped to spend the night with the woman he couldn't get out of his head.

Hazel was gone. Isn't that what Jolie said? Or did she just say that she wasn't here?

Maybe it was just as well.

CHAPTER 27

THE STREETS OF ABILENE were quieter now. The distant clamor of rowdy cowboys faded as Seph wandered aimlessly. His feet carried him toward the edge of town. Thoughts of Hazel swirled in his mind. Why couldn't he get that woman out of his head?

He stood in front of a church and admired its simple beauty. The exterior was recently painted bright white, making it more visible in the dark than the other buildings in town. A soft glow of warm light brightened tall windows on either side of the large door at the front and center of the structure.

The faint strains of a hymn reached his ears. The melody tugged at something deep inside him. It was hauntingly familiar. He realized with a jolt that it was the same tune Yodel often played on his harmonica. But it sounded different here.

Seph approached the steps, cautiously. Reverently.

He had never been inside a church before, but the idea of opening the door and crossing the threshold felt right. It was as if his footsteps were meant to carry him here. And the giant doors were an invitation to enter.

A faint creak echoed through the sanctuary as he pushed the door open, and stepped inside. He turned to make sure the door closed gently and quietly. He looked around slowly and felt something he hadn't known he needed.

A few people sat scattered among the pews with their heads bowed in prayer. Seph removed his hat and wandered deeper into the entryway, then stepped lightly up an aisle. He chose a spot and sat on a bench in the middle of the front row.

For a moment, he simply stared at the altar. Except for the cross, he didn't know what to make of the religious symbols and artifacts he saw. It felt like he was staring into the heavens at night, only he was inside. He didn't know what to do, so he just sat there, letting the stillness settle over him. Like a blanket.

After a few minutes, a young man in heavy robes approached quietly and sat beside him. "Can I help you?" the man gently asked.

Seph turned to him, flipping his hat in his lap. "I ain't never been in a church before," he admitted. "Figured it was about time I saw what it was like."

The man smiled warmly. "Well, you're here now. I'm Brother James," he said, extending his hand. Seph took it, his grip firm but uncertain. "Would you like to pray together?"

Seph hesitated. "I wouldn't know what to say." But after listening to Lullaby's prayers the past two years he probably could have come up with something.

"You don't have to know," Brother James said. "Sometimes it's enough just to listen." The man recited a short prayer and said. "May you find comfort in God's presence, friend."

After their brief visit, Brother James gripped Seph's forearm as they stood. "You're welcome here anytime," he said. "Our doors are always open."

Seph nodded. "Thank you."

As Brother James moved away, Seph sat back down, letting his thoughts wander. Ten minutes later, the scrape of footsteps caught his attention. A young woman in a bright blue dress slid onto the bench beside him. She smiled nervously, her hands folded in her lap.

"I'm Irene Fallstaff," she whispered loudly. "I've been praying for a strong husband. And here you are."

Seph blinked, unsure how to respond. A hot rush flushed his cheeks as Irene giggled nervously. "We're having a picnic tomorrow, just up the road. You should come. It's half a mile to the north. Can't miss it."

Seph tipped his head forward. "I'll think about it, ma'am. Thank you."

With that, Irene was gone.

Fifteen minutes later, Seph stood to leave. As he walked toward the side aisle, he noticed someone sitting alone in the shadows of the back pews. The woman lifted her head, and his heart stopped.

It was Hazel.

She wore a plain dark dress. Her expression was contemplative. Seph froze, blinking in disbelief, before speaking. "May I sit beside you?"

Hazel looked up, startled, but nodded faintly.

Seph slid onto the bench beside her. "I'm so glad I found you," Seph said quietly. "Jolie said you weren't there. I thought she meant you were gone."

Hazel smiled shyly, her gaze dropping to her hands. "It's my day off," she said softly. "This is where I come to be alone. It's peaceful here. This is where I remember happier times."

Seph stole a glance at her. She was every bit as beautiful as he remembered, but there was something different about her now.

"Do you remember me?" he asked, fearful that she did not.

Hazel placed a hand on his shoulder, her touch light but steady. "Of course. I'll never forget you, Mr. Vermillion. Long as I live, I'll never forget *you*."

"Do you remember when you asked me to take you away?" Seph asked.

Hazel's smile faded, and she looked down, dejected. "I gave up asking cowboys to take me away with them. Now I talk to God instead."

Seph hesitated before asking, "Would you like to go for a walk?"

Hazel nodded, and together they left the church. They walked in silence to the cow camp. Charlie was asleep and Lullaby waved his hat in greeting as Seph fetched his bedroll.

Seph reached for Hazel's hand and they strolled to a sheltered spot along the riverbank, a good distance from the cow camp.

They stood for a moment, gazing up at the heavens. The stars sprayed across the sky like scattered candles, their brilliance mirrored in the still water below.

"Would you go with me," Seph asked quietly, "If I said we could ride away right now?"

Hazel's answer came slowly, her voice soft but firm. "No. I don't want to marry a man who knows my past." After a pause, she went on to say, "Of all the men that have ridden through town, if one could tempt me to change my mind, it would be you, Mr. Vermillion. But once a year, when you come to town, let's indulge the fantasy of being newly married. I'd like that. The rest of these cowboys blur together in my mind. But you... you have a special place in my heart."

Seph rubbed the back of her neck gently and kissed her softly. "What if I don't come back?" he asked. "Cowboying is dangerous."

Hazel's smile faded. "I'd be sad. I live a sad life. Maybe that's the way it's meant to be. But if you didn't come back, I'd cherish your memory. So, if it's just the same to you, I'd like to have you come back."

Seph looked at Hazel, wrapped his arms around her, and said, "Long as you're here, I'll keep coming back. Would you lay with me on my bedroll, Mrs. Vermillion?"

It was just after noon the next day as Seph, Dusty, and Stoke made their way to the small jail in the middle of town. The building was a simple, single-story structure with iron bars visible from the outside, weathered wood siding, and a sign that read "Marshal's Office." Inside, the smells of tobacco and coffee greeted them.

Scorch looked up from his cot behind the bars as they entered. "Dusty, Seph, Stoke," he croaked, scrambling to his feet. "You come to spring me out?"

Dusty crossed his arms. He spoke slowly, "Depends. You ready to own up to the trouble you caused?"

The marshal, a wiry man with a sharp mustache, leaned back in his chair, eyeing the trio. "I don't know what you boys see in him," he said. "Didn't he try to kill you?"

Seph stepped forward. "He made a mistake, Marshal. Nobody would deny that. But he didn't light that fuse. Clive did."

The marshal snorted. "Sure, but this kid made it possible."

Scorch pressed his face against the bars. "I swear, Marshal, I ain't gonna mess up like that again. I'll ride straight and narrow. I promise. Just give me another chance."

Dusty turned to the marshal. "We're not asking you to pardon him. Just let us handle him. Kid owes me more than you can collect sitting him in that cell."

The marshal eyed Scorch, then Dusty. "You think he's worth another chance?" The tone of his voice made it clear that the marshal didn't see any potential in Scorch.

Dusty hesitated before answering. "No. But I reckon I'll give him one anyway."

Seph stepped closer. "Dusty, he worked for Clive. We can't pay him for this year—but what about next year? What do you say?"

Dusty groaned and stepped closer to Scorch's cell. "Clive tried to kill me, Scorch. And you helped him."

Scorch's voice cracked. "I swear, Mr. Deatherage, I'll never do nothing like that again."

Stoke piped in, "Why don't you just shoot him and be done with it?"

Dusty sighed. "That'll do, Stoke. That'll do. I won't pay you for this year, Scorch, but I'll advance you a month's wages that you can spend now. You mess up again, and you're on your own."

Scorch nodded fervently. "I won't let you down, sir. I promise."

The marshal shook his head in disbelief. "Before you go, I got a question." He slid his desk drawer open and held up Scorch's stick of dynamite. "Where has this been all summer?"

Scorch scowled but answered honestly. "Well, it spent the last two months in my boot."

The marshal shook his head and rolled his eyes. "Do you smoke, kid?"

Scorch hung his head. "Heck, no. I can't afford tobacco."

The marshal chuckled. "Tug that boot a yours off." After the prisoner did as told, the marshal said, "Now remove the other boot. The marshal laughed so hard, he almost cried. "I have to tell you kid, that stick of dynamite wouldn't have blown up anything. It all leaked out into your boot and onto your socks.

Seph leaned over and looked at the dark, greasy stains on Scorch's gray sock. On closer inspection, he noticed yellow, crystallized beads on the fabric.

He understood why the marshal asked Scorch about smoking, with all that explosive material in Scorch's boot.

The marshal shook his keys and freed Scorch. "He's your problem now. Setting him free will save Abilene a fortune. This kid eats too much." He tipped a shoulder at a tray with dirty dishes piled high.

Dusty fished a few coins from his pocket and tossed them onto the marshal's desk. "For your trouble," he chuckled, then turned to Scorch. "Come on, kid. Don't make me regret this."

Their next stop was the bank, where the rest of the Deatherage outfit waited in line.

Passersby began to worry that they were going to rob the place. The Mud Creek National Bank was a grand structure with tall windows and ornate carvings framing the entrance. Seph glanced at Stoke, who adjusted his hat nervously. "First time opening a bank account?" Seph asked with a grin.

"I never even thought of having a bank account before," Stoke admitted.

Inside, the bank was bustling. Tellers in crisp shirts stood behind the counter, while customers lined up to conduct their business. The smell of ink and fresh paper were unfamiliar and mingled with the faint scent of wood polish. The sound of clinking coins and chattering patrons made the bank feel almost festive.

Dusty led the group to an open counter. "Afternoon," he said to the teller. "We're here to open accounts for my boys."

The teller, a middle-aged man with thin spectacles, raised an eyebrow. "All of them?"

Dusty nodded. "Every man who worked this drive gets a share of the net. They earned it."

From behind them, a deep voice chuckled. "A cattleman who shares his profits with his crew? Now I've seen everything."

The group turned to see Mr. McCoy, the cattle baron that Stoke and Seph had met the previous year in the barber shop. "Glenn Deatherage," McCoy said, tipping his hat. "You're an unusual man. Most trail bosses barely pay their men enough to drink away their misery."

Dusty shrugged. "A man works hard, he deserves to feel like he's part of something bigger."

McCoy smiled faintly. "You've got an outfit to be proud of. And I admire you, sir."

As the process began, Seph couldn't help but smile at the excitement among the cowboys. Hork and Conjure whispered jubilantly about their newfound wealth, while Yodel and Lullaby stood quietly, their expressions proud.

Stoke, standing at a counter with his hand resting on a stack of bills turned to Seph. "Feels strange, don't it? I'd almost rather keep it on me than hide it away here."

Seph nodded. "I think this is what cattlemen do, Stoke."

The teller handed Seph a small booklet. "Here's your account, Mr. Vermillion," he said with a smile. "Welcome to Mud Creek National Bank."

Seph took the booklet. His name was neatly written on the cover and it was spelled correctly, with both L's in the million part of his name. He held it for a moment. It wasn't money, but it could be turned back into money. The teller explained that they could access their funds through a correspondent bank in San Antonio, and Dusty confirmed that was what he did.

Even the wary cowboys felt proud to have bank accounts.

Scorch frowned in a corner but didn't complain.

Torp held up his book. "Hey, lookee here. I'm a cattle baron now."

Dusty chuckled. "Well, you are on your way. That's for sure, son."

The cowboys laughed and slapped each others' backs and shoulders.

As they stepped out into the late afternoon sunlight, Seph looked back at the grand building. Someday, he'd put that money to good use. A strong sense of accomplishment settled over him.

They had made it.

Seph stood by the battered chuckwagon with his hands on his hips and stared into the distance. Lullaby and Yodel sat nearby, Yodel's harmonica resting on his knee. It was the quietest the camp had been in ages.

Dusty approached, "Got a minute, Seph?"

"Sure, Boss," Seph replied, turning to face him.

Dusty gestured toward a pair of logs twenty yards away. "Let's sit a spell."

As they settled onto the logs, Dusty stared at the ground. His hands were clasped between his knees, and he cleared his throat before finally speaking.

"I've been thinking about this drive and everything that's happened," Dusty began. "If it weren't for you, I don't reckon I'd be here. Clive... well, he dang near got the best of me. That tonic, too." He shook his head. "The herd would've been lost. The ranch gone. Everything my family built. But you, Seph... you saved it. And you saved me."

Seph didn't know what to say, so he just nodded. His throat felt tight and a burning sensation blossomed behind his eyes.

Dusty leaned back, his eyes softening as he looked at Seph. "I never had a son, but if I did, I'd want him to be just like you. You've earned the right to be promoted. I'd like to see you ramrod this outfit."

Seph's eyebrows shot up. "Ramrod? Dusty, no. I'm just a drover."

Dusty chuckled. "Oh, you ain't just a drover. You've taken on big responsibilities. Not just this year, but last year too. You are ready."

Seph shook his head, smiling faintly. "Someday, yes. When I'm ramrod, I want to be the best there ever was, but I ain't ready yet. Last year, Dunk told me I had to be good at everything first. I'm still learning. Give the job to Stoke."

Dusty frowned thoughtfully. "Stoke? That hothead?"

Seph shrugged. "He's earned it too. He's tough, and the men respect him. I'll back him up if he needs it."

Dusty sighed, but his lips twitched upward in a grin. "All right. What about top hand, then?"

"Can you have two?" Seph asked, glancing over at the fire where Yodel and Lullaby sat quietly. "I'd give it to Lullaby and Yodel. They've been with you forever. They've earned it more than I have."

Dusty leaned forward, resting his elbows on his knees. "And what about you? What do you want, Seph? Can you answer me that?"

Seph hesitated, his gaze shifting to the horizon where the sun painted the sky in shades of orange and red. "With Chops gone, I'd like to be wrangler next year. Maybe after that, I'll try my hand at scout. If you still need a ramrod then, I reckon I'll be ready after that. What's the rush?"

Dusty threw his head back and laughed, a deep hearty sound that echoed through the camp. "You're somethin' else. Alright. We'll take it one step at a time, then." He paused, and his laughter faded into a wistful smile.

Seph said, "I got a question for you, Boss. Let's say a drover wants to get married. Could he build him a cabin on the ranch for his wife?"

Dusty scratched his chin. "I ain't thought of that." He looked back at Seph, and said, "Is there something I should know?"

Seph shrugged. "What if there was?"

Dusty said, "I'd have to think about that Seph. Take it on a case by case basis. But if it was you, my answer would be yes."

Seph nodded thoughtfully. "Good. Good to know. Now, what about you?"

Dusty leaned back. "What do you mean, what about me?"

Seph laughed. "You ain't getting any younger. Why don't you get yourself a wife? Then you won't have to say stuff like, *If I had a son, I'd want him to be just like you.*"

Dusty laughed. "I suppose you're right. Truth is, I have been hankering to do just that." Dusty stood and yawned. "We leave for home tomorrow. Better get some rest."

Seph nodded, watching as Dusty walked back to the fire. Rising slowly, Seph stepped away from the camp.

Win trailed behind him. They rarely tied or hobbled the ghost horse anymore. Instead, they let him go where he wished. Win followed Seph to the place where Seph and Hazel had spent the night before.

The river shimmered in the distance, and above, the stars spilled across the heavens in a breathtaking spray of light. Seph rested his hand on Win's neck and the horse nuzzled him gently.

He looked out at the horizon. Behind closed eyelids, he relived his precious moments with Hazel. She was his favorite memory. He longed to dash off into the night and tell her that the boss said she could live with him on the ranch. But Hazel didn't want that. Maybe she would feel differently next year.

Seph bowed his head and said a prayer.

Then he spoke to Win as if he were his childhood pal, Slaw. "How about that, partner? You asked me to take you along with me so you could see everything through my eyes. Hope you enjoyed the wild ride this year, Mr. Townsend Ballard."

Seph gently rubbed the spot between Win's ears. "What are we gonna do about you, Win?"

What's next? Buffalo hide hunters are everywhere. A raging turf war spreads across the prairie. The Deatherage outfit is tangled in its bloody path.

Snap up your copy of Devil Buffalo before the buffalo vanish.

ANOTHER ADVENTURE

Seph Vermillion's next adventure is called Devil Buffalo, Book Three in the series.

A raging turf war spreads across the prairie. The Deatherage outfit is tangled in its bloody path.

This is Seph Vermillion's third trip up the trail. Now he's the wrangler. The horses are as wild as the longhorns, and a rogue stallion is determined to steal them. Seph must break the mustangs, keep them from bolting, and defend them from a relentless thief. Without a strong remuda, the drive is doomed.

Rival gangs of hide hunters have driven a buffalo herd into a deadly frenzy that threatens to engulf everything in its wake. Each outfit fights to claim the most skins while driving the others away. Every hunter dreams of felling the notorious Devil Buffalo. A ruthless buffalo assassin is on a mission to wipe them out. A fierce band of Comanche and Kiowa warriors will stop at nothing to end the slaughter. The cowboys are caught in the crossfire.

When a thunderous stampede consumes the herd, the Deatherage outfit stands to lose everything. Even the bravest men shudder at the sight of the mythical buffalo. Extracting longhorns from its ferocious grip is nearly impossible. The quiet prairie explodes into a battlefield. Rifles crack. War cries pierce the air. Bison rampage. Every attempt to reclaim the herd comes at a deadly cost. Cowboys perish in the dust. Seph's friends have all but given up. Will anyone survive this accursed drive?

The buffalo are vanishing. The people who depend on them are forever changed. The plains will never be the same. After all they've endured, will the Deatherage outfit also be forced to surrender their beeves and go bust?

Barrel into the third installment of this thrilling western adventure series.

https://www.amazon.com/dp/B0F48J5DKZ

A Tip of the Hat

A Tip of the Hat

Thank you for signing on with the Dagger D, Angry R, and for reading *Dead Heat*. You've spent months in the saddle, eaten way too much trail dust, and galloped into town with the herd. It's been a pleasure having you along.

If you enjoyed the ride, I'd be most obliged if you could share your thoughts with a review. Even a few quick words or brief thoughts can make a big difference, and help folks discover my fiction.

It's an honor and a privilege to write for you. Your emails are welcome in my inbox and you can reach me at dave@itsoag.com

I look forward to many more journeys together... if the good Lord's willing and the horse don't buck.

With gratitude,

David Fitz-Gerald

GHOSTS ALONG THE OREGON TRAIL

If you haven't read the series, Ghosts Along the Oregon Trail, why not start today?

Embark on a harrowing trek across the rugged American frontier in 1850. Your wagon awaits, and the windswept wilderness calls. This epic adventure will test the mettle of even the bravest souls.

Delve into an unforgettable saga of empowerment, sacrifice, and the haunting echoes of a harrowing journey. Immerse yourself in an expedition where every decision carries the weight of life, death, and shattered dreams.

Ghosts Along the Oregon Trail was written as if it were a single volume rather than a series of five novels. It has been divided into five books which split the Oregon Trail into segments, or legs, of the journey. Readers will enjoy this series most when read in order, beginning with *A Grave Every Mile*. Hop aboard!

About the Author

David Fitz-Gerald writes westerns and historical fiction. He is the author of more than a dozen books, including the series, Ghosts Along the Oregon Trail set in 1850. He's a multiple Laramie Award, first place, best in category winner; a Blue Ribbon Chanticleerian; a member of Western Writers of America; and a member of the Historical Novel Society.

Alpine landscapes and flashy horses always catch Dave's eye and turn his head. He is also an Adirondack 46-er, which means that he has hiked to the summit of the range's highest peaks. As a mountaineer, he's happiest at an elevation of over four thousand feet above sea level.

Dave is a lifelong fan of western fiction, landscapes, movies, and music. It should be no surprise that Dave delights in placing memorable characters on treacherous trails, mountain tops, and on the backs of wild horses.